HE

called himself both a man of business and a man of morality.

Slave-stealing was his trade, and he served his wallet while he served his God, and found profit in both.

SHE

had known only bondage from her day of birth.

She had neither religion nor morals nor knowledge of the world. Her only wisdom was the wisdom of the blood, her only power that of her dark beauty.

Yet as this strange pair made their way through a South of decadent gentry, brutal lawmen, wandering gypsies, and violent mountaineers, one step ahead of capture and death, it began to be hard to say just who was freeing whom . . .

Other SIGNET Titles You'll Enjoy

☐ **THE CONFESSIONS OF NAT TURNER by William Styron.** The record-breaking bestseller and Pulitzer Prize-winning novel about the devoutly religious, well-educated Negro preacher who led a violent revolt against slavery. (#Y3596—$1.25)

☐ **PARADISE FALLS by Don Robertson.** An epic chronicle of America during the 35 years following the close of the Civil War, a gangster-business-man-kingmaker, a Madame who opens a house in Paradise Falls and a miners' revolt—this is Paradise Falls. (#J3762—$1.75)

☐ **IMMORTAL WIFE by Irving Stone.** The dynamic story of Jessie Benton, whose marriage to John Charles Fremont, daring young topographer of the unexplored West, made her one of the most beloved, hated, feared and feted women in American history. (#Y3803—$1.25)

☐ **LOVE IS ETERNAL by Irving Stone.** The poignant and deeply memorable story of the tumultuous courtship and marriage of Mary Todd and Abraham Lincoln. (#Y3802—$1.25)

☐ **ANDERSONVILLE by MacKinley Kantor.** The Pulitzer Prize novel of the infamous Civil War prisoner. (#Y3543—$1.25)

THE NEW AMERICAN LIBRARY, INC., P.O. Box 2310, Grand Central Station, New York, New York 10017

Please send me the SIGNET BOOKS I have checked above. I am enclosing $_____(check or money order—no currency or C.O.D.'s). Please include the list price plus 10¢ a copy to cover mailing costs. (New York City residents add 5% Sales Tax. Other New York State residents add 2% plus any local sales or use taxes.)

Name_____

Address_____

City_____State_____Zip Code_____
Allow at least 3 weeks for delivery

The Slave Stealer

By Boyd Upchurch

A Signet Book

Published by The New American Library

© By Boyd Upchurch 1968

All rights reserved, including the right to reproduce this
book or portions thereof in any form. For information address
Weybright and Talley, Inc., 3 East 54th Street,
New York, New York 10022.

Library of Congress Catalog Card Number: 68-12133

This is an authorized reprint of a hardcover edition published
by Weybright and Talley, Inc. The hardcover edition was
published simultaneously in Canada by Clarke, Irwin &
Company Limited, Toronto and Vancouver.

SIGNET TRADEMARK REG. U.S. PAT. OFF. AND FOREIGN COUNTRIES
REGISTERED TRADEMARK—MARCA REGISTRADA
HECHO EN CHICAGO, U.S.A.

SIGNET BOOKS are published by
The New American Library, Inc.,
1301 Avenue of the Americas, New York, New York 10019

FIRST PRINTING, MAY, 1969

PRINTED IN THE UNITED STATES OF AMERICA

To Fern

Chapter One

It was a country younger than the life-span of some of its citizens, and it had known wars. It had challenged the first power of Europe and brawled with its New World neighbors to the north and south. Always its borders had sounded to war whoops, now dwindling to the death rattle of a savage race. Half horse and half alligator, it had conquered forests and swamplands, prairies and mountains.

In the year 1858 the Republic was at peace.

Peace lay over the land as the hush before a summer storm, for on the horizon thunderheads gathered and lightning flickered. All heard the thunder, and many made the thunder. Of those who made the thunder, some were called fire-eaters, and some were called abolitionists: they were for slavery, and they were against slavery. A few men made the lightning.

Among men who made the lightning were those who moved alone against the slave power to wrest the bondmen from the kitchens and fields of their masters: these men were slave stealers.

Few names of the slave stealers would survive; they moved in shadows, and their records were kept, if kept at all, in hidden places. Holding in common anonymity and a quality of courage that permitted them to fight without banners or expectations of an honored grave, they differed in motives. Some walked into violence for love of the oppressed, some went in hatred of the oppressor—and some were mercenaries, hired liberators selling freedom for a profit.

Few of their names would survive, and these are names of lightning: Fairbanks! Fairfield! Tubman! Ross!

There was another by the name of Solomon Villaricca.

Presently, he felt no affinity with lightning.

By avocation he was an ornithologist, by trade a peddler, and he was of the Israelite persuasion. As an amateur ornithologist, he kept records of bird sightings to help establish avian migratory patterns on the North American Continent. As a peddler, he traveled the Southern Appalachian Highlands dealing in fabrics, hardware, household utensils, and runaway Negroes. As a Jew, he did these things for the glory of God, the betterment of mankind, and to raise enough money to open a store in Cincinnati.

The violin was one of his lesser hobbies.

At the time he met Dixon Kelly, on an early afternoon in April, he was attempting a composition Mozart had written at the age of nine. If a child could write the music, Solomon reasoned, a man of twenty-six should be able to play it, but his logic was proving so unsound that the melancholy which had drawn him to the instrument was giving way to disgust at his own lack of talent.

Another handicap was his beard. Throwing it over the chin rest interfered with the strings. Tucking it under put an inch of padding between him and the instrument with which he was trying to establish rapport. It was a handicap he had to tolerate. The beard was his trademark as a merchant, his greatest distinction as a man, and a badge of Orthodoxy which was growing lamentably rare among Cincinnati Sephardim.

He drew one pleasure, at least, from his musical exercise—the feeling of relief he felt when his wife tapped, opened the door, and said, "Sol, there's a man in the parlor."

He followed Leah down the hall, sniffing the fragrance of lilac water which rose from her hair to mingle with the Sabbath redolence from the kitchen. His thin, sensitive nose fluted among the odors to compose a symphony of scents. When he walked into the parlor, the symphony soared to a crashing finale in the reek of bourbon.

"Mr. Kelly, my husband, Solomon Villaricca."

Leah turned and fled to the kitchen.

"Dixon Kelly's the name, and I don't mind telling you I heard your fiddle from the back, and you sounded real professional."

Kelly was dressed to match his odor, which reflected a

8

taste in whiskey as perceptive as his taste in music. His free hand held a beaver hat, out of style but expensive, as his right hand mangled Solomon's in salutation. His gray overcoat had lapels of sealskin, and the white scarf around his neck was relieved by pink polka dots which matched the color of his hair and nose.

"Thank you for your kind remark, Mr. Kelly. What may I do for you?"

"Mr. Blood at the Quaker store sent me. He said you were going South, Sunday." He sidled closer. "I got a little job down there, if you know what I mean."

"Perfectly, Mr. Kelly. My office is in my carriage house. Come with me."

Solomon took his shawl from the coat tree and invited Kelly to precede him through the door. Outside, he led his visitor around the house to the rear, keeping to the board-walk to avoid mud from an earlier shower, marking the well-curried Morgan before the buggy at his hitching post, and wondering what had prompted Blood to send Kelly. It was not prudent to advertise in this trade, and Blood knew it.

Always, Blood assigned him the slave to be freed, paid the fee (minus the broker's commission, which was in truth a donation to the Society of Friends), and named no names other than that of the slave to be picked up. The procedure protected the Underground Railroad, the slave's benefactor, and Solomon; and it also spared Solomon the bother of collecting his fee.

Probably, Blood had sent the man because time was running out, Solomon decided. Assignments were usually made weeks in advance of Solomon's departure, but up to now, forty-eight hours before he left for the South on his bona fide commercial rounds and only five hours before his Sabbath commenced, there had been no word. He had been anxious for days, finally depressed, and to ward off the hypos, he had taken to the violin.

"I keep my office out back," he told Kelly as they walked across the gravel-covered stable yard, "because my wife doesn't like the odor of tobacco, but mostly because she doesn't know the full extent of my business in the South."

"Tell the truth, I'm consternated myself. Hebrew merchants ain't usually nigger stealers."

"Moses married an Ethiope," Solomon explained, as he unlocked the office door. "Least I can do for Moses is lend a hand with his in-laws."

The office, separated from the carriage house by a brick partition, held a desk, stove, two chairs, coal bin and scuttle, and a brass spittoon. Light entered through a barred window by the door. On the wall behind the desk was a large Colton map of western Virginia and the Carolinas, eastern Kentucky and Tennessee, and northern Georgia and Alabama.

"Bite off or light up," Solomon invited, draping his shawl over a peg and going to the stove to rouse the embers from his morning fire. "I'll have it warm in here, directly. Winter's hanging onto spring, this year, like an unpaid madam."

He adjusted the draft on the stove, dropped in a lump of coal, and turned to find Kelly had removed his overcoat and was seated before the desk. Brushing off his hands, Solomon walked behind the desk and sat down.

Kelly's overcoat was rendered modest by his suit of brown and yellow, patterned in squares large enough for a checkers game. From compassion or by accident, Kelly had relieved the pattern with a pale blue tie which was saved from abject humility by a diamond stickpin.

Kelly's chest was swiveled toward the window. The diamond sucked in the pale light from the clouded sky and shot the rays directly at Solomon. It was at least three carats, he estimated, and since it drew his attention so obviously, he let admiration show in his eyes.

"Beautiful stone you have there, Mr. Kelly."

"Won it on the Louisville boat. Man covered an eight-hundred-dollar pot with it."

"He stood to win twice what he anted," Solomon said. "Nevertheless, it's a beautiful stone."

As he looked, he felt avarice, but avarice he considered the least deadly of sins. Avarice, like absinthe, was deadly only when guzzled; it was bracing when sipped. Yet, it was a sin. He admitted his sin and hoped that it would be weighed against his sense of justice. In fairness to the stone, it deserved to be delivered from such a background, and Solomon was a just man.

"I gather from your taste in music and from your dress that you're a merchant of parts, Mr. Kelly."

"No, sir. Just a horney-handed Mick trying to make a dollar. I keep a tavern down on Front Street."

"Your customers must be mostly rivermen."

"Deckhands and dock handlers. I keep gamblers out. There ain't no sharpies at my tables."

"As one commercial man to another, how's their credit?"

"It ain't. They pays me first, or no room and board. If they welsh at the tables, I'll drop them. They know it."

Though three inches shorter than Solomon, Kelly was half again as wide. His fists, matted with pink hair which crept down between the knuckles, resembled mallets. For those fists, dropping a man or a mule should be easy.

"What's your business at the South, Mr. Kelly?"

"I got a little black girl down in Georgia I'd like brought to Cincinnati."

"She'd be seized and transported back," Solomon said. "Even freed Negroes aren't safe in Cincinnati."

"I make provisions."

Kelly pulled a document from his coat pocket and handed it across to Solomon. It was a typeset bill of sale with details of the transaction handwritten in the blank areas. For $1,500, it transferred ownership of Melinda, a Negro female aged about sixteen, from Mr. and Mrs. William Blake of Blake's Crossing, Cherokee County, Georgia, to Mr. Dixon A. Kelly of Louisville, Kentucky. It was dated July, 1857, and signed by Mr. and Mrs. William Blake and Dixon A. Kelly.

"Are these signatures authentic?"

"You damned right they are!"

Solomon's regret was not feigned. "Mr. Kelly, you don't understand. I don't deliver slaves to Cincinnati. I take them to the closest station on the Underground Railroad, and they're sent to Canada. My religion forbids me to transport a servant from one master to the other."

"*You* don't understand *me*. Them signatures is real because Jack the Artist did them up for me, at five dollars a name."

Solomon was puzzled. If Kelly ran a tavern on Front Street, won eight-hundred-dollar diamonds in card games, and associated with criminals as notorious as Jack the Artist, he could hardly be the selfless benefactor of a slave girl.

Solomon handed back the bill of sale. "Where's Blake's Crossing?"

"A few miles north of Canton, on the railroad twixt Marietta and Ellijay."

Solomon let his eyes register disappointment. "I don't go that far south."

"Blood told me you covered North Georgia."

"Only as a merchant. Not to free servants. Distance increases my risks. When the risk is too great or the profit uncertain, I don't undertake the job."

11

"I'll make your profits certain."

"Assuming you could, what's your interest in the girl?"

"I love her."

"You love her!"

"Yes, sir."

Solomon had known slave-quarters Lotharios, but "love" was not in their lexicon. Kelly's wholehearted use of the word made his pursuit of the diamond seem shabby. Faced with this embarrassing irrelevancy, he shrugged his shoulders. "Believe me, Mr. Kelly, I'm a man of the world. Your feelings I appreciate. But it is written, a Jew taking a woman for purposes of fornication shall be put to death."

"I ain't good at them highfalutin words, but if you mean something dirty, you can put your religion to rest. On the grave of me mother, it's marrying the girl I am."

Again the Irishman's voice rang with the flat, clear tones of truth. Solomon, himself a man of ritual, was impressed by a white who would honor a darky with the rites of marriage. If Kelly meant what he said, the marriage would explain why Blood had sent him here, but Blood was a romantic. He still glowed over the Maynard wedding, three years ago, where the dark bride had been smuggled from Mississippi to her white groom by the Underground Railroad to put the seal of marriage on a love which had aroused the admiration of Ohio.

Maynard was a trustworthy mechanic. Solomon had doubts about Kelly, but Kelly had obviously met with Blood's approval. Romantic or not, the Quaker was a sound judge of character.

"Why don't you go South and buy the girl?"

"I tried. I offered fifteen hundred for her, three hundred more than the market, but the Blakes wouldn't sell."

"How did you meet her?"

"Working a Mick gang down there, building a railroad. I needed a cook. Somebody told me about Mellie, and I went over to the plantation and hired her out. That's where I got the Blake signatures . . . and that's where I met Mellie."

Memories of Melinda wrought deep changes in Kelly. His direct gaze grew pensive. Lines softened around his mouth. The bibulous nose seemed less porous.

His transfiguration both allayed Solomon's doubts and alerted him to an opportunity. From such a swain there was far more to be gained than merely a diamond. His mind soared with an idea . . . Here was his store on John Street!

"Tell me about Mellie." Solomon's voice was gentle.

"She's a drawers buster. She ain't no high yellow, but she ain't no shine, neither. She's got a head like the Blessed Virgin, but underneath her Adam's apple she's pure Jezebel. They got a hole down in Kentucky what can suck you to it if the wind's blowing right. Mellie can do it at twenty paces, with no wind blowing. On the grave of me sainted mother, I swear she's a drawers buster."

Solomon leaned back and listened, his hands stretched palm to palm along his cheek. Kelly expressed himself well for a man with a limited choice of words; his imagery revealed Celtic imagination. Solomon leaned forward to open a bound account book.

"You've given me a good general idea, but I need details. How tall is she?"

" 'Bout teat-high on me."

"How big a foot?"

" 'Bout so?" A handspan.

Solomon jotted notes. "Her waist?"

"So." Two handspans held about two inches apart.

"That small! Her hips?"

"So big. She curves out pretty fast. Might say she's waspy-assed."

"Breasts?"

"Small, but they stick out."

Solomon looked at his notes. "Say she's a size ten, with a five and a half shoe."

"I never thought about her like that."

"You implied that her features weren't Negroid. Could she pass as a white?"

"No, sir. Maybe a Dago or a Hebrew, but not a white."

"So, Mr. Kelly, and could she pass as my sister!"

Solomon's anger flared unnoticed. "Hell, Mr. Villaricca, you couldn't pass yourself off as a Hebrew without that beard and skullcap you're wearing."

Mollified by his readmittance into the white race, Solomon leaned back.

Kelly's answers had dispelled some of his doubts and left his mind free to concentrate on his fees. His tone became brisk.

"First, I have to consider the distance to the nearest Underground Depot, in this case more than a hundred miles. Every minute that I'm on the road with a fugitive, my life's in danger. I have to be compensated for that risk.

"Second, North Georgia is my regular trading territory.

It gives me five hundred a year income. Those people trust me as Solomon Villaricca, the merchant. Once I steal from them, I become Solomon Villaricca, the thief. Obviously, my goodwill is gone. It will take at least two years to build up customers in a different territory. So, there's a thousand dollars lost. . . ."

"I'm willing to pay that, right now." Kelly leaned forward, reaching into his pocket, but Solomon held up a hand.

"One thousand dollars only pays for the loss of goodwill. There are other considerations.

"After I have reached the relative safety of the Underground Railroad, *I* am still not free from harm. I'll have to go with her to Wheeling, Virginia, and bring her downriver. Otherwise, the Railroad would send her straight to Canada.

"For two weeks, I'll be under the guns of the slaveowners, six additional weeks hauling her through some of the roughest country in the world. That's two months' time invested.

"Considering the danger, the delicacy attendant upon traveling with a female, rental on my equipment, room and board for two months, loss of goodwill, hindrance to my selling from having the fugitive—even in the mountains I'm still in the slave states—I wouldn't touch the job for less than two thousand five hundred dollars."

"God damn!"

Kelly's eyes glazed. His jaw quivered. He sat silent for a long moment, and when he spoke his voice echoed from some chamber of horror. "Blood figured you wouldn't charge me more than a straight thousand."

So, Ely Blood's estimate of the Irishman's wealth supported his own. Solomon's usual fee was two hundred and fifty dollars.

Solomon mouthed a few platitudes to give Kelly time to recover. "Mr. Blood is a religious man who sometimes overlooks commercial considerations. I, too, am a religious man, but I'm also a man of business."

"Every time I'm doing business with a religious man, I get chivied." Kelly lowered his face into his hands.

"I'm not an abolitionist," Solomon explained to the Irishman's cowlick. "I work for pay. How much would *you* charge to go as far into the South as Georgia and steal a servant from her master's kitchen?"

It was a rhetorical question, but Kelly answered with eyes shut and mouth muffled. "Not more'n a thousand."

"Then you're fifteen hundred dollars braver than I, Mr.

Kelly. Such courage I admire." Solomon's tone was cutting. "Say what you will about the Southerners, Mr. Kelly, they are not made of molasses candy."

Kelly raised his head. He was dazed but recovering.

Solomon resumed his sales talk. "You offered fifteen hundred for the girl, and you were turned down. So, she must be worth at least two thousand on the market. I ask two thousand five hundred. Deduct fifteen hundred for my expenses, and I am letting you have a two-thousand-dollar girl for one thousand dollars. Is this a bargain? I should have my head inspected. I am losing one thousand dollars before my wheels take one turn south."

"I feel for you, Mr. Villaricca, losing all that money. But I ain't got two thousand five hundred, lest I sold my tavern. Then I wouldn't have no way of taking care of poor Mellie."

"Mr. Kelly, if you can't afford my services, then you can't afford my services. But I'm reasonable. You can give me half now and half in September, on delivery."

"I'll level with you. I got a thousand. I could raise another thousand, maybe, between now and September by setting in on my own games. I couldn't touch fifteen hundred. Be Jesus! It's hard to fill an inside straight, and I don't deal every hand."

"You offered the Blakes fifteen hundred. How could you expect me to charge less?"

" 'Cause I'm buying stolen goods. Stolen goods don't go at more than half price."

Horror and indignation mingled on Solomon's face.

"Mr. Kelly, do you buy at the fence?"

Flustered by the transformation and shamed by the indignation, Kelly blurted, "Mr. Villaricca, I'm a good Catholic."

Solomon was diverted by the irrelevancy. "Surely, the girl's not a Catholic. Are you willing to marry outside your faith?"

Happily again on safe ground, Kelly said, "No, sir. I aim for Mellie to take instructions."

"Look, Mr. Kelly," Solomon leaned forward, his voice dropping to a confidential level, "for you, I'm willing to make concessions. I'm a sentimental man. You love this girl. Am I one to keep Romeo from his Juliet? For you, I'll make it two thousand even. One thousand down, and one thousand on delivery. And you throw in the diamond."

"Be Jesus, Mr. Villaricca! This stone's worth eight hundred dollars!"

"At four hundred dollars, you're robbing the man."

"For two thousand, I'd shake. But the stickpin stays with me." Kelly turned to get up, and the diamond flashed in the sunlight.

"From my heart, I thank you for turning down my offer." Solomon heaved an audible sigh of relief and settled back in his chair. Taken by the gesture and the remark, Kelly asked, "Why thank me?"

"For taking the guilt of Melinda's fate off my conscience."

"And how would I be doing that?"

"You were willing to marry the girl. You stood ready to put the seal of God on our transaction. I sat here talking about profit and loss. Me you made feel like a money changer in the Temple. Now, I ask you, Mr. Kelly, I should worry? So, I should be ashamed of trade when you, a practicing Catholic, are willing to sacrifice a spiritual union for the sake of a bauble you stick on your tie?

"Maybe you don't consider marriage a holy union. I hold that fleshly delight, inside the bonds of matrimony, is the closest to religious exaltation that the man of earthly interest may reach. Indeed, that is true for the female, especially for the female."

Solomon leaned forward and dramatically lowered his voice. "Steal a glance at the face of your beloved when she approaches her moment of ecstasy. Notice her indrawn look, her closed eyes, the raptness of her countenance. Adoration, sir! Sheer apotheosis! Will you not agree, sir, that there are spiritual values in the raptures of married love?"

"You damned right!"

The Celt was salivating. His fingers fumbled at the stickpin, and Solomon's oratory became a chant. "So, you will deny the girl! You will leave her to the ruttings of some black stud in the glades of Georgia while you, her White Knight of the North, sit above the Ohio and fondle a trinket instead of the melons of her breasts." Solomon's voice mixed scorn with sadness. "And you are the spiritual one!"

"You fucking right I'm spiritual, Mr. Villaricca."

Kelly's hand swooped up and zoomed down, striking the desk with a thud that shook the carriage house. When his hand drew back, the diamond, quivering on the shaft of the pin embedded in the wood, seemed to dance in the sunlight.

An hour later, after an interrogation so detailed that it covered the distance of the backyard pump from the back porch of the Blake mansion and so broad in scope that it uncovered the name of Mrs. Blake's married sister in Dalton, Georgia, Kelly wrote out a draft for one thousand dollars. He paused before he handed the check to Solomon. "What warrant I got you'll bring her back?"

"My life, my liberty, and your remaining one thousand dollars."

"Guess that's good enough," Kelly said, handing Solomon the check.

"Before we shake on this transaction," Solomon said, "I want one provision clear. You pay me the remainder once I get the girl to Cincinnati. When she gets here, she's a free woman as far as I'm concerned. If she decides not to marry you, that's your little red wagon."

"She'll marry me," Kelly said emphatically. "The lass is eager . . . But there's one thing . . ." He fidgeted uneasily, groping for words, ". . . I ain't paying these prices for used goods. I ain't marrying no girl what ain't no virgin."

"That guarantee," Solomon said with gentle indulgence, "you'll find in the Ten Commandments. I am a married man."

Kelly rose and extended his hand, getting four loosely folded fingers in return, waved off Solomon's offer of an escort to his buggy, and bade good-bye with a cordiality that disturbed his host. The man who minutes before had been moaning over price swaggered off with the air of a grubstaker who has seized a gold mine for back payment on his stake.

Solomon, however, felt his own measure of exultation as he led his driving horse out of the stable. He had completed a transaction which had set the opening date of his store forward by three years. He regretted that he could not tell Leah of their good fortune, and though the regret tempered his exultation as a tradesman, as a Jew he felt exalted. In the past, slave stealing had furnished less than a fourth of his annual income, but the activity lent a dimension to his trips South that profit could not give them. Now, when he had despaired the most, it was as if God had emerged from a cloud and said, "Go down, Solomon, and make Melinda free."

And, for this once, the profit was commensurate with the peril.

He danced a ballet around the routine of harnessing,

swaying to the music of his thoughts. He liked Southerners —he had married one—and he shared their passion for excitement. He slapped on the breast harness with a military thump and threaded the traces through the shaft holes smoothly to the right and smoothly to the left . . . Southerners kept arranging the cards of life in the manner of rummy players too drunk to care that the deck was running out . . . He snapped the final trace to the whiffle tree and waltzed back three steps to the sound of hands clapping appreciation.

Leah had been watching his antics from the back porch, and she called, "Take a bow, Sol."

He doffed his skullcap and bent low.

"I'll declare, Sol. If I live to be a hundred, I'll never understand you. One minute you're moping around the house like a man with the vapors, and the next you're out in the backyard doing a buck-and-wing."

"The sun came out."

"You going downtown?"

"Yes, ma'am."

"Get back before sundown!"

"I will."

He pirouetted and managed a graceful leap onto the buggy. At the snap of the reins on her rump, the hackney flowed into a trot with the ease of a falcon riding an updraft of air.

Leah, leaning over the banister, waved him out of sight, feeling pride in the man whose easy erectness on the buggy's seat matched the grace of the pacing horse.

Yet, when she returned to the kitchen, she went about her tasks with worried abstractedness. All morning he had moped, sawing his fiddle like a man on the verge of hypos; then, a person who was not even a gentleman had called, and Solomon was happy.

At such times, she felt apart from the man of long silences and hidden joys who read the Scriptures more for the poetry than for preachments and read them less than he read the Greeks and Shakespeare, who quartered his Sabbath studies between the Torah and the Rambam, with a full half going to Audubon.

Leah smiled as she poked a fagot into the stove.

Solomon thought he aspired to Orthodoxy as an ideal of behavior when, in truth, he was compressing himself into a mold never meant for his spirit. He would be aggrieved if she voiced her thought, but it was true, and she brushed off his imagined disapproval as she clapped the wood dust from her hands.

His attitude supported her argument. Once, she had asked him how he prepared matzos for Passover on his commercial journeys before their marriage.

"Hoecakes," he said. "They taste foul enough."

In other ways, his unorthodoxy had charmed her. During his first visit to her home, on a commercial journey South, he hardly noticed her, she thought, although every female in Chattanooga noticed him. He had called on her again, in August, on the return leg of his journey, and he had proposed in a manner unsuitable for one who read the classics. "Miss Levy, you're going to like Cincinnati. A hired girl at the North works harder for less keep than the coloreds do here."

Her acceptance had been equally abstruse. "But, sir, is the Ohio as wide as the Tennessee?"

"Not wider, but much deeper, ma'am."

"I just love deep rivers, Mr. Villaricca."

Then, he had left her to speak to her father. When she inquired about his conversation of her father, the answer was enigmatic. "He didn't exactly ask me, Leah," her father said, and added, "You're marrying a very strong-willed man."

After three years, she still did not have a maid, except on Tuesdays. As Simon the Just had said, there was law, worship, and generosity. What Solomon lacked in law and worship he fulfilled with generosity.

But she could not justly complain of him as a provider. Perhaps, in two or three years, this Trade Fair might come to something, and his shop had always been in the rear of his house.

Yes, she had gotten the better part of their marriage. So far, all he had achieved were the services of a domestic, a dancing partner, and a companion who could not share his love of birds, poets, and Quakers and who could not bear to watch his sparring matches at the Turnverein.

She shared his faith, however, and lamented with him that so many of the Congregation were turning away, marrying Gentiles, moving west, and she sensed in his unorthodox Orthodoxy a promise for the future. Winds of change were blowing in Cincinnati, and Solomon's faith could bend without breaking.

But shared faith was not enough for a woman married to

a man who could not truly fear even the Lord because he did not know fear, and in the fullness of days, she prayed that he might come home to another besides herself. Great, then, would be the rejoicing.

She smiled in candid self-appraisal as she gathered the candles for the table. Until that day, he would never be checked or reined, but afterward, the stallion would be gentled.

Tonight, she would read to him from the Book of Job:

> Hast thou given the horse strength?
> Hast thou clothed his neck with thunder?
> The glory of his nostrils is terrible.
> He goeth to meet the armed men.
> He mocketh at fear and is not affrighted.

No, she corrected herself. Better not those verses. Solomon might listen with an ear different from that which she intended and be burdened with an awareness of her knowledge and her fears.

Solomon took Kemble Street east to Cutter and south to Fifth, picking the least muddy route past the building which, with the help of the Lord and Kelly, he would open next March as the Cincinnati Trade Fair.

Except for the absence of snow, spring had made no appearance in Cincinnati. Even with the sun now shining in a clearing sky, it was chilly enough for steam to rise from the fresh droppings of horses. Solomon had yet to see one green shoot from a crocus, and the odor of mud from the rain had a brittle tang.

At Fifth and John streets, he slowed as he drove past the building he intended to lease. An ordinary eye would have seen a two-story cotton warehouse which had lost so much trade to New Orleans that the present tenants were in a mood to swap their lease for part interest in a small livery stable. No matter. From this spot, come next March, he would fire the shot that would be heard around the merchandising world.

His idea was so simple that he praised the Lord for sending him Kelly to speed its consummation before it was hit upon by some scheming Yankee in Boston or clever Jew in New York. He intended to put twelve different shops under one roof, selling noncompetitive goods.

Customers would swarm to a store where they could buy anything from shoes to saddles without traipsing all over town. Bad weather would help rather than hinder trading. Money from rents on the other eleven apartments would afford him an income and pay the rent on his own section, ladies and gents ready-to-wear.

He had thought of calling it a "compartment store," but rejected this as clumsy and uninviting. The name Trade Fair was a Brueghelesque carnival with codpieces atilt, dignified by connotations of honesty and square dealing. The name had been his brainchild, but Leah's imagination had produced the motto: "Fair trades at Trade Fair."

Trailing clouds of expectation, he drove past the building and on toward the Bank of Ohio.

Kelly's draft was on the bank Solomon used, no remarkable coincidence since there were but three banks in downtown Cincinnati. However, he was grateful for the opportunity to check Kelly's credit before Sabbath put an end to his activities.

"Hello, Mr. Villaricca," the teller greeted him. "Figured you'd be long gone by now."

"Leaving Sunday. This thing any good?"

The teller looked at the draft. "With that name on it, it's as good as the Philadelphia Mint."

As Solomon deposited the money and arranged for the storage of the diamond in the bank's safe, he felt oddly deflated. The teller's attitude toward the draft implied that he had been outbargained by an Irishman. As he reined the mare north toward the Quaker Store, he dismissed the thought from his mind. Avarice punished by begetting more greed, and the hour deserved untainted joy.

This day was maple taffy and the smell of hot buttered popcorn. Sunlight gilded the city from a sky now blue. Under the trotting mare, Race Street unreeled as pastel buildings echoing the "gees" and "haws" of wagoneers whom he saw as knights of commerce jousting for positions in traffic. Miami Canal, flashing beneath him, glittered silver.

Solomon enjoyed his visits to Blood even on less momentous occasions. It was the Quaker who had enlisted him as a mercenary in the war against slavery. Blood wanted all men to be free and all free men to be Quakers. Solomon was drawn to the older man because he shared Blood's first passion and was amused by the latter.

Solomon figured he had two hours of sunlight left when he dropped his reins over the hitching rack outside the store, scraped the mud from his boots, and walked into the sprawling frame building. Blood was at the counter with a woman customer. Simon, his eldest son, was serving a man in the hardware section, while Levi, the younger, was sorting goods and placing them on shelves.

Solomon waited until the woman left and exchanged greetings with Blood. "Your gentleman, Kelly, came by."

Blood was abrupt, almost hostile. "He wasn't mine, and I doubt he's a gentleman."

"Reservations you have, Friend Ely?"

"It's not for me to pass judgment on a man, not even a popish tippler, but if thee took the job, I hope thee charged him well."

"I did, and I've come to tithe."

"Leave us go into the back, Solomon. Simon will mind the store."

Going into Blood's office was usually a cabalistic pleasure for Solomon as well as a necessity. Blood was more than simply a conductor on the Underground Railroad, he was a yardmaster and division superintendent. His store was watched by agents of the marshal's office for violations of the Fugitive Slave Law, by deputy sheriffs holding warrants for runaways, and by that peculiar breed of Northern jackel which sought profit by kidnaping and transporting back to the South fugitives and even free Negroes.

Solomon was troubled by Ely's manner as he followed him into the office. When Ely closed the door and offered Solomon a chair, Solomon remained standing.

"I charged him two thousand dollars and collected one thousand. I've come to tithe."

"Good, but I want no part of Kelly's money."

"You sent him to me!"

"True. But when I spoke to him, I could not think clearly. His talk of the girl, his manner, and his clothes scrambled my senses. Now, I hold grave second thoughts."

"Then you *have* passed judgment on the man!"

"No. There is still room for doubt. It may be that Kelly's intentions are honorable. More likely, thee's furthering an assignation between him and the black. If such be true, I want no part in the matter."

"Yet, you sent this man to me."

"Why not, Friend Solomon? My way is narrow. I have Jesus Christ to consider. There may be loopholes in thy law. But I cannot share in thy profit, not at the risk of my profits in the hereafter."

Blood's smug piety had often amused Solomon when

directed at others. Now that it was directed toward him, Solomon's chest swelled, his fists clenched, and his voice rose above conspiratorial levels.

"Granted, Friend, that my religion gives me no I.O.U. from God which I cash at the wicket of heaven. Granted, I have no Jesus Christ. But there are over twenty books to the Talmud. Should I hire a lawyer to find a loophole? Where would I find such a lawyer, and who would pay his fee?

"Mark this, Ely, my God is your God. But God is my partner in my business. If I compromise my partner by making a procurer of Him, then you, too, compromise Him. Kelly I listened to because you sent him."

Ely Blood was aware that Solomon in his wrath was not to be taken lightly. The Jew was a slave stealer who lived under the threat of violence and could react with violence to do quick and permanent harm to Ely. More important, there was truth in his argument. If a sin were committed in smuggling the girl out of Georgia, Ely was a partner to that sin.

Ely was honestly placating. "Calm thyself, Solomon. 'Tis not that I relegate thee to a lesser circle because thee's a Jew. Truly, I felt that thy law might permit thee absolution for an unwitting sin. Perhaps there will be no sin. Mayhap my prickings come only from the knowledge that this man is popish and a tavern keeper. Possibly I wrong the man. We cannot all be Jews and Quakers.

"Still, I must try to predict what pitfalls lie ahead, so I will make thee a proposition. Thee may write me a check for the full two hundred, and I will not cash it until thee and I attend the wedding of Kelly and the black. Is that fair?"

"That is NOT fair! I am pledged to deliver this girl, and Villaricca always delivers. If it is assignation Kelly wishes, then you will have redeemed your soul for two hundred dollars."

Solomon's voice grew hoarse, the veins stood out on his temples, and he leaned menacingly forward. "For two hundred dollars you have redeemed your soul. And I? If I don't return, then I have sold my life for a two-thousand-dollar contract. Now, I ask you, does it not seem strange that a Jew's body is ten times the price of a Christian's soul?"

"You win, Solomon. Write the check."

Solomon sat down, wrote out the check, and handed it to Ely, who looked at it ruefully. "I've not had time to think this matter through, Solomon, but it seems that you and I have our souls in mortgage to an Irish tavern keeper."

Solomon, remorseful over his outburst, covered unease with badinage. "Mind your 'thee's,' Ely."

"Customs must be watched, and I forget. Thee wear that skullcap to the privy, Friend Solomon?"

"Should I catch an early death of cold? . . . Now, to the girl, Melinda. Near the town of Canton, in North Georgia, do we have friends?"

Ely walked to the map and said, "Our closest is a widower by the name of Burl Gaines whose farm lies about twelve miles west of Ellijay, Georgia—here. From the Gaines' farm north, we have nothing until thee reaches Smith at the Knoxville Station or Gresham, up here, at the Sycamore Station. Now, Mr. Gaines. . . ."

Solomon's mind focused as the Quaker's calm voice moved into areas where life or death might depend on the information his words carried.

Driving west after the meeting, Solomon knew how Hector must have felt when the balance of his fate sank low and Phoebus Apollo left him.

Sunlight still slanted along the street, but it was merely sunlight. Drawn out by the clippity-clop of his horse, Twelfth Street was a monochrome of gray cleaving the massed drabness of buildings which echoed the creak of carts and the courses of draymen, those scullions of the town's trade, who would soon be turning home to drab houses and drab wives. The afternoon tasted of sulfur and molasses and reeked of asafetida.

Blood's grave second thoughts disturbed him because they matched so well his own first thoughts. In his eagerness to obtain the commission from Kelly, he had let himself be mesmerized by a diamond and Blood's fancied endorsement of the man. Thus rendered witless, he had sipped absinthe and found it hemlock.

Ethics he could ignore. He had a wife to feed, and a slight overcharge of seventeen hundred and fifty dollars for the delivery of a slave was not the Medusa he was bending to kiss.

However vague the Law might be on other points, on one it was chillingly specific—a Jew who delivered a woman for purposes of fornication would be taken from the altar and be slain.

Yet, Ezekiel said, "The wickedness of the wicked was upon them." If Kelly had lied when he vowed to marry Melinda—if he had feigned the aura that glowed around his pink head when he remembered her—then the lie was Kelly's. He had told the Irishman that the girl was free when she reached Cincinnati, he had been suspicious enough to put that clause in the contract, and Solomon had no way of judging whether the man's love was sacred or profane. Melinda would have to decide that for herself.

There was another argument in his defense which was valid: His duty to God was far less defined than his commission from Kelly. He had taken half pay from the Irishman, and if he failed to honor his covenant with Kelly, to that extent he was unworthy of God's Covenant with Israel. He did not relish going South as a skullcapped procuror for a tavern keeper. On this, the deepest and most dangerous expedition of his career, he preferred to walk in the paths of righteousness, but his pledge had been given, and Solomon Villaricca would remain true to himself.

Besides, there was a thousand dollars awaiting his return. He smiled to himself—with two hundred of the thousand, he'd find himself a Talmudic lawyer to look for loopholes.

Tomorrow at the synagogue he would go to the *Mishna Torah* and see what Maimonides said about witless transgressions and sins of exuberance. The task appalled him. Often, he arose from the Rambam more confused than when he sat, and it made for a sad Sabbath—all Maimon and no Audubon.

With time to spare before sunset, he relaxed as the mare jogged southward on Baymiller until he topped a rise and looked into Kentucky at the hills beyond Covington. Humped and stark from winter, the hills were like gray hippopotamuses wallowing on the banks of some invisible river, dark, wide, sinister—the river of the tragic land, the river of the South.

Rio de Muerte!

He was disturbed by the fancy which had come to him in a language he had spoken rarely since childhood. Always, in the past, the silent flutes and drums of April had called him south.

He loved the South with the passion of a saint for a trollop. He loved her flashing cardinals and her carrion crows, her carefree poverty and her guilty wealth. He loved her people, soft of voice but swift to anger, whose gentle

25

manners veiled violence. He loved the lushness of a land so fruitful of flowers and prodigal of trees, so quick to yield to brush and broom sedge.

He was disturbed and perplexed.

He was no stranger to fear. Fear walked beside him on the roads of summer, but the fear was of a specific threat. Now, as he looked at the hills beyond Covington, his mind was roiled by a dread of something out of space and out of time, except that it lay somewhere southward, and with no definition except in the honeyed and musical name he spoke aloud, "Melinda."

Chapter Two

"Melinda does right well with her cooking," Mrs. Blake agreed with Solomon's compliments on the soup, "and we have another girl, Beulah, who's an excellent cook. But Beulah's so much stouter than Melinda we give her the heavier housework."

Her words fluttered above the shutter-muted strumming of katydids and tree frogs in the Georgia twilight. Phoebe Blake confused him. She had confused him for the three days he had known her. At the moment, with Melinda standing impassive and listening by the pantry door, he could not tell if the girl's mistress was damning her with faint praise or tactfully balancing compliments to her servants in the presence of one of them.

Solomon bent again to his soup, where there was certainty.

From the far end of the table, Bill Blake spoke without shades of meaning. "Mellie's the best damned cook in Georgia, if Brother Smith'll excuse my Anglo-Saxon."

The circuit-riding preacher on Solomon's right was bent so low over his bowl that the candles highlighted his cowlick. He nodded his agreement or forgiveness without interrupting the rhythm of his spoon, which was synchronized with the rise and fall of his Adam's apple above his turned-about collar.

It was soup made from sugar crowder peas, small, wrinkled, brightly green, picked in the sweetness of their adolescence, and boiled to a point where they saddened

27

the taste with the ephemerality of all delight. He had thought the soup an accident of picking in the garden and timing in the pot—until he tasted the corn bread, a crisp brown crust that, after dunking, held the flavor of the peas long enough to dispel sadness and leave only delight. He was bowed in adoration over the bowl when Blake shattered his bliss.

"Mellie's smart, too. She don't know a Jew from a Jew's harp, Sol, but when I told her about your kushnat, or kashnit, she scoured every pan in the kitchen to get shed of the pork. She switched over to cooking with butter like she'd done it all her life, and, I'll swear, I can't tell the difference.

"Fellow offered me all the money in Georgia for her last summer, three thousand dollars, and I turned him down flat.

" 'Course, my nigras think you're a holy man with that skullcap and comforter. Little Jimmie T. watched you set up your altar, day before yestiddy, and he told all the hands in the quarters about your solid silver candlestick."

Solomon's hand had not wavered in the easy flow of the spoon to his mouth and his face had not changed expression. So, Kelly was a liar!

Kelly had offered three thousand dollars, not fifteen hundred. Solomon had been hornswoggled. He had walked almost a thousand miles to steal a girl for two thousand dollars, when Kelly had legitimately offered three thousand to her owner. Solomon could easily get four thousand for the girl from the Creoles at the Charleston market! Through the duplicity of the Irishman, Solomon Villaricca, misbegotten son of Israel, was risking his life and walking two thousand miles for the rare pleasure of being cheated at one dollar a mile!

"Would you care for a second helping, Brother Smith?"

"Don't mind if I do, Sister Phoebe. I declare, between your dinner wine and Mellie's cooking, I'm apt to leave here a drunkard and a glutton."

Solomon bent to his soup to calm his anger.

When Solomon shoved the bowl back and sat upright, he was composed. The Lord had visited this disappointment upon him as punishment for his avarice. The Lord had tempted him with the thought of the Charleston market, and he had put the temptation behind him. He had sinned, suffered, and repented; he had been tempted and resisted temptation, all in the pause of a supper conversation. It was nobler of him to imperil himself in the cause of true love than to profit from the carnality of a Creole. Kelly was a liar and a cheat, but he was also a lover; the three talents did not necessarily conflict.

Solomon declined more soup and spotted a flaw in the perfect jewel that was Melinda. In ladling the soup into Brother Smith's bowl, she flecked his coat and brought him a damp towel with low apologies.

While Brother Smith finished his second helping, Mrs. Blake leaned toward Solomon and said, "Mr. Villaricca, do you know that our nigras think you're descended from King Solomon?"

"As a matter of fact, ma'am, I am."

"Be careful there, Sol, or Phoebe'll have me eating in the kitchen," Bill Blake interjected. "Phoebe's descended from Edward the Third. You notice I always walk behind her. I do that because she's royalty—and to get a better look at her bustle."

"Oh, hush up, Bill! —Bill always guys me about the Turnipseeds, Mr. Villaricca. They kept a large estate in England, near Bristol. That's my family, the Turnipseeds. The Blake family was kept not far from there, at Dartmoor."

"She means that English prison, Sol. Over in England they call Dartmoor the Blakes' summer resort."

"Bill Blake, you quit maligning your family like that, you hear! You let *me* malign your family.—Mr. Villaricca, I'm fascinated by your ancestor. Compared to how long King Solomon's been dead, King Richard just took sick. You must have found a wonderful genealogist to trace y'all that far back."

"No, ma'am. It's just mathematics. Since my forebears double with each generation, back that far we were related to every Jew in Palestine. We're all of one tribe."

"There are twelve such tribes," Brother Smith interjected from above his emptied bowl. "They used to be thirteen, but one got lost somers."

"By the way, Brother Smith," Mrs. Blake said, "one of the reasons I wanted you to meet Mr. Villaricca is that he's educated, too. He'll have to tell you the name of the school he went to. I just can't pronounce it."

"Yeshiva Rambam Torah," Solomon said, "in Cincinnati."

"Ah, yes," Brother Smith nodded knowingly. "My own alma mater is Emory, at Oxford, Georgia."

Solomon was surprised. "I understood that Emory was a Methodist institution."

"I started out as a Methodist when I got the call," Brother Smith admitted, "but when I was about halfway through my studies, the Holy Ghost and I got together and decided we couldn't abide the Methodist practice of sprinkling at baptisms. Sprinkling just dilutes the sin and spreads it out. The only way to wash that sin clean off is to douse the sinner, send him under, not once but three times. There's no sense taking half measures with the devil . . ."

Solomon had learned during Mrs. Blake's piano recital before supper that Brother Smith's conversation followed Newton's laws of motion. He had a gilded cross in his pocket he had intended to give to the preacher as a page marker for his Bible, but at no time had Brother Smith permitted a pause convivial enough for gift giving.

When he talked, he cocked his head and peered from beneath bushy brows as if searching the face of his listener for evidence of sin, and the stare made Solomon feel uneasily that he was in the presence of a sin fighter of heroic mold. For Brother Smith, the devil was a real person with whom he wrestled so often that, surely, Satan must have grown muscular from exercising with Brother Smith alone. Yet, Brother Smith had powerful allies in his fight. He was on first-name terms with each member of the Holy Trinity.

Despite his distaste for Smith's peculiar logic, Solomon was grateful to the preacher. Brother Smith's monthly visit to the Blake Plantation was the occasion for Solomon's invitation to the Sunday supper, and the monologues gave him an opportunity to consider his opponents, the Blakes.

"Now, foot washing don't only get the cracks between the toes, it teaches humility . . ."

William Blake dismayed Solomon.

Tall, with lanky brown hair and the cragged face of a Scottish laird, he had the energy of mind and body to produce one of the best managed plantations Solomon had found in the South. He was a veteran of the Mexican War at sixteen, and he had taken over the plantation from his dying father at twenty. His slaves obeyed him with promptness and respect, and he had control of his wife.

Solomon had arrived at the plantation on Friday, a few hours before Sabbath, and shown his wares. Mrs. Blake wanted two yards of silk, but Bill, called in from the fields, thought the price too high and had vetoed the purchase. Mrs. Blake had accepted her husband's decision without fluttering or fretting.

True, Bill had slipped down to the caravan last night and bought four yards of the silk, but his wife had not persuaded him to change his mind. She was unaware of his act; he had sworn Solomon to secrecy. He and Bill had sneaked to the barn, this morning, to sample Bill's home-made whiskey. Neither act revealed cowardice or moral weakness, Solomon well knew, because in this region, clandestine behavior and furtive pleasures were standard practices among males.

Obviously, Blake was a man who tolerated no opposition and was accustomed to command. He was not a man to leave the recovery of a stolen slave up to authorities. He would come after his property and its thief.

Solomon lamented that the Lord had not seen fit to provide him with a less formidable opponent.

Then, there was Phoebe Blake.

"When I decided to convert to the Baptists, the Lord said to me, 'Brother Smith, you go whole hog. You go over to the Hard-shelled Baptists.' The good God know's I'm not a man for half measures . . ."

Phoebe Blake's smile flashed easily from gray eyes so cool and direct that they touched her mirth with wistfulness and gave him the mildly perplexed sensation of one who is sure he has seen a wraith haunting the rose arbor of a summer's noon.

Her manner was regal but so devoid of patronizing airs that Solomon, four years her senior, deferred to her with pleasure and was flattered by her attention. Slender to the point of angularity, she had an easy grace more sensual in its dignity than the mincing flounce of her serving girl, moving among them now with the vegetable dishes.

"What is to be will be if it don't ever be . . ."

On their visit to the barn, Bill Blake had told him that Phoebe was a graduate of Cox Female College in La Grange, and, lowering his voice in the presence of cows, had confided in awe, "She reads books."

Solomon knew this from her sister, at whose home, near Dalton, he had stopped on his way down for a supposedly commercial call. He had brought her Scott's *Peveril of the Peak* from her sister, and Mrs. Blake had accepted it graciously, barely glanced at the title, and laid it beside her to continue her questions about her sister's family "up

North." He had expected more enthusiasm from a lover of literature in an area where books were rare.

Yet, she must read. He had seen books on the shelves in the drawing room.

Melinda was bringing in the main course, leg of lamb sliced in the kitchen, creamed corn, sliced okra fried in butter, baked sweet potatoes in their shells with their honey oozing out the ends, and, rarity of rarities, baked wheat flour bread. Even before he tasted it he knew that this was an orchestrated meal, harmonized, blended, balanced. Watching the girl who had prepared it, her deft movements matching the chiseled quality of her features, he surmised that she was Nubian or Ethiopian, and from the smooth arch of her brows, with possibly an intermingling of Semitic blood. For two thousand dollars, in any event, she was a bargain.

"Say, Sol," Blake remarked, "I been reading in the Atlanta papers about this fellow up in Illinois, Abe Lincoln, who's been stumping against the Kansas-Nebraska Act. I would dearly love for those abolition agitators up North to come down here and get a firsthand view of what's going on."

"Now, honey, let your victuals hush your mouth."

"With the average planter down here, it's 'root hog or die.' About a third of a working nigra's labor goes to his own support, and they don't all work. Out of fourteen on this place, Mellie and Beulah are house help, Jimmie T. and Sassafras are babies, Bob's Will is just a quarter hand, and Fred's too old to do anything but scare crows."

"Now, Bill, you're working yourself into a lather."

"By God, I'd like to have that woman—what's her name? Stowe?—I'd like to have her come down here and see me working alongside my nigras."

"Honey, there's no sense in getting your mind all ruffled at the table. Now, hush. I have something important I want to ask Mr. Villaricca."

She turned to Solomon, focusing a look on him that singled him out from all the men of the world for her special attention. "Brother Smith and Bill have about argued themselves out on a religious question. Now, Mr. Villaricca, you're a Bible-reading man. Relying on your special astuteness, I'm going to ask you to settle a question. Does a nigra have a soul?"

Solomon was often asked to settle religious questions because as a Jew he was considered a preacher and an authority on the Bible by country folks. As a merchant, his answers were usually more temporizing than final, though freely given. After he had taken Melinda, he would not have to worry about his position as a salesman, but Melinda was present, and he had not acquired the Southerners' indifference to Negroes. For a moment, he felt ill at ease, but it suddenly occurred to him that Mrs. Blake's question was an opportunity to ingratiate himself with the slave girl.

"Before I judge, I'd like to hear the arguments. Brother Smith, you're the senior member present, what is your position on the matter?"

Melinda was placing dessert before them, peach cobblers topped with whipped cream. Brother Smith had been hanging off the edge of Blake's political conversation like a hurricane off the coast, and he came roaring ashore.

"In my theological studies, I have found no rule either for or against the proposition that a nigra has a soul. So, I approach the subject in the light of pure logic. Either your nigra is a simulacrum of a man, or he's a man. I argue he's a man. Why? Because he stands on his hind legs, he walks, and he talks. Now, an ape stands on his hind legs and walks, but he can't talk. A parrot can talk, but he don't stand on his hind legs and walk. Now, a nigra stands on his hind legs and walks and talks."

Solomon nodded at this masterful definition, the knowing nod of one educated man to another.

"Now, I have saved the souls of many nigras, some right here on this plantation, and a saved nigra's soul is white. When I stand at the gates of heaven to greet the souls that I've saved, I'll shake hands with them nigra souls just like they were whites."

Brother Smith's summation was hastened by the peach cobbler, and he lifted his fork.

"That's a generous emotion," Solomon said, somewhat surprised at the source of the affirmative speech. He turned to Blake, "You're the negative, I take it, Bill. What's your argument?"

Bill, too, was eyeing the peach cobbler.

"My argument is short and sweet, Sol. I've heard tell that the thing that distinguishes a man from a brute is the ability to reason, and I've never met a reasonable nigra."

Melinda had paused by the door to the pantry.

"It's not within my province to assert flatly that the Negro does or does not have a soul," Solomon began, "but

33

it's also out of my province to decide whether a white person has a soul or not. First, we have to decide what a soul is. If Bill's definition of reason were the only gauge, then an unreasonable white person would be without a soul—lunatics and children. If, on the other hand, souls were apportioned purely on the basis of race, an octoroon would have one-eighth of a soul, a quadroon one quarter, and so forth. We would be conducting our thinking into unrewarding channels.

"How can you assume a soul exists in a person? Only by his works. Now, it is obvious to me that Mrs. Blake has a soul of rare vintage, expressed through her music and the delicious strawberry wine. On the other hand, I am certain that your girl Melinda has a soul, evidenced by this splendid meal she has created." He raised his eyes. Melinda stood in the doorway beaming. "Brother Smith has a soul certificated to by his profession. That leaves Bill and me.

"I will have to leave that matter for further consideration, but there's one thing I feel reasonably sure of: The colored person has as much right to a soul as a white person."

"A decision worthy of your great-great-grandpa." Mrs. Blake said.

Surprisingly, Brother Smith took umbrage, possibly because he had finished with the clobbler. "No, you can't figure a preacher has a soul just because he answered a call to the church. No, sir. Why, Brother Villaricca, I'm in a constant struggle with the devil. Last month, I was down in Atlanta, and there was a low comedy playing there in the opera house. I'll have you know I was tempted by them playbills. Why, the devil took me by the hand and led me right up to that there ticket seller, and I was just reaching into my pocket to buy a ticket when the Holy Ghost came up . . ."

Again the hurricane swept inshore, and Solomon ate his cobbler in genuine enjoyment while vast forces of good and evil clashed around him. Melinda removed his dish, and Bill lit a cigar, while Brother Smith, head cocked, eyes peering first at Solomon and then at Bill, recounted his trials and tribulations. Solomon was aware of a clatter from the kitchen as Melinda went about washing the dishes, and he was also aware that Mrs. Blake had quietly departed.

Taking advantage of Mrs. Blake's absence, Brother Smith

crowned his list of tribulations with a quick digression. "But, boys, when that little rascal, lust, starts grabbing at my gonads, it takes a whole battalion of angels lined three deep along the way to keep my feet on the straight and narrow.

"Up in Ellijay, where I got my congregation, there was this beautiful little blue-eyed blonde, just flowering into womanhood, who always took a seat in one of the front pews. Now, one thing that really makes a woman beautiful is a good case of salvation, but if you take a woman that's already beautiful and pour the Holy Ghost into her, boys, you got a flower that's begging to be deflowered.

"Now, boys, I was sorely tempted. This little girl, Eulalee was her name, I can name her 'cause she's since got married and done had two beautiful little boys, got me so stirred up I figured there was just one way to solve this problem. Now, I have to be wary in my own congregation . . ."

Brother Smith never revealed his solution to the problem of Eulalee, because Mrs. Blake returned, obviously upset.

"I declare, Bill, that girl's got the vapors. She was handling Mother Turnipseed's Spode like it was pewter . . . I'm sorry, Brother Smith. You were saying you were in Atlanta."

"Talking about Atlanta reminds me," Bill broke in. "I got to go down to Atlanta to pick up that T-frame from the foundry for the sorghum mill. I don't like to leave Phoebe here without any protection, and as long as you're on the place, Sol, maybe you wouldn't mind sleeping in the company room while I'm gone? Brother Smith's sleeping there tonight, but Monday and Tuesday it'll be empty. Then I can catch the train in the morning and be back Wednesday evening at four."

"I'd be happy to have you as a guest, Mr. Villaricca."

"The pleasure is mine, ma'am."

Jehovah had blessed him. In the house, with Blake gone, he could be in communication with Melinda while he planned her escape.

"Now, Bill, I don't want you going down there and sitting in front of the Kimball House to watch all those hussies walking back and forth to show their ankles to the drummers."

"Honey, when I stay at the Kimball House, I'm not interested in just looking at ankles . . . Sol's an ornithologist, Brother Smith, and he thinks he spotted a bird

35

up on the ridge that shouldn't be this far south at this time of the year . . . Say, Sol, why don't you take old Fred up with you, morrow morning? He's about eighty, but he can spot a jaybird at a thousand yards."

"Honey, just what did you mean about the Kimball House?"

"Pudding 'n tame."

"Brother Villaricca," the preacher said, "I took studies in natural history at Emory, and we touched on ornithology. It is useless to try to uncover the workings of God which in the fullness of time shall stand revealed . . ."

Melinda came in to whisper something into Bill Blake's ear. Her master's answer cut off Brother Smith's monologue in the middle of a subordinate clause modifying a subject Solomon had forgotten.

"Looky, Mellie, I have guests. I can't carry you to your quarters. You've got a full moon out there, and you don't need the lantern. Mr. Villaricca doesn't know the path, and he does need the lantern. Now, you get that black behind of yours down the path, or I'll whip you till your nose bleeds."

"Massa Blake, whupping or no whupping, I's gonna sleep right here on the floor les' you carry me. I ain't gonna go down that path by that spring without no lantern."

Blake, his anger ebbing, looked at her and shook his head. "Brother Smith, you baptized this girl. See if you can talk some sense into her."

Smith turned to the frightened girl. "Child, have you ever seen a ha'nt?"

"No, sir."

"Were you born with a caul?"

"Don't know."

"A caul, a veil over your face?"

"No, sir."

"You are not the seventh daughter of a seventh daughter?"

"No, sir, I is the only of a third or fourth. I don't recall just which."

"Then, you know it would be impossible for you to see a ghost?"

"I don't want to see none."

"Ghosts can't harm you. They are transparent spirits without hands to claw or teeth to bite. They can't harm you, and you can't see them. Why are you troubled?"

"Rawhead and bloody bones got teeth."

"Indeed, but they have no musculature. Without jaw muscles, they can't bite."

"I go by that spring, and old Chippie start rattling his chains and moaning, he scare me to death."

Brother Smith shrugged his shoulders and sighed. "I fear, Brother Blake, that logic is lost on this child."

"See, Sol, I told you you'd never find a reasonable nigra."

"Perhaps I might help," Solomon offered, "since it is I who am depriving Melinda of the lantern."

"You're welcome to take a swipe at it, Sol. Maybe you can save her from a whipping."

Solomon removed the cross from his pocket, his intended gift for Brother Smith, and stood. He leaned forward far enough for his beard to block the lights from the candles beneath him and to give a chiaroscuro effect to his face, except for the reflection of the more distant candles in his eyes. He held the cross above him and tilted it to let the mica flakes embedded in the gilt glitter in the candlelight. His voice dropped to a tremolo, gentle and hypnotic.

"Melinda, are you a Christian?"

"Yes, sir."

"Do you believe that God is good?"

"Yes, sir."

"You know, then, that once the Glory of God surrounds you, no evil can come to you?"

"Yes, sir."

"You know evil spirits cannot live in the presence of good spirits? Brother Smith will bear me out on that statement."

"True," Brother Smith intoned. "The two spirits are mutually exclusive."

"Melinda, you recognize the symbol of your church, this cross?" Solomon raised a long, slender finger and pointed to the upraised cross, thinking El Greco himself should paint such a scene.

"Yes, sir."

"There are three points to this cross, and these points are symbols." The pointing finger touched lightly as the voice intoned hollowly, "Here is a power against which no evil may stand."

Slowly, keeping the cross aloft, Solomon moved around the table with stately stride, saying, "This cross I will give to you, to have and to hold, from this day forward, forever and ever, amen. Take it with you tonight, and as you walk down the path, hold it before you and above you, touching each point in turn, thusly, and say aloud, 'Aroint thee, witch. Thy husband's to Aleppo gone, he's master of the Tiger.'

"Now, Melinda, can you remember the spell?"

"Yes, sir."

Avidity and interest had replaced the fear in her eyes. He bent slowly from the waist, holding his arm rigid. "Take the cross, Melinda."

She reached.

"No, Melinda. Your left hand. So. Hold it above your eyes. Now, say the charm."

He repeated the incantation in the sepulchral voice he had chosen and was astounded by her vocal mimicry when she repeated his words without a shade of dialect and with his very same intonation.

"Now, I'll walk with you into the backyard and set you on your way. When you get to your cabin, place the cross above your bed. It will give you protection throughout this night, and all the nights of your years."

He led her through the pantry into the yard, repeating again his improvised chant as she held the cross. In the moonlight, the mica flakes sparkled with each beat of her pulse. "With this cross, Melinda, you may go anywhere without fear, to the spring, into the wood, and even to the graveyard at midnight to lay the troubled spirits of the dead."

Suddenly he bent down and whispered, "Meet me at the spring in an hour when I go for water for my mules." Raising his voice, he said, "Go, Melinda, and fear no more."

He watched her for a moment as she walked steadily down the path, holding the cross aloft in the moonlight and casting the nonsensical spell with her words.

Upon his return, Bill Blake was complimentary. "Good work, Sol. She's so scared of ghosts that I had to put a lamp in her cabin, and she burns more oil than the big house."

"What's this Chippie she's afraid of?"

"Papa Blake had a slave who was too old to work and given to night roaming. Papa put chains on his legs to keep him from wandering off and getting lost. He hobbled down to the spring one night and either died and fell into the spring or fell into the spring and drowned. Ever since then, the nigras swear they can hear his chains rattling and his moaning down by the spring."

"The darkies have some interesting ghost tales, Mr. Villaricca," Mrs. Blake said. "I'll tell you some, but let's go back in the drawing room where it's less stuffy. If y'all take your cups, I'll fetch the coffee pot."

Brother Smith dropped behind with Solomon as they filed out. "I was interested in that incantation you taught her. Does it really lay the spirits?"

"Invariably," Solomon assured him.

Solomon was half an hour late at the spring. In the distance, the slave quarters were dark, except for a single light from Melinda's cabin. The cabins were huddled in the moonlight like unsheltered chickens in a drizzle. Bending to fill his bucket, he heard Melinda's voice from the slight rise above him. "Mr. Ricky, I do wants to thank you for the cross, and I want to thank you for what you said about us having souls."

"Come closer, Melinda, and talk lower. I'm late, but you knew I would come, didn't you?"

"Oh, yes, sir. I been waiting."

"You have the cross?"

"Yes, sir. It scares off ha'nts. It truly do."

"Tomorrow, I'll bring you a gold cross on a golden chain that you can wear around your neck. Then you can keep the big one over your bed."

"I thank you, sir."

"Is it safe to talk here?"

"Yes, sir. I reckon this is 'bout the safest place, lest Brother Smith comes down."

"He'd have no call to. Beulah took the house water in, didn't she?"

"Yes, sir."

"Melinda, do you remember Dixon Kelly?"

"Oh, yes, sir. Deed I do, sir."

"He's waiting for you in the North, at a city called Cincinnati, Ohio. He wants you to come to him."

"You mean he wants me to run off?"

"Yes, he wants to marry you, Melinda."

"Lordy, mercy, Mr. Ricky, I thought he was just guying me."

"No. He was serious. He's in love with you, Melinda."

"Lordy, Mr. Ricky, he done gone crazy. I can't marry no white man."

"You can in Ohio, Melinda."

She giggled, low and throaty. "Mr. Kelly, he mighty raunchy."

"Melinda! He has the most tender affection for you. He wishes to make you his wife. Would you be willing to marry him?"

"Mr. Ricky, I'd be mighty proud to marry Mr. Kelly. I'd be mighty proud to make free. I'd be mighty proud to sing in heaven at the throne of Jesus, and I'll be singing in heaven with Jesus before I make free and marry Mr. Kelly."

"Do you trust me, Melinda?"

"Sho I trust you, Mr. Ricky."

"Then I'm going to trust you. You know what would happen to me if I help you make free and get caught?"

"Sho, Mr. Ricky. You'd get hung dead."

"You wouldn't like to see me hanged, would you, Melinda?"

" 'Course not, Mr. Ricky."

"Then, I'm going to tell you something very secret. This is a secret between you and me. Mr. Kelly sent me all the way down here to carry you back to Cincinnati. Are you willing to go North with me?"

"Mr. Kelly do that?"

It was purely a rhetorical question; he could tell from her knitted brows and her look of wonderment.

"He did, indeed, Melinda. Will you come?"

"Mr. Ricky," she blurted, "I don't want to go off and leave Massa Bill. Who'd take care of Massa Bill if I ain't here?"

Solomon was taken aback. "Why, he's got his wife to take care of him—and Beulah."

"Beulah, she's no-count. Miss Phoebe, she gets cranky. Massa Bill needs me."

"He threatened to whip you, tonight."

"He don't mean nothing, Mr. Ricky. He always threaten to whup me. He's the kindest man. I got a lamp in my cabin. And I got a bed and a counterpane. Brother Smith, he done give me a Bible with pictures of Jesus. I dearly loves Massa Bill."

"Melinda, you're swapping a lamp, a Bible, and a counterpane for your own house, your own carriage, and a husband. Mr. Kelly's a very important man up North."

"Mr. Ricky, I'd sho like to have them things, and I sho

like Mr. Kelly, but I ain't never been up North. I likes it fine right here in Georgia."

"Then, why did you come here tonight?"

"I just wanted to thank you for my cross and for saying us colored folks got souls."

"I'm sure you're welcome!"

Villaricca grabbed the bucket in one hand, the lantern in the other, and walked down the path to his caravan. In his anger and disgust, he sloshed his trouser leg, and had his religion not forbidden it, he would have turned the moonlight blue with curses.

Truly, it was no dishonor to be an unwilling bondman, but somewhere, there must be a special imprecation to invoke for a serving maid who kissed the hand that cuffed her.

Was it the hand that cuffed her? Solomon set the half empty pail beside the van, ripped off his boots, jerked off his trousers, and crawled to stretch himself on his bunk and consider the situation.

Solomon remembered how Bill had come skulking into the caravan Saturday night to buy those four yards of silk, saying that he wanted it for two petticoats to be made by Beulah for his wife's Christmas.

Solomon had taken Blake's words at face value. Now he wondered. Four yards! Two petticoats for his wife— and a chemise for his concubine? Ordinarily, Solomon would not have associated the open-mannered Blake with a nocturnal prowler of the slave quarters, especially a man married to Phoebe Blake. On the other hand, Blake was not exactly a spiritual man, and even Solomon had felt carnal stirrings toward the slave girl.

"Who'd take care of Massa Bill if I ain't here?"

Was Melinda's superficially innocent remark truly innocent?

Whatever her reason, Melinda did not care to go North.

"Villaricca delivers the goods" had been a motto true for generations, honored from Lisbon to London to Philadelphia. Would that motto survive, now, in Cincinnati?

One thousand dollars! Enough money to stock the entire ready-to-wear compartment at the Trade Fair, more than enough for two years' rent on the building. All gone! Gone at the whim of a simpering servant girl who thought she had a soul.

Oh, Melinda! Melinda! Should he hog-tie her, gag her, throw her into the hidden compartment beneath his bunk, and drag her to a freedom she did not want?

He moaned.

He had worked from false premises. He had assumed that all slaves wanted freedom. He had accepted without question Kelly's word that the girl shared his passion, trusting that only the simple words to her that Kelly awaited her would send her, ass over appetite, to Cincinnati. Folly wide the mark! Melinda had the house servant's instinct for recognizing a person of breeding, and a girl fresh-ripped from the Congo would have known that shanty Irishman for a lout. All the same, Kelly was the world's most abysmal cocksman if the girl preferred slavery with Blake to marriage with him.

He thought of the massive fists of Kelly. The man who broke this news to the Celt would not only lose a thousand dollars, he would lose his jawbone to the ass.

Moaning and muttering his lamentations, Solomon tossed for a full fifteen minutes before he realized he was still wearing his coat and shirt. He arose to remove them and lay down to lament some more, when suddenly he was granted a rare insight.

He sat up, swinging his legs over the edge of the combination bunk, false-bottomed merchandise drawer and stowaway's compartment with sliding escape hatch. Lamentation, he was suddenly aware, was nothing more than an old Hebrew trick for diverting the mind emotionally to give the intelligence a clear shot at a problem. While he had lain moaning and groaning, his mind had been working to solve the problem from an entirely different approach.

Villaricca would deliver the goods!

He could not force the girl to come against her will, but he could force her to change her will. He could not make her want to come, but he could make her fear not to come.

Melinda was not the key to the solution of the problem. That key was the majestic mistress of the plantation, Phoebe Blake.

Only a moment ago, in his anger, he had considered the possible infidelity of Bill Blake. Suppose Phoebe Blake suspected an illicit liaison between her husband and Melinda? It might well be that the disputatious banter between the Blakes reflected deep-lying hostilities and doubts. Could it be, he wondered, that those cool, gray eyes of Phoebe Blake did not smile as readily as her face because they could not smile?

If such doubts existed, they would explain her damning

a great cook with faint praise. It would even explain her lack of enthusiasm for an author, however popular, whose romances must needs seem shallow and whose pratings about chivalry ring hollow to a woman who had ripped the beguiling mask from the face of chivalry and romance, Southern style.

It did not matter if her suspicions were false or true. To make Solomon's plan workable, they needed only to exist.

He had two days in which to find out, and if the Lord saw fit for him to prey on the personal tragedy of a gifted and gracious lady, so be it. God, Himself, had set the pattern. Big fish ate little fish. An innocent child might waste away from the inroads of tapeworms, but who could, therefrom, question the goodness of God? God must also consider the welfare of tapeworms.

Solomon slept.

Bill Blake left for Atlanta at seven-thirty, Monday morning, in the carriage of Brother Smith, who was dropping his host off at the railroad station prior to returning to Ellijay.

Solomon's caravan was parked on the edge of a pine grove facing a pasture, and he had a clear view of the big house across the pasture. He had finished breakfast after a pleasant awakening by the field Negroes singing as they swung along the path by his wagon on their way to work. Presently, he was boiling eggs for his lunch, when he saw the carriage pull away from the house.

Watching, he saw the preacher's buggy swing off the road and across the pasture toward him. Solomon walked out a ways into the pasture to meet it.

After greetings, Bill said, "I told Uncle Fred to stay in his cabin, it's the third by the path as you go toward the house, case you wanted to use him. He's the best goddamned scarecrow in Pickens County, and he's got a good eye for birds."

"That's mighty nice of you, Bill. Can he ride a mule?"

"Sho, and he'll enjoy the outing if you can keep him awake."

Solomon shook hands with the two men and assured Bill that he would take good care of his wife. Brother Smith gave his last and shortest injunction, "Have a good trip North, Brother Villaricca, and go with Jesus."

They were gone, splashing across the small branch that

43

drained the spring, and Solomon turned back to throw more eggs into the boiling water.

A few hours alone with a garrulous old man should afford him useful information about the Blakes.

He bridled his mules and threw a balanced sack with his eggs and his field glasses over the jack and mounted, leading the jenny toward the line of cabins, seven in all, which lay west of the path. He stopped before the third cabin and yelled through a half-open door that sagged on its leather hinges. "Fred!"

A tall, gaunt, and slightly stooped Negro came out of the doorway, looping a single left suspender over his right shoulder.

"Yes, sir, Mr. Ricky."

"Mr. Blake says it's all right for you to come up on the ridge with me and help me try to find a bird. Want to come along?"

"Yes, sir. I'd 'preciate that."

He walked over to the jenny, led her to a nearby stump, climbed up on the stump, and swung aboard.

Fred fell in behind Solomon as they jogged down the path toward the road. "Looks like we're in for a warm day," Solomon said.

"Yes, sir. Sure do look like a scorcher."

As they passed the rear of the Blake House, Solomon remarked, "Very nice house Mr. Blake has."

"Yes, sir. Real fine house."

"Could use a new coat of paint, though."

"Yes, sir. Getting a little scaley in spots."

They emerged from the pathway onto the road and followed it northwest for a quarter of a mile. There, the road turned almost due west and began a winding ascent of the ridge. For a space, the road cut a red gash through a stand of hardwood, and Solomon commented favorably on the timber. "Yes, sir," Fred agreed. "That red oak makes mighty fine lumber."

"Sometimes it warps, though, and the knots pop out."

"Yes, sir. Man got to be careful curing that old red oak."

Solomon knew that he could say the sky was red and the old man would agree. Fred was "following behind the man," a polite practice of Negroes that did nothing to stimulate the conversation, yet the talking lent a pleasantly desultory note to a pleasantly languid scene, and through it he was gaining, he hoped, the old man's trust.

Pine stumps along the way emitted the drowsy odor of resin, complementing the drowsy hum of insects from either side of the road where bees were plundering Cherokee roses. Once a coach whip fully eight feet long slithered across the road before them, but the snake was too far away to frighten the mules.

It took almost an hour to reach the ultimate crest of the ridge because the road wound sharply to avoid outcroppings of boulders, leprous with gray lichen, as large as small houses. Road building in North Georgia, Solomon knew, was an art that had never been discovered; yet, he rarely grew impatient, because the bend in the road always lured him with the promise of some grand vista.

After they topped the crest, he was rewarded with such a scene.

They were on the western slope of the spine, riding parallel to the crest, when the road passed over an outcropping of granite so sheer it cleared the treetops below and gave them a view northwest. Far away, through the cloudless air, he could see a mass of mountains tumbled against the horizon and of a color so blue that their hue seemed to diffuse upward and stain the sky a deeper blue.

"Fred, this is our observation point."

"Yes, sir."

"We'll tie the mules down here in this grassy spot and go up under that oak tree above the trail. It'll be cool up there, and we'll have a view across the ravine. Reckon you can make that climb all right?"

"Yes, sir."

They dismounted. Solomon carried the bag with the eggs and his field glasses, while the old man scrambled up the hillside with something approaching agility.

"We'll sit here and lean against the tree. Don't make any sudden movements. Keep your eyes on that area, there, starting with the hickory tree on the spur and working back up the hill. I'll look down the ravine. If you spot any bird that's got red on it, tell me. By the way, have you ever looked at anything through field glasses?"

"No, sir. Don't rightly reckon I have."

"Here, take a look at that hickory. Slide the barrel of the glasses slowly back and forth until it comes into focus. That way, you'll be able to pick out single leaves on the tree."

Solomon adjusted the glasses to fit his own vision and handed them to Fred. The old man's hands trembled as he held the glasses. He looked through them quickly with-out making any attempt to focus and handed them back.

"Yes, sir. They sure make things clear."

Fred had seen nothing through the glasses. He was afraid of them.

They sat in silence for fifteen or twenty minutes, when out of the corner of his vision Solomon caught a glimpse of a cardinal fluttering below the trees. It flew across the ravine and perched in a sumac bush not twenty yards away in Fred's sector. Fred said nothing.

"See anything red, Uncle?"

"No, sir. Not yet. Just an old blue jay."

"What I'm looking for is a rose-breasted grosbeak. He'll have a black coat, a white breast, and red around the throat like he's wearing a red bandana."

The cardinal swayed in full view with no halloo from Fred, who was scanning the area with the intensity of a ship's lookout.

"Fred, you see that sweet gum tree down yonder, just to the right of the bend in the road?"

"You mean that tall one?"

"Yes. Isn't that a red bird near the top."

"Now, that might be a red bird, but I thought it was an old mocker."

Solomon lifted the glasses. "I guess you're right, Uncle. It's a mocking bird."

"Thought it was a mocker the minute I seed it."

The only tall tree by the bend in the road was a scraggly longleaf pine. Fred, the keen-eyed bird scarer of the Blake Plantation, could not see fifty feet.

"Well, we've worked long enough. What say we take a little nap?"

"Yes, sir. I could use a little catch-up sleep."

"Well, let's stretch out, then. No sense wasting all this cool shade."

Solomon slid down, pillowed his head on a root, and closed his eyes. Fred did likewise, saying, "If Massa Blake come up the trail, I hear him, and I wake up, or I catch hell."

"You wake me up, too," Solomon said. "I don't want to borrow you to work, and we both go to sleep on the job."

In a few seconds the old man was snoring.

As a source of information about the Blake family, Solomon felt he might have drawn a low card from the pack when he got Fred. So far Fred had told him nothing, not even that he was half blind, but he did not want to give up on the old man. If he had concealed his blindness from Blake for so long, he must have a form of cunning, and since he had learned an approximation of Solomon's name so quickly, he must be in close touch with the house girls.

Solomon's summons to Fred had been an order of the master. Taking a nap on the job was stealing the master's time. Fred would awaken refreshed, pleased with his theft, and grateful to the man who had permitted it.

Solomon drifted into a deep sleep.

He awakened first when the sun neared zenith. Quietly he sat up, stretched, and took the eight eggs and a packet of salt out of the bag. He reached over and shook the old man. "Wake up, Fred. Dinner's ready."

"Lordy, Mr. Ricky, that was surely a wonderful nap. I do thank you for it."

"I took one along with you, but I don't want you telling Mr. Blake we spent most of the morning up here asleep."

"I won't tell him. No, sir."

"All we got is eggs and water, but that ought to keep us till suppertime."

"I surely like eggs, sir."

"It's half and half, Fred. Four for you and four for me."

Fred was an egg-lover. He ate the four eggs in eight bites.

Solomon took a swig from the canteen and passed it over to the old man. "Uncle, you know I'm an Israelite. We were slaves, once, just as you black people."

"Yes, sir. I hear talk about Moses leading them Children of Israel to the land of Canada."

"You know Moses married a black girl, Uncle?"

"I don't rightly recollect."

"He sure did, Fred. Almost broke up his family over it. His brother, Aaron, got so mad he tried to take over from Moses. His sister, Miriam, she went around bad-mouthing Moses, too, but the Lord didn't like it when they started talking against Moses. You know what the Lord did, Uncle?"

"No, sir." The old man was interested.

"The Lord stuck up for that colored girl. He chastized Aaron and turned Miriam into a leper. And the Lord didn't let up till Moses' family took that black girl in."

Old Fred's eyes glowed with belligerency. "Them white

47

folks ought to let Moses be. He want to fuck that girl, that he's business."

Solomon nodded agreement. "That's right. Then there was King Solomon—he's the one I'm named after—he got a hankering for the Queen of Sheba. Some say he had a pickaninny by that girl, a boy who grew up and got to be King of Ethiopia. What do you think about that, Fred?"

Fred thought for a moment, and then he cackled with laughter. "Them Children of Israel, they sho must like they's poontang."

Solomon waited for his mirth to subside and said to him, "Some black girls are right pretty. That girl, Mellie —she strikes me as being a prime piece. You ever get into that, Uncle?"

"No, sir." He shook his head slowly. "I get my ass whupped."

"You mean Mr. Blake's saving that for himself?"

"If he is, he don't tell me."

"Then why would he whip you?"

"He won't. Beulah, she whup me. Beulah's my woman."

Solomon felt like a boxer feinted out of position. To gain breathing space, he clinched. "Does Mr. Blake whip his hands?"

"Not that I recollect. Miss Phoebe, though, she whip hell out of them uppity house niggers."

"Miss Phoebe whips her maids?"

"She sure do. Miss Phoebe, she quality folk. She don't take no sass from no nigger."

"You mean the girls sass Miss Phoebe?"

"No, sir. She whup them so they won't sass her. She get a little drunk, she frail hell out of them."

"You mean Miss Phoebe gets drunk?"

"She sure do. She drunk most of the time. She drink wild strawberry wine. Lordy, Mr. Ricky, she must have barrels. She don't have no truck with tame strawberries. I sure hate to see May come. Summer's all right, out in the fields, scaring crows out of the corn. Fall's good, riding to town on the cotton. Winter's best, with the crop laid by, setting inside roasting goobers. Come spring, I'm out in the woods picking strawberries. If I don't pick a gallon a day, I catch it. Even Jimmie T. pick strawberries."

"Does Miss Phoebe let her hands see her drunk?"

"No, sir. Nobody but Beulah and Mellie."

"Then how do you know she drinks?"

"Beulah tell me. Beulah lives with me."

"Mr. Blake must know she drinks."

"No, sir. She honey and pie to Mr. Blake leaves. Then she get drunk and whup Beulah and Mellie."

"If they get whipped, they must be scarred. Mr. Blake isn't blind. He could see from the blood and bruises that the girls had been whipped."

"No, sir. She got a little whip I made for her that don't cut they hides. I got a peach tree switch, and I shined up some leather. I wove that leather round that switch. It ain't very long, but it swishes, and it hurts. She keep it hid in her drawers so Mister Bill won't find it."

"Well, Uncle, this is all very interesting, but I don't want you telling anybody you told me this, least of all Beulah and Mellie."

"I don't tell them house niggers nothing."

"I don't want Mrs. Blake ever to know that you told me this. If she ever finds out that I know she drinks or that she has that whip hidden in her room, I'll know that you've talked too much. If you talk too much, I'll let Mr. Blake know that you can't see fifty yards in front of you, and he'll have you back behind a hoe. Is that clear?"

"Yes, sir. But I thought you being a child of Israel and a slave like me, you'd like to hear it."

"I enjoyed hearing about it. Now, go get those mules!"

"Yes, sir, boss. Deed I will."

Solomon rode down the hill with Fred trailing him at a respectful distance. His anger against the old man slowly subsided under the lulling sway of the mule's motion and the pleasant odors of mule and harness leather. Take mule sweat, he thought, I like to smell it because it's plain and honestly animal. Man sweat I can't abide because man is supposed to be more than animal.

Behind him rode a hurt and sullen old man who was not responsible for his thoughts, because his thoughts sprang from a background for which he was not responsible. Granted, the old man might be forgiven for weaving a whip to be used on the backs of serving girls, there must be a line, somewhere, where even the most lenient judge stopped understanding and initiated punitive action.

Once back in Cincinnati he must go to the seminary and look up in the commentary "Forgiveness, limits of."

They turned a bend in the road above the red oak grove and the plantation lay below them. Solomon reined in his mule and motioned Fred to ride up.

In the clear air, the buildings and fields were so plainly visible that Solomon could see chickens pecking in the yard behind the house. He marveled at the symmetry of fields so rare in this unsymmetrical land, the blue-green of the wheatfield to the left of the house, the dark green of cotton, and the bright green of corn to the right, and the red thread of the road looping among the fields to be lost in the forest. Beyond the forest was another ridge line, and far to southward, almost lost in the blue haze, he could distinguish the soaring knob of Kennesaw Mountain.

From his eminence, he felt suddenly the arrogance of a hawk looking down on a cluster of chickens, and he shoved the mood behind him. If he slipped one inch in caution, he might lose a mile to danger. He was the chicken. The hawks were down there.

"Look, Uncle," he said, "isn't that a beautiful scene?"

"Yes, sir, Mr. Ricky." The reprieve granted by Solomon's tone brought a happy smile to the old man's face. "You knows I can't see it, but if I could, it would be the prettiest sight I ever did see."

"Forgiveness, limits of" might be extended to cover the evils of senility, Solomon decided; but, down there, in the white house gleaming in the sunlight, a lady of quality moved lithely and in grace. Only the shadows in her eyes gave a hint of the twisted mind behind them, of the inhumanity that put her beyond the limits of human forgiveness.

She who loved the whip would be flayed by whips, and though innocence would suffer, innocence would flee, and flee to a man who was younger than eighty years of age.

He thumped the mule's ribs with his heels and headed downward.

Mister Dixon Kelly had better start filling those inside straights. Melinda was on her way.

Chapter Three

"If I reasoned as Brother Smith does, Mrs. Blake, I might be reluctant to offer you an after-dinner drink . . . 'Cursed is he who putteth the cup to his neighbor's lips.' But this is sparkling Burgundy, the veritable essence of French *joie de vivre*." He cradled the bottle in his hands for her viewing. "It's offered to you as a token of my appreciation for your hospitality and to honor graciousness and vivacity which make the sparkle of the wine pale by comparison."

"Why, Mr. Villaricca, after such a charming compliment I would be happy to accept a glass of vinegar."

"This is vintage '48, a dry spring followed by a wet summer, not a large harvest but an accomplished harvest. *Voilà!* I invite your attention."

Deftly, he inserted the corkscrew and popped the cork, topping the bottle into his glass before filling hers. "To my absent host and to my hostess, *shalom!* May your years be long and your children many."

"To our charming guest . . . I declare, this is good. It's been years since I tasted sparkling Burgundy. Papa used to have it served on ceremonial occasions."

"Your father must have been a man of discriminating taste. Certainly, in his choice of daughters. Your sister is likewise a lovely woman."

"Amelia was the prettiest thing. I was the happiest girl at her wedding because I was so glad to get shed of her. Does that sound mean? I knew I didn't have a chance to catch a beau with Amelia around the house."

"Your father's plantation was near Rome, I recollect."

"That's where we went to live after we left Alabama. Our family plantation was originally just north of Mobile. Papa had such a deal of trouble with yellow fever we had to move north. I was just eleven when we left, but I remember to this day the big house, the azaleas in the moonlight and the big, fluted columns on the veranda. Not the little square poles you see on the front porch here. There were oodles of servants, liveried, too. I reckon I'll always be an Alabaman at heart.

"Still, I got much to be thankful for. Bill is a good husband, and the rest of my family made out well too. My brother James has six hundred acres down near Covington. Brother Harry is a representative down at Milledgeville. My first cousin Lamar Turnipseed is high sheriff up in Ellijay. Yes, Turnipseed is a big name in North Georgia."

From the southwest, they could hear the rolling rumble of thunder. Phoebe listened while the sound rippled and died.

"My, this is good wine. It arouses fond memories. I think of Papa, poor, impractical Papa. He thought goobers would replace cotton as a cash crop. He came north and settled on the Coosa River. My mother—Mama could get a little bold with her language—always said that 'Coosa' reminded her of something little girls had . . . But, I'm talking too much.

"You'll forgive me, Mr. Villaricca, but it's not often that I have an intelligent man to talk to. Are you comfortable down in the grove? Do our nigras pester you?"

"Not at all. Little Jimmie T. ambles down, now and then, for a licorice drop, and he always thanks me prettily."

"I just love that little pickaninny. If anything ever happened to him, I'd die."

"He's certainly a well-mannered little fellow."

"I been thinking about teaching him to read. When I get old and blind, like Mama got, I'll need somebody to read to me."

"That day is not inevitable, Mrs. Blake. May I offer you more wine?"

"If you'll join me."

"Gladly."

"I usually limit myself to three glasses before I go to bed."

"Wine's very relaxing, and it induces sound sleep," Solomon commented as he poured, thinking that she must have had at least six glasses of vintage '58 strawberry before dinner.

He had been troubled at dinner. The chicken and dumplings were delicious, the service faultless, and Phoebe Blake a glittering hostess who had discussed music with some understanding, but he had picked up with his salesman's instinct a definite feeling of hostility from Melinda, directed not at Mrs. Blake but at him.

"I may stretch my limit tonight, since I've got such a charming guest. Usually, I don't stretch my limit, except for love or money, but I feel safe around anyone wearing a skullcap. Here's to Solomon Villaricca, the Wandering Jew.

"My, this is delicious wine. Do you mind if I call you Sol, like Bill does. Mr. Villaricca sounds so formal."

"Certainly not. I prefer Sol."

"Then, you call me Phoebe."

"Phoebe. I dearly love that name. Greek for the goddess of the moon. I believe the Romans called you Niobe."

"You know, Sol, wine is a marvelous drink. You take a few glasses, no more than three or four, mind you, and all the little cares and worries dwindle away. You can think about things that really matter, things like family.

"You know, Sol—well, you don't know, because I haven't told you—Bill doesn't like for me to talk about family, because Bill isn't really family."

She leaned forward and lowered her voice in the warm intimacy he found so flattering. She pronounced her words carefully to keep them from slurring. "Bill's father was a riverboat gambler. Now, I know that sounds romantic, but it was a small boat on a short river. Papa Blake won his first slaves from a drunken planter in a card game.

"I know that y'all up North don't go in for breeding like we do down here, Sol, but I would put the Turnipseeds up against the Howards or the Roanokes or even the Washingtons. More than the Washingtons—they seem to have run out with George. Of course, my first cousin Lamar, up in Ellijay, drinks a little too much . . . What do you want, Mellie?"

Unobserved by Solomon and silent in her cloth slippers, Melinda had entered the room.

"Miss Phoebe, it's fixing to storm, and I wondered if I could go home early. I's through in the kitchen."

"Have you lowered all the windows?"

"Yes, ma'am. Do you want me to take out the wine-glasses?"

"If I wanted you to, I'd tell you to. You've got the lantern?"

"Yes'm."

"Then you may go."

"Good night, Miss Phoebe."

"Good night, Melinda . . . Melinda, mind your manners. Aren't you going to tell our guest good night?"

"Good night, Mr. Ricky."

"Good night, Melinda."

After she had gone, Phoebe Blake said, "Imagine the insolence of the girl. A body would think she's minding my p's and q's. I don't know what's got into her, lately. Did you notice how she defied Bill last night? And she's been positively sullen all evening. She's got the vapors."

"Have you had a doctor in to see her?"

"We got old Mary down in the quarters. She's good at herbs. I have Doctor Cartwright's manual on the disease of nigras. I think she's suffering from dysaesthesia Aethiopica, and getting worse . . . Shall we have another nip, Sol? I see your glass is empty."

"My pleasure, ma'am."

Solomon poured, thinking that jealousy was the most beautifully just of the cardinal sins because it carried its own punishment. He who distrusted those he loved suffered for that disloyalty with the self-flagellation of his own imagination. The charming lady across from him who delighted in wielding the whip on her servants would be no less sparing of herself.

"If I may venture an opinion about Melinda, I don't hold with Doctor Cartwright, although I respect his scholarship. My diagnosis of Melinda's ailment is quite different. How old is your girl?"

"Seventeen."

"Ah, so I assumed. Freshly blossoming into womanhood. From her the air of languor, the detachment, the inattentiveness, I feel her ailment is far more universal than dysaesthesia. Now, Phoebe, I make no pretense at being a doctor, although I once considered the profession and took a few courses in the apothecary's art, but I think I recognize her malady."

He took a sip from the glass to heighten the dramatic

54

tension. "No, Phoebe, I diagnose her ailment as lovesickness. That girl is in love."

"Why, Sol, who could she be in love with?"

"You would know better than I, Phoebe. Is there some young buck on the plantation or on an adjacent farm who might have struck her fancy?"

"There's only Mr. Peter's crazy Will, across the railroad about a mile, but he's so touched and taken with night wandering that the patrolers don't even bother with him anymore."

"Last night, she spilled Brother Smith's soup as she leaned over. Is it possible that she might have developed a case of puppy love over Brother Smith?"

"Heavens, no! Brother Smith is all of thirty-five."

"But young girls are often smitten by older men."

"Brother Smith baptized her. He's her preacher. Nigras don't look on preachers as men. They're something way out yonder."

"Mind you, Phoebe, I don't suggest it's Brother Smith. I merely inquire. Unions between the races sometimes occur at the North. So, I'm sure that black hearts can be taken by white manhood."

"It wouldn't be Brother Smith," Phoebe said slowly. Then she repeated, as if talking to herself. "No, it wouldn't be Brother Smith."

Suddenly, she seemed to rouse herself and asked, "You say your studies have touched on medicine?"

"Indeed. I once aspired to the profession of healing, but my father's death put an end to the ambition."

"I wonder . . ." She sipped slowly as she debated some inward problem. Finally, she resolved it. "Solomon, would you think me very bold if I touch on a rather indelicate matter?"

"Certainly not, Phoebe. Anything you say to me is held in the deepest confidence."

"This isn't as if I were asking a doctor for free advice, because you aren't a doctor. But I have a chum down in Marietta, Lucy Belle Barrington, and she's been married three years without having any children."

"That's not unusual. Leah and I have been married four years without children. Of course, I'm gone from April to September."

"But Lucy Belle tries hard, and the doctor says she's healthy as a brood mare . . ."

"Actually, Phoebe, there are only a few days in a month in which a woman is receptive, and even then, it's difficult to conceive unless it's during the full moon. It may be that her cycle is out of phase with the moon, a common enough occurrence in modern times, when women are courted by artificial light. In olden times, women were courted only in the light of the full moon, and moon barrenness was unknown.

"Another theory holds that a woman should be completely relaxed. Perhaps your friend is trying too hard, and her anxiety makes her nervous. Perhaps she resents her husband's advances. She might suspect him of infidelity. Something must prevent her from relaxing."

"What you say seems sensible, Sol, but maybe she finds it hard to relax under such beguiling circumstances." Phoebe's drawling accent on the word "beguiling" gave a faintly ironic edge to her remark.

Solomon was convinced that "Lucy Belle" was Phoebe Blake, and Phoebe Blake had left herself vulnerable to his next thrust, but Solomon delayed his attack in order to establish himself more strongly as a man of religious character.

"Has she tried prayer?"

"Lucy Belle and I aren't religious. But don't you ever dare breathe a word of this to Brother Smith. He'd just die."

"Don't you believe in prayer, Phoebe?" Solomon's question was not a delaying tactic but asked out of sheer curiosity.

"I don't bend the servile knee to anybody or anything. God and I have a working arrangement: He runs heaven without my advice, and I manage this house without running to Him with my troubles. I heard old Mary, down in the quarters, praying to Him to give her a little piece of calico. You know what? Well, you wouldn't know because you weren't here. But the next Saturday, I went down to Canton and bought a bolt of calico and laid it outside her cabin. I would have signed it, 'To Mary, from Jesus,' but she can't read. Religion is good for nigras."

"Well," Solomon leaned back. "It might be that Lucy Belle is relaxed enough, and, as you say, she's healthy. The fault could be with your friend's husband. Do she and her husband hold much slave property?"

"They're rather rich. They have about forty nigras."

"Do you think her husband may have a Negress as his concubine?"

"Why, Sol, she wouldn't tell me. I'm her best friend. She'd be ashamed to let *anybody* know that."

"Sometimes, the vital juices are diluted by excess. From what I've seen of the Negro wenches, few would attract a man of discriminating tastes. But it may be that he has a girl of unusual attractiveness, such as your girl Melinda. I've heard stories from the freed Negroes in the North that amalgamation exists. Of course, their tales are probably told to discredit the South."

Phoebe spoke softly, but there was horror and disgust in her voice. "Sol, amalgamation does exist."

Solomon feigned disbelief. "Such a practice is surely out of harmony with the Southern male's sense of chivalry. The Southern woman is known to be such a paragon of virtue that she is enshrined, embowered, and encastled, as it were, in the heart of the Southern male. Surely, such dishonor is not common."

Phoebe's eyes saddened. "The Southern white woman's kept in a castle, all right, with the drawbridge drawn up and the casements shuttered. But that's not always to protect her honor. Sometimes, that's to keep her from seeing out."

A bolt of lightning struck nearby. The house shook with the thunderclap that followed. Solomon flinched, but Phoebe, intent on the storm within, did not pause.

"You, being a man, can never know the degradation a woman feels when the very girl who removes her slop jar might be the secret concubine of her husband!"

There was an awesome sincerity in her voice and intensity. He felt strangely ill at ease, although she was responding as he had wished. It was the subject, he decided. Southern women did not discuss the matter even among themselves, never before a stranger, and he had gained entry to her secret thoughts only because she thought him a man of religion.

"Phoebe," he said without ceremony, "there's enough left in this bottle for two more glasses. Shall we make it a dead soldier?"

"Pour up," she said flatly.

He sought the even tempo of small talk. "That last bolt of lightning hit close by. I hope it didn't strike one of the cabins."

57

"If it did," she said, "there'll soon be a delegation of fully grown men up here to ask me, a woman, what to do."

She settled back with her glass, and when he told her he hoped to leave Wednesday, she suggested that he ride down to the station on the morrow and reserve a boxcar to convey him and his caravan to Ellijay. Thus, he would be able to leave later on Wednesday and arrive earlier in Ellijay with the mules fresh. Besides, it might rain and make the roads impassable.

It was an excellent suggestion, he agreed, and as he spoke, the rain started with a hesitant patter on the roof and rose to a steady drumming. She asked about his mules, and he told her he had rigged the tarp to protect them.

"The hands won't be working tomorrow," she said, "because the fields will be wet. Why don't you bring your fiddle, Sol, and let's give the nigras a violin and piano duet. They just love music."

He assented, and they talked for a while of the program they would present.

He had underestimated her capacity for wine. When time came to retire, she led him to his bedroom upstairs with no observable stagger; but he had drunk enough to watch her progress with more than objective interest.

He was glad to be alone, glad for the opportunity to wash his socks and rinse the taste of Burgundy from his mouth. As he stripped to his drawers, he weighed his evening's work: He had planted the seed, but the harrowing had not been done properly. Phoebe required stronger wine than Burgundy to produce the catastrophic hangover which would spur her to beat some sense into Melinda's head.

When he walked to the washstand, he found no water in the pitcher, and the washbasin was soiled from last night's occupancy.

Solomon was exasperated. Sock washing was as much a ritual in his life as prayer, and he cursed the girl, Beulah or Melinda, who was responsible for this gross negligence.

His exasperation soared to fury when he discovered the chamber pot had not been emptied from the night before. In disgust, he placed it as far away from his bed as the room permitted and used the window.

He blew out the lamp and crawled into bed, onto a mattress of goose down so soft it seemed of little greater consistency than air. With the crash of thunder outside and the driving spurts of rain against the windowpane, he welcomed the enveloping warmth, but as he sank deeper into the pillow, he caught the unmistakable odor of evangelical sweat.

They had not changed the bed linens after Brother Smith.

He groaned and wadded the pillow beneath his head to give his nose more clearance.

In the morning, when Phoebe awakened sick and mean with a hangover, as he had planned, and wished to wield the whip, he would volunteer to hold high the butt of the girl responsible for this debacle.

Solomon awakened to bright sunlight streaming through the window and the sound of a knock on the door.

Broad, black, and beaming, Beulah stepped in. Solomon raised himself onto one elbow.

"Beulah, will you bring me some water for my pitcher, clean out my washbasin, and empty my chamber commode?"

"The chamber commode, sir?"

"That thing." He pointed to the offending pot.

Beulah giggled. "Oh, you means the slop jar. How it get way over yonder?"

"I put it there. It stank. Somebody forgot to empty it. Somebody forgot to put water in the pitcher. Somebody forgot to clean the washbasin, and somebody forgot to change the bed linen."

"Reckon Mellie forgot to tell me we was having company in the company room. Now, don't you fret none, Mr. Ricky. I'll be back directly."

She swooped down on the chamber pot, cuddled it in her elbow under one breast, grabbed the washbasin, tucked the pitcher in a nursing position, and waddled out, still giggling over "chamber commode."

From the window, it was a beautiful day. The storm had swept away, and the sky was azure. Along the slopes that rose behind the house, the trees were still drenched in shimmering raindrops. He could smell the odor of wet shrubbery from the garden below, where the roses flashed scarlet and white and the red earth seemed redder against the brighter green of the grass. On the topmost limb of a peach tree near the barn, a brown thrasher swung and sang to the morning.

Georgia, he thought, was too good for the likes of Georgians.

There was only one place setting at the table when he entered the dining room. Melinda lounged by the pantry door.

"Am I too late for breakfast with your mistress?"

"Miss Phoebe feel poorly this morning. She say you go ahead without her. She say she see you this evening. Want some coffee now, sir?"

"Yes, Melinda."

She brought it promptly. It was very good, but recalling the night before, when there had been sugar and cream on the table, he asked her if the items were still available.

"Oh, yes, sir. I forgot."

She was definitely hostile, and he felt that she was unwisely so. She might blame him for the hangover that caused her mistress to feel poorly and brought the threat of the whip closer to her, but Phoebe would wait until he left before she used the whip. It was to Melinda's interest to keep him in the house as long as possible.

Bringing cream and sugar, she said, "I got buckwheat cakes, eggs boiled, or eggs fried in butter. Miss Phoebe said you wouldn't want any bacon, ham, or sausage, but I got it if you wants it."

"It's kind of you to make the offer, but I'll take the buckwheat cakes."

In five minutes, she returned with a platter of buckwheat cakes, but she forgot the syrup and butter.

By now, he was definitely irritated. He had been more than considerate of the girl simply because she was going to be his traveling companion on a long journey, but the time had come for him to put her in her place.

"What's wrong around here? Are you girls holding a forgetting bee? Beulah forgets to clean up the guest room because you forgot to tell her I'll be in it. Then, I come to breakfast, you forget to serve half the food."

"Yes, sir. It sure is a forgetful place. People don't only forget what they're supposed to do. They forget what they say they're going to do."

His reprimand was sidetracked by her remark. *She* was rebuking *him!* Suddenly he remembered. He had promised her a cross to wear around her neck, and he had forgotten. He should have known better. An item of jewelry that sold for ten cents after a hundred percent markup was a bagatelle to him, but to her, it would be the equivalent of crown jewels.

He had thought her hostility sprang from fear of the

60

whip, and it had been nothing more than resentment over his failure to deliver a geegaw. All things were relative. The lash was a part of her morning's routine, but the loss of a trinket was a pain too great to be borne.

"Yes, Melinda, we do forget. Sunday, down by the spring, I promised you something. This evening, I'll give you my bag to take to my room. You open it, and you'll find a package for you. . . . Now, I mustn't forget Beulah. Your package will be white, wrapped with a red ribbon. Beulah's will be blue, wrapped with a white ribbon. Now remember, you have my permission to open the bag. The white's for you, and the blue's for Beulah."

"Why, bless you, Mr. Ricky, I surely will remember. Can I get you some more buckwheat cakes, Mr. Ricky?"

"You may, Melinda, and more coffee, please."

His second batch of pancakes were folded over and held by toothpicks. There were three. Inside were delicious cores of strawberry jam, blackberry jam, and crab apple jelly. They were frosted over with powdered sugar. Solomon ate with gusto and profuse compliments under the beaming gaze of Melinda.

On the afternoon of this second day, Solomon brought gifts. For Melinda, he brought the golden cross on a golden chain and a bracelet of imitation pearls. For Beulah, in the blue package, he brought a golden bracelet and a string of glass beads, knowing full well that he would be out of the state before Beulah's golden bracelet stained her wrist with telltale green. For Phoebe Blake, he brought along his violin and an executioner's ax in the form of a large bottle of cognac, a brandy of rare bouquet, compelling taste, and eighty proof.

The soiree was a success, not so much from the quality of the music presented but from the quality of its reception. Phoebe opened wide the windows, and the Negroes sat on the porch. As an audience, they were uncritically responsive to the moods of the airs they heard, and as slaves, they held an obvious and unalloyed affection for their mistress.

At the end, he and Phoebe joined in "Oh, Susanna" and sent them homeward clapping their hands and singing, "Go Two in a Row, Chinkapin Hunting."

The evening's music was a pleasant prelude to a supper of savory beef stew. Phoebe sparkled with the afterglow of the entertainment. Yet, she seemed tense, and her gaiety had pensive moments. Solomon thought her mood might be the result of her missing her afternoon's intake of alcohol because of the musicale.

When they retreated to the drawing room, Solomon was only mildly surprised that her china closet contained brandy glasses. He had noticed that her piano was well tuned, and when she swished the brandy in her glass with a practiced motion, he was more than ever aware that she was a woman who paid acute attention to her hobbies, music and drinking.

"Sol," she said, "you've only been here since Friday, but you're already an old friend. I'll miss you when you're gone."

"Thank you, Phoebe."

"I wonder," she said, taking her first sip of brandy. "This is delicious, but it's almost as strong as bourbon."

"The cognac is kosher, but what are you wondering?"

"Well, you partly answered my question. You wouldn't try to get me drunk and seduce me on sacramental wine, would you, Sol?" She shook an accusing finger in his direction.

"It would be sacrilege," he said, "but very pleasant."

Somehow, he was not surprised at her remark, and his own answer pleased him.

"Now, I warn you, Solomon Villaricca, the minute you start to take off that skullcap, I'm going to scream . . . How was your trip to the station?"

"Muddy." He heaved a sigh and shrugged his shoulders. "And your Marietta and North Georgia Railroad should be cursed with a plague of train robbers. For a boxcar to Ellijay, they charge me two dollars."

Phoebe was sympathetic. The planters along the route, forced to use the M & NG, called it the tapeworm because it drained all the money from the area.

They veered into a discussion of religion after he had asked her bluntly if her husband was aware of her attitude toward prayer.

"I don't keep secrets from Bill. He doesn't care. He prays himself, but he says he gets to his knees to give God a fighting chance."

She inquired about the Hebrew faith, and inspired by her interest, he spoke of rituals.

After he had spoken at length, she said, "Sol, you've got the most soulful brown eyes I ever did see. And that nose of yours isn't Hebraic. It's a keen, aristocratic nose. I bet when you held your *bar mitzvah*, the girls were lined up around your house . . . Now, why don't you eat pork?"

Last night, he had thought her habit of changing topics was the result of her drinking, but now, as the brandy warmed him, he felt he had done her an injustice. Her mind caught juxtapositions of ideas and held them quickly to the light, but she invariably returned to the main thread.

When she had exhausted her questions on Judaism, he was surprised when she leaned forward and said, "Sol, I believe your religion is the same as family to me. We want to be part of a tradition or something greater than ourselves because we're not sure of ourselves. Do I make sense to you?"

"Not exactly. But I think you're on the verge of letting me in on a great truth, and I'm waiting."

"Remember Sunday night, when Mellie was scared to go to her cabin alone and without the lantern? Bill's threats did not convince her, and neither did Brother Smith's peculiar logic."

Solomon's mind leaped into rapport with her at the use of the word "peculiar" for Brother Smith's logic.

"Then, along comes good old Sol," she continued, "but he didn't tamper with her superstition or threaten her. He used her religion to persuade her to go home alone. You used her religion as a superstition. Don't tell me you didn't. And that little incident told me more about you and religion than all the little skullcaps you can ever wear."

"Phoebe, you have a very analytical mind. Shall I pour?"

"Go ahead, but don't you get drunk . . . Now, you listen. I need tradition for reassurance. Not like Bill, who makes his own traditions as he goes along.

"Take you, Solomon Villaricca. You're not content just to be Solomon Villaricca, so religion makes you something. I'm not saying we're weaker than the Bills of this earth, I'm just saying we've looked into a chasm, so we cling to bushes for support. We want to reassure ourselves by being *something*."

"Phoebe Blake," he said, with genuine admiration, "you are that rarest of all creations, a profound woman. I propose a toast."

"Go ahead, Sol, but go easy on this brandy. It's strong. And I know you're not used to drinking sacramental wine by the glassful. Doesn't matter to me, I can drink you under the table."

She was chiding him, swinging into a rare mood under

the impetus of the brandy, and he was being drawn into her wake. In the three nights he had been in her company, he had drunk more alcohol than he usually drank in three months, and enjoyed it more. He lifted his glass, feeling a sudden glow in his mind, in the room, and emanating outward to cover half of North Georgia.

"To Southern womanhood."

"To Southern womanhood," she echoed, "white or black."

Suddenly, she raised her voice. "Mellie, quit standing behind that door and come in."

Melinda opened the door and walked in.

"Girl, how many times do I have to tell you that I don't want you eavesdropping?"

"Miss Phoebe, I just got to the door. I swear."

"You took a long time coming through. Are you done with the dishes?"

"Yes, ma'am. And I wanted to thank you and Mr. Ricky for the music. It was real pretty."

"Thank you for your courtesy, Melinda, and good night."

"Good night, Miss Phoebe. Good night, Mr. Ricky."

"Good night, Melinda."

She turned with a swiveling of the hips which he recognized as Phoebe Blake's manner and left the room.

"You must have given her a Yankee dime, Sol. She's been a lot more friendly toward you this evening."

"I brought her some trinkets."

"You shouldn't have done it, Sol. It'll upset Beulah."

"I thought of that. I brought Beulah a gift, too."

"My, you're going to lose money on this visit. Two bottles of wine for me and jewelry for the servants have eaten up your profit on four yards of silk."

The woman was diabolical. He had not heard Melinda approach the door, but she had, even while intent on talking. There had been no overt display of hostility from Melinda yesterday, yet she had sensed it. Now she spoke of Bill's purchase of the silk, even to the amount of yardage.

Solomon said, "You are very intuitive, Phoebe."

"I don't believe in intuition. God gave me an analytical mind, and it would be an abomination not to use it. Besides, my servants answer my questions when they're asked . . . I wanted to get Melinda out of the room because she's the next subject on my agenda. You didn't know that I had an agenda, did you, Sol? Well, you

64

wouldn't know, because I haven't told you. But I am a woman who has a purpose to everything that I do. Finish your glass, Sol, and pour us another. Then, hang on to your skullcap!"

He poured, and if he remembered correctly, this was their fourth glass. It was beginning to affect him, and he was a two-hundred-pound man. He wondered about the approximately one hundred ten pounds of woman across from him.

"I've run a few tests on you, Sol, and you've passed them all. I know that you're a strong-minded man, not a prude, and that you're a man of broad sympathies who can keep a confidence. So, I'm going to ask you to do something for me that is very irregular. I want you to take Mellie to the North with you."

Her quietly uttered words burned the air between them.

"Phoebe, are you out of your mind? That girl's worth two thousand dollars."

"Solomon, you sound like a slave trader. You can't put a price on a human being."

"I don't. But you Southerners do." He sat back, making no attempt to conceal his amazement. He had not expected it to happen like this. He had expected to steal the girl, not to accept her as a gift, and he felt suddenly disinherited.

Gratefully, he let her continue talking.

"You've been too long at the South, Sol, and I'm disappointed. Sell Mellie! Why, I wouldn't be able to sleep nights. In the first place, she doesn't belong to me. She was a part of Papa Blake's estate. Bill would never let her be sold. He would not even let her be sent away, because he doesn't think she's intelligent enough to take care of herself, but I want her to be free while she's young.

"With girls like Beulah, it doesn't matter. Beulah's happy. But Melinda is made of finer fiber. She's too intelligent, too gifted, and she could earn for herself far more than Bill and I could ever give her. If she could reach Canada, there are African societies up there that would educate her, and she's capable of being educated. Here, it's against the law for me to even teach her to read."

Solomon was as confused as an expert pool player watching the right ball sink into the wrong pocket, but he had to admit that he knew little about the inner thoughts of a flagellant. It was possible, even probable, that Phoebe was setting the stage for one last, glorious orgy with the lash.

"Phoebe, I appreciate your humanity, but it would be murder for me to try to take her to the North. If I were caught trying to smuggle a slave out of Georgia, I'd be lucky to get to prison. A mob might hang me on the spot. A sheriff might shoot me."

"Nonsense, you would never be caught if you kept to the mountains. Those hillbillies would never turn you in. They hate us. And I'm sure you'd be more than a match for the back-country sheriffs."

"But what about feeding her?"

"She would feed you. She's got a genius for anything edible. She knows all about herbs and roots and berries."

"Bill would put out a reward for her."

"Indeed he would. But few of those mountain towns have telegraph wires."

Solomon's mind began to function. He was in a bargaining arena, and here was familiar and beloved ground.

"True, but the few towns that do have are the ones I do most of my selling in. I couldn't stop in those towns with a fugitive slave in my possession. I wouldn't be able to call on at least a third of my customers." He shrugged his shoulders. "Phoebe, as a human being, I love you. Believe me, I am your friend. For so gracious a woman as you, I would gladly put my life in jeopardy. But, I have to think of the money. I'm a commercial traveler, and I have a wife to support. As a merchant, I go proudly. As a thief, I skulk."

"Solomon, my family has never been in trade. I know little about money. How much would you lose if you took her with you?"

"At least a hundred dollars."

"Oh, my, I could never reimburse you that much. I might be able to raise a hundred dollars, but I would have to write to my brothers, and that would take two weeks. Bill comes home tomorrow, and I have to do it while he's away."

"Phoebe, for you I will split the loss, fifty-fifty. Make it fifty dollars, and the girl goes with me."

"Solomon, I only have thirty dollars."

"Phoebe," he clasped an anguished hand to his brow, "thirty dollars for a thousand miles. For that, the Marietta and North Georgia Railroad would charge you sixty."

She sat for a moment, considering. Then she smiled, a bit sadly, he thought, and said, "I haven't been completely honest with you, Sol, but it wasn't that I didn't intend to.

I just remembered. Papa Blake gave me a twenty-dollar gold piece before he died. I never thought of it as money, it was sort of an heirloom, but I will give you that."

"Phoebe, it hurts my heart, but business is business."

"Then let's get on with it."

She rose and walked over to a breakfront. He did not watch her but sat swishing the brandy around in his glass. The fifty dollars would help reimburse him for the loss of the girl's true market value. It was unfortunate that a woman of such social grace should have to pay for the shrewdness of an uncouth Irishman, but this was business. You made a little, and you lost a little.

"I heard you Hebrews were sharp traders," she said behind him, "but I never dreamed I'd be giving up my souvenir of Papa Blake."

"If you're a Jew, you're a sharp trader," he said. "If you're a Gentile, you're an intelligent commercial man."

"Really, I'm grateful to you, Sol, and I believe in paying my way."

She did not hand him the money but laid it on the table beside him. He did not count the scrip when he picked it up, nor did he bite the rim of the gold piece. In her world, honor was a part of her way of life, and he pocketed the money quickly to get it out of sight.

Leaning back, his fingers fluting the stem of his glass, he said, "Phoebe, I don't feel good about the gold piece, so I'll tell you what I'll do. I'm generous. Tomorrow, before I leave, I'll drive by the house and drop off that bolt of silk. You will have enough to make drapes for your drawing room windows."

"Why, Sol, that's right kind of you."

"You are the kind one, Phoebe. To grant freedom to such a girl. But the girl, she is devoted to you and your husband. Maybe she won't care to come."

"You leave that to me," Phoebe said. "I'm very resourceful."

He winced inwardly for Melinda.

"And what about Bill?"

"Bill worries me the most. I'll have to put the blame on you because I've got to live with him. But his train will not arrive till four o'clock tomorrow, and by that time, you should be twenty miles into the mountains. There is no night train to Ellijay, so you'll have fifty miles headstart. He won't be able to telegraph to Ellijay because the telegraph station closes when the last train passes. By the time he finds out that Mellie's gone, the operator will be gone home."

She had outlined an itinerary it had taken him an hour to plan on Sunday.

He hunched forward in the chair, a woebegone and worried look on his face, and she said, "It's a brave thing you do, Sol, but I sensed that you would do it from the moment that I met you. You cheer up now, and pour us another drink."

His reason for drinking was done with, but he automatically poured, grateful that the end of the bottle was in sight. The drink he lifted to his lips marked a milestone in his life. It was the first time in his memory that he had ever taken a purely social drink.

"To Melinda, God keep and guide her," Phoebe lifted her glass, "and may He watch over you, Sol, on the road North."

She shifted position on the setee with a rippling movement that made him acutely aware of the heavy, ripe, and yearning-to-be-made-fertilized body beneath her changeling's face. His glance fell to her ankles, slender, tapering, and lovely. Suddenly, he did not want this evening ever to end.

"Phoebe, you're not an abolitionist, are you?"

"Sol, I hate and despise slavery. I think it's an unalloyed evil. It's evil for the slave, and it's evil for the slave master. I would like to see it dug out, root and branch, from the soil of my beloved country."

There was a flame in her eyes, and if she were acting, she was acting and not pretending. Before his eyes, she had completely disassembled the woman with a whip and had created a woman who sent his mind soaring with her words.

"I think slavery is an evil for the nigras because we smother them with authority and take from them any independence of action. In turn, they smother us because they demand so much of our attention, give us so much pleasure, and create in us so much shame. We Southerners are like little boys playing with their jimmies . . . Why do I like such crude figures of speech, Sol? You tell me. You're a scholar.

"You know why we Southerners are supposed to be careless and even lazy? Maybe we are, but we didn't start out that way. We fought against our nigras' slipshod way of doing things, and we lost. We became like them, not they like us. When you fight against something, day after day, and can't win, then you give up and drift with the tide. We've drifted on a black tide.

"Bill worries about their expense to our bodies and to our time, but I worry about their expense to our other faculties. Behind a mule, you may find a plowboy poet, but if you lived a thousand years, you'd never hear song from the throat of a slave driver."

As she spoke, the girl flickered behind the woman's eyes, for a moment dark and brooding, now lit with a phantom radiance, suddenly focused with intense sincerity—yet, always she kept her cool, immaculate poise.

"Phoebe Blake," his voice swelled with emotion, "you have about you a quality of spirit that's as gossamer as the wings of a dragonfly, but you're the earth mother. You deserve to be fertilized. You should and you will spawn children like a queen bee. Before you die, your sons will stride this earth as princes among men, because you're a queen among women.

"You're the queen bee.

"Do you know how a queen bee is fertilized? She takes off on her powerful wings and flies straight up, straight into the sun, mind you, into the empyrean, higher and higher." He made a fluting, spiral motion with his fingers toward the ceiling, raising himself on one arm to get greater height. "Behind her comes the drones, beating the air with their wings in their passion and their frenzy. But the weak ones falter and flutter back to earth. The strong beat upward, higher and higher, until only one is left. He, the strongest and the best, mates with her in one self-destroying burst of ecstasy, and so dies."

"Dulce est pro vagina mores," Phoebe intoned.

"What man could ask more than to soar into the empyrean realms of that gossamer-winged mind of yours, mate with you, and die?"

"I declare, Sol, you're a little mixed up, but you're good. And you're right. Bill would kill the man."

"But you see what I'm trying to say, Phoebe? I'm trying to express something very beautiful and personal. My soul is talking to your soul. Who would expect to find the warm heart of an abolitionist behind the cool, poised, and beautiful face of . . . of that paragon of virtue, Southern womanhood? Who would expect to find the Norn Mother in a sweet potato patch?"

"Sol, you're sweet, but girls don't like to hear talk about getting fertilized. You didn't get *that* out of Sir Walter Scott."

"Phoebe, you don't understand."

She did not understand. Her smile, wavering mistily in the lamp's glow, was the warm, indulgent, and slightly mocking smile of a teacher who watches her brightest pupil spelled down, in a moment of inattentiveness, by the class dunce.

She thought he was drunk, and she was right, but she did not understand, could not understand that he was telling her the truth.

She could not understand that he had found in her such clarity of thought and nobility of emotion that his very soul aspired to mingle with that intellect. She could not understand that she epitomized those virtues he so admired, the spirit never to submit or yield, the pride and independence that would not permit her even to bend the knee to God, that coolness and propriety of feeling which let her pick and choose from the pathos of this world to find the correct one, the proper one, to respond to with her emotions.

Poor Phoebe, too selective in her emotions ever to know the grandeur and warmth of such a love as his own, a love all-encompassing in its ability to understand and forgive. Yes, and forgive.

A great and pure emotion welled in his breast. What mattered if in the privacy of her boudoir she bent the lash to a sullen girl too insolent to empty a slop jar; it was her queenly right to wield the whip, as it was her right to grant freedom. For the privilege of opening those sweet thighs to the benediction of Solomon's wand, he would hold the whip for her when her graceful arm grew tired.

"Phoebe, I truly do love you." He lifted his hand to his eye and brushed away a fleck from the tides of his emotion. "You are the most gracious lady, the sweetest, most luscious, most desirable girl I ever did see, and you make the best wine south of Schenectady, New York."

She arose in alarm. "Why, Sol, you *are* drunk! You're crying. I'm going to put you to bed."

"Phoebe, just let me sit here and tell you how beautiful you are. Besides, I don't think I can get up."

"Sol, get up now, you hear!"

The imperious command in her voice aroused him. With effort, he rose from the chair. Her wiry fingers seized his arm, steadied him. She guided him to the stairs, grabbing a candle as they passed the candelabra by the doorway.

"Phoebe Blake, I fear I got a little sentimental, but write this down in your senior class book from Cox Female College and sign my name: 'Roses are red, violets are blue, sugar is sweet, and so are you.' "

"Solomon Grundy, born on Monday, too bad you got drunk on Tuesday. Now, here are the steps. Right foot, up. Left foot, up."

They tacked down the corridor, each leg of their course marked by protestations of affection from Solomon. When finally he stood in his bedroom, after Phoebe had lighted his lamp, he was almost sobered by its spotlessness. Fresh flowers stood on the dresser. Fresh linen was on the turned-down bed. Although he could not see inside, he knew there would be water in the pitcher set in the gleaming porcelain bowl.

"Last night they forgot the slop jar."

Phoebe lifted the lid and checked it and set it near the bed. "If you get sick, throw up in the jar. Now let me help you out of your coat."

"You drank as much as I did," he said. "Long about now, I should be helping you unlace your corset."

"I'm used to drinking," she said. "Anyway, I don't wear a corset."

As she unfrocked, detied, and unshirted him, Solomon declaimed, "Phoebe Blake, when they put that noose around my neck as a thieving slave stealer, I want you to know, right now, that my last thoughts will be of you. Yes, ma'am, when that coarse hemp is rubbing against my delicate skin, you know what I'm going to tell them? . . . Well, you don't know because I haven't told you . . . I love the way you put that sentence in. I'm going to say to that hangman, and to that multitude gathered around the foot of my gibbet, 'I only regret that I have but one life to lose for Phoebe Blake.' "

"If they catch you, you send me my fifty dollars back. You hear? Now, sit down."

He sat on the edge of the bed while she tugged and pulled to remove his boots. "Now, I'm not going to help you out of your breeches. Not a man as potent as you are . . . Relax your foot . . . You'd fertilize me through the ether.

"Now I'm going to blow out the lamp, and you can finish."

"Thank you very much, Niobe."

"The Romans call me Diana. I just tell you that to show my smart." She stooped and blew out the lamp, standing for a moment in the doorway, her candle aloft. "Thank you, dear Solomon, for all that you are doing."

"Phoebe Blake, I'll consider it an honor and a privilege to be hanged for you."

"Good night."

In the morning, Solomon awakened to wave after wave of nausea heaving in the pit of his stomach. He rolled over and sat for a moment on the edge of the bed, and his movement set up sympathetic vibrations in his skull pan. For a moment, he sat perfectly still as his brains sloshed back and forth. He rubbed his clammy forehead with his clammy palm, wondering how one thin envelope of skin could hold inside it so much misery. His hand shook visibly.

Water.

He rose and negotiated the distance to the water pitcher in the manner of a newly risen patient who has spent too long abed. Gratefully, he gulped down a glass of water, feeling its cool trickle down his throat, but when it hit his stomach it spewed up again. Holding his hand to his mouth, he dashed for the chamber pot and stood above it, retching.

When the spasms ceased, he sat again on the edge of the bed, his dehydrated body crying for water that its seared or pickled stomach could not hold. Yet, he was oozing moisture from his pores.

Memory struck. It hit him with the force of a sledge-hammer in his stomach and chest cavity, and he cringed under its blows.

He remembered his lewd, lascivious glances at Phoebe's ankles. He remembered his beautiful sally about fertilizing her and dying. God, how poetic! Memory piled layer after layer of remorse on his already aching skull.

"I love you, Phoebe," he remembered, and the maudlin tears. But, oh, the crowning wit, the cleverness, of that Latinized vulgarity, *"Dulce est pro vagina moreis."*

Remorse became shame, and shame became anguish. He fought off the strong desire to crawl under the bed covers, put the pillow over his head, assume a fetal position, and never arise again.

He forced himself to remain upright, knowing that the

only spark of dignity left to him was in the courage to stand up like a man and face himself. So, half-naked in the sinister sunlight of a July morning in Georgia, a morning racked by the din of singing birds, he faced himself.

In vino, veritas, and, God, the *veritas* hurt worse than the *vino.*

Solomon Villaricca!

Gentle-minded student of Maimon?

No. Prurient peeker-upper of women's dress.

Hawklike plucker of bondmen from bondage?

No. Slimy silverfish slithering out of damp, dark places.

Gentleman and esteemed guest?

A lewd and vulgar oaf who had violated the first law of hospitality by attempting to seduce the wife of his absent host.

He bent down and picked up his crumpled trousers.

He was buttoning the last button on his fly with unsteady fingers when Melinda knocked on the door. At his invitation, she entered, smiling so freshly, moving with such unhampered energy, that waves of envy swept shoreward between his waves of nausea.

She held a decanter on a tray with a pitcher of fresh water and a glass. Bourbon was in the decanter.

"Mrs. Blake send her compliments, Mr. Ricky. She say she won't join you for breakfast, but she say you might 'preciate a little bracer."

One glance at the brown liquid made him want to retch.

"Set it on the chifforobe, Melinda."

Melinda obeyed. Then, furtively eyeing the door, she moved closer to him and lowered her voice. "Mr. Ricky, I wants to go North with you."

Solomon, his bodily ailments forgotten in the shock of her request, fought to keep his voice low. "Child, has that woman whipped you already?"

"No, sir. She ain't whipped me."

"Did you talk to her about going North?"

"No, sir. I don't want to get you hung."

"Sunday night, you didn't want to go. What changed your mind?"

"Sunday night, I was scared of ha'nts. I didn't want to go out in them dark woods in that little old wagon. Why, Mr. Ricky, one little old screech owl light on that roof, we both be dead!

"But yo' cross works just fine. I done tried it out. I went

73

down to the spring, last night. I set there near an hour. Them old ha'nts don't bother me 'tall."

"What about Mr. Blake? You said you loved him."

"Deed I do. Mr. Blake, he's a real kind man. But I wants to marry with Mr. Kelly."

"Melinda, pour me a drink!"

Bill Blake had been correct about unreasonable Negroes. She poured and left. He drank and gagged. After washing his face and hands, combing his hair and beard, and after finishing his dressing, he tried a second and a third. The third went down easily, and the fourth was delightful.

The fifth was illuminating.

His remorse had been caused by his nausea.

He could not understand why he had been so upset over offending the hospitality of Bill Blake. Blake, in Atlanta, was probably well taken care of by now. And Solomon Villaricca had not made that vulgar remark in Latin. It was the immaculate Phoebe who had said, "Sweet it is to die for pussy."

Suddenly, he felt a new wave of remorse.

The fertility approach had been too subtle. A straight "what's good for the gander's good for the goose" argument might have succeeded, and he might at this moment be cupping in his palms the low-slung, pear-shaped breasts of Phoebe Blake.

Maimon would not approve, but Maimon had never seen Phoebe Blake.

Standing beside the open door of the boxcar on the loading platform, Solomon could see less than two hundred yards southward to where the railroad tracks curved out of the forest, and northward less than a hundred yards before they curved again into the dense woods. The clearing in which the station was set, at the intersection of the railroad and the road, was only about an acre, and it oppressed him with its smallness in the leagues of woodland surrounding it. It was an artifact, smelling of creosote, hot iron, and cinders, which made the wilderness more sinister by this puny intrusion.

Standing there, he had the eerie feeling that the glade might be a bubble in the forest of eternity and that he would wait forever for a train going nowhere. His feeling had some basis in reality. The ten o'clock train from Marietta was already the ten-twenty train, and it was making a fair bid to be the eleven o'clock train.

74

He heard the key clicking in the station office and walked over to a bench by the doorway and sat down. When the key fell silent, the stationmaster, who was also the telegrapher, called from inside, "That was Bronson Station. Train just left there."

"Where's Bronson Station?"

" 'Bout three miles south of here, as the crow flies."

"Takes fifteen minutes to make three miles?"

"That train ain't no goddam crow, mister, and she's got a hill to climb. You'll hear her when she hits the grade."

Solomon figured that fifteen minutes of Marietta and North Georgia Railroad time gave him another half hour and started to doze, when his ears picked up the sound of drumming hooves. He aroused himself to await the diversion of a passing horseman. Phoebe Blake came galloping from the forest, riding sidesaddle with the flamboyance of a circus rider. He rose to his feet as she wheeled the horse onto the platform, waving a greeting.

He walked over to help her dismount, but she had swung to the platform before he could reach her and was extending a gloved hand. "Solomon, I just couldn't bear letting you go off without saying good-bye. I got the silk and that charming little 'thank you' note, and I'm going to paste it in my class yearbook, right beside that poem which goes, 'Roses are red, violets are blue.' "

"I suppose I should apologize for some of the personal remarks I made last night, but seeing you, now . . ."

"Solomon Grundy, don't you dare take one thing back you said. After all, what does a handsome man talk about when he's alone with a girl who's worth her salt? The price of cotton?"

The stationmaster-telegrapher emerged and shouted greetings. Phoebe inquired about his health and his family, asking of individuals by name. To Solomon, watching as she chatted, she was even lovelier by sunlight than by candlelight.

She was dressed in a gray tweed riding habit, white ruffled blouse, gray boots, and a jaunty riding hat. She wore gauntlet gloves, and from her left wrist dangled a riding crop.

"I was going to add, Phoebe, that I have to make another personal remark. Your dress is very becoming."

"Like it?" She whirled in front of him.

"It must have come from London."

"The cloth did. Beulah made it to a pattern Bill furnished

75

her. It was my birthday surprise. Course, I knew about it days in advance."

"It's lovely, indeed. But your riding crop must surely be from England."

"Old Fred plaited it for me."

"Did he?" Solomon feigned astonishment. "May I see it?"

She handed him her infamous whip, and he hefted it, slapping it against his palm. It was polished, pliant, well balanced, and flexible.

"He has talent," Solomon commented, handing it back. "That's a professional piece of work."

"He had inspiration," she said. "I told him I was going to whip the house nigras with it, and he put his whole heart into making it."

She grasped his arm and looked up at him, her eyes luminous and wide with mock sympathy. "Sol, honey, I hope your poor little old stomach didn't churn and burn this morning. If you'd asked that queen bee, Phoebe Blake, she would have told you that brandy causes the most excruciating hangovers of all, especially kosher brandy."

"Was I sick! But your bracer braced me . . . Truly, I enjoyed my visit, Phoebe, and I'm flattered that you should come down and see me off. I'm lucky to be here. The train's half an hour late already."

"This train's always half an hour late. I hear it now. It's running an early late this morning."

Far away and dimly, he too could hear the chug-chug-chug of a laboring engine.

"Did you get the merchandise aboard, all right?"

"Safe and sound. A little sad and weepy. I gave her paregoric, and she's asleep, by now. What did you tell her?"

"Can you imagine that ungrateful wench? I told her I was sending her North because I loved her and wanted her to be free. Do you know—well, you wouldn't because you weren't there—that she didn't say one word about hating to leave me and Bill. All she could moan about was leaving Jimmie T."

As she spoke, the engine hove into view around the curve, throwing smoke from its cinder catcher, wheezing steam from its driving cylinders, and slowed to a clanking stop a few yards before the siding switch. The switchman dismounted from the cab.

"Now, Sol, I want to warn you about Mellie. She's a very intelligent girl, and she's got a genius for cooking.

But she's got an impish sense of humor that borders on insolence. If she gets away with one thing, she'll try one little thing more. If you aren't strict, she'll get out of control.

"Now, you won't have to whip her. She hasn't had anything but a spanking since she was born, and that was from her own mammy. Give her a tongue-lashing when she needs it, but tell her why you're scolding her. Always tell her what she's done wrong.

"Now, she's a card when it comes to joking. . . ."

He listened and was listening when his boxcar was hitched behind the engine, run forward, and backed up to hitch onto the rest of the train. He was getting his final instructions when he stood in the partly closed door as the train eased away from the station.

Phoebe stood on the platform as the locomotive rolled into the green ravine that the tracks cut into the forest and waved until his boxcar rounded the curve. Solomon, leaning out, lowered his arm sadly in farewell to the gallant lady he might have wronged so mightily in his thoughts.

He had to find out if he had wronged her.

He edged around the blocked wheels of his van, making his way to its rear. He climbed inside and opened the lid of the chest. He lifted the false bottom containing fabrics and leaned over to gently slap the sleeping girl awake.

"Yes, sir." She opened drowsy eyes.

"Melinda, we're on our way. Tell me, did Mrs. Blake ever whip you?"

"No, sir. Miss Phoebe never whipped nobody. She sharp tongued, but she kind."

"Very well, Melinda, go back to sleep."

He closed the covers of her hiding place, locked the door of the van, and made his way forward. Forward of the van, he took the key from his pocket and placed it in the slit pocket inside his boot, and then he remembered the money. He reached for his wallet. It was all there, the thirty dollars in scrip, twenty dollars that he habitually carried, and the beautiful gold piece. He bit the rim of the coin, and satisfied with its softness, slipped it into the hidden boot pocket with his key.

He had believed the scurrilous tale of a lying and jealous old Negro against the evidence of his own senses, and in doing so, he had wronged a noble woman. He had seen her solicitude for her servants and had felt their love for her, yet he had not believed. He had watched her free a valuable property from the highest of motives, and he had attributed her act to jealousy.

"As a man thinketh, so he is."

Solomon thanked God for the deliverance of the slave girl and asked for greater understanding so that he might put his trust in those deserving of trust.

It took two and a half hours to make the two-hour journey to Ellijay.

On the railroad map, Ellijay resembled a metropolis, fitting terminus for the mighty Marietta and North Georgia Railroad. When he felt the train slow and pass over a switch point, he went to the door of the boxcar and looked out. He could see a cornfield, and over in the far corner of the cornfield was the city of Ellijay.

The train turned away from the town on a Y-track, stopped, spurted steam, and backed up, switching onto the opposite leg of the Y to back into the station.

Solomon changed doors and got his first view of the city unobstructed by cornstalks, a twin row of unpainted frame and log buildings strung along a streak of exposed red clay and dominated by a brick courthouse and the one painted building in the collection, a white frame church with a steeple. The church must be Brother Smith's, and even at the distance, Solomon could see that Brother Smith had opposition in Ellijay. He could read signs on three saloons.

He had hitched his mules by the time the train creaked to a stop, but when he shoved back the door of the boxcar and laid his planking between the door and the loading platform, he found that the platform was too narrow to maneuver a span of mules. He unhitched the outboard animal and maneuvered with the inboard mule only. Even so, the turning circle of his front wheels brought the outboard wheel within scant inches of the edge of the platform. For shuddering minutes, he had visions of a four-foot drop to the ground and an hour's long repair job in Ellijay.

He started his maneuver in view of a group of station hangers-on far down the platform in the shade of the station shed. When he had completed the turn and was hitching the outboard mule to the wagon, one of the men detached himself from the crowd and walked down the station platform. Solomon was bent over, snapping the last trace to the singletree, when the man asked, "Air ye Solomon Villaricca?"

78

Solomon turned to his questioner, a heavy-jowled, fat man wearing a horse pistol strapped to his right leg, blue jeans stuck into knee boots, blue shirt, black hat, and a sheriff's badge.

"Yes, Sheriff, I am. You don't happen to be Lamar Turnipseed, Phoebe Blake's cousin?"

"I happen to be. That's a mighty nice rig you got there."

"Thanks, Sheriff."

Red-faced, pig-eyed, with a flat snout for a nose, Lamar Turnipseed was a disappointment to Solomon. He had expected the Ellijay representative of the North Georgia Turnipseeds to be tall, lean, and to speak with a cultivated accent. Nevertheless, he was flattered that Phoebe had seen fit to write her cousin about him.

"I'll get aboard with you," Sheriff Turnipseed said, "and direct you down to the livery stable."

"That's mighty kind of you, Sheriff, but I'm heading straight out of town. I'd like to visit with you, but I'm running late."

With an agility commendable in one of such heft, Turnipseed swung himself onto the seat of the van. "This ain't no social call. I'm impounding this here wagon."

"Impounding the wagon! Sheriff, I'm a peddler. This wagon is my livelihood, and I don't owe anybody in Georgia a dime."

"I ain't impounding it for debt. I got a telegraph warrant here in my pocket, sworn out agin' you by one Mrs. William Blake. You're under arrest."

"Under arrest!" Solomon's jaw went slack. "What for?"

"Nigger stealing . . . Now, git yo goddamned ass up here, and git this rig moving!"

Chapter Four

" "Go in there," Sheriff Turnipseed said.
"Stand there," Sheriff Turnipseed said.
"Face the wall," Sheriff Turnipseed said.
"Shut up," Sheriff Turnipseed said.

In the one-room sheriff's office facing a barred cell, he was entered on the rolls of the jailed in the presence of the jailer, one Whitey. He answered precisely the precise questions relative to his name, age, place of residence, place of birth, occupation, previous criminal record, literacy or illiteracy.

"Search the prisoner, Whitey."

Whitey ordered him to put his hands against the wall while he rifled his pockets and removed the purse hanging around his neck. They took his watch, handkerchief, and Barlow knife. Sheriff Turnipseed counted the money and locked it in a drawer with Solomon's other possessions, but they did not find the key to his van and the gold piece in his boot.

"Lock the prisoner up, Whitey."

The cell was an extension of the sheriff's office, but with all-brick floors, walls, and ceiling. It was windowless and without furnishings, except for a sanitary pot and a blanket laid on the floor in one corner. The apron of bricks extended four feet into the sheriff's office area. On the edge of the apron, halfway between the desk and the bars, was a brass spittoon centered on a brown doily of near misses.

Turnipseed finished his paperwork, rose, stretched, and said, "I'm gone, Whitey."

When Turnipseed left, Whitey moved from his bench to sit in the sheriff's chair, using the desk as a foot rest. He pulled a twist of tobacco from his dirty jeans, brushed off the dust, and bit off a very large chew. Already, the acrid stench from the spittoon irritated Solomon, and he moved farther down the line of bars, knowing that the contents of the cuspidor was in for a roiling.

Solomon studied Whitey, trying to figure from the man's appearance if he were normally a friendly or hostile person, sympathetic or indifferent, sociable or reserved.

In color, Whitey was almost albino. His wispy hair was blond, his skin dead white. Although he was skinny to the point of emaciation, pouches below his eyes drew his lower lids downward to reveal an abnormal amount of white below the washed-out blue of his irises. His gaze held the dull vacuity of a molting reptile's, and the pale fringe of his lashes was almost invisible. The only color in the face was the yellow tobacco stains on his crooked teeth, and that color was visible most of the time, since he breathed through his mouth.

Whitey probably suffered from adenoids, Solomon decided, and after the jailer emitted his first gob of tobacco juice, Solomon figured he was also nearsighted. He spat in the general direction of the cuspidor, using dead reckoning rather than sighting, and he was a poor navigator.

Solomon could read nothing from the agglomeration of features that made up his face, neither sympathy nor hostility, kindness nor cruelty, thought nor emotion, life nor death.

"Sir," Solomon asked with a maximum of humility, "how long do you think I'll be here before I'm hauled before a magistrate?"

Whitey looked in Solomon's direction, but his eyes focused some distance behind Solomon in the manner of a white Southerner looking at a Negro. "I don't give a shit how long you're there. You can stay there till you rot."

Solomon returned to his thoughts and to the greatest lesson adversity had taught him. He was too trusting.

He had trusted Phoebe Blake. He had believed her impassioned utterance against slavery. A cynical, worldly man would have taken her words at their true value and would have got off the train at Jasper and cut across country. That man with his calloused sensibilities would be free.

It was clear to him what had happened. She had really galloped down to the station to telegraph her cousin in Ellijay, not to bid farewell to her good friend and co-conspirator, Solomon.

But she did not know where he had Melinda!

She had assumed that Melinda was in the van, and he had verified her assumption, but no one knew about the hidden compartment. If Sheriff Turnipseed was no better at searching vans than he was at searching prisoners, he would never find Melinda. He might break down the door of the caravan, but to find Melinda, he would have to chop it into kindling wood.

Something had to be done about Melinda, and done quickly. No doubt the paregoric had worn off, and she was awake. Driven by hunger, she might release herself through the bottom of the van and escape into the night, only to be recaptured. Or she might lie there, growing too weak to move and waiting for a knock that would never come. Probably, a week or so after his trial, when the authorities auctioned off the van, she would be nosed behind the arras.

Solomon turned again to Whitey, who was staring into space and slowly chewing his cud. From his belt dangled the key to the cell and Solomon's dilemma.

If he could get the wispy jailer close enough to the bars to grab him, he could choke him into unconscious-ness, take the key, and escape. But how to get him to come to the cell? It would never do to ask for water or food. He knew from Whitey's answer to his question that jailer would never respond to that gambit.

Southerners were supposed to be hypersensitive about remarks reflecting on their ancestry.

It was that simple! He could not only get Whitey to the bars, he could get him inside the cell.

"Whitey, I asked you a question a minute ago, and you didn't know the answer. I suspected you wouldn't because I can tell from looking at you that you're a moron."

"I ain't no Moron. I'm a Baptist."

"Coming from a man of normal intelligence, that might be a witty remark. Coming from you, it's just another gauge of your abysmal stupidity.

"Probably it's a matter of inheritance. I suspect that the prostitute who whelped you was too feebleminded to collect

82

for her favors, or she was doing her brother a good turn."

Whitey looked at him with something resembling curiosity stirring in the vacuity. "Is that grammar?"

"I'm calling you a dumb son of a bitch."

Whitey's slack lips tautened into the semblance of a grin. "I ain't as dumb as you are fellow, 'cause I ain't coming in there after you."

Solomon sat himself in the corner farthest from the spittoon. His one attempt had failed, and he could think of no other.

Solomon figured it was about two o'clock. In another two hours, Bill Blake's train would be arriving at Blake's Crossing. He could be here by eight o'clock if he pushed his horse. After Blake got here, a hearing before a magistrate might become an academic matter. If Turnipseed found Melinda, he might get his hearing, but then the trial would become an academic matter.

Solomon would have no defense. He could technically claim a sale, but he had no bill of sale, and fifty dollars was hardly the going price for a seventeen-year-old Negro girl. Even if he threw in the thirty dollars he had in his strongbox in the van, such a sum would seem more like a desperate excuse than evidence. If he told the truth—that Phoebe had sent Melinda North in his care—his only witness would be Melinda; and any Negro, free or slave, was not allowed to testify at a trial involving whites. Melinda was a thing, a piece of evidence against him.

Why had Phoebe done it?

With absolute certainty, he could consider himself a convicted felon, as of this minute. If he remembered correctly, the penalty in Georgia for aiding a fugitive slave was seven years. In seven years he would be thirty-three, an old and broken man, if he survived the prison sentence.

He would have to write Leah and tell her to sue for divorce on the grounds that he was a convicted felon. She would then be automatically entitled to his full estate, which should tide her over until she could remarry. It would be hard for her to live him down. There would be whispers in the synagogue. His bright, vivacious Leah would be referred to as the woman who married the felon, but—in time—the whispers would die. In time, the name Villaricca would be forgotten, and his very bones would be dissolved by the slow fire of quicklime in an unmarked grave at the Milledgeville Prison . . .

Seven years in a Georgia prison! O Lord, how could a

son of Israel withstand seven years of sowbelly, cornbread, and blackeyed peas? Even the peas and cornbread were cooked in pig fat, and no doubt, the Sunday delicacy in prison would be pork chops.

Solomon sat and faced the wall and prayed.

For a full hour he prayed, starting in seminary-learned Hebrew interspersed with Ladino, and the burden of his opening lament was the phrase that sealed the wisdom of his fate-harassed and wandering tribe, *"Dino d' malkuto dino."* He had failed to follow the precept of his fathers; he had broken the law of the land, and he must suffer.

He had taken that precept lightly, heretofore, but considering it behind the bars of a prison gave it profound meaning.

Accepting his fate, he asked that he be permitted to endure with dignity the seven years of the locust. He asked that Leah be permitted to marry well, preferably a Spanish Jew of orthodox faith. He asked that God grant him a taste for pork in order that he might endure with less discomfort. He asked that God permit his success with the compartment store and not permit other merchants to steal his idea before he was released.

Even as he prayed, Solomon was aware of external happenings. He heard the swish and splatter of Whitey's near misses behind him, and his nostrils burned with the acrid odor of tobacco juice. Under the circumstances, Solomon did not consider it in the least irreverent to ask God to improve Whitey's aim. Almost immediately thereafter, his ears caught the gong of a direct hit. Solomon considered the sound a good omen.

Finally, he made his supreme request. He asked that he be given an understanding of the mind of the woman who had betrayed him. "O Lord, how does she profit by this betrayal of your son who trusted her? Reveal the workings of her mind to me, O Lord, lest I bear witness to this woman's perfidy in heaven. And give me the strength, O Lord, not to trust. Let my trust be only in you, O Lord."

"Hey, Villaricca, no matter how long you look at it, you ain't gonna find no hole in that goddamned wall."

Sheriff Turnipseed had returned. Bleary-eyed from drinking, he stood in the middle of the room, hands on hips, smiling jovially. "Well, Whitey, how'd you make out with the prisoner?"

"He called me a son of a bitch, Sheriff."

"Now, Whitey, he had no call to do that, did he? He

don't even know your ma, like I do. Have you fed the prisoner?"

"Hell, no, Sheriff. He's a goddamned Holy Roller. He's been squatting over there in the corner talking in unknown tongues."

Sheriff Turnipseed roared in laughter. "He was wailing, you pink-eyed son of a bitch. He's a Jew. Now, haul ass over to your ma's and see if you can dig up some cornbread and turnip greens."

"I'd rather have a couple of boiled eggs, Sheriff."

"See if you can get the prisoner a couple of boiled eggs, Whitey."

Whitey sauntered out, and the sheriff, reeling slightly, went to his desk and sat down. "Seems like your prayers have been answered, Villaricca. You got a friend in court. Reverend Smith will be over in a little while to testify for you. I checked on that rig of yours, and you had it locked, but it don't make no difference. I smelled all around it, and I couldn't smell no nigger. So there's no evidence against you."

"If Brother Smith is testifying, then I'm to see a magistrate?"

"Sho nuff."

"When?"

"Well, that depends. He ain't on duty yet."

Turnipseed tilted back, pulled an inkwell and pen out of his desk, and bent over some forms he was filling out, writing laboriously and looking down at the paper with one eye closed.

Solomon clutched the bars, thinking there was something very irregular about these proceedings. The courthouse was a brick structure down the road. If he were going to be hauled before a magistrate, it must certainly be done before nightfall; and it was already past three. Surely, there was no night court in Ellijay, Georgia; but the judge was not yet on duty.

It was also rather unusual for a sheriff seeking evidence to go over to the nearest saloon and get drunk, particularly if he were going to smell out the evidence. After three drinks, the sense of smell was deadened.

And what value was Brother Smith? Character witnesses did not testify at an arraignment; certainly not at an arraignment for a capital offense.

"You know," the sheriff said to him, without looking up, "if you prisoners knew how much you cost the county, then you'd think twice before getting locked up. Hell, room and board ain't the half of it. You ain't seen so many goddamned forms to fill out since Buck was a heifer, and they ain't just any old piece of paper you write on. These are legal papers. You don't just write down on them what comes to mind. You got to be legal-like, and that takes time. Yes, sir, if you goddamned prisoners knew how much you cost the county . . ."

Whitey ambled in with a slab of cold corn pone. "The hen didn't lay today, Sheriff. All ma's got is this pone."

"Whitey, I keep telling your maw that goddamned hen's a rooster. Well, give him the goddamned cornbread."

Whitey stuck the pone through the bars. "No, thanks," Solomon said.

Whitey ejected his cud into the spittoon, sat down on the corner of the sheriff's desk, and started to chew on the pone.

Brother Smith came briskly through the door. "Can I speak to the prisoner, Brother Turnipseed?"

"He's all your'n, Brother Smith."

Smith advanced to the cell and stuck his hand through the bars. Solomon clasped it, feeling human dignity flow back into him from the preacher's grip.

"Now, don't you worry, Brother Villaricca. Trust God and me. We'll get you out of this. We must render unto Caesar the things that are Caesar's, but be fortified. We are not put here to store up the riches of this earth, but to store up wealth in His kingdom, which is heaven."

Solomon would have never suspected that he would listen with such interest to one of Brother Smith's impromptu sermons. It seemed to hint at a pattern. Sheriff Turnipseed's lecture, a moment before, had also leaned heavily on economics. Now Brother Smith, like a prison chaplain, urged Solomon to take comfort: It was easier for a camel to crawl through a needle's eye than for a rich man to enter the kingdom of heaven.

Brother Smith was pitching into the theme that the streets of heaven were paved with gold as God's way of showing contempt for that metal when his sermon was brusquely broken into by Sheriff Turnipseed. "All right, Whitey, release the prisoner and bring him before the judge."

Solomon was led out of the cell and ordered to stand before the desk. Sheriff Turnipseed removed his badge, slid it into his drawer, and brought out a gavel. He rapped three times on the desk and said, "Now, hear ye. Court of the Honorable Justice of the Peace, Lamar Turnipseed, Third District, County of Gilmer, State of Georgia, is now in session."

Phoebe had been right in saying that Turnipseed was a big name in Georgia.

"Prisoner is charged with aiding and abetting the escape of a fugitive slave, not specified, in complaint brought by Mrs. William Blake, alleged owner of said property. How say you to the charges, defendant? Guilty or not guilty?"

"Not guilty."

"How say you to the defendant's character, Brother Smith?"

"Reckon I can't say much about his character, Judge, but he's got a kindly way with nigras, and he's a religious man."

"Let the record show, and so state, that in the pursuance of his duties, the Sheriff of Gilmer County did inspect the van of the defendant and found no evidence of a fugitive. Since no further evidence has been offered to attest to the claims of the plaintiff, the defendant is released to the custody of a citizen of good standing in the community to await further depositions from the plaintiff. Bail is set at fifty dollars."

Sheriff Turnipseed took the fifty dollars and other possessions of Solomon from the drawer and shoved them across the desk to him. "You pay your fine to the judge."

Solomon pushed the money back, and Turnipseed counted it again. In the process, his fingers paused, he scratched his head, and he finished the count hastily. "Say, where's that gold piece?"

Now Solomon understood. His prayer was answered.

Slowly and reluctantly, he reached into his boot and drew out the coin. He started to retrieve twenty dollars in scrip, when the sheriff extended a pudgy hand. "Just a minute. There's a little more business before this court. You called Whitey a son of a bitch. For insulting an officer in the performance of his duty, you're found guilty of insulting an officer in the performance of his duty. That'll be ten dollars plus ten dollars court costs."

"Sheriff, or Judge, how do you figure ten dollars court costs?"

"Five dollars board and room, five dollars livery fees. Now, get out of here before I jail you for contempt."

Solomon was a free man and in no mood to question

the legality of court decisions. Right about now an irate horseman would be thundering out of Blake's Plantation who would cheerfully deprive him of his remaining rights to life, liberty, and the pursuit of happiness.

He swirled, stalked out of the courtroom-jail, and loped obliquely across the road to the livery stable, glancing at his watch before putting it away. It was five-thirty, later than he had thought.

Brother Smith sprinted to overtake him. "Brother Villaricca, I got a message here from Sister Phoebe."

Solomon broke his stride. "And what kind words does our good sister have for us?"

"She sent me this telegraph." He held a sheet of paper in his hand. "It says here, 'Tell Sol to get out of town fast. Soon as Bill hears about our little misdeed he'll come running. Tell Sol love of money is root of all evil. I just couldn't bear to part with Papa Blake's gold piece.'"

"Do you know what she means, Brother Villaricca?"

"It means I've been slickered out of seventy dollars."

Solomon resumed his stride and Brother Smith his trot. "Brother Villaricca, I'm a man of God, and you're a man of God. You can talk to me in full confidence and with a free heart. What did Sister Phoebe mean by y'all's little misdeed?"

Solomon stopped at the open door of the stable and looked down at the preacher. Brother Smith's eyes were licking their chops and his feet were spread apart in the stance of a small dog eager to leap for a bone. Beyond the preacher, the stable boy sprawled against the wall, snoring softly. Solomon put a gentle hand on the preacher's shoulder. He paused for a moment, staring off into the distance. He thought of the biblical injunction against bearing false witness and, at the same time, that an eye demanded an eye. He took his choice.

"Brother Smith, there are some subjects that gentlemen do not discuss with one another."

The stable boy aroused himself and said, "That'll be fifty cents, mister."

Solomon looked at him over Smith's shoulder. "Fifty cents for what?"

"Feeding and watering them mules."

"In harness? Doesn't matter. You got five dollars waiting for you down at the sheriff's office. Right, Brother Smith?"

"Right. Five dollars livery fee . . . Tell me this, Brother

Villaricca, does she have some weakness? . . . Now, I know she drinks, but . . ."

"You sure of that, Brother Smith?" The stable boy was demanding more assurance.

"I think that's what he said. Go over and ask him."

The boy turned back to his nap as Solomon climbed to the driver's seat.

Brother Smith was tugging at his boot as he maneuvered onto the road. "Does she have some weakness other than drinking that I can help her overcome?"

Solomon halted the mules. "I don't know if it can rightly be called a weakness, Brother Smith. But talk to her alone, sometimes, and see if you can get her to come right out and confess her sins. But, Brother Smith, I feel I've got to warn you, don't let her get you *too much* alone. And, Brother Smith . . ." Solomon paused to look up and down the road, checked the sleeping stable boy, and leaned low.

"Yes, Brother Villaricca."

"When you start talking to her, if that little devil lust starts grabbing at your gonads, you coldcock the little bastard . . . Giddap!"

Both mules lunged forward at the crack of the lash, raising a cloud of red dust around Brother Smith, who stood immobile, oblivious to everything but his own thoughts.

According to Ely Blood, the Gaines' farm was ten miles west of Ellijay on the road to Dalton. Blake, at his starting point, was thirty miles away. It was now almost six, which meant that Solomon could figure on, at most, three hours to get to a farm he had never seen, find a man he had never met, and get Melinda, himself, and the van hidden for the night.

It was against his principles and practice to put the whip to animals he would have to walk nine hundred miles, but if they did not get the first ten miles behind them in a hurry, the remaining eight hundred ninety would be scratched. He lashed each animal once, putting a prayer behind the whip.

Possibly because they had been pent all day in boxcar and stable, the mules responded with élan. Through some chemistry of mules, they matched their strides at the onset, moving with a coordination that gave a wonderful rhythm to their rumps and at a speed which would have frightened an engineer on the Marietta and North Georgia Railroad. Aft of the rumps, the rhythm was quite different. The van slewed, skittered, careened, and bounced on springs built more for strength than resilience, more for the protection of the axles than for the comfort of the riders. He braced both feet on the dashboard and alternated his weight between his buttocks and his thighs to lessen the torture to his spine.

Melinda must be taking a pounding in the chest, but she lay on quilts. At least, she was being battered in comparative comfort.

For a full three miles, the mules galloped down a road stretching straight and level through cornfields, sorghum fields, bean fields, and pinewoods, laying a blanket of red dust along the hedge of blackberry bushes that choked the birn. As the hills closed in and bends began in the road, they swung into an easy canter, still in unison. For three miles they cantered, for three more they trotted. When they finally decided to walk, they had crested the long incline, and the weight of the van behind them kept them moving at a brisk pace.

As the evening shadows crept over the fields and the lonely call of the whippoorwill sounded against the even more melancholy and distant baying of running hounds, Solomon came to the place engraved on his memory that Friday afternoon in April in Ely Blood's office: "A gray, unpainted house built parallel to the road and about fifty yards back from it to the right as you head toward Spring Place. It's atop a knoll. The driveway's lined with oak trees, and the barn's off to the right of the house. There's a sweet-gum in the frontyard, and the kitchen's an ell jutting back from the right of the house. The owner's name is Burl Gaines. He's a widower with three sons. Put thy trust in him, Sol, for he's a good man."

Solomon wheeled into the driveway and drove toward the house, admiring the well-tended cornfield on his left and the fenced pasture on his right. It was an unusual cornfield in Georgia that was well hoed in late July, and between those stalks, there was no grass. A sleek Clydesdale horse ambled up to the fence from the pasture to get a better look at the mules. Surprisingly, no hounds came yelping from the house in greeting and in challenge.

Solomon reined his mules near the barn and climbed down. From the barn's shadowed interior, he heard the swish and splatter of milking in progress.

"Hello, the barn!"

"Be right with you," a voice called from inside.

Solomon walked off a way to look over the farm from the eminence. Behind the house, the ridge crested under a stand of tall pines. Before the house, the fields stretched on either side of the road, ending in a far arc of trees which followed the winding embankment of a creek. Southwestward, where the road bridged the creek, he saw the unmistakable blue-green of alfalfa. On the slopes to westward were apple and peach trees. It was a farm that might have been in Ohio had the house behind him been painted.

As he stood, a voice behind him asked in the twanging accent of the mountains, "What can I do fer ye, mister?"

Solomon turned to face a tall, bearded man wearing overalls and boots and carrying a pail of foaming milk. His rolled sleeves revealed arms as big as young saplings, and his face, heavy-browed below a receding hair line, was handsome although battered. His gray eyes were neither friendly nor hostile.

"My name's Solomon Villaricca. I'm looking for Mr. Burl Gaines."

"You're looking at him."

"I'm a friend of Ely Blood. He sent me."

Gaines set the pail down and extended his hand, smiling. "Pleased to meet you, Mr. Villaricca. How's old Ely?"

"Good, the last time I saw him, back in April."

"How're his boys?"

"Levi and Simon are just fine."

"And how's his wife, Rebecca?"

"His wife, Hannah, does well."

Gaines dropped his easy affability. His body tensed, and his eyes grew wary. He threw a quick glance in the direction of the road. "Reckon you'll do," he said. "Are you in trouble?"

"Bad trouble, Mr. Gaines. I've got two hours, maybe three at most, before they get here."

Solomon sketched the story of the day's events, highlighting Phoebe Blake's behavior at home against the background of the farcical trial and fine arranged at her instigation. "Sheriff Turnipseed," he finished, "thought it was all a big joke, but when he finds out from Blake I really had the girl, the only person left laughing will be Mrs. Blake."

"Where's the girl?"

"In the van. She's been there all day without eating, and she's taken a fearful pounding."

"Let's get her out of there."

Solomon was already unlocking the door. He climbed in, followed by Gaines.

"She's scared of the dark," Solomon said, as he raised the lid of the chest. "I gave her a dose of paregoric so she could sleep on the way up. It wouldn't have lasted too long, and she probably heard the sheriff when he arrested me. Lord knows what state she's in."

He lifted out the interior shelf of merchandise.

Melinda lay like a little black doll in a coffin. Whatever claim she had on womanhood had vanished, and a very young and very frightened girl looked up at the two bearded faces peering down at her.

Her face was tear-stained, her arms were folded across her breasts. Clutched in hands that quivered visibly, she held the gilded papier-mâché cross that Solomon had given her, four days or four centuries ago.

"Melinda!"

"Mr. Ricky."

Her voice was so low it was almost inaudible, and it was shaky with relief or terror. For the first time in five years of slave stealing, Solomon felt compassion.

He reached down and lifted her from the chest. She was weightless in his arms. Gently, he sat her across the aisle on another chest, bracing her lest she fall.

"Are you all right, child?" Gaines asked.

"Yes, sir. I's all right. I weren't scared in the dark, Mr. Ricky."

"Melinda, this is Mr. Gaines. He's a friend. He's my friend. He's your friend. And he's a friend of freedom."

"Pleased to meet you, Mr. Gaines, I'm sure." She attempted a gracious smile in the manner of Phoebe Blake, but her attempt flickered, twisted. Her mouth screwed up. Her lower lip began to tremble. She lowered her face into her hands.

Gaines put his arm around her shoulder, speaking with a gentleness awesome in such a large man. "Child, you needn't be frightened anymore. You're safe now."

"I ain't crying 'cause I's scared, Mr. Gaines. I's crying 'cause I's happy." She lifted her face to him. "I heard them arrest Mr. Ricky, I thought they'd done hung him. When them old mules started running like that, I thought the devil had done took hold of that wagon and was dragging it straight to hell. I grabbed my cross to scare off the devil."

She looked at Solomon. "I ain't scared of the dark no more, Mr. Ricky. Honest I ain't."

"Can you walk, child?" Gaines asked.

"Yes, sir." She stood up, took one step forward, one back, and sat down.

"Good. How would you like some ham hocks and butter beans, roast beef, baked sweet potatoes, turnip greens, and all the milk and cornbread you can eat, plus hot buttered biscuits and blackberry jam?"

"I sure would like that. I's starved."

Solomon stood silent as Gaines spoke, knowing the big man was lulling her with the sound of his voice. "All right, then, Melinda. You go on over to the well and wash up. There's a wash pan on the bench, and you can see the privy. I want to talk to Mr. Ricky."

"Is it all right, Mr. Gaines, if I get my belongings out of the chest? I brung my belongings with me."

"What do you need, child?"

"I need my soap and my towel."

"You brought a soap and towel?" Solomon broke in. "I told you to bring just what you needed."

"I reckoned I'd need a soap and towel. But I brung all my belongings, 'cept my lamp and my counterpane."

"Melinda, you'll be the death of me yet." Solomon reached above her head to a merchandise rack and brought down a towel. From a drawer in the merchandise chest, he took a bar of perfumed soap. "Here, these are for you."

She held the bar of soap in her hand, wonderingly, and raised it to her nose to smell it. "This for me to wash with?"

Solomon tried a jocular note. "Unless you want to eat it."

"I might do just that," she giggled. "It smells like candy."

"All right, you go over to the porch and wash up, Melinda. We'll be there directly, and I'll bring your bandana."

Melinda jumped from the van and scampered to the house, her terror wafted away on the odor of verbena.

Solomon turned to Gaines. "I'd better have a look at this," he said, reaching into the chest for her bandana. "I told her to bring just what she needed."

He untied the bandana, and Melinda's earthly possessions lay before them. Besides a chunk of lye soap and a rag of tattered toweling, they consisted of a faded calico dress, a white chemise made from sacking, a pair of shoes, her cloth shoes, the dark serge dress with the white piping around the sleeves and collar she had used as a maid's uniform, the imitation pearl bracelet, a brass finger ring, and the Bible Brother Smith had given her, which she could not read.

Solomon looked down at the collection with the same feeling of embarrassment he might have felt from looking into a private diary. Here lay the reward for years of devoted effort by a talent approaching genius, and the only item worth over twenty-five cents was the uniform that marked her bondage.

"She was their cook for three years," he told Gaines, "and she's best I've ever eaten after."

Gaines said, "She could have worked there forty years and not added one jot or tittle to that collection.

"We'll take out her Bible and jewelry and burn the rest. She's about the same size Mrs. Gaines was. We'll move the mules into the barn, and I'll show you where she can sleep."

"There's a moon out tonight, and they can see the van from the road," Solomon pointed out. "Don't you think I ought to put the van behind the barn?"

"No," Gaines said slowly. "I want them to see it. My two grown boys left for Dalton this morning with a load of hay, and I can't protect you except with me and the young one. We've got to use guile instead of force."

Gaines was talking as if to himself, as if he had been figuring all possible plans of action and was now selecting the best of them. Solomon felt such confidence in the man that he did not protest what seemed to him the obviously wrong course to take. He unhitched the mules and led them into the barn, where he gave them water and feed while Gaines took the milk to the springhouse.

Solomon's confidence in Gaines was reinforced when he came back and took Solomon into one of the stalls, kicked away the straw, and raised a trapdoor revealing a small cellar. They descended, and he lighted a lantern. It held a cot with blankets and a pillow.

"I'll leave the lantern burning," he said. "She might be more afraid of the dark than she lets on."

Walking back to the house, Gaines said quietly, "Of course, Mr. Villaricca, I can't guarantee your safety tonight, anymore than you can guarantee the girl's safety on your way North, but there's one promise I can make. If the girl leaves here in the custody of her master, I'll be dead."

He spoke in a matter-of-fact voice, but Solomon knew that he spoke the truth.

As they stood on the back porch, taking turns with the washbasin, Solomon complimented him on the beauty of the fields spread below them in the light of the setting sun.

"My boys and me work hard. I had a better farm down in the lowland, but I couldn't abide the slaveowners, and they couldn't abide me. Have you any weapon?"

Solomon told him no and explained. "I wouldn't kill a man protecting my property because I haven't got any property worth killing a man over. I depend on my fists for self-protection. Killing is against my religion."

"I reckon it's against mine, too," Gaines said, "but it ain't against theirs. I'll sleep you upstairs, and I'll give you a Bowie knife to take to bed with you."

As they spoke, the baying of a lone hound on the ridge behind the house was followed by the excited yelping of the pack. Solomon was saying he would kill to save a life of a friend, when Gaines held up his hand for silence. On his face was the raptness of a musician listening to and understanding the harmonics of an angel choir.

Eastward, a blue-white hunter's moon, fast yellowing in the twilight, rose over the ridge, and the high-pitched strumming of insects was dying into sibilance from the valley below. A night breeze stirred fitfully from the fields, bringing the odor of timothy and pine, the clean smell of growing corn, and the rich sweetness of alfalfa. Behind them, the tall pines soughed and tossed their tops in unison like a gaggle of strolling geese. But all sights, sounds, and odors were lost in the baying of the hounds.

Near and loud and far and soft, the pitch changing as the pack dipped into ravines and loped over crests, the mournful ululations flowed with a current of excitement that made the human heart beat faster and human muscles tense for the chase.

They listened for a long minute, Gaines' face keening to the thrill of the hunt and glowing in pride at his hounds, while Solomon listened with deepening sadness. Solomon thought of the fox.

"My youngun's going to be late for supper," Gaines finally said. "Old Cap struck a scent northeast of the knob, and they're hightailing northwest. If it's the fox I think it is, he'll take them over the main ridge and down the creek southwest. Then, he'll circle back northeast, up that creek down yonder, and head back toward the farmhouse. Come morning, the dogs will be right back where they started, their tails down and their tongues out, but they'll be happy."

"Won't they catch the fox?"

"Hell, no! They don't want to catch it. They just want to chase it . . . Come on, let's eat."

Melinda ate with them at the kitchen table.

Burl served her with the politeness he would have accorded a white woman and, Solomon suspected, with far more gentleness.

Solomon spoke of the problem of housekeeping for a widower with three boys. Gaines said, "Housekeeping's no chore. All the boys are neat, but, Lordy, do I have a problem with their language. With no woman around to make them temper their tongues, they all cuss a blue streak. Don't reckon I set them much of an example. Thank the good Lord, they don't fight. Burl Junior can whip Jackson, and Jackson can whip Lafe, so they manage to keep discipline among themselves. Any one of them does the work of four hired hands."

Solomon took an avuncular pride in Melinda. At the table, she imitated manners of her mistress, but no amount of formality could hide the appreciation with which she ate. Gaines was pleased by her running comments on his cooking, all flattering. Solomon had feared she might not be a credit to Dixon Kelly, but observing her in surroundings similar to those she would find in Ohio, he felt Kelly might not be a credit to her. In justice to Phoebe Blake, she had given the girl little in the way of worldly goods but much in the way of gentility.

After supper, Solomon showed her the clothes he had brought from Cincinnati—boys' jeans, a heavy denim shirt, and brogans. She was appreciative, but when Gaines told her that a lady up in heaven wanted her to have something and took her in to show her his late wife's wardrobe, she clapped her hands in delight.

Surprisingly, the dresses of Mrs. Gaines fitted her, even a pair of high-buckled shoes. Gaines let her select the dresses, a white one for summer, feminine with frills, and a heavier dress with a cape. He added stockings, a hat with a veil, two petticoats, a pair of gloves, and a carpetbag to carry them. Solomon understood and appreciated the gift of the veiled hat and gloves.

"I declare, Mr. Gaines, this is just like Christmas," cried Melinda.

"Girl, we'll have to burn your old clothes."

"You go right ahead, Mr. Gaines."

She went with Solomon and Gaines into the kitchen where the cooking fire still burned on the raised hearth and watched as Gaines poked her clothes into the fire. As the remnants of her bondage burned, Melinda seemed pensive and a little sad.

"Upstairs" in the Gaines' house was a sleeping loft, and Solomon's bed was a pallet laid over straw.

Entrance was gained through an aperture four feet by three feet wide in a corner of the ceiling that was reached by rungs nailed to the wall. Solomon could lie unobserved in the shadows and view the room below for its entire length.

Solomon stretched out with the Bowie knife beside him. Sleep would be impossible, he knew, but he might get a little rest.

Below him, Gaines was bent over his account book, entering on his daily record the purchase of a van and its contents and two mules. Solomon had figured a price of two hundred dollars would represent a hardship sale and had written out a transfer of ownership. He had thought this bill of sale a needless subterfuge, but Gaines was a thorough man. Good lying, Gaines said, took far more skill than telling the truth, and that was the best argument for honesty he had found.

Solomon had climbed into the loft shortly after eight. Approaching on to nine, he heard the back door slam. Gaines, whom he could see clearly in profile, did not look up as he called, "That you, Lafe?"

"Yeah, Paw."

"Supper's on the table."

In a few minutes, Gaines finished with the account book and went to the kitchen. Solomon could hear the murmur of conversation as the father told his son of the evening's happenings. Gaines came back, put his account book into a drawer of the library table, and picked up a farm journal.

Despite himself, Solomon was growing drowsy, when his senses alerted to the drumming of hooves in the distance from the Ellijay pike. He listened closely. More than one rider approached—Blake and the sheriff. In their estimate, two would be enough to capture a frightened girl and a meek man of God.

He could hear them turn at the approach road and thunder toward the house. There was no window in the loft, but the moon shone brightly through cracks in the chinking, easily bright enough to reveal the van from the road.

Gaines rose at the sound, reading glasses and magazine in

hand, opened wide the door, and looked out into the moon-light.

Gaines called a greeting which was not answered. Sheriff Turnipseed brushed past him into the room, followed by Blake, still dressed in his town clothes with the high collar, but now wearing a pistol strapped to his leg. Behind the two, Whitey sauntered in, his mouth slackly open.

"Where'd you get that van out front?" Turnipseed demanded.

"Bought it off a peddler, Sheriff. It warn't stole, were it?"

"Whitey, get back and watch them horses. Gaines, I'm gonna have to search this house."

"You got a warrant, Sheriff?"

"Hell, think I carry warrants around in my pocket? I can write out a warrant as judge in this here county."

"I never rightly figured you for a judge, Sheriff. You got your appointment signed by the governor?"

"Quit arguing with him, Lamar," Blake said. "Just search the goddamned place." Blake had already brushed past the two men and was stalking into the bedrooms below. Solomon could hear him opening wardrobes. In Solomon's range of vision, the sheriff was talking. "I'm telling you not to try anything, Gaines."

"Who is that man? Is he an officer?"

"I deputized him. That peddler just stole his nigger."

"He stole that girl? My, my, he really hornswoggled me with his soft talk. I believed every word he said. He told me he was taking her over to . . ."

Blake, moving toward the kitchen, whirled.

"He told you what, mister?"

Gaines, ignoring the belligerent Blake, feigned a look of cunning. "Say, Sheriff, is there a reward out for them two?"

"Hell, ain't nobody had time to post a reward. The girl was just stole this morning."

Blake turned on Gaines. "Mister, if you're hiding that pair or withholding information, you'd better start talking."

"He's right, Gaines. If you're withholding information as to the whereabouts of them two, you're obstructing justice. You're guilty of aiding and abetting."

"Now, Sheriff, how in hell would you know I'm withholding information if I don't tell you what I'm withholding?"

"I got ways of making you talk, mister," Blake said. He was much smaller than Gaines, but his anger made him appear far more formidable.

"Yeah, I reckon you have, mister," Gaines said mildly. He called toward the kitchen. "Hey, Lafe, we got company. Mind your manners and come in and say hello . . . Yes, mister, I reckon you got ways."

Solomon craned his neck to see the kitchen entrance. As he watched, the "youngun" came sauntering through it, a piece of cornbread in his hand.

He was a very handsome young man of about nineteen, with the blue-black hair of a Welshman and smiling, mobile features. He was shirtless and barefooted, with broad shoulders tapering to narrow hips. Solomon figured there was not an ounce of fat on his six-feet-six frame that supported about two hundred eighty pounds. He grinned a welcome. "Hello, Sheriff, you pot-gutted lard ass. Have a good day over in Ellijay beating up drunks after you jailed them?"

"Hello, Lafe," Sheriff Turnipseed said.

"This gentleman, here, was just telling me, Son, that he has ways of persuading people."

"He means legal ways," Sheriff Turnipseed said hastily, and Blake let the interpretation stand. "That van out there is evidence you're withholding evidence."

"Hell, Paw's easy persuaded," Lafe said, walking over to the fireplace and sitting down on a stool. "Just give him a dime, and he'll tell where Grandmaw hid her snuff."

Casually, the boy picked up the hickory nut rock from the hearth. It was half the size of a man's head, and he tossed it idly from hand to hand.

"Yeah, there's ways of persuading me. But one thing's been bothering me, Sheriff. Suppose you pick up this peddler, and he's found guilty. Does that cloud my title to his cart?"

"Well now, that would depend . . ."

"Hell, I ain't looking for legal advice. If you don't catch him, I know my title's good. What I want from you is an agreement, here and now. Nobody in the county can impound the cart but you."

"He'll honor the bill of sale," Blake said.

"That right, Sheriff?"

"That's right, Mr. Gaines."

"Well, now, Sheriff, I got my legal business over with you. You, mister. I don't like you busting into my house like you did. It's going to take a little more persuading from you."

Solomon could see Gaines' face clearly in the lamplight. The avarice and shrewdness in his eyes seemed real when

99

he looked at Blake and asked, "Mister, how much you willing to pay me for the Jew and the girl?"

They were real! Solomon saw the scheme in all its diabolic simplicity.

He who had prayed to God that day for the strength not to put his trust in others was again betrayed. Gaines had left the wagon in full view to attract them to the farmhouse. He had drawn up the bill of sale in order to gain legal title to Solomon's property. He had put Solomon into a room without an exit to prevent his escape, and he had armed Solomon to justify his murder at the hands of the authorities. Lafe Gaines had not been joking when he said that Gaines would betray his own mother.

"I'll give you fifty dollars for the girl, but I won't give a dime for the Jew. He's Turnipseed's responsibility."

"You sure ain't being generous, mister, offering fifty dollars for a girl that's worth a thousand."

"You aren't buying the girl, goddamn it! You're supposed to be a law-abiding citizen. I don't have to give you a dime."

"No, you don't have to do anything, mister. But I say you're going to volunteer a reward of one hundred dollars."

Above them, Solomon planned his moves. Gaines had made a fatal error in giving him the Bowie knife. His thumb along its edge told him it was razor sharp.

Blake was aggressive. He would climb the ladder, with the sheriff covering him from below. But the sheriff was a tosspot, and his reactions would be slow. Solomon would cut Blake's throat with a swish of the knife, and his body, falling, would confuse the sheriff long enough for Solomon to drop the eight feet onto the sheriff. With luck, he might break Turnipseed's back or knock him unconscious. No matter what happened, Gaines must die: Unless he died, Ely Blood would never know what happened, and others would be sent to this house.

Solomon felt a surge of elation. He had all the advantage!

Blake and Gaines would die! That would leave a befuddled sheriff and a boy. Solomon knew his knife, and his quickness overmatched the heft of the boy. As for the sheriff, Solomon would slit his throat with as much compunction as he would feel from sticking a pig and go armed into the moonlight against the vacuous idiot who guarded the horses.

He crouched in the darkness, muscles coiled, knife at ready, exhilaration pulsing through him like a galvanic flow. His moment had come, and he was ready to meet the moment. He licked his lips as he counted the deaths: Blake's from necessity, the Gaineses' from duty, and Turnipseed's and Whitey's for the sheer joy of it.

Old gods faltered. Moses was toppled by Alaric, and Attila scourged David. The gods of battle were trumpeting for blood, and the newest knight of heathendom was readied for the fray.

Over the pulse that pounded in his ears, Solomon heard the devil's bargain being drawn, and he smiled a sardonic smile in the darkness.

"Hell, I don't have but fifty dollars. Think I carry a goddamned safe around in my saddle bags? . . . Hey, Lamar, you got that fifty dollars you fined that pious thief?"

"Sho, boy, but that's county money."

"County money, hell! You didn't get that lard ass on sheriff's pay. Throw it in the pot!"

Turnipseed reached down in his jeans and pulled out the wad of Solomon's scrip. "Count it," he said to Gaines.

"I aim to," Gaines said. He uncreased the bills one at a time and counted them slowly.

"This man's stalling, Lamar," Blake said. "Like as not, he's got the girl in the barn."

"Don't worry, mister," Gaines said. "They won't get away . . . Well, appears to me it's all here.

"Now, you'll find the peddler and the girl between here and Dalton. They was going to catch the train to Chattanooga. My boys, Burl Junior and Jackson, give them a ride. My boys are taking a load of hay to Dalton."

"When did they leave?"

" 'Bout six-thirty. Now, that Jew's a smooth talker. He can tell you any story and make you believe it. He might tell them the truth, for that matter, and bribe them into letting him and the girl hide in the hay. So, when you overtake that wagon, if him and the girl ain't sleeping on top of the hay, you tell my boys you want to unload that hay and search it. If they give you any sass, you tell them their paw said he'd whip hell out of them if they don't let you search that hay."

"They going to drive all night?" Blake asked.

"Maybe. Leastwise till moonset."

"All right, Gaines, I'll buy your story. But if we don't get that girl, I'm coming back for that money, and the sheriff's going to seize that van."

"Mister, I'll make you a proposition. If you don't find

101

that girl, you'll find twice the number of bills you left here waiting for you when you get back. That's a Burl Gaines promise."

"He always keeps his promises, Bill," the sheriff attested.

Blake was appeased enough by Gaines' cooperation to ask, "My horse is nigh winded. Have you got a saddle horse I could borrow, Mr. Gaines?"

"I got a Clydesdale. They ain't much for speed, but they're sure as hell strong. Course, I'd have to charge you a little rent."

Blake did not even ask the rental fee. He turned to Turnipseed. "I'll take Whitey's horse, and he can ride mine back to Ellijay. At an easy trot, we might catch them by moonset."

"Bill, you don't want to ride all night. Why don't we get back to Ellijay and telegraph the sheriff in Dalton to pick them up?"

"Hell, no! The sheriff in Dalton might be another one of Phoebe's cousins!"

"What about Phoebe? You going to leave her down there all alone with them niggers?"

"Brother Smith was kind enough to ride down to keep her company . . . Now, I've run you out of excuses to sit on your lazy ass. Get moving!"

Solomon lay back on his pallet, listening to the hoofbeats recede into the distance. The tensions which had keyed him to murder relaxed, and his whole body quivered.

Inscrutable were the ways of the Lord. He had trusted, and he had been betrayed. He had prayed for the strength to distrust, and belatedly, he had distrusted. In his distrust, he had been disloyal. In his disloyalty, he had planned the murder of a staunch and true friend.

If the events of the day held any religious significance for him, they only served to show that he was a very poor student of theology.

Self-recrimination was a sour mash in his mind that suddenly bubbled with a yeasty influx. He remembered Brother Smith, pounding leather through the night for his imagined tryst with Phoebe Blake, that little devil, lust, grabbing at his gonads.

An hour before daybreak, Solomon was heading due north with his van, Lafe Gaines leading the way. Melinda trailed them astride the Clydesdale in deference to her new brogans. The extra horse had been brought along by Lafe to be used as a third draft animal in the roughgoing Burl Gaines had promised them, and Lafe would ride it home once they had reached the Toccoa Road.

It was Burl's plan that they cut north over the ridge, following an old charcoalers' trail, and then northeast up the valley to cut into the road to Toccoa six miles north of Ellijay.

Young Lafe was their guide through a darkness so dense that he must have found the way by his sense of smell. For the first quarter of a mile along a farm access road, the going was easy. Then, for no reason that Solomon could determine, Lafe veered off onto an old trail overgrown with brush.

The slope was beginning to rise, steeply in places, and the mules had to strain. Stars were visible through a narrow opening in the treetops. After a particularly arduous struggle, they came to a brow of a hill, and Solomon asked, "Is this the top of the ridge?"

"Hell, no, Mr. Villaricca. We got an hour yet before we reach it. We couldn't make the climb in the dark, nohow."

"Call me Sol, Lafe. It's easier to handle."

"All right, Sol. Let the mules rest a spell."

Here, Solomon unraveled a minor mystery. "Why did your papa promise to give Blake twice his money back?"

"Paw didn't say twice the money, he said twice the number of bills. He cut the bills in two. Blake'll get his money back, and the sheriff'll get title to your property, but neither'll be worth a good goddamn."

Solomon walked back to Melinda. Her legs were spread almost horizontal on the broad back of the horse.

"Melinda?"

"Yes, sir."

"Know how to find the North Star?"

"No, sir."

"I'll show you, and it may be the most important thing I'll ever teach you . . . Look up yonder." He pointed to the northern skies. "Can you see the Big Dipper?"

"Yes, sir. There." She pointed.

"Now, take the two bright stars in the handle of the dipper and make like you're drawing a line through them away from the bowl of the dipper. Can you see the bright star that your line points to?"

"Yes, sir, I believes I do."

Her answer was a politely phrased negative, but it did not matter. It was merely a first lesson.

"That's the North Star. In the next week or so, I'm going to teach you to find it in your sleep. As long as you can see it, you'll never be lost. Makes no difference if you're alone in the woods, on top of a mountain, or crossing fields, as long as you follow that star you'll be going in the right direction. If you and I are separated, you sleep in the woods in the daytime, and you travel by night. You always follow the North Star."

"Yes, sir."

"Sol," Lafe said, when Solomon rejoined him, "you'd better brake the wagon down this slope."

Ten yards down the incline, Solomon clamped the brake shoes onto the wheels, and the van sledded over the brush on its wheel rims, forcing the mules downward at a pace which threatened their legs. As he despaired the most, the mules plunged into a sizable creek at the bottom, and the van slued in the water and came to a rest closer to the opposite bank than the mules.

He jockeyed the mules up the bank, but the ledge undercut by the stream balked further progress until he and Lafe levered the wheels onto the bank. After minutes of intense effort, the mules stood snorting on solid ground.

Somewhere in the darkness, a bird twittered. The east grew gray.

At the bottom of their third crest, as they rested from the climb and Solomon gathered courage for the ascent, the light had grown strong enough for Solomon to see ahead.

What he saw made him yearn again for darkness to cover the sight.

"There she be," Lafe said, and there she was.

Solomon was sometimes afflicted by a fear of heights, but this was the first height he had ever seen from the bottom that put a dull ache in his scrotum. Soaring leagues above them, almost perpendicular, the ridge lifted, its sides covered with longleaf pine whose needles would have made slippery going on a flatland. Ground fog steaming up from the trees obscured the summit in a cloud of the mountain's own making.

"You mean to tell me, Lafe, that men drove wagons up that?"

"Not wagons. Two-wheeled carts."

"How can an animal get a foothold on that incline?"

"We'll make it, Sol. We got two mules, a draft horse, two strong men, and a boy!" Lafe guffawed and pointed to Melinda seated demurely on the Clydesdale.

Solomon looked and also laughed.

The trousers fitted the boy well, snugly adhering to the curve of the hip. The shirt fluffed out over an unusual set of pectoral muscles, and the heart-shaped face beneath the hat brim would have made a eunuch yearn for the unattainable.

"Looks like my idea isn't going to work."

"What y'all laughing at, Mr. Ricky?"

Lafe howled in the exuberance of youth. "We're looking at the cutest little boy that ever unbuttoned a goddamned fly. Jesus Christ, Sol! You put that little tooty in smelling distance in front of me, and I'll tote this goddamned wagon over the hill!"

As Solomon helped the girl dismount, Lafe said, "You stay way up in front of that lead horse, black girl, or you're going to hear cussing like you never heard before."

Lafe secured the towline to the front axle bar and led it between the mules to the shoulder harness of the horse in the lead. He cut down hickory saplings and trimmed them, showing Solomon how they would help the animals by inserting the saplings between the spokes of the rear wheels and lever down on the spokes, using the rear axle housing as a fulcrum for their levers. Cursing, lashing, and caterwauling, he started the Clydesdale, the mules following.

Fortunately, the trail was overgrown with brush which provided the animals with traction. Solomon took one rear wheel, Lafe the other. Straining, struggling, slipping, the animals started the ascent; levering his bar and braking, Solomon felt most of the propelling force came from him.

His movement and Lafe's were similar to rowing, but in motion only. Once a spoke moved its maximum distance, one man would hold while the other removed his pole and levered the trailing spoke. On an incline which Solomon would have sworn varied less than twenty degrees from the perpendicular, merely holding the bar in a braking position took almost his full strength; additional strength for levering came to Solomon from desperation and to Lafe from profanity. Prying, holding, prying, holding, they inched sixteen hundred pounds upward with, it seemed to Solomon, only moral support from the animals.

At one point, they appeared to be blocked by a windfallen log partly imbedded in the loam. Sweating, groaning, praying, and cursing, they got the light front wheels over, but the weight on the rear would not permit them to budge the van. Solomon felt a cold and growing panic as the two men braked the wagon and weighed their plight. An overhang from the log blocked the wheels and made the barrier impassable.

Solomon, out of panic, said inanely, "Maybe we can pry the tail up, levering on the log?"

"Yeah," Lafe agreed, "if we had a goddamned tree as a crowbar and could stand out in the air."

Cutting the log into pieces and digging it out would have been a day's work for two men while a third braked the wagon. They stood there, sweating, defeated, holding onto their braking poles, until the boy exploded in disgust, "Fuck this shit, Sol. I'm going under. You just whip that goddamned horse when I yell."

Solomon held onto the brake bar with one hand and grabbed the whip the boy tossed him. Lafe crawled under the back of the wagon. Squatting, he braced himself against the fallen log. His giant muscles bunched. He grunted, and slowly the heavy rear end of the wagon rose from the ground.

Whip in hand, Solomon waited for the wheels to clear the log. The whip crackled at the same time Lafe yelled. The animals lunged forward, dragging the wagon a full eight feet up the slope, well clear of the sprawling Lafe, who leaped to his braking bar and shot it home.

He stood behind his wheel with a look of utter disgust on his face. "Did you see them goddamned beasts? They dragged that wagon ass over appetite once they felt that whip. Them bastards been soldiering on us all the way up the hill. Sol, I don't like to whip another man's beast, but if you give me the word, you and me won't have to raise another hand."

Solomon had heard mule skinners say that driving a mule took talented cursing, that a mule would slack off if given the opportunity, but he had always dismissed the tales as mule skinners' hyperbole.

"I usually use prayers, son."

"Hell, them mules don't know nothing about God."

Solomon considered his aching body and tossed the whip to Lafe.

Lafe's profanity and lash were far more effective than Solomon's prayers had ever been. Paced by the willing horse, the mules moved the wagon four times as fast as they had with the assistance of the men. Their last twenty yards was up a slope so steep that Solomon had trouble negotiating it afoot. When he finally reached the summit, the wagon was there, balanced on the razor back, with Lafe sprawled on the turf beside it. He threw himself on the ground beside Lafe, rolled over on his back, and looked up into the brightening sky.

For such effort, Dixon Kelly was getting the bargain of his life.

Lafe was still gasping for breath when he shouted, "Jesus Christ, Sol, look at that!"

Solomon looked.

Not over twenty feet away, Melinda stood on a boulder looking down into the valley below, her arms resting easily by her sides. Golden light, flooding the crest in parallel rays through the tree trunks, plainly revealed her in profile. Her buttocks curved outward in a smooth arc that met the supple lines of her back, and her breasts crested forward. She held her hat in her hand, and the chiseled molding of her face gave her the appearance of a bronze statue. Solomon appreciated the boy's enthusiasm.

"By God," Lafe said, "for a thieving nigger stealer, you're doing right well. If that ain't chocolate-flavored eating pussy, I don't know my poontang. What do they call her, Sol?"

"Mellie, they call her. Melinda's her name. But lower your voice. She's only seventeen."

"Seventeen! Hellfire, she's five years past nigger prime. I could take a little of that right now. Hey, Mellie, how about you and me going off into the bushes for a spell?"

Mellie was embarrassed, indignant, and highly pleased.

"You hush your mouth, white boy."

"Lafe," Solomon asked, "how can you think about something like that just after you've hoisted a wagon to the top of a mountain?"

"Hell, Sol, I can think about it in church. 'Specially in church. Best piece I ever got was at a prayer meeting down in Ellijay. Won't never forget that one. Ever'body in the congregation was after it, including the preacher, but little old Lafe was the one to put the prong to it, three times without decunting.

"Reckon she must have liked it, too, 'cause she got married about a week later and had two boys in less than two years. Lordy, that poor husband of hers must have that little thing of his'n worn to a frazzle by now."

Solomon rolled over in the grass to face Lafe, asking

107

softly, "You're not talking about little old Eulalee, are you?"

"How in the hell did you know that?" Lafe looked at Solomon with sheer incredulity on his face. "Jesus Christ, I reckoned she'd done spread it around a little before I got to it, but I sure in hell didn't think she'd spread it all the way to Cincinnati!"

Going down the ridge might have been more dangerous than difficult, but Lafe, the marvelous boy, used the towline from his jury rig to reeve the wagon down the slope, anchoring the bight of his line on the boles of trees. All the mules did was guide the vehicle, and in a short time, they were camped in a green glade at the foot of the ridge to breakfast.

It was a pleasant spot surrounded by live oaks, mossy boulders, and a brook. On the hillside westward, the morning was dropping golden light which, reflected into the dale from the forest, gave a greenish cast to the shadows. Solomon's nose relished the cool, rich odor of the dewy moss around them.

Melinda took over the preparations for breakfast with speed and efficiency, while Solomon and Lafe squatted on their haunches and rested.

"How much farther, you figure, before we hit the Toccoa Road?"

" 'Bout six miles, but that's going to take us about three hours, I reckon, 'cause we'll have to cut down a few trees. We'll come out about six miles north of Ellijay, and you'll have a straight shot north for a spell. If they got that road cut through north of Ivy Log, you could be clear across the Carolina border by noon tomorrow."

"How long will it take you to get back home?"

"About two hours at a trot."

"You'll have to go through Ellijay?"

"Sho."

"What if Sheriff Turnipseed sees you coming south along the road north of Ellijay?"

"None of his goddamned business where I come from . . . But if you're worried about him tailing you that way, forget it. Way Paw figured, Sheriff Turnipseed ain't going to be anywhere near Ellijay." Lafe looked up at the sun. "I calculate that right about now, him and Blake's getting their asses whipped hard about three miles east of Dalton.

"They're going to try to search that hay wagon for you and the girl. Burl Junior and Jackson ain't going to let them, 'specially when the sheriff tells them that paw's going to whip them both if they don't let him search it. They going to study that remark. Hell, Paw can't whip either one of them, and he knows it."

"Both Blake and the sheriff have pistols," Solomon reminded him.

"I hope them pistols don't have sights on their barrels," Lafe guffawed, " 'cause them barrels going to hurt something terrible when Burl Junior and Jackson rams them up their asses."

"Are Burl Junior and Jackson as big as you?"

"Hell, Sol, I'm their little brother." Lafe roared again, slapping his haunch with his hand. "I ain't but nineteen. I ain't got my full growth yet. I can't even whip Paw. Burl Junior'd done beat the shit out of the old man by the time he was sixteen. Paw says, when we can whip him, we got our full growth."

"As I make it out, none of you boys like Sheriff Turnipseed too well."

"Oh, he's all right, the lard-assed son of a bitch." Lafe's face grew suddenly pensive. "Reckon I shouldn't talk so bad about a poor old cripple like the sheriff."

"Why, I didn't know the sheriff was a cripple," Solomon remarked with genuine surprise.

"He ain't, yet," Lafe chortled, "but he will be in about half an hour."

As Solomon listened to Lafe's detailed description of the fighting prowess of the Gaines boys, he recalled the remark of a salesman in Cincinnati who had also journeyed the South. "As long as a Southerner is throwing around his 'goddamns' and 'sons of bitches,' you're safe. When he quits cussing, he's dangerous."

Lafe, in Solomon's opinion, had perfected the regional knack for swaggering with the mouth. His language had power and beauty. Profanity flowed from him with a splendor that awed rather than offended Solomon; he used it with admirable accuracy for emphasis. His frequent references to the process of elimination were delivered with a purity and lack of pruriency that marked him a poet of the alimentary tract. For religious reasons, Solomon never took the name of God in vain, but Lafe broke the commandment with such abandon that Solomon felt the greatest contribution Christ had made to this boy's Christianity was in lending his name as a swear word.

A whole day with the boy would have driven Solomon

to lunacy, but as an eye-opener before breakfast, he was bracing. Talking was another expression of two hundred eighty pounds of energy which marked the boy as more a force of nature than a human being.

Gaines had given Solomon two slabs of bacon, a straw hamper of eggs, an extra pound of coffee, and a sack of buckwheat flour. Melinda had the fire started and was cooking breakfast. Lafe eyed her admiringly as she swayed back and forth between flipping flapjacks and turning bacon.

"Sol, how much you figure a girl like that's worth?"

Melinda was in easy hearing distance of the booming voice.

Lowering his own voice, Solomon said, "About a thousand dollars."

"Jesus Christ! I'd give that much to stroke her velvet ass . . . Jesus, that coffee smells good . . . Say, Solomon, we'll be going up the old Cherokee Trail. Right along here's where General Jackson drove them poor red-assed bastards out of Georgia."

"Are you a student of history?"

"Student, hell! I got eyes. See that beech tree over yonder with the growed-over slashes on its trunk? Them's blaze marks put there by a tomahawk. Show you more of them when we go up the trail."

"Breakfast ready," Melinda called.

She had spread an oilcloth upwind from the fire and had placed two tin plates with accessories.

"Where's your plate?" Solomon asked her.

"I's waiting till I's done serving y'all."

"You eat with us, Melinda. We haven't got time to stand on ceremony."

"He's sho right, gal. If that cute little ass of yours ain't out of Georgia pretty damned quick, Blake's going to have it back down on his farm. Just thinking of that pretty little ass getting whipped comes nigh on to breaking my heart . . . Goddamn, these are the best damned buckwheat cakes ever slid down my gullet."

Solomon and Melinda were spared further conversation by twelve buckwheat cakes, fourteen slices of bacon, and six cups of coffee from a pot that held ten.

In the next three hours, Lafe proved his investment in food well spent. Half a mile up the trail, an uprooted tree blocked the trail, seasoned hickory. Lafe chopped through it and rolled it aside in ten minutes. He walked ahead of

110

the team, chopping down saplings with one hand on the ax handle as an ordinary man would use a hatchet. Once again, he performed the feat of lifting the back wheels of the wagon over a fallen log. Yet, three hours later, when they crested a rise and Solomon could see the red streak of the Toccoa Road below them, Lafe's perspiration was no more than normal for the heat and humidity of a late July forenoon.

"There she is, Sol. Downhill all the way, and nothing in front of you that you can't roll over with the wagon. When you hit the road, turn left, and you're headed North."

"Lafe, there's no way I can thank you and your pa."

"Hell, forget it," Lafe said, embarrassed. He went back to unhitch his towline, and Solomon walked forward to survey his approaches to the road. Melinda had climbed up on the driver's seat of the van to rest, when Solomon caught her saying again, "You hush your mouth, white boy!"

He turned to see Lafe walking away from the front of the van, coiling the rope which he then looped around the horn of the horse's shoulder pad. When he rejoined Solomon, he was grinning.

"Say, Sol, there's one way you can thank me. I could take that little black girl down in the bushes for a spell. She's ready and willing."

Solomon managed a smile. "I just heard her different."

"She meant yes. No girl, black or white, ever says no."

"She's spoke for, Lafe. I'm taking her to Cincinnati to get married."

"That don't make no fair thee well. Her buck up North won't know. Anyhow, it don't make no difference to a nigger."

"It does to me, Lafe."

Lafe was not grinning any more. "I can't wear that thing out. There'll be plenty left for you. You'll get your share on the road North."

"It's not for me, Lafe, and it's not for you."

"Look, Sol, I've worked my behind off from three-thirty this morning till right now. I done earned that poontang. I was asking you just to be polite. You don't own the girl. You got no more right to her than I got."

Solomon noted with clinical detachment that Lafe had used up several sentences without a "goddamn."

"Be reasonable, Lafe. I don't own the girl, and you don't either."

"Reasonable! Sol, a stiff prick can't reason. After I whop it to her a couple of times, then we can set down and hold a prayer meeting."

Solomon braced himself with genuine sadness. He knew that he had feared this climax.

He grasped at the straw of Lafe's racial loyalty. "Lafe, her buck up north is no buck. The man who's waiting to marry her is a white man."

"White man marrying a nigger!" Lafe grinned again, broadly. "What'll them goddamned Yankees be doing next? Goddamned dee-generates, that's what they is. You ain't telling me you aim to keep old Lafe Gaines from his pussy on account of some niggerloving Yankee?"

Solomon heard his "goddamned" as the peals of hosannah, but his hopes faltered when Lafe turned and strode back to his horse, where he unsheathed his hunting knife and cut a length of rope from the coil on the harness knob. He turned and walked back.

"Sol, you got your choice. I can coldcock you and tie you up, or I can just tie you up. I can't have you on my back when I'm knocking off a piece, but I tell you now, next to poontang, I like fighting."

"Coldcock." The term struck Solomon's ears with irony. The one thing most needed in this crisis was a cold cock— Lafe's.

"Lafe, I'm opposing you on moral grounds. I'm a religious man, but I'm a practical man. If I oppose you on moral grounds, and you tie me up, then I'm not morally responsible for what happens. Right?

"Being a practical man, there's something else I've got to think about. I've got a delicate nose. Melinda's mistress was kind enough to tell me it looked aristocratic. Now, I want to keep my keen, aristocratic nose, and I don't want to have a headache for the next two weeks. So, if you want to tie me up so that I won't be morally responsible, I might even ask you to dedicate a few strokes to me. Tie me up, boy."

Solomon crossed his wrists and extended them. Lafe, grinning, came forward saying, "Goddamn, Sol, I just knew you'd come around to . . . Ugh!"

Lafe's breath exploded in one anguished gasp as Solomon's boot whammed into his scrotum. Before his jack-knifing body struck the ground in its agony, Solomon whipped the knife from its scabbard. As the boy thrashed on the ground, his hands clutching the spot where so lately a light and pleasant passion had throbbed, Solomon stood over him, knife poised.

When the spasms eased, Lafe rolled over to a sitting position and looked up at Solomon with hatred and anger.

"You kicked me in the nuts, and as soon as I can straighten up, I'm going to kill you, knife or no knife."

"You're not going to kill me. When I tell you why I did that, you'll ride home thanking God for the toe of Solomon Villaricca. Now get up and get on that horse. You're not hurt."

"Not hurt!" Incredulity edged out the hatred and anger in the boy's eyes. "You just nutted me, and you say I ain't hurt."

"Look, Lafe, you're going to do what I tell you, or you're going to catch hell from your pa. Now get up and get on that horse. I got some private business to talk over with you."

Either the mention of his father or the appeal to his curiosity chastened Lafe. Still bent, groaning, and clutching his crotch, he gingerly mounted, lolling backward to avoid his normal center of gravity. Leading the horse, Solomon made his way to the road below and stopped. Still keeping his distance, the knife at ready, he tossed the reins up to the rider.

"I want you to know, Lafe, I didn't kick you out of anger. I did it to help you."

"Tell my balls that, goddamn it! I got to ride on them for the next two dozen miles."

"Listen, Lafe," Solomon's voice was deadly serious. "That girl up there on the hill is afflicted. In about three weeks, you'd have got a sore on your lips. By and by, you'd have got scabs all over your body. Then your hair would start to fall out. Pretty soon, you'd have what they call locomotor ataxia. You wouldn't even be able to walk without saying, 'My left foot goes here. My right foot goes there.' That'd be bad enough, but in about a year, you'd get what they call general paresis. Your brain would get soft. Your pa and brothers would have to feed you, and you'd slobber all over yourself, like a baby.

"What do you think I'd feel like if I let that happen to you, after all you and your pa have done for me?"

Lafe was dumbfounded. "You mean to tell me that pretty little thing's got the queen's pox?"

"The worst kind," Solomon assured him. "The French."

Lafe's face grew whiter. "Goddamn!" He spoke in hor-

113

ror. "Jesus Christ!" For a moment, he was dazed by his narrow escape and sat in silence. Finally, he said, "But you're taking her North to marry a white man."

"So," Solomon gave an expressive shrug to his shoulders, "and who worries about a Yankee degenerate? But if something like that should happen to you, the next time I was through here, your pa would kill me."

"You won't tell pa, Sol?"

"Lafe, after all you've done for me, you should ask?"

He handed the knife back to Lafe, patted his leg in a friendly gesture, and slapped the rump of the Clydesdale. He raised his arm in farewell as the horse ambled down the road, but the boy, bent over his aching testicles, did not look back.

Solomon turned and strode back up the hill, his boots crunching into twigs, old leaves, and the green shoots of poison ivy. Although he breathed a prayer of thanksgiving for his deliverance, his own testicles twinged with sympathetic pain, and he was shaken and sick to his stomach.

He wished God had chosen another method of delivering him.

Melinda was still perched on the seat of the van when he strode up, and there was concern and curiosity on her face.

"Mr. Ricky, why'd you kick that white boy?"

It seemed to Solomon that it was obvious why he had kicked Lafe, and it irritated him that she should ask. He reflected a moment. She was only seventeen, and it was probable that she questioned him in all sincerity. He could not be brusque with the innocence he had so recently fought to protect.

"He wanted to copulate, Melinda."

"Copulate, sir?"

Solomon searched for a suitable synonym.

"He wanted to do something to you, Melinda."

She thought for a moment, and then she giggled. Her mirth was not the mirth of innocence. The giggle was a dark, liquid sound that flowed with the wine of rampant femininity. "Whyn't you let him, Mr. Ricky?"

As he looked up at her, two clear and distinct recollections came to his mind. One was of Phoebe, standing on the station platform idly swinging her riding crop. "She has an impish sense of humor that borders on the insolent, but never let her become insolent." Following the image of

Phoebe, he saw the face of Lafe saying, "You'll get your share on your way North."

Melinda's giggle was a threat to discipline. But worse, far worse—in the coquetry that prompted it and in the wanton beckoning behind it lay a vital danger to his immortal soul.

Cold hauteur was in his features and cold anger in his voice. "Get inside the van!"

His tone erased her coy smile. Crestfallen, sheepish, and a little frightened, she jumped from the seat and scampered to the rear of the vehicle. When he shot home the bolt of the padlock on the door, the sound carried the thud of anger.

He climbed onto his seat, yelled "Giddap!" to the mules, and trundled down over young water oaks and sumac bushes to the road below. He reined the mules left toward the blue barrier of the Great Smokies.

Solomon Villaricca was rolling North.

Chapter Five

All afternoon, he strode before the mules, setting a pace which cut five-mile segments every hour from the red ribbon looping ahead of him over hills and around mountains. His legs moved with a metronomic beat through the settlement of Toccoa and over the Toccoa River, fifteen miles, twenty. Stopping neither for food nor calls of nature, he slogged through the sparsely settled piney woods country, twenty-five miles, thirty.

If Burl was right, he had one day free from Blake's pursuit. If Lafe was right, he had two. But he would be pursued. This girl meant trouble, not merely from the rear, but from all sides, for she was one-hundred percent, grade A, choice prime poontang. It was not a van rolling behind but Pandora's box, and she would keep the lid clamped from here to Wheeling, should he live so long.

Half an hour before sunset, he pulled off the road to set up camp and complete his correspondence before dark. He wanted to post letters in Blairsville because a mail wagon ran from there to the steam railroad at Rabun Gap, and his mail would be in Cincinnati in three days—even less if the Southern postmasters were fast readers. Blood must be notified as quickly as possible that his escape route had been changed.

Originally, he had planned to leave Georgia northwest through Columbus, Tennessee, and the Tellico Plains to join the Underground Railroad at the Knoxville Station. Chance had put him on the Blairsville Road, a shorter route out of Georgia but a longer route to the Railroad. At the moment, his overriding desire was to get out of Georgia.

His new route led along the eastern fringe of the Great Smokies to Asheville and northwest through the valley of the French Broad. With his commercial stops, it would take three days longer to get to the Railroad, but he would join it a day's journey north of Knoxville, at a Quaker meeting-house near Sycamore, Tennessee.

When he had stolen a slave, his procedure was to keep Ely as closely informed as possible of his whereabouts. Blood had avenues of intelligence from these mountains. If Solomon were jailed, lynched, or bushwacked, Ely would break the news to Leah and, if need be, help her settle the estate.

Ordinarily, Solomon took the stolen slave to the nearest Depot and put the fugitive in the hands of a Conductor, but he had been commissioned to deliver Melinda to Kelly. The Underground Railroad was organized to assist runaways fleeing to Canada, not to accommodate slave stealers.

He followed a creek downwind from the road to conceal the odor of his camp smoke and halted the van in a cane brake close by an elm grove. He opened the door to find the girl sitting meekly on a chest, and she scanned his face for signs of anger. Her own face was tear stained.

"What you been crying about, girl?"

"I reckon I's homesick, sir."

"I should put shackles on your ankles to make you feel at home. You can take a bath in the creek yonder, while I make camp. You can fix supper."

"Can I use the sweet soap, sir, and the big towel?"

"They're yours, and get a hairbrush out of that second drawer . . . Go upstream, but don't go too far. If you hear anybody coming, hide."

Soap, brush, and towel in hand, she emerged, ready to sprint in the direction he had pointed, when he stopped her. "Girl, how good are you at imitating bird calls?"

"I can mock a mockingbird real well, sir."

"Can you make this sound?"

He pursed his lips and throbbed the call of the whippoorwill.

Instantly and without a flaw, she repeated a sound he had spent hours perfecting. Suddenly interested, he asked. "How about this one?"

He tilted his head and trilled the notes of the hermit thrush.

She watched him intently and said, "Would you do it again, sir?"

She studied his lips as he repeated the call.

She placed both hands to her mouth, spread her lips with the little fingers, and trilled the liquid notes of the hermit thrush, the most beautiful and difficult call in his repertoire and one he had spent days perfecting.

"Where'd you learn that?" he asked in astonishment.

"I just learnt it from you, sir. But I likes best of all to mock the mocker."

"That'll do, girl! . . . Now, when you're away from camp and spot danger, give me the call of the whippoorwill. When you're ready to come back, give me the hermit thrush. That's the call I just taught you. If I don't answer, keep hidden until I do. Remember. The hermit thrush means that the coast is clear, but the whippoorwill means danger. Now, skeedaddle!"

He watched her waddle into the underbrush with her brogans and went about the business of setting up camp and watering and feeding the mules. Upstream, a bullfrog harrumphed for more rum and fell silent. The girl had found a pool. A jaybird's shrill chatter told him she was disrobing, and the resumed croaking of the frog told him she was lolling in the water.

He started a fire and turned to his correspondence, choosing his most difficult letter first, the one to Leah. For his wife, he usually wrote much and said little, composing letters so devoid of specific information that their composition taxed him.

North Georgia
29 July 1858

My darling wife,

Again I take my pen in hand to tell you all is well with me and hoping you're the same.

It has been a serene journey since I wrote you last. Business is good and business is bad. The weather is holding good for the most part and the streams are fordable. Tomorrow night is Sabbath and I shall light the candles, etcetera.

You will note that my draft from Chattanooga was 48.53 higher than the same from there last year. Cotton prices are holding and prosperity in the lowlands means a better market for beef, pork, and corn in the highlands. You would think that the planters would raise their own corn, but the price of cotton drives all else from the land.

Your parents are both doing well and I spent a pleasant outing with them on Lookout Mountain.

118

I mention my commercial success with trepidation for the journey is not over, and I don't like to plan on money that I haven't earned. Recently I heard a Christian sermon based on the subject that the love of money is the root of all evil. I was highly impressed by the arguments given and might have been more so had I not discovered that the preacher was requesting a sizable donation.

He looked at the paragraph and thought of the anguish behind it and the anguish he could cause by adding that he had donated seventy dollars to the preacher's cohorts to spare himself seven years in prison or death at the hands of a slaveowner whose property he now had in his keeping.

My dearest, did you know that the streets of heaven are paved with gold to show God's contempt for that metal?

He wrung four more paragraphs from his brain and closed:

The journey has been so uneventful as to be tedious, but I am fortified by the memory of the beautiful woman who lightens my burdens with the knowledge that it is for her well-being that the tasks are done.

Your devoted and faithful husband,
Sol

Writing to Ely posed a different problem. Ely's information had to be as specific as Solomon could make it, and for Ely alone. He wrote to Ely's son Simon at Simon's home address. Any letter to the Quaker store would be opened by every postmaster south of the Line and the postal authorities in Cincinnati.

My dear Simon:
Yours of the 20th inst. received. Thank you for your inquiry regarding my health. I spoke to Doctor Gresham about the extract of sycamore and he feels that would be the best prescription.
The merchandise should be at the railhead on Wednesday, August 11. It is my feeling that the market value of the wares greatly exceeds the list price. Some of the objects may be subject to pilferage, so I shall escort the merchandise to Wheeling. And downriver by boat or train, depending on the exigencies. In any event, you may inform your client that the merchandise should be on your shelves in time for the September sales.
Enclosed is a missive for delivery by your kind hand.

Yr. obdt. servant, etcetera,
S. Lomon

He folded Leah's letter inside Ely's and heated his wax, sealing the two letters as one.

He was boiling ears of corn when a hermit thrush trilled from the underbrush. Slightly vexed by the realization that she had been away for almost half an hour, he answered.

She broke from cover, running barefoot, draped with the towel to pad the shoes which she had tied by their laces and hung from her neck. Her brush was stuck in her belt, the soap bulged in her shirt pocket. She held her hands cupped together, and there was excitement in her eyes. "Mr. Ricky, look what I done found!"

He looked down at the objects she held, oval-shaped fungi which resembled the desiccated fetuses of brown squirrels.

"And what is that?"

"Sponge mushrooms, sir. They's the best tasting mushrooms there is. I got them for supper. I can throw them in the water and boil them a little and cut them up and fry them in the butter Mr. Gaines give you, and they go real good in scrambled eggs."

"Girl, are you trying to murder me? How do you know they aren't toadstools?"

"I knows mushrooms, sir. Looky." She dropped one into the boiling water, scooped it out with a ladle, and swallowed it. "Now, if I's dead by suppertime, don't you eat none."

She was beaming and alive twenty minutes later at his frank approval of the omelet she had prepared. Small, chewy, and tasty, the mushroom chips gave a flavor and character to the eggs he had never experienced before.

As twilight deepened around them, he said, "You think you can stand being penned in the van for the next two or three days?"

"Yes, sir."

"Maybe now and then we can stop to let you out for exercise. Would you like that?"

"Yes, sir. I'd like it fine."

"How do you like those clothes?"

"They fits me fine, sir."

"I noticed you didn't wear your shoes back to camp. They hurt your feet?"

"No, sir. They fits me fine."

"Be easier, though, if you went barefooted."

"Barefooted's fine, sir. That lets my feet breathe."

"Those trousers are a little tight around the waist."

"Yes, sir. They's a little binding."

"Come morning, I'll give you material to make yourself a dress to wear on the road. Would you like that?"

"Yes, sir. I'd truly like that."

He sipped his coffee. She was not "following behind the man" because she was polite. She was scared. He had been angry with her this morning, and she was being careful not to say anything that might offend him. Possibly, she really did not know why he had been angry. He remembered Phoebe Blake's injunction never to chastize her without explaining the reason.

"Girl, you remember I got angry with you this morning?"

"Yes, sir."

"You know why?"

"No, sir."

"Do you know you're an attractive girl?"

"Attractive, sir?"

"You have magnetism for men. You draw men to you."

"That mean I's pretty, sir?"

"You're pretty, but that isn't what draws men. You tempt them."

She cocked her head and leaned forward slightly. "That bad, sir?"

"It can be good or bad. If you do it just for the fun of it, like a Jezebel, it's sinful. If you save your tempting for your bespoken husband, it's good."

"How does I not be tempting, sir?"

"You must be modest around men. Don't smile at them sideways. Don't swing your hips when you walk. Don't giggle low in your throat."

"Does I do that, sir?"

"Not deliberately, I'm sure."

"Then, why's I tempting, sir?"

He was slipping into a quagmire, and his struggles were taking him deeper. "If I knew, I could make a million dollars teaching girls to be tempting."

"If they all wants it, why's it sinful?"

"It's not sinful, I told you, if it's used right."

She looked at him dazedly and then asked, "Why'd you get mad at me, sir?"

"Because you told me I should have let Lafe do it to you."

She understood and answered with a hint of defiance.

"I didn't want no truck with that white boy. But he worked like hell to get us up that hill. He didn't deserve no kicking."

"Your sense of justice I appreciate. I did not want to kick the boy, but I promised Mr. Kelly I'd get you back to him without letting anybody do it to you. Then, when you said what you said, I thought you were tempting me."

"You mean I ain't supposed to tempt *you*, Mr. Ricky?"

"Particularly not me, girl."

"Sir, I thought you was a man of God."

"In my fashion, I am. I live by the Law God handed down to Moses. Do you know the Commandments: Thou shalt not steal, kill, bear false witness, worship graven images?"

"I heard talk about them, sir."

"Under the Law given by Moses, I'm forbidden to commit adultery."

"Adultery, Mr. Ricky?"

"That means a man shouldn't do it with any woman but his wife."

She seemed befuddled.

"Mr. Ricky, was Moses a married lady?"

"Of course not! He was a man who spoke for God."

Even more puzzled, she shook her head. "I just can't figure God out, sir."

"Don't try to, girl. Just don't tempt me."

She looked at him intently. "You mean, sir, you don't want me doing it to you 'cause that's sinful?"

"That's about it, girl."

Suddenly she flashed him a warm and comforting smile. "Lordy bless you, Mr. Ricky, don't you fret none. I gives you my spoken word that I won't do it to you, no matter how much I wants to."

She was a brown pixie leaning forward to reassure him that she would not ravish his six-feet-two frame, and the incongruity caused him to laugh. "I thank you, Melinda. I truly thank you. Now that I feel safe in your company, I'll show you again how to find the North Star."

In the morning, he gave her the fabric and the sewing equipment she needed for a dress to replace the boy's clothes so useless as a disguise and so uncomfortable. Her task would make her confinement to the van easier, he hoped.

At Blairsville, he posted his letters and headed due east toward the Valley Town pike. Sightings of Brasstown Bald to the south told him he was keeping to his pace of the previous day.

By five o'clock, he had crossed the Hiawasee and was headed north-northwest toward the Carolina border. Half an hour before Sabbath sundown, he parked on the banks of the Hiawasee south of Valley Town, unsure whether he was celebrating his last Sabbath in Georgia or his first in North Carolina.

When he opened the van, Melinda cakewalked out in a calico dress of red on white, fully trimmed and hemmed, with pleats in the waist that forced the skirt into a bouffant ballooning around the hips. Her dress was made with a flair and in a style more appropriate for the pages of *Godey's Lady's Book* than the roads of Carolina.

"I puffed it out, Mr. Ricky, so folks won't see my butt shake."

She strutted away from him a few paces, turned, and walked smoothly back, and the fluffed skirt concealed her sway and quiver. He observed the neckline canceled the gain in propriety below the waist; it was cut so low it revealed the beginning swell and cleft of her breasts. But the glow of pride in her face edited all but the praise from his remarks.

"Artful . . . Most becoming . . . Well sewn."

As he set up his candelabra, she asked and received permission to bathe in the river with her sweet soap. It was sheer extravagance—the soap she used cost over a penny a bar—but if the perfume from the soap cut down the Negro odor in the van, the security was worth a penny a week. So far, he had not picked up her scent, but apparently, he was not gifted with the Southerner's ability to smell a Negro.

Despite her objections, he insisted on boiled eggs only for supper and told her, "If you haven't finished the supper dishes by sundown, don't finish them."

She returned early from her bath to chide him for washing his socks. "I do it for you, Mr. Ricky. I don't mind they stink like carr'on. You walks all day, and your feet can't breathe in them boots."

"I always wash my own socks, girl. It's sort of a ritual, like yonder candles, though it's not for God. It's for me."

She looked into the van at his candelabra with the candles in place. "They's pretty, Mr. Ricky, but your tablecloth's a little wampy. You going to hold a meeting, sir, when you lights up?"

"Sort of."

"Is that your altar?"

"That's as good a word as any."

"You going to read from the Scriptures, sir?"

"Yes."

"Would you read out loud, sir?"

Wringing out his socks, he thought for a moment. He appreciated an audience for his readings, but his Bible was in Hebrew.

"Be glad to, girl, if you'll lend me your Bible."

They passed Murphy, North Carolina, at dawn, and Solomon relaxed. There were three roads north out of Murphy, and if Blake had followed by horseback, he would have to give up the chase, here. No one in the sleeping village had seen Solomon pass, and no one could, if they would, tell Blake which road he had taken. Blake was too intelligent to attempt to pursue him into this wilderness.

In western North Carolina, the populace was indifferent to slavery and hostile to slaveowners. Solomon's greatest danger lay in the local sheriffs and Federal marshals.

He could foresee Blake's strategy.

The Southerner would box him in by telegraphing his description to the sheriffs at Chattanooga, Knoxville, and Asheville, hoping to hold Solomon within the triangle until he had reward notices printed and distributed by mail to the post offices. If the reward were high enough, say two hundred dollars, the entire population would become Blake's confederates. Few citizens of the area held antislavery or antilowlander sentiments worth more to them than two hundred dollars.

Ironically, the farther north Solomon got, the greater his peril became. Asheville would be dangerous by the time he arrived, and within two weeks, Blake could blanket Tennessee, Virginia, and Kentucky with his posters. Solomon had estimated that it would take him two weeks to get to the Quakers at Sycamore, Tennessee.

Without the Underground Depots, he reflected, he would not have the slimmest chance to get this girl out of the South.

He was not long in discovering that the black girl had at least a minimal ability to act independently.

Saturday afternoon, he let the girl out to exercise and had permitted her to skip ahead of the van looking for berries along the roadside. Here the road cut through a stretch of timberland. Danger seemed alien to this sunlighted woodland, and he was drowsing on the wagon seat when the sound of drumming hooves surprised and alerted him.

He leaped from the wagon to open the door for the girl, intending to call for her, but the road where she had been stretched empty ahead of him. Topping the rise behind him, however, a quarter of a mile away, a band of horsemen approached at a full gallop.

He ran forward and grabbed the head harness of the jack, leading the team to the side of the road as the horsemen came nearer, yelling and caterwauling at the sight of the van. The riders thundered by without slowing, a band of youths, drunk and skylarking. The trailing lad fired a pistol over the heads of the mules, and, screeching, yelling, laughing, the boys were gone.

When the sound of their hooves had died, Melinda rushed from the woods, terror-stricken. "They shoot you, Mr. Ricky?"

"No, girl. They were just trying to scare the mules."

"They scared me, sir. When I heard them coming, I ducked in the bushes and prayed like hell to God and Moses. I was scared for you, Mr. Ricky. Deed I was."

North of Murphy, he began commercial calls on farmhouses, each time concealing her in the compartment, but on the road he let her out of the van more often. No stage lines traversed the area, and the few travelers they met were mountain folks.

She amused him. Once while riding beside him along the southeastern approaches to the Great Smokies, she exclaimed, "Mr. Ricky, look at that old red squirrel!"

He looked and saw the squirrel, alertly erect, forepaws held before it, jaws aquiver. His gaze dropped to Melinda who sat alertly beside him, her hands dangling from her extended forearms, her jaws quivering.

Her mind had facets that hinted of talents more profound than mimicry.

One Sunday morning, when she was walking beside him, he noticed she seemed pensive.

"Don't be sad, Melinda. Just a few more weeks for to tote the heavy load."

125

"I ain't sad, Mr. Ricky, I just ain't got my sleep out. I likes getting up and starting the fire. I likes the way morning smells in the woods, and them old mules snorting and pawing, and the way the wagon creaks when it starts rolling. I likes the rolling along, Mr. Ricky. Why, sir, I sure would like to keep going—go to the South runs out and go to the North runs out."

"What would you do when you got to the edge of the world?"

"I been thinking, Mr. Ricky, I'd take a lot of that fishing line you got back there, and I'd catch me a flock of wild geese, and I'd tie that line to they's legs, and I'd fly right off to Jesus."

On a drowsy afternoon of the first day of August, they were traveling the stretch of country south of the Little Tennessee River, when Melinda began to sing an old hymn in a plaintive, rather pleasant voice:

> How tedious and tasteless the hours
> When nothing in Jesus I see.
> Sweet prospects, sweet birds, and sweet flowers
> Have lost all their sweetness to me.

She pronounced correctly words he knew were not in her vocabulary as she sang the song, and she had said "the" and "their" instead of her habitual "de" and "der." He had assumed that the Negro accent was the result of a malformation of the palate. Even the Northern Negroes he had met spoke with the flat, guttural accent general, he had thought, throughout the black nation. Melinda had pronounced the words correctly.

The revelation inspired a plan which might lighten the tedium of the days ahead, particularly after they reached the Railroad, when his commercial calls would cease.

"Melinda, when you get to Cincinnati and get married, you'll be expected to talk like a lady."

"I reckon I is a lady." She giggled her low giggle.

"You sound more like a pickaninny. Your words are wrong, and that's bad grammar. Now, you don't want to use bad grammar, do you?"

"No, sir, I sho don't."

"Say 'sure,' not 'sho,' Melinda."

"Sure not sho, Melinda."

Her answer demonstrated the scope of his task, and he

was on the verge of dropping the whole idea when it occurred to him that her limited vocabulary was his greatest asset. For such a small house, it should be easy to tear down the bricks and replace them with new ones. "Say, how'd you like to learn to talk like white folks, maybe even learn to read and write? What would Kelly think if you walked up to him when you met and said, 'How lovely to see you, my betrothed'?"

"Somebody say that to me, I'd shit!"

She needed coaching in more than grammar.

From Murphy to Waynesville took seven days, but his teaching duties and the charm of the girl's company made it a short week.

During her lessons, she was a superb student. With faultless diction, she would say, "I am a girl, I shall talk as a girl. That is a book. Those are books. These are shoes . . . Mr. Ricky, look at dat ole mountain ober dere! Don't it 'pear jest lak a humpin' rabbit?"

Seated behide him, scented alternately with verbena or lilac, she fascinated him with her mental agility and maddened him with her short span of attention. He limited her lessons to no more than fifteen minutes to keep from overtaxing her and permitted her to gambol ahead, barefoot, picking berries, throwing stones, or merely scuffing her feet in the dirt. On the downhill grades, when they could ride together without burdening the mules, he would clap for a lesson, and she would come running and eager for the change in amusements.

He wrote out the alphabet slowly and laboriously, in script and block letters, and she was able to memorize it almost at one sitting, demonstrating an unusual rote memory. She passed the tests he gave her with flying colors, but once the lesson was over she would slip back into her old speech.

She had the curiosity of a child, delighting in trivia around her, but she made no attempt to organize her knowledge, except in the area of edible plants—a throwback to some survival instinct of her savage forebears, he presumed. Outside of that area, her fancy fluttered like an undiscriminating butterfly, and time seemed to eddy and slow down around her.

Often, he let himself be drawn into her eddies.

She wore the ring he had first seen at the Gaines farm, her cross, and the pearl bracelet awake, asleep, and probably while bathing. Once, as they rode along, he asked her to remove the ring to let him judge its value She complied, and he hefted it in his palm. It was a gold-plated trinket of little value, but he said, "Girl, this looks like fourteen carat, pure virgin gold. Who gave it to you?"

"Pudd'n tame."

"Bet you found it."

"No sir-ree, bobtail!"

She was flattered and made shy by his interest but would tell him no more. She wanted him to think she had a beau, and he pretended to think so, teasing her into giggles. Her behavior surprised him because it was so similar to an adolescent white girl's, and since it was the only secret she had, he did not press her to tell.

She lived only for the moment. She never mentioned the Blakes, except in casual references, and she never wondered aloud about Kelly or Cincinnati. Her one abstract interest seemed to be in his religion.

"Sir, is you a Methodist Jew or a Baptist Jew?"

"Jews aren't Christians. Methodists and Baptists are Christians."

"Why ain't Jews Christians?"

"We don't accept Christ as our savior."

"How you get to heaven if you don't 'cept Jesus?"

Teaching her grammar was difficult enough. Theology would have to wait. "Jews go to a different part of heaven."

She seemed saddened by his remark and sat in silence for a while. Then her face glowed with a new curiosity. "Mr. Ricky, do they cut that little thing off you Jew babies?"

"Of course not! Who told you that?"

"Brother Smith. He say a lady cross the waters spent her life looking for the one they cut off Jesus."

Solomon laughed aloud, thinking of the vast new fields of profanity that might be opened to Christians if the foreskin of the Christ child were found. "I couldn't think of a more unusual relic."

"What's a relic, Mr. Ricky?"

Her mind seized on juxtaposed ideas quickly; she was witty. After two days of intensive drilling, she still used " 'I is' " between lessons rather than " 'I am.' " With exasperation he asked, "Why do you have such trouble with those little verbs?"

"I ain't having no trouble with my little verbs, sir," she giggled. "You is."

On the fourth day north of Murphy, he noticed a used primer in a farmhouse and bartered a bread knife for the book in a straight swap.

Melinda was as nervous with the book as Uncle Fred had been with the spyglass. He returned to paper and pencil for her lessons. Again she did well, but once the lesson was done, English, as he spoke it, became a dead language.

Yet, she was sensitive to the language. Once as he drove down a stretch of road lined by dense forests, she asked in a desultory manner, "Mr. Ricky, 'fore you got me, didn't you get mighty lonesome riding down these roads all by yourself and sleeping alone in the woods?"

He started to tell her that the Lord was always with him, but shied away from the possibility of a religious discussion. "Not at all, Melinda. The moon's my constant mistress, and the lonely owl my marrow. The flaming drake and the night birds make me music to my sorrow."

"Mr. Ricky, that's the prettiest talk I done ever heard."

She astonished him. He often mixed quotations and ragtags of poetry into his conversation, and no other listener had ever commented on his borrowed beauties. Here, on a dusty road in Carolina, an illiterate slave girl had "cotched" him at once.

"I cheated you, Melinda. I didn't say that. Those words are from a poem."

"What's a poem, Mr. Ricky?"

"It's like a song, except the music is in the words."

"Say some more."

"Well," he said, "let me think . . . I remember these lines because they always reminded me of me:

> With a host of furious fancies
>   Whereof I am commander,
> With a horse of air and a burning spear
>   Through the wilderness I wander.
>
> A knight of ghosts and shadows,
>   I summoned am to tourney,
> Ten leagues beyond the wide world's end.
>   Methinks, it is no journey.

She shivered deliciously. "Them's real pretty words, but they's scary. I don't want any them nights of ghosts and shadows."

"It's a different kind of night. It's a k-n-i-g-h-t knight. A knight was a man on horseback wearing shining armor who went around rescuing girls in distress. Nowadays, we wear skullcaps and drive mules."

"You know anymore of them poems? Some that ain't so scary?"

A mental glance over the poetry he remembered revealed only dirges and elegies written in graveyards, but her eager face inspired him to ransack further until he came up with one stanza of the clown's song from *Twelfth Night,* which he recited.

"It sho does have music, I could sing that."

It was tragedy, he thought, that a girl with such an appreciation of the language had so little interest in learning it.

"Say it again, sir."

He recited it again, she listening intently, and there was a moment's silence.

She began to sing it. Her improvised tune had a reedy, bucolic charm, Elizabethan in flavor, and her voice fitted well with the song. She had given him an exciting idea which he was considering when she suddenly veered onto a new tack with the abruptness of Phoebe Blake.

"Mr. Ricky, if you gets us some lettuce today, I can make a salad that's best you ever tasted. But I needs to put a little bacon in it, just little-bitty chunks. You won't even notice the bacon, Mr. Ricky. It just flavors the lettuce."

"I'll get the lettuce at the next farmhouse. You fix yours like you want it. I'll eat mine raw."

On that afternoon, he pulled off the road farther than usual and half an hour earlier, taking a side road along the north bank of the Little Tennessee River. Upstream, he found a beech grove where the road ended.

As Melinda took her evening bath, he tuned his violin and practiced the tune she had composed. When she returned, he asked her to sing the song to music. He repeated the words to her, fitting them to the bars of music, and she listened, humming softly to herself. Then, she stood on the bank, looking out over the river, and sang in faultless diction the words to the old Elizabethan song:

> What is love? 'Tis not hereafter.
>> Present mirth hath present laughter.
> What's to come is still unsure.
>> Then, come kiss me, sweet and twenty.
>> In delay there lies no plenty.
> Youth's a stuff twill not endure.

130

In her singing, the song achieved a beauty beyond its sound, and she was less the singer than the receptacle of her song. Even as he played the high and reedy notes that matched her soprano, he knew that here on the banks of the Little Tennessee, among the pale boles of beech enfolded in the red light of the sunset reflecting from clouds massed eastward—here, where a daughter of Africa sang the words of an English poet to the music of a Jew-errant —an event was taking place which would live as long as his memory lived.

When her song was ended and his violin laid aside, she stood in silence looking out over the gurgling water, and around them the forest was silent. It was full seconds before the evening chirping of birds and chittering of insects again engulfed the glade.

"If we'd done that in New York, we'd both have made a hundred dollars."

"They pay people to sing, Mr. Ricky?"

"Yes, and some are paid very well."

"How do you get hired out?"

"First you learn to read and write."

She looked at him and smiled in sad despair.

Long into the night, he lay on his bedroll at the door of the van, looking up at the stars and mulling over the incident and the girl.

She tantalized him with glimpses of deeper dimensions to her mind. Somewhere inside the girl was a substratum of intelligence and sensibility; if he could overcome her natural frivolity and lengthen her span of attention, he might yet teach her to read and write, to speak with enough force to articulate the emotions that moved her.

There were other dimensions to the girl, less ethereal, which also opened new areas of self-knowledge for Solomon. At times, when she yawned and stretched on the seat beside him, he felt the enfoliations of his culture and religious disciplines peel back like the leaves of an artichoke, and he would hastily mutter a prayer.

Still, it was the undeveloped child rather than the developing woman that caused his greatest frustration and aroused his greatest compassion.

Two days out of Waynesville, camped on the banks of the south branch of the Tucksaga River, he hit on an idea that lengthened her span of attention by a country mile.

He was seated at the camp table writing a letter to Leah, when Melinda rushed up weeping. She had lost her pearl

131

bracelet in the river. To him, her tears were out of proportion to her loss, but he laid aside his letter to attend her sorrow.

Concealed by a sliding panel at the end of the chest was a money box bolted to the floor of the wagon. He kept his jewels, so-called, in the safe because they were tempting and easily pilfered.

He picked out another bracelet and turned to leave the van, when he noticed her open primer. She was still struggling to complete the first lesson.

Rejoining her, he said, "Here's your bracelet, and here's your book. You get the bracelet when you read to me the exercise at the end of the first lesson."

Melinda reached for the book.

Until midmorning of the next day, she stayed inside the van. He could see her poring over the primer through the window behind him, when he rode the downgrades. Before noon, she jumped out of the van and came running up beside him. "Mr. Ricky, soon as we's going downhill, I wants to show you I done won back my bracelet."

Finally, seated beside him, she read hesitantly: "The boy saw a dog. The dog ran. The boy ran after the dog. The girl said, 'Be kind to the dog. The dog is a dumb animal. Boys and girls should be kind to dumb animals.' "

She had done it. With profuse compliments, Solomon took the bracelet from his pocket and presented it to her.

At the next campsite, he used more finesse in presenting the prize.

Among the jewels, there was a single item of value, a string of imitation pearls worth almost two dollars which he had acquired as a part of the close-out sale at which he had bought the bracelets and other trinkets. After supper, he brought out a hand mirror.

He handed her the mirror, holding the closed pearl case in his hand. "Melinda, since you like pearls so well, I want to show you something very valuable."

He opened the box and let her look at them lying on their velvet lining. As she oohed and aahed, he drew them out and draped them over his hand, turning them to let them shimmer in the firelight.

She was mesmerized.

"Now, look in the mirror."

As she looked, he stepped behind her and draped the strand over her neck, letting the pearls hang as a single strand. "They can be worn like this."

He wrapped them twice around her neck and hooked the clasp. He stepped back and watched her preening herself in the mirror. Indeed, the pearls were lovely. They gained luster against the ebony of her neck, and if she was rapt in self-adoration, she had ample reason.

"Your neck is like the tower of David hung with a thousand bucklers," he spoke with a spontaneity that drifted into a self-conscious silence before a girl who was paying him no heed. But in the silence, the wind rustled through the willows and ferns, whispering to him: A garden enclosed is my sister, my spouse; a spring shut up, a fountain sealed.

He unclasped the pearls from a neck that bowed reluctantly. "Melinda, how'd you like to own these?"

She did not answer but got up and shuffled down to the stream, head drooping and shoulders sagging. Mystified, he put the pearls back into their case and waited for her to have her cry out. When she returned, smiling sheepishly, he repeated his question.

She sat down across from him and said, "Mr. Ricky, I done took yards of your best cloth, and you done give me two bracelets and two crosses. Them pearls is too good for a no-count nigger. You save them pearls, and you give them to your wife. They's for a fine lady. They ain't for me."

"My wife has three such strands. I don't intend to give these to you. I expect you to earn them."

"I reckon I'd do anything to earn them pearls."

"Then you learn to read, you hear! No sense you being a 'no-count nigger' all your life. There are just ten exercises in this book, and you've already learned the first. I'm going to tear out the last reading exercise at the end of the last lesson. I'm going to put it in the box with these pearls. The day you can pick up these last two pages and read them, that day you've got yourself a string of pearls."

That night as he laid out his bedroll, she came to the door and asked, "Mr. Ricky, can I burn the lantern a little late tonight?"

When he rolled into Waynesville the next morning, he stopped at the general store to get an extra gallon of coal oil and a slate with chalk for Melinda, picked up some beefsteak at the butcher's shop, and walked across the street to the post office to mail Leah's letter inside a note to Ely confirming his schedule.

The postmaster, who was also county recorder and the town's apothecary, was weighing his letter for charges, when footsteps sounded the length of the store behind him, moving with the measured tread that carried a man of authority. The obsequious smile of greeting on the postmaster's face confirmed the evidence of Solomon's hearing. He knew without looking behind him that the man would be broad of beam, pussel-gutted, and that his face would carry a set expression of officious impersonality. Solomon handed over the required coppers to the postmaster and turned. His imagination so matched the reality that the hands hooked over the gun belt and the star on the shirt were superfluous.

"Mister, you own that rig across the street?"

Solomon slumped a little to conceal his height and smiled his most ingratiating smile. "Yes, sir, captain."

"I was a mite curious. Went over to Asheville, yestiddy, and the sheriff over there had a circular. Got a reward out for a nigger girl. Seems a Jew driving a rig like yours run off with her down in Georgia. From the looks of your van, I might get a mite suspicious, 'cepting I know Cherokee Indians. Any damn fool can tell you're the Cherokee, but that sheriff over in Asheville ain't no damned fool."

Genuinely alarmed by the sheriff's warning, he decided to avoid Asheville by backtracking to Quallatown and taking the road over the Great Smokies the hard way—up and over. The route would lengthen by a day his arrival at the Sycamore Station, but a day late through Quallatown was better than never via Asheville.

Near noon, he topped a shoulder on the southwestern edge of Balsam Mountain and halted the van to boil eggs for lunch. He risked letting Melinda out to look at the view across the valley.

Before them, six miles away, towered the most formidable physical barrier they would face, the Great Smokies, soaring a mile into the sky. On this side of the mountains, the sky was a clear blue dotted with random clouds. On the far side, a cloud bank massed beyond the range, outlining the peaks against its white. It was as if the teeth of a jagged comb were carding the clouds, letting tufts drift through to dapple the eastern slopes of the Smokies with shadows. The cloud shadows speckled the dark blue of spruce and balsam on the higher ridges, which were swashed with the pale green of the balds. Lower on the slopes, the bright greens of maples, buckeyes, and chestnuts shimmered. The girl stood beside him in silent awe.

The clouds beyond the mountains disturbed him. A storm might be brewing.

After he had shooed her back into the van, he trundled into the valley, heading southwest to ford the north branch of the Tucksaga and begin the long ascent of twenty-odd miles. He rolled through the hovels of Quallatown and headed northwest, into the mountains. A mile beyond Quallatown, he let the girl out of the van.

It was safe to release her. They had entered the mountains, and he knew they would meet few travelers, if any, on the wild road ahead, until they descended into Tennessee on the far side.

Melinda was excited and gay, flitting in among the trees and out again, calling his attention to the sights, such as a tulip tree fully four feet in diameter and soaring two hundred feet. "Lordy, what a heap of kindling that tree would make!"

He had not truly gauged the height of the mountains from Balsam Mountain, which was dropping away below them to a lump on the valley floor. Near two o'clock, they took a turn to the northwest, where the road climbed into a ravine cutting off their view of the distant range of the Blue Ridges eastward, and suddenly, they were travelers in another land at another time. The familiar trees of the Piedmont Plateau had given way to Canadian hemlock, spruce, fir, and balsam. Now they had entered a dark, Germanic forest, and Solomon half-expected to find, around any bend in the road, a gingerbread house with a witch waiting at the gate to turn Melinda into a chocolate cooky.

They were approaching the area where the peaks were blocking the clouds, and the cloud mass piled against the windward slopes was threatening to pour over the crests. Already, some of the peaks were wreathed in mist. The tops soughed faintly in the rising breeze. Once as they passed through a narrow defile, he looked up, and the lowering clouds, moving fast, gave him the sensation that the earth was scudding westward and rising. He had to lower his eyes to regain a sense of the world's stability.

As they climbed, the air grew thinner, more transparent, the odor from the thickening stands of balsam and spruce seemed more pungent, and even the quality of the sounds changed. Breast harness jingled more loudly on the mules, the squeak of axles and the thud of wheel rims on the loam grew more distinct. He listened as a man might listen to the beating of his own heart in the deeps of night, vaguely apprehensive.

The afternoon grew cooler under the vanguard of haze that the advancing clouds threw under the sun. Even so, perspiration beaded his face, and the mountains around him shimmered in the eerie light. Overarching spruce turned the road into a tunnel lighted by a slit of gray. This was the black forest of Loki, Frei, and Thor. Here in the gathering gloom, the trees awaited the return of old gods or the entrance into their demesne of a propitious sacrifice. Beside him, the mules kept plodding, the clip-clop of their hooves beating a steady cadence for his own feet to follow, and before him, the black girl skipped and ran. He was thankful that the mules were brutes and that the girl's exuberance and ignorance guarded her against the funereal woods. They had climbed from the region of Hansel and Gretel into a Cimmeria inhabited by trolls and hobgoblins. He would, he thought, be less surprised than startled to hear the eldritch cackle of beldams from the silence.

Ah, that was it, the silent forest!

Suddenly, he found himself listening to the silence. It had not struck him before, but the dissonance of the harness jangle, the creak of the axles, and the crunch of the wheels into the loam were sounding so distinctly because they were the only sounds. No insects chittered, and no birds sang.

With the arch of the black balsams almost closing above them in the gloom and silence, the fog came lower, misting now between the tops of the highest trees on the ledge to his left. Humidity increased to the point where he could taste the air he breathed, and the balsams, black, watchful, malevolent, exuded an odor of grave clothes.

Now the tendrils of fog looped the boles of the trees, and there was nothing definite anywhere. No definite light moved among these unseen crags, no definite shadows. There were no outlines to the trees along the dwindling perspective of the road. Cold congealed the perspiration on his face that oozed in viscous droplets to his sodden neckband. He plodded upward through a limbo of formlessness where no light gleamed and no darkness fell, where perspiration formed on cold brows and raindrops fell without rain.

Then, the witches laughed.

Out of the silence and gloom came the sound-shrill,

136

raucous, demoniac, triumphant. It began with a low chuckle, breaking against him from all sides, and rose to high, rasping, and looping cackles of glee. Ahead of him, the swaggering girl moved through the sound unheeding, swinging her hips with exaggerated gestures, scuffing the balls of her feet in the soft loam. She did not hear the sound.

He was hallucinating.

He staggered under the weight of horror. The sacrifice had walked into the dark woods. The mountains had driven him mad!

"Mr. Ricky, them old crows is talking. They's lost. I heard one say, 'Come over this way, Blackie, or you going to run into the side of the bank.'"

As she spoke, without looking back, the cawing of the crows dwindled down the valley, and he walked upright but ashamed. He, a would-be ornithologist, had been frightened out of his civilized wits by a flock of crows, while a girl who believed in ghosts and witches had recognized the sound from its beginning. Hell! he thought, she believes in ghosts for the same reason a white child believes in fairies: she *likes* ghosts.

"Melinda, it's getting cold. Get that coat Mr. Gaines gave you and put it on."

She scrambled into the van and came out, barefoot still, and strutted ahead of him, posing. "How I look from the side, Mr. Ricky?"

"Just fine, Melinda."

"How I look from this side?"

"Better. Twice as good."

Her antics and his anger at himself for his irrational fright lightened his mood, even as thunder rolled off to the southwest, its echoes reverberating between the invisible peaks. Melinda fell back to walk beside him.

"Aren't your feet cold?"

"No, sir. My feet's like my face."

She turned to face him, walking backwards. "Mr. Ricky, why don't you Jews eat bacon?"

She was hungry, and he was glad that he had not told her about the slab of beefsteak he had bought in Waynesville.

"We have to keep the price of pork down for you colored folks."

She turned with a flip of her hips, saying elaborately, "I thank you, Mr. Ricky. I truly thank you."

Overhead and far away, the thunder rumbled again, shaking the gloom in the narrow defile traversed by the road. Melinda, skipping occasionally, dropped back again. "Mr. Ricky, we going to spend the night in these mountains?"

"We should reach the crest before nightfall."

She looked up at him, and in the half-light, her face seemed ashen and drawn. "Mr. Ricky," her voice quavered, "I's scared."

"Don't you fret now, honey," he said, putting his arm over her shoulder, "because you've got the meanest Jew in Christendom to protect you."

"Mr. Ricky, that's the first time you ever called me honey. Why don't you call me honey?"

"Because I've been trying to teach you to talk correctly. 'Melinda, honey,' is redundant. 'Melinda' means 'honey.' If I called you 'Melinda, honey,' that'd be the same as saying 'honey-honey' or 'Melinda-Melinda.' You wouldn't call me Mr. Ricky-Ricky."

She grinned, cakewalking ahead of him, her shoulders arched far back, and looked behind, calling, "How'd I look from the back, Mr. Ricky-Ricky?"

"Right pert, Melinda, honey."

His estimate of their time of arrival at the crest fell short by almost twenty-four hours.

Past five in the afternoon, they climbed above the fog, moving out of it as amphibious mammals might emerge from a sloping sea bottom onto shore. From above, the fog bank lay as smooth and even as the surface of a pool and rising above it the highest peaks seemed islands. They had not emerged into sunlight but into an overcast day with the clouds so low that southward he could see a peak arise from the fog bank and lose itself in the clouds.

Judging westward to be the region of the thunder, he reckoned the road was bending southwest to skirt the edge of a rhododendron bald which lay on a gentle incline to his right and covered an area over a quarter mile in diameter. As they skirted the bald, going slightly down for the first time in eight miles, he looked westward across the bald and saw a squall sweeping toward him. He yelled to Melinda to get inside the van and wheeled the mules off the road, turning them in a small circle to trample the rhododendrons.

Moving fast, he unrolled the side tarp, tamped the edges into the ground, unharnessed the mules, and led them under the tarp. Grabbing his sack of purchases from Waynesville from beneath the driver's seat, he made it inside before the rain struck.

From the first sibilant hiss on the roof, he felt this was no sudden summer shower but the beginning of a major weather front rolling up from the Gulf. He called to the girl to light the lantern as he laid out his purchases on the chest. He turned and handed Melinda the slate with its chalk, saying, "Here's something I picked up at Waynesville to help with your lessons. Ever see a slate before?"

"Master Blake had one. He let me draw birds on it when I's a little girl."

Holding the items in her hand, she sat down on the chest and began to weep.

He chucked her under the chin. "Don't weep. It's not the Louisiana Purchase."

She tried to smile, and the attempt threw her deeper into tears.

He patted her shoulder and walked to the door, looking out at the rain, wind-driven now and sweeping in sheets over the tops of the balsams below them.

He avoided sentimentality on professional grounds. Sympathy was an indulgence no peddler could permit himself who serviced this territory, but with the girl, he was finding that he had not perfected his craft or guile. Gratitude for a simple kindness touched him because it indicated those kindnesses had been so few. He turned from the rain, asking brusquely, "Girl, can you cook with charcoal?"

"I seed it done, sir. I ain't done it myself, but I knows I can."

"Good," he said, "and while you do, I'll rig up my hammock."

"Where you put a hammock, Mr. Ricky?"

"This van comes equipped for sleeping accommodations for both sexes," he said. "My bedroll has lashings on the corners I tie to the axles and hang suspended above the ground in wet weather."

"Mr. Ricky, no sense you sleeping under this old wagon. You catch your death of chill.

"You sleep right there on that other chest where it's warm and dry. Nobody's going to pay us no never mind up here in the mountains."

She was arguing for his health, but her eyes pleaded her

own fear. Solomon, in the act of removing his poncho from its peg, paused.

Ordinarily, he slept on the chest when traveling alone. In the past fortnight, he had slept outside the entrance to protect her from intruders. Frightened by this desolate heath on the rain-flailed roof of the world, she wanted a human being near her in the darkness.

And if he refused her plea from any pretense of modesty, his refusal would be hypocrisy because it sprang from fear of his own concupiscence.

Smiling, he turned to her, replacing the poncho.

"Seeing as how you promised not to rape me, reckon I can risk it."

Chapter Six

He awakened to a brass sun blaring through the doorway and to silence on the roof. Across the aisle, Melinda's rales told him she still slept. He eased to a sitting position and pulled on his boots and crept out of the van, closing the door behind him to shield the girl's eyes from the glare.

He stepped into the wet smell of a morning on an archipelago in the sky. Enisled mountain tops dotted densely banked and scallop-surfaced clouds below him which stretched to the horizon. Above, the sky was blue and clear, and around him, the sodden bald glittered. Solomon spread his arms to the east and thanked the Lord for the risen sun, for truly, this sun was a benediction.

Time no longer moved in his behalf. By now, the posters were being distributed, and a day's traveling time lost now meant a more dangerous day added to his journey as he approached the Underground Depot. Checking the condition of the road, he knew it would be noon or later before he could venture onward without risk of miring.

At any event, the girl would have a morning free for study, and Solomon was mildly surprised by the pleasure the thought gave him.

They pitched camp that evening on the western slopes of the Great Smokies, and she completed the fifth lesson that she had studied during the day. With the slate and chalk, he taught her how to write her name, and within half an hour, she could write it without reference to the sample. She used the Spencerian script demonstrated in the book, and her power of mimicry seemed to extend even to her fingers. Her handwriting was better than his own.

Having mastered her own name, she asked him to write his for her to copy. Keeping faith with her pronunciation, he signed himself "Sol Ricky."

She was seated across from him, practicing, when suddenly she looked over and asked. "Mr. Ricky, what's my last name?"

He was stretched out on the chest, his head on his bedroll, Maimon's *A Guide for the Perplexed* propped on his stomach, and he answered without looking up, "You don't have one."

"Why for ain't I got no last name?"

A hurt expression in her voice drew his attention. He looked over, "It's not the custom," he explained. "Some servants take the names of their masters, but usually they get permission to do so."

"But I's free. I wants a last name like the human I is."

Her lower lip was beginning to tremble. He sat up. "Don't start whimpering, you hear! It's nothing to fret about. Why, girl, you can name yourself. Not many people in this world are privileged to name themselves. Take any name you like, and I'll show you how to write it."

She brightened up, to his immense relief. "What'll I call myself, Mr. Ricky?"

"That you'll have to decide for yourself. But be careful. Once you've signed that name to a legal document, it's yours forever. You can't go back and change your mind. Before you sign it, make sure it's what you want—some simple name, easy to remember, like Melinda Jones. But you've had enough for today. Put the book away, and go to bed. I'm blowing out the lantern and going outside."

As he stretched out in the darkness, she called to him, "Mr. Ricky?"

"Yes."

"What's a legal document?"

"It's any paper that goes on record, like a marriage license."

"After I's married, my name will be Kelly?"

"Yes."

"You said names mean something. What does Kelly mean?"

"I don't know. It's an Irish name."

"You know any African names, Mr. Ricky?"

"Scads of them. Congo . . . Zanzibar . . . Kiliman-jaro . . . Cape of Good Hope."

"Melinda Congo Zanzibar! Lordy, I'd never be able to spell that."

As the pearls drove her to read, the search for a surname spurred her to write. Between the Great Smokies and Wears Cove, she ran through the alphabet from Astor to Zilber-man. The road was downhill most of the way, and she rode beside him, asking him to spell out names that struck her fancy. Perelman appealed to her, but he dissuaded her from a Jewish surname.

He felt he would never be crowned with laurels as a teacher, but the Lord had given him luck in stumbling upon methods to arouse his student's interest. Without a doubt, any high-minded pedagogue would have questioned the ethics of using a string of pearls bought at a remainder sale to lure a student to read, but Solomon felt like a gambler with a hot pair of dice. She had mounted a Faustian attack on the book, and the words she was learning as a beginning speller were not "dog" and "cat," but "Jefferson" and "Adams" and "Washington." Whenever he found the op-portunity, he wove in some tidbit of information regarding history, natural history, or the preferred modes of conduct in a polite society.

As a teacher, he was also learning.

On a downgrade through the wild country north of Sevierville, when the heat of the afternoon had driven Melinda to the seat beside him, she laid aside her book and asked, "Mr. Ricky, when I's married up to Mr. Kelly, I'll be a lady. Does I get to sleep late, like Miss Phoebe, and drink wine?"

Solomon feared a misconception was forming in her mind, and he took immediate and drastic steps to halt it.

"You'll find very few ladies like Miss Phoebe anywhere at the North. Mr. Kelly is rich, perhaps richer than Mr. Blake, but bond servants are not permitted at the North. If you have a servant, you must pay her well for her work. Northern housewives take pride in doing their own house-work."

"What they do 'cepting cook?"

He wanted his answer to be specific, and thinking back over a day in the life of his wife, he started: "You get up in the morning about an hour before your husband and start the fire in the bedroom to make it comfortable for him when he awakens. Then, you go down to the kitchen and start the kitchen fire. Say it's a Monday, in winter, and a wash day—Tuesday's ironing day, Wednesday's baking day, and so on. You draw the water for the wash pots and build a fire under the pots. If you've got a cow and chickens in the back lot, you go out and feed them, gather the eggs, and milk the cow."

"I can't milk, Mr. Ricky. Old Fred did all our milking."

"A Northern housewife takes pride in doing every job and doing it well. So you learn to milk, and you milk."

Step by step, he pyramided the tasks awaiting her, urging speed at every turn. It took more than the allotted half hour to get her up from the cellar where she selected the breakfast preserves and back into the kitchen to prepare breakfast. She was ten minutes late awakening her husband. She sped through the after-breakfast cleaning of the kitchen and rushed to the washing pots, back into the house to make beds, clean, and dust. Then, her noon meal was upon her, and she had to rush through it to time it for the arrival of her husband, who wanted his dinner hot. Before his tread sounded on the front porch, Melinda was already complaining of weariness from the seat beside him.

"Don't give up, Melinda. Your day's just starting."

At full throttle, he drove her through the afternoon chores, leading up to the preparation of the big event of the day, supper.

"Supper will be in the dining room, so that means you set the table, spread the linen, set out the china, see that the silver is polished . . . Wait a minute! You've forgotten the milk in the cellar! Well, good thing it's winter. Go get it. Churn it." He allowed her ten minutes to take a quick bath in the water she had been heating on the stove and don a fresh dress for the arrival of her husband.

"When he gets home, he'll be tired," Solomon warned, "so he'll appreciate it if you'll lead the horse and buggy to the barn, unhitch the horse, feed it, and curry it if needed. Before you do that, though, better set your husband down in the parlor with the evening paper and a glass of his favorite wine so he can relax . . ."

"What the hell he been doing?" she exploded.

Quickly, he explained Kelly's tasks, supervising the help and entertaining guests at the tavern. "His work's very important. But you've got to get back to the house, check the meal. Better trim the candles in the dining room. Attention to details make a neat housewife. Husbands dislike sloppy housewives . . ."

He let her preside graciously at the meal, taking care to conceal her anxiety to get back to tasks—sewing, mending, odds and ends of work not accomplished through the day. Melinda listened with growing horror as he recounted a day in the life of Leah Villaricca. "You may get to bed a little late. If so, crawl in very carefully in order not to disturb your husband. Remember, he needs his sleep."

"Mr. Ricky, I be so draggle-assed by time I finish, I just flop on that sewing room floor. Don't worry 'bout me waking him up. . . . Does I get paid for all that work?"

"Of course not. You're his wife, not his hired hand."

"Master Blake, he say I'm not stout enough for housework. He make that broad-assed Beulah do all the housework."

"Well, if you're not strong enough to keep up your end of the work, Mr. Kelly might be prevailed upon to hire you a colored maid."

"No sir! I ain't having no uppity nigger in my house getting paid to do what I can't do. If she stout enough to do all that, she stout enough to knock me on my ass if I tells her to do it."

"You're the lady of the house. You're supposed to tell her what to do."

"I know that. You know that. She don't know that."

Melinda had a point there, Solomon admitted.

"Mr. Kelly, I work harder for him than I ever done worked for Master Blake. What do I get for making free?"

"Mr. Kelly will love you as his wife. Mr. Blake valued you as his property. If you don't work, then you're a shiftless housewife, and Mr. Kelly won't love you anymore. Besides, freedom is not freedom not to work. Freedom is freedom to work. If you're free and you don't work, then you're free to starve to death."

"Mr. Kelly, he let me starve to death after you done carried me all the way up North?"

"No, he wouldn't do that. But if he didn't love you anymore, then he'd be free to make you work."

"But if I's free, how's he going to make me work?"

Somewhere in their volleying conversation, his definition of Freedom had been shuttled aside, but he still had the Truth. "He could beat you."

She thought for a long moment. Finally, she said, "Mr.

Ricky, I been thinking. I'd sure 'preciate it if you'd turn this wagon round and carry me back to Georgia."

"Next wide spot in the road," he said. "But you may just as well throw your book away, because you won't be needing to read where you're going."

"Don't I get the pearls?"

"Pearls! What's a slave doing wearing pearls? If Miss Phoebe saw you strutting around the house with a string of pearls that she couldn't afford, she'd tear them off your neck. And you can throw away your slate, because you won't need any name but Mellie, and they won't let you write that. Whoa, mules!" He reined back on the mules.

"What for you stopping for, Mr. Ricky?"

"I'm taking you back to Georgia, to die in the cotton fields and corn."

"Then you go back without me. I done found out where that North Star is." She hopped down from the wagon, strutting ahead, making a big show of her independence, swinging her hips from side to side in an exaggeration of the forbidden walk. He clucked the mules forward, following her, and she called back, "I's going North, and I's going to tempt people. I done figured out my name. I's calling myself Melinda Jezebel.

"I know Mr. Kelly. He real raunchy. When I gets through with him, he'll be doing the cooking."

She strutted ahead of him with her flamboyant walk. She was a drawers-buster to a fare thee well. Her attitude was familiar, her manners outrageous, and she was committing a breach of discipline with that provocative behind; and he only chuckled.

They were five days crossing the valleys of the French Broad and the Holston, and in those five days, he sold less than fifty cents' worth of goods. It seemed locusts had swept through the land, denuding it of hard money. He was reduced to straight barter, swapping his wares for honey and whiskey, worth more than money on the Cincinnati market but hard to carry.

For Melinda, the trip from the Smokies toward the Cumberlands was a progress in education marked by place-names. Lesson six she completed at Sevierville, seven near Dandridge, eight at Panther Springs, nine near Rock Springs. On the southern side of the Clinch River, two days out from the Sycamore Station and two days behind the schedule he had posted to Ely Blood, Melinda won her graduation gift, the pearls, plus a bonus he had not intended to give her.

On the morning of the day of Melinda's triumph, he discovered why the countryside was bare of money through a chance encounter with a mountain family.

Melinda was studying in the van when he topped a rise and saw below him a farm wagon crawling up the hill about a hundred yards ahead and below him. He dropped back a few paces, rapped his signal for her to get inside the chest, and swung up to the seat. On the road, he had found that his customers responded more favorably to him when he was seated on the van. The sight of a man standing by the road and waiting put them on the defensive, possibly in fear that the standing man was a highwayman.

There were three occupants in the wagon, a man in overalls, a woman in a sunbonnet, and a small, shirtless boy seated with his legs dangling over the tail gate.

When they got within speaking distance, Solomon asked, "Would the nice gentleman and his lady have need of pots, pans, ax heads, calico, gingham, or a fine piece of denim for a shirt for that handsome boy?"

"Got need of them, mister, but ain't got ary penny."

"Jeff, I got that dime. Victor rightly needs a shirt. Mister, how much you charge for denim?"

"Seven cents a yard, ma'am. Finest quality Watertown."

"Save your dime, Mag," the man said, talking low. Solomon heard her say, "Eleven cents at Dandridge . . . he needs a new shirt . . ."

The man halted the mules but paid no further attention to Solomon. Solomon needed no attention. He dropped to the ground and went to the rear of the van, bringing out the roll of denim, a pair of scissors, and a cheap Barlow knife.

He held up the denim, "Notice the weave, ma'am. A shirt from this will wear till the boy outgrows it, and it can still be used as patching for overalls or for a bonnet. For your boy, I will give two extra inches, because they grow fast at his age . . . That's a nice basket of oats you have there, sir. Never would you find such nice, fat oats on the Carolina side . . . Feel the texture of this denim, ma'am. It is made to last. Notice the close weave."

"It's mighty fine material, sir. I'll take a dime's worth."

Solomon unscissored his carpenter's rule, measured out a yard and a half, plus two inches, and cut it for her as she

147

worked at the knot which secured the dime in her handkerchief. While she fumbled, Solomon again praised the oats, saying, "Sir, if it pleases you, I'd be willing for your wife to retain the dime and add a Barlow knife for the boy, in exchange for the hamper of oats."

"Mister, the hamper's worth a dime, and there's a bushel of oats there worth twenty cents on the market."

Solomon reached into the hamper and ran the oats through his fingers, letting the Barlow knife dangle in full view of the boy. "No, sir," he said, "these oats will go for twenty-four cents, maybe twenty-six. But that's on the market. You'll be selling to the market. Those storekeepers in town are sharpies. They'll try to make you think they're doing you a favor by taking them off your hands at half price. Your wife keeps her dime. My mules get the oats. Your boy gets a shirt and a Barlow knife. You can keep the hamper. Now I ask you, sir, where can you make more people and dumb brutes happy with oats worth fifteen cents to you than right here?"

Jeff, impassive on the seat, said nothing. He was thinking.

Solomon stood with his hand on the side board of the wagon, the Barlow knife glinting in the sunlight. The woman held the dime, waiting. The boy crouched near the tail gate, ready to lunge for the knife.

"I reckon it does get a mite expensive to drive two mules."

"Sir, sometimes I must go without corn myself to feed my beasts. Times are indeed hard, sir."

"You admired them oats . . . Well, I'll do it, mister."

Solomon smiled at the boy and handed him the knife. Restraining his eagerness, the boy walked forward and took it, looking at Solomon. "Air ye a Gypsy, mister?"

"Hush, Victor."

"It's all right, ma'am . . . No, son, I'm a Hebrew."

The father stepped back into the wagon and lifted the hamper. "Where do you want these, mister?"

"Right here in the side box. I'll take them."

He opened the feed box and poured the oats from the hamper, handing it back to the mountaineer.

"Good day to you, sir, ma'am, and son. My name's Solomon Villaricca. I travel these parts often, and if I'm ever able to be of service to you in the future, it will be my pleasure."

148

"We'ns the Hammonds, sir. We live down the road a spell, by the river. And a pleasant day to you, sir."

"Go with God, sir and madam. May your years be long and your children many."

Back on the seat, Solomon clucked the mules forward, realizing suddenly and a little sadly that he would never again come this way, unless the Irishman welshed on his final payment for the girl or in the unlikely event that the Cincinnati Trade Fair proved a complete failure. If the latter occurred, then he would be back, but probably not until the summer of '63 or '64.

Far off to the southwest, thunder rustled through the summer air like an echo of phantom artillery. Southwestward, the clouds floated in fleecy battalions. If a storm were brewing, it would be beyond his horizon, on an arc between Chattanooga and Murfreesboro (although he was not thinking in place-names), and the sound came from far away, as far, perhaps, as a landing on the distant Tennessee River near a little church called Shiloh.

He turned and slid back the window. "Melinda, did you ever see a Gypsy?"

"No, sir. But I seed a blue-gummed Geechee, once."

"I saw a blue-gummed Geechee," he corrected her.

"Next time you see one, Mr. Ricky, don't let him bite you. They's poison."

Since the boy, Victor, was wondering about Gypsies, he must have seen some recently.

Solomon had seen Gypsies, once only, twelve years ago. His grandfather had permitted a band to camp on his farm, and Solomon had played with one of the boys, Rudolf Bartok. They were Ungar Gypsies from Ireland, he recalled, who spoke with an Irish brogue when they were not speaking Romany.

If the tribe had moved into Tennessee, it was no wonder there was no money around. They combed the countryside with glib and expert salesmen; and if he were traveling behind Gypsies, he would be lucky to find anything left even for barter.

Near noon, Melinda stuck her face in the window. "Mr. Ricky, when we stops for dinner, you can get them pearls out, 'cause I've done won them."

"You sure of that?"

"Yes sir-ree, bobtail!"

Noon found them on the heights overlooking the valley of

the Clinch. He led the mules off the road into an oak grove which crowned the brow of a small hill. He felt safe, now that he was nearing the Sycamore Station, but he drove the van off the road to leeward and far enough to be out of sight of wayfarers. He went down the slope a short way to give the smoke from their cooking fire enough space to diffuse below the skyline.

Melinda had prepared a dish the night before of boiled dry butter beans which hardened in its own sauce. Today, she would add water and bring the dish to a boil as she stewed tomatoes in sugar. The mixture of the beans and the tomato sauce eaten with chopped onions and dunked cornbread was delightful. She went about preparing the meal while a crock of buttermilk cooled in a shallow saucepan filled with water.

As she worked, Solomon, in the van, removed the last pages of the primer from the pearl case; he wrapped the case in white paper and tied it with his last bit of red ribbon.

Melinda looked up from the skillet and saw the package in his hands. "Lordy bless you, sir, but you didn't have to wrap that. I know what's in it."

"It's a graduation present," he said, "and it's customary to wrap graduation gifts."

"Mr. Ricky, I got to be excused. Would you just stir these tomatoes, real slow and easy, while I go? The beans'll keep boiling theyselves."

He squatted, stirring slow and easy. She was learning, he thought. Two weeks ago her request would have been phrased a little differently.

She gulped her meal. Solomon ate slowly and sipped his buttermilk with majesty. No matter how urgent the occasion, she had to mind her manners.

Fretting and fuming, she sat with folded hands as he slowly unfolded the pages and read them, guarding the sheets from her eyes.

He read a tale told for children of a hen that went into the woods to scratch, was frightened by a falling acorn, and ran clucking to the barnyard to tell the sheep that the sky was falling down. The sheep told the mule that the world was coming to an end. The mule told the horse that the world was burning up. The horse fled from the barn, telling the other animals to flee to the millpond, the barn was on fire.

150

The farmer, coming from the millpond, stopped the stampede and asked what was going on. He traced the story back to its origin and told them the truth—the chicken had been frightened by a fallen acorn.

He handed the pages to Melinda, saying, "All right, girl, here's your exercise. Read it with expression, if you can, and I'm going to judge you on how well you understand it. There's no sense reading something if you don't know what it says. Now, go over under that oak tree, hold the paper like this, and read it out loud."

Her hands were visibly trembling as she took the sheets from him and walked away to stand ten yards in front of him, looking down at the paper. Slowly, she began to read, "Henny-penney, Farmer Brown's red hen . . . went . . . into . . . the . . . woods . . . to . . . scratch . . . for . . . acorns."

She paused for a moment, looking down at the pages. He could see her lips moving, and he saw the expression on her face change from fear to triumphant confidence.

When she resumed reading, it was no longer with the hesitancy of a child. She read accented sentences with the stresses laid on the proper words, and the rhythm of the sentences flowed naturally. He sat amazed, for she was reading ahead of her voice, and she was practicing elocution. At times, he felt she was practicing oratory.

When the sheep said "baa-baa," she raised her voice and bleated.

She faltered only once, when she came to the word "pasture," but she erred on the side of correctness. "What does 'past-yoor' mean, Mr. Rickey?"

"Paiss-cha, he answered, pronouncing the word in her dialect. "But you said it correctly when you said 'past-yoor.'"

"This book's wrote in Yankee talk."

She completed the story, folded the sheets, and curtsied. He clapped, loud and enthusiastically. "Melinda, that was very good. In fact, it was excellent. I'm giving you an 'A.'"

"Can I have my pearls now?"

"No. You still have your comprehension test. For that, I have only one question. That story has a moral. It points out a lesson for all of us. In just one sentence, tell me what that story is trying to tell us that we should not do."

She thought for a moment. "It says we ought not to

151

believe just anything a chicken tells us, 'cause chickens is natural-born liars."

"That's close enough, Melinda. Now, I'm giving you the pearls, but first I want to give you a graduation speech.

"You are a gifted girl. You have imagination, intelligence, even talent. It's up to you to develop your gifts. If Mr. Kelly will permit you, and he probably will, you keep on with your learning.

"Now, when you get up North, you're going to meet with disappointments. People of your race are not always welcome. You will have to harden your heart to slurs, even cruelty. You will have to find inside yourself the strength to withstand these things, and the best way to do this is to cultivate the joys of the mind. Reading will help you find a quiet place inside you where you can go when you are weary and troubled.

"Now, that's my graduation speech to you. Since you're graduating at the head of your class, you're entitled to deliver the *magna cum laude* address yourself. Anything you wish to say?"

"Yes, sir, Mr. Ricky. I got one thing to say. Give me them pearls."

He handed them to her, graciously, wondering if his speech had made any impression.

He held the mirror for her, and she unclasped them, wrapping them twice around her neck. "I likes them best this way in the mirror, but I can't see them when I wears them."

"They accent the structure of your neck better that way. You have a long neck."

"Like that tower builded by David?" she asked unconsciously, her attention focused on the pearls. "I truly love these pearls."

"Better than your ring?"

"Yes, sir. Mr. Ricky, can I wear them now?"

"Certainly. They're yours."

"I like pearls better than anything, even rhinestones. I reckon I got to clean the dishes, but I'm so happy I'd just like to set here awhile . . . Sir, if you didn't have that beard, I'd kiss your cheek."

"Have you ever kissed a white man?"

"Sure. I kissed Old Massa Blake, and young Massa Blake when he came back from the war."

"Did Mister Blake ever ask you to kiss him?"

"He make me kiss his butt, once."

"What!"

"Yes, sir." Her eyes glowed with the memory. "When I's a little girl, he take me swimming. I say I can throw a rock across a creek. He say he kiss my ass if I do. I say I kiss his if I don't. I didn't."

"Did you swim with him with no clothes on?"

"Hell, Mr. Ricky, come summer I didn't wear no clothes, nohow."

"When did you start wearing clothes?"

She giggled. "When Mammy saw fuzz."

By pushing his pace, he might have reached the Quaker meetinghouse shortly after nightfall, but tonight marked the beginning of his Sabbath, and he preferred to observe it alone. Once aboard the Railroad, his nights would be spent in the presence of Quakers.

They forded the Clinch in midafternoon. Melinda wanted to bathe in the river, but he denied her permission. The river was too wide for her concealment. "We'll find a place," he assured her.

Approaching five o'clock, traveling downward through a narrow glade, he saw a kingfisher wing past them in the opposite direction with a fish in its beak. He plotted its course and said to the girl, "Melinda, the wind has whispered to me, telling me that soon we'll come to a pool of deep water where you'll be able to bathe."

"I sure hope that wind ain't lying, sir. Dirt's sticking out my ears."

Half a mile farther, they came to a rill that flowed across the road from their right, joining the small branch that paralleled the road. Here the glade narrowed, and he spotted the marks of deer hooves cutting across the road, leading to a narrow run through a clump of alders. He stopped the mules and walked along the deer run for thirty yards or so. It led him to a point of rocks above where the valley narrowed between two cliffs, and below the rocks was a large pond formed by a landslide. On his side of the pond, the bank was lined with small willows and sumac bushes which had gained a foothold in the disintegrating shale. The far end was shadowed by overhanging oaks and hickory trees.

He returned and led the mules through the alders, beating his way as he went, and parked not far from the promontory jutting out from the invisible pool. Then, he invited the girl down to see his discovery.

"Lordy, Mr. Ricky, I thought you was guying me. I didn't know the wind talked to you."

She believed him, and he could not mislead her. "It didn't, Melinda. I saw a kingfisher coming up the ravine with a fish in its beak . . . Now, you can take your bath while I set out my candles."

She looked up at him. "Mr. Ricky, can I go to meeting with you?"

"Certainly, long as you keep quiet and don't go to sleep."

"I loves to watch candles burning. They's like live pearls, 'cept they's yellow."

She walked ahead of him a few feet to the ledge of bare rock, evidence of some primeval fault slippage, and stood for a moment in a semimilitary stance, arms folded beneath her breasts, legs apart, erect though relaxed. He moved to the ledge alongside her and turned to speak, when he noticed the expression in her eyes.

She was looking over the pool with a longing that bespoke deprivation, the look of a landlocked mermaid, and in repose her face was regal. "Melinda," he said, "sometimes I'd swear that you're a white girl with a black skin."

"I don't want to be white, Mr. Ricky. Being colored don't help none, but it ain't shameful."

"I'm right proud to hear you say that. I'm glad I'm Hebrew. Gentiles can get real mean."

"I don't mean that, Mr. Ricky. They's some nice white people, like you and Jesus. Master Blake, he nice. Miss Phoebe, she cry when she send me away. Mr. Kelly, he send for me. Mr. Gaines, he give me clothes. Lafe, he want to do it to me. I ain't met nothing but good white people."

She turned to face him, eagerness replacing the introspection in her eyes. "Mr. Ricky, I been thinking, I don't want to be white, but I don't want to be colored, either. I wants to be a fish."

"I was just thinking that you reminded me of a mermaid. Do you know what a mermaiden is?"

"Don't rightly."

"It's a woman who's fish from her hips down. She's half human, half fish."

"Don't want to be half nothing, Mr. Ricky. I wants to be all fish. I wants to live where it's cool all the time and everthing's clean. I just hang there in the water till I gets

154

tired of being there, and then I flips my tail and swims off. No arms to get tired, no legs. Just flip my tail and go . . . Mr. Ricky, you must be tired and hungry. I'll go fix supper, and you can wash up."

As he followed her down the trail, he said, "I always wanted to be an eagle and soar among the clouds with the sun at my back and the earth spread out below me."

"Eagles's got claws," she said.

Later, after he had taken his bath and relieved her at the fire, he let her go swimming while he went about setting up his candles.

He was bothered by a vague feeling of unease as he dusted off the forward cabinet, polished the seven-pronged candle stick, and took out his white tablecloth. Perhaps, he had overdone the warning about the treatment she might expect in the society she was to enter. Might be she would captivate every white person she met. With the current popularity of *Uncle Tom's Cabin* in the theaters of the North, there was surely a public predilection toward Topsys. Even so, she would meet with a measure of snubs and hostility, and he must arm her, now, as best he might.

He resolved to pray for the girl this night, pray for her safe delivery, and ask that if Kelly be the Pluto that Ely feared, then God grant her grace as Proserpina, for, come Hell in Cincinnati or high water on the Ohio, she would be delivered.

He folded his tallis across the chest and went out into the sunlight to chop a reserve supply of wood for morning's breakfast.

Chopping at a windfallen log, he gained a keen, aesthetic joy from the bite of the blade into the seasoned wood. Would to the Lord it were as easy to cut one's way through human entanglements. Should he, a white man, be saddened by the sadness of a darky? So, she liked white people as individuals—just wait until she bucked against them as a group!

Well, he held a mighty keen ax for cutting through human entanglements. Sixty-six point six times thirty pieces of silver—the traditional price for a slave. Six sixty-six— the Mark of the Beast—on Friday the thirteenth.

To rid himself of his mood, he swung the ax with such fury that he was drumming a tattoo against the log, when above the thuds he heard from the pond below the call of the whippoorwill.

Before the alarm died in his ears, he had flipped the ax in the air, caught it by the shaft, and was racing toward the pond, running low for concealment. He scrambled along the ledge, fully expecting to find the girl struggling in the embrace of some impromptu mountain swain or being chased through the trees by a Tennessee satyr.

As he broke through the sumac to a clear view of the pond, the whippoorwill sounded again, to his right and farther down the glade. He slid to a halt on the loose shale of the ledge. With his hearing no longer distracted by the thud of the ax, he recognized the call of the whippoorwill as—the call of a whippoorwill.

His grip relaxed on the ax handle. He squatted to catch his breath, drawing his handkerchief to wipe the perspiration from his forehead. On the far side of the pool, Melinda stood unharmed in ankle-deep water near the bank, reaching up for fox grapes on an overhanging vine, turned partly away from him.

Breathing a prayer of thanks, he turned to go, when he was struck by the lines of her, the swell of calves and thighs, the convex arc of buttocks, the concave arc of her back, the flat plane of her stomach, the swell of taut, high breasts, the curve of her neck, and the dynamic line of her lifted arm. Burnished by the slanting rays of the sun, she was a bronze of Virginal Innocence.

When he turned to go, she plucked the cluster of grapes and bent to rinse them, turning in his direction in a motion as fluid as a leaping fawn's, and he paused. Her pose, bending downward, was more delightful than the former. She had been lithe and graceful. Now, the swell of her buttocks, the arch of her back, and the ballooning of her breasts projected a voluptuousness as delicate as a kiss remembered from a dream. Marveling at her, he turned to go as she tossed aside the grapes to soap herself.

He could not turn and go. She was Susanna, and he was all three of the elders without impediment of age, with six months of celibacy and three weeks of close but circumspect association with yonder nymph. He tried to pray, but the swelling at his groin told him that prayer was an ounce of prevention when he needed an approximate ninety-five pounds of cure. He was sinful, low, and lewd, playing Peeping Tom, but his eyes commanded his will, and he was watching visual music roll in swelling diapasons from

156

breasts, from hips, from thighs, across the sheen of the pool, as she curved, twisted, and bent.

If the Commandments were literal, he had stolen, had borne false witness, and now he coveted his neighbor Kelly's forsworn wife, his neighbor Blake's maidservant, and surely his neighbor Melinda's ass. And it was written that he who lusts after a woman in his own heart has taken her in the flesh.

She spread her legs and leaned backwards to rinse the water from her hair, and he lusted for her. Watching her, shadow-dappled now, sliding under water to rinse and rising in delightful convolutions, he knew that his desire was sin, and he would have to answer for his sin in heaven. So, if he must pay the price, it was only just that he sample the merchandise.

Trapped by the logic of theology, he slipped out of his clothes and dove into the pool, almost cleanly.

When he surfaced a fourth of the way across the pool, swimming toward her, she was modestly seated in water high enough to cover the lower third of her breasts.

"What for you come here for, Mr. Ricky? You know I's taking my bath."

On the point of telling her truly of the whippoorwill's false alarm, he remembered the injunction of Maimonides that the hand of tenderness should not be laid upon a woman unless preceded by words of tenderness. This was no place for factual explanations, and he waded closer, intending to sit beside her, but there was no upward slope to the bottom. The Jezebel was tempting him by exposing two-thirds of her breast from a standing crouch.

Laughter and invitation in her eyes told him she knew the purpose of his coming. With the sure instincts of a female, she realized that their relationship had shifted. She was no longer a black girl plucked from servitude; she was the eternal Delilah, the beckoning one, the dark and secret mistress of the dark and secret dream.

Long time she had waited his coming, waited while the swords clashed at Karkor, waited in the ruins of Samaria, by razed Jerusalem, knowing he would come as Moses came, as the first Solomon. Long time she had waited, knowing that if it were not here they met, by a pool in Tennessee, they would have met at some bazaar in Baghdad, some bistro of Kharkov, some *estaminet* at Bizerte. Long time she had known he would come, borne on the tides of the centuries out of the abyss of time, and she had plotted his course from the day Adam walked east from Eden. He knew of her knowledge from an axiom of her race voiced once by a fellow bird-watcher: "Them children of Israel—they sho must like they's poontang."

So be it, he was here. Selah! Since this meeting was fore-ordained, predestined, and inescapable, he bowed to fate with the poise of a practiced sinner.

"After all the book-learning you got from me, you still don't know why I'm here?"

"I reckon." Her lips were prim, but her eyes laughed.

"I was lonesome for your nearness, for I feared that you were sad at heart, and so I came to the edge of the water to call for you. Yonder in the sumac bushes I stood and watched you picking grapes. The joints of your thighs were like pearls, your navel a round goblet wanting not liquor. When you bent, your two breasts were like young roes that are twins. For a moment, I was another Solomon, and you stood in the pools of Heshbon by the gate of Bath-rabbin. I thought: A garden enclosed is my sister, my spouse, with pleasant fruits, camphire with spikenard and saffron, calamus and cinnamon."

The laughter was gone from eyes grown deep and as soft as the low notes on a bass fiddle. She said, very low, "I ain't learned them words yet, Mr. Ricky, but they's sure pretty."

"So, I came to that garden, Melinda, for you are fair. There is no spot upon you."

"I got a strawberry on my ass."

"You have come with me, Melinda, from the den of the lions, come over the mountains of eternal smoke. You have ravished my heart with your eyes. You have put out the lights of my soul with the lights in your eyes."

"I don't want to do that, Mr. Ricky. You got the prettiest eyes I ever did see in a white man. You got colored folks eyes. When you ain't mad about something—when you's sad—your eyes cry without making no tears. That's why I sometimes make out like I don't hear you, 'cause you make me want to cry, and when I cries, I make your eyes cry. I don't want to make your eyes cry. I likes to make them laugh."

She was drifting toward him, arms spread and floating on the water. Tears glistened in her eyes.

" 'Scuse me for crying, now, Mr. Ricky, but I thinks you's the prettiest man. Ever since that night I first saw you up close, talking about Moses and Jesus, when you come to dinner and said us colored folks had souls, I been . . ." She choked up, stood silent for a moment to regain her composure, and lifted her eyes again to him. "Mr. Ricky, I's going to break my spoken word . . ." She paused slightly, looking at him with an ineffable gentleness mixed with an iron resolve. "Mr. Ricky, I's going to fuck you."

He reached out and cupped the nape of her neck in his palm, shaking her gently. "Melinda, Melinda, you must never use that word!"

"I cain't he'p it." Her soft dialect lapped his ears. "I's jest an ign'ant niggah. I wants to talk lak you wants me, but I jest cain't . . . 'Scuse me foh cryin' . . . When I seed you jump off that rock with yo' dick hard, I damned near come in my drawers, 'cepting I ain't wearin' no drawers . . . Lawdy mercy, Mr. Ricky!"

"Not here, Melinda. On the bank. In the honeysuckles."

"I got the hankerin', Mr. Ricky. I gotta git it here, and I gotta git it now."

She was taking the pillar of Solomon, and glorious was the taking thereof, using it as a handle to turn him over on his back while her slippery and water-buoyant legs slid over and around him. With deft and gentle hands, she manipulated until he was hers, but the waves created by the urgency of her passion threatened to drown him in the most pleasant death ever suffered by a man. His frantic heels caught in the muck, propelling them backwards and shorewards, she riding him like a boy on a dolphin, until his head slithered into the shallows where he could support them above the water with his elbows. She was lashing him with her body, and his buttocks moiled the bottom as he rose to meet her. He looked up and saw her eyes squinched shut in an intense ecstasy as animal moans and whimperings came from her throat. Then, he forgot her in his own long-pent and explosive expression, and they went limp together.

Relaxed and lying on him, she sighed, " 'Scuse me, Mr. Ricky. Now, you can do it to me."

Solomon grasped her thighs, slid her over his shoulder, stood up, and walked onto the bank with his burden, patting her rounded buttocks as he walked. "I'm going to use a little finesse. I'm taking you over to the honeysuckle vine, tramp us out a bower, and take you in a nest of flowers."

159

"Watch out. Bees likely sting your ass."

Later, she complimented him on his efforts, "Mr. Ricky, you right nice. You so slow and easy."

"You sound like an expert," he muttered in the gathering shadows. "How many men have you done this with before?"

He was drowsy with the euphoria of spent passion, but her answer shocked him fully awake. "Just one, Mr. Ricky. Brother Smith, he do it to me."

"Was he any good?"

"He all right. He slobbered, and he keep saying, 'I's coming, Eulalee, honey.' Hell, he know my name ain't Eulalee."

"How'd he get you away from Bill and Phoebe Blake?"

"He take me down to the creek and baptize me. I don't have nothing on but my white shimmy, like he tell me. After he duck me, he start feeling my tiddies. Next thing I know, he down there whamming away."

She paused, silent with the memory of her first lover, and Solomon lay beside her, speechless. Finally, she said, "Ever' time I get in the water with a preacher, I get fucked . . . 'Scuse me, Mr. Ricky. What do you call 'getting it?' "

"Ladies don't mention it at all. If they have to, they say 'making love.' "

"I reckon I'd better say 'making love,' 'cause I reckon I's still a lady."

"Why do you keep saying you reckon you're still a lady?"

"Brother Smith, he say when I let a preacher do it to me, it don't count. I's still a lady."

"I reckon you are," he said drowsily, cuddling her in his lap. Somewhere below them a whippoorwill fluted its ironic call through the darkening glen. Close by, an opening primrose threw its lemon fragrance into the air. Forspent with loving, Solomon slept.

He awakened to starlight and felt her fingers fluting through his pubic hair as she softly hummed "The Rock of Ages."

O, how low the righteous had fallen! Solomon Villaricca, keeper of the Law, guardian of the seed of Judea, decorous, disciplined, one who walked humbly before his God, was fit only for the company of Bacchus, goathooved Pan, and the drooly-crotched satyrs. Solomon, son of Aaron of the line of Villaricca, husband of Leah the faithful, lay naked in a starlit glade in Tennessee. He had transgressed. He had proved faithless to Leah. He had violated his promise to Kelly. Now he had come to this estate, lying in lewd embrace with a dusky harlot who hummed a Christian hymn, and he was enjoying himself!

His hand slipped up and cupped her breast, his fingers rolled her nipple, hard and swollen, and she turned herself to him with a sigh. Once more the pipes of Pan went keening through the glade.

When she returned from her toilet, he was gentle but firm. "Get your clothes on, Melinda. We're going back to the van."

She dressed, and they circled the pool to his clothes. He donned them, and they walked back to the deserted supper pots. In silence, they ate a cold meal.

He let her finish her meal before he spoke.

"Melinda, what we did must never be repeated. Adultery is a serious offense. I have broken God's Commandments. If my wife knew this happened, she'd be very hurt."

"Don't tell her, Mr. Ricky."

"I won't. And you must never, never, tell Mr. Kelly about Brother Smith and me. Tell him you sat on a picket fence, because Mr. Kelly's dead set against girls who aren't virgins. If he knew of this, he would spurn you. On the other hand, if you show him the merest portion of the skill and enthusiasm that you have shown me tonight, he'll cherish you forever.

"More important, I get as sluggish as a hibernating bear when I've been with a woman, and I'm supposed to be a knife honed to a sharp edge for one purpose—to get you safely to the North. I must stay alert because our safety depends on my alertness.

"You must promise me that you'll be very careful and not tempt me. Your freedom and my life depend on my alertness."

"I sure will, sir. I don't know what I'd do without you."

"Very well." He assumed formality. "It's two-thirty, now. You get to bed."

When he went into the van to fetch his bedroll, his eyes caught the pale gleam of the candelabra. He went forward and put away his Sabbath gear, and he emerged from the van muttering in Hebrew. Melinda, standing aside to permit him exit, asked, "Sir?"

"I said, 'Remember the Sabbath Day and keep it holy.'"

"I'll do that, Mr. Ricky, come Sunday."

Outside, he lay looking up at the stars. This day, he had violated the *hilkot 'abatim* in his treatment of a servant. More, he had shattered the Commandment against adultery while violating the Sabbath, and neither deed reflected honor upon his father and mother. As he saw it, he had three Commandments left intact from this journey: He had not murdered anyone; he had not taken the Lord's name in vain; and he had worshipped no graven images.

Languor and the sadness of satiety he felt, but not a whit of remorse. On the contrary, in justice to the black, he had to admit that she was perhaps the liveliest female he had ever experienced.

"Erwachen!"

He awakened to the command and the toe of a boot nudging his ribs. His head lay in the shadow of the van, and in the light of a sun which had already cleared the eastern ridge, he could see plainly the face of the man looking down at him, a Teutonic Moses. Beyond the man, two others sat on horseback, both blond like the older man, and one carried a rifle. Above him, the bearded man was very big, but it was not his size which dismayed Solomon—it was the cocked pistol he pointed at Solomon's head.

As the rifleman watched, the youngest man of the trio swung from his horse and went to the van. Solomon rose to his feet.

The retribution of the Lord had been swift. Under ordinary conditions, three men on horseback would not have been able to ride undetected within twenty yards of him, alseep or awake, but under ordinary conditions, he would have awakened at the first glimmer of light. Now he stood in the midst of his captors, while his alertness lay like a tarnished blade in the bower by the pool of Heshbon.

A volley of German came from the van, and the young man emerged, dragging a sleepy-eyed Melinda into the sunlight. He practically threw her in front of the big man, talking excitedly. With his limited knowledge of German, Solomon could understand only isolated phrases of his speech, "She is black" and "Surely, he is the Jew."

He clapped the patriarch on the shoulder, *"Wahrlich, er ist Villaricca!"*

Melinda looked at Solomon. "Is we cotched, sir?"

"Looks that way." Solomon shrugged.

She edged closer to him, frightened, and the man on horseback, thin-faced and hard-eyed, swung the muzzle of his rifle toward them, pointing, and called to the younger man, "Look at them, Little Franz. It's Death and the Maiden."

His German could not hide his derision and contempt, and Solomon hated the man.

The two men afoot conferred briefly, and the patriarch, whom the young man called Big Franz, turned to Solomon.

"Sprechen Sie Judisch?"

Solomon knew some German but less Yiddish—Spanish was his second language. His knowledge concealed might work to his advantage, and he would yield no advantage. God had made His displeasure known to Solomon; now Solomon would make his displeasure known to God. At the first opportunity, he would enrich the soil of Tennessee with three dead Germans.

"Je ne parle pas Français," he said.

Chapter Seven

He came, finally, to the Sycamore Station, but he came as a captive, slumped beside Big Franz on the driver's seat with the girl locked in the van. He saw the Quaker meetinghouse, an unpainted frame building, grow more distinct through the trees to the right of the road. He watched as the building seemed to swing past them at the hub of Gothic corridors formed by the straight trunks and high, overarching boughs of loblolly pines. He looked as the perigee of the church's apparent circuit swung past them and the intervening trees narrowed and finally closed the aisles of his vision. A bearded mass of plaintiveness topped by a yarmulke, he looked and thought of God and planned murder.

He reckoned their destination to be the village of Cumberland Gap, twenty miles away. Twenty miles was six hours at this pace—the German was not forcing the mules—but here, the road was generally upgrade. In two hours, they would top the plateau and go downhill into the valley of the Powell River. Then, the mules would step up the pace.

He could count on five hours before jail.

Big Franz had given his pistol to Little Franz, who was riding ahead, and removed the whip from the socket on Solomon's right and laid it on the seat to his left. Leading Big Franz's horse, the rifleman rode ten yards behind to get a clear shot if Solomon leaped and, incidentally, a clear view of Melinda if she dropped through the escape hatch and broke for the woods.

As morning wore on and heat waves gave a subaqueous shimmer to the road ahead, Solomon could think of nothing. Weaponless, boxed in by hostile horsemen fore and aft, with a giant riding beside him, he had only the bitter consolation that these men were avenging angels of the Lord. Inwardly, he smiled at his dark fancy. If so, they should at least speak Aramaic—certainly not German.

Incredibly, an hour before zenith, Big Franz shouted to the boy ahead, who turned, waved, and urged his horse forward at a gallop. Solomon watched as the rider disappeared around a bend and the tattoo of his horse's hooves died in the distance. Solomon had caught the words *"Jude"* and *"Freundin,"* and he assumed that the lad was riding to tell the sheriff at Cumberland Gap they were bringing in the Jew and his woman friend.

These men were not avenging angels. They were mortals, and they had made a mortal error.

They were not over half an hour from the Powell, and the river had a rapid current. When they forded the stream, Big Franz would be struggling to keep the mules headed upstream, and the rifleman would be fighting to control his mount and the trailing horse, riding closer in the lee of the van. One blow would knock Big Franz from the driver's seat. When his unconscious body struck the water, his friend would be given a choice—save Big Franz or shoot at Solomon.

If he risked a shot, he would be firing from the back of a jouncing horse, and he would not be able to dismount and reload in waist-high water. With the loaded handle of the whip, Solomon could club him to death in the river.

If he went to the aid of his friend, Solomon would have time enough to drive the van upon the bank, around the curve, and get Melinda through the hatch with their bags before he sent the mules trotting westward. They could flee into the woods and wait for nightfall.

Somewhere in this area was a Quaker by the name of Gresham who would send them North.

So, his plans were laid. He could only wait while the wagon rolled toward the river.

At the point where they finally began their descent into the valley, the road swung southwest along the lip of a swale which cradled a grove of oaks. As Solomon looked at the scene, he realized that his mind was tuning itself to a higher pitch to meet the approaching crisis; his senses were functioning on a higher level of awareness.

His vision seemed invested with a sense of touch. Behind a thin stand of pine fronting the road, his eyes felt the gnarled boles of the oak trees, and their ancient shapes had the gentleness of the hands of a beloved grandparent. In front of the oak foliage, the pines, mast-straight and limbless except in their topmost reaches, conveyed the visual roughness of pastels slashed over oils of green. He felt the brown bark with his vision.

When they rounded the bend, the road stretched west-northwest for over a mile, downgrade. Through the gap in the trees, he saw, far off, the long-sought ridge of the Cumberlands. Beyond the mountains, he could sense the curve of the earth, could feel his line of vision diverging from the planet. He saw infinity.

His mind soared with an awareness which matched the acuity of his vision and let him feel the ultimate blue in the blueness of the skies, weigh the buoyancy of the clouds and swing with them through the currents of the air.

Odors grew keener. He distinguished the hollow, autumnal smell of oak humus beneath the astringency of pine. He caught the faint pungency of sun-warmed paint from the van, the smell of leather from the harness, and the dear, familiar odor of the mules.

He knew that nothing had changed in nature. Earth had been beautiful forever. Only because he was poised on the brink of a terrible and desperate action did this receptivity exist.

He was awed and grateful and somewhat wistful.

But the van was rolling toward the river. He remembered to feign fear, and he cast a worried glance behind at the rifleman.

Wolf-lean, hard-eyed, slouched, the rifleman rode with the rifle slanted over the pommel of the saddle. The steel sheen of the weapon was shroud gray, its firing hammer curved forward like the neck of a striking viper, and the stock had the high gloss of a coffin. Solomon's vision touched the instrument and felt the shape of death.

I am going to die, he thought.

He had watched the hill people drive nails into trees with such rifles at thirty paces. It was not an outside chance that the man behind was a marksman—it was a certainty.

The rifleman's skill explained the dismissal of the horseman with the pistol. His captors were superbly confident that he could not escape the rifle.

They were correct. Solomon had looked upon the face of his executioner.

His heightened awareness sprang not from senses honed for combat but from the compassion of God, Who was granting His once-beloved son this final draught of life before he was taken from the altar to be slain.

Solomon Villaricca would die with his brains splashed in a dwindling line up the dirt of a road in Tennessee. No rabbi would dispatch his soul in faultless Hebrew, no cantor chant his liturgy.

No! His epitaph would be delivered in a flat Tennessee drawl by the sheriff who cleared his slayer at the inquest. "The nigger-stealing son of a bitch oughta knowed better than run."

This was no way for a gentle Jew to die—catapulted onto Abraham's bosom by a minié ball. It was not fitting that a son of Israel should be slain on the noon of a Sabbath, forgotten in the delights of adultery and slain impenitent after committing murder. Only mad dogs and Anglo-Saxons were shot down on the roads of Tennessee.

His name would be stricken from the scrolls of Israel; Gentiles would toss his dishonored flesh into a hole in the sod of Tennessee. For a little while, the grass would grow over his mound. Then, winter would come, and these hills would stand barren beneath an aching sky. Winds would blow whorls and eddies in the fallen leaves that drifted over his grave. Cold and slanting rain would pound the leaves into mulch above him, obliterating even the sight of his mound. He who had walked so splendid in the sun, who had loved justice and mercy, would melt into a grave unmarked on earth and unrecorded in heaven.

Rat thoughts scurried from the image of death in his mind.

He could drop the Law and accept Christ. As a Christian, Christ would accept his sins, because that was part of the contract.

No, not that! It would not be just for a Landsman to add to the burdens of Jesus. Jesus had his hands full in the likes of Brother Smith.

Strangely, his mind's oblique collision with the memory of Brother Smith steadied him.

167

He must have thrown a fit, he thought. If he sought instant conversion, Mohammedanism was his logical choice. He could kill the Dutchmen and be ushered into heaven for slaying the infidels.

It was not eternity he wanted but the Cincinnati Trade Fair. Above all, he wanted to see tomorrow's sunrise.

He could buy tomorrow by doing nothing. Seven years of sowbelly in a Tennessee jail would be penitence enough for sins to placate any god. But the girl in the van trusted him, and she was a note for one thousand dollars collectible in Cincinnati. Already, he had sunk seven Commandments into her, free of charge. He would throw in the eighth, save his worldly investment, and let the rifleman fire at will.

As Solomon keyed himself once more to high resolve, the wagon emerged onto the bluff overlooking the river.

To the left of the road, the hillside had been cleared for farming, and the field stretched down to the line of trees marking the river's course. Less than half a mile away, he could see the slot in the trees where the road forded the river and curved south to angle up the incline.

On that curve, yonder, his body would lie in the dust of the road, its toes pointed to the sky, and its eyes staring into the sun. He could see the scene as if he were standing and looking on it with living eyes, could see the hole above the brow, the gelatinous globs clinging to the roadside bushes, see the thin, aristocratic nose that would never again quiver to the scent of lilac water rising from Leah's hair.

He broke.

Tears swelled in his eyes. His musculature went limp and began to tremble, completely out of control. He could not even beat his breast in lamentation for the soul of Solomon Villaricca, blown into interstellar space by his nova of self-revelation. He could do nothing because he was nothing.

He who had worn the tallis as a godly man was neither a man nor of God; he was a gutless poltroon who had feared man and God equally because he was fearful. His prayers, skullcap, candlestick, tallis—all the jujus of a savage. His fear of God was not religion but cowardice, and the cowardice stood before him now, naked of its pious posturings. If he had honor left . . .

Honor! He shamed the word by thinking it.

If he had honesty left, he would turn and grovel before the German with the rifle because he feared him more than he feared God. Verily, this was the truth! He would turn and give thanks to the rifleman for sparing him the minié ball. He would pray to the rifleman to let the water of the river splash high over the footboard to hide the dark stain of his disgrace, which would soon be showing on the crotch of his pants.

His struggle to control his bladder helped control his nervous dissolution. He won, and the quivering in his muscles ceased. The sobbing was harder to quiet, and lastly, the tears quit flowing. When he was able to raise his head and look again at the river, he found they had turned off the road and were following a wagon trail due north through the forest. They would not cross the river.

He braced his left foot on the footboard, dropped to his right knee, and urinated to the side of the van. When finished, he took his yarmulke from his head and tossed it into the bushes without ceremony. It was senseless to peacock in the uniform when he did not belong to the army.

For over a mile, they drove through the forest, until it broke from the woods onto a broad, well-graded work road which bisected fenced fields and pastures dotted with cattle. Finally, the road ended at the bar of a T-marking, the intersection of the work road with an east-west road surfaced with gravel along the edge of a forest to the north. Big Franz turned right, and Solomon saw, two hundred yards ahead, a settlement set back in a cove.

Twelve large houses, six on each side of the road, sat before a large stone building divided in the center by an arcade. Farther up the slope to his left, against a backdrop of pines, stood a white frame church with a steeple.

Drawing nearer, he saw each house had been decorated along the porch and eaves with elaborate wood carvings, and the logs used in their construction were symmetrical enough to have been turned on a lathe. Each was fronted by a flower garden behind a picket fence.

He had been brought to a Bavarian village whose neatness was far from the customary chicken-infested, hog-littered, dog-plagued settlements of the Cumberland, and it was not even on his map.

With the horseman swinging ahead to open the gate,

Big Franz drove the van under the arcade, which led, Solomon could see, into a livery compound.

Big Franz halted and motioned Solomon to get down. Unattended, Solomon followed the German to the rear of the van, which he casually unlocked and turned, handing Solomon his key as he called inside, *"Kommen, Mellie."*

Solomon stood looking at the key in his hand, befuddled, when his wonderment was cut short.

Melinda came to the doorway of the van.

She wore her pearl necklace and her cross, her ring and bracelet, and, in eighty-five degrees of heat, she wore the heavy dress with the cape that Gaines had given her. In her hand were white gloves and on her feet were high-buttoned shoes. Without a doubt, she was the most gorgeously attired female ever to step from the door of a van in the history of itinerant trading.

Big Franz recovered first; he offered his hand to the lady. Lightly and gracefully, she stepped to the ground.

"Melinda," Solomon said, "they're not taking us to a ball."

"I knows it, Mr. Ricky, but I's going to wear my finery once before I's hung."

"Child, they're not hanging you. You're worth more to them than a herd of cattle."

Franz pointed to a doorway and said, "In."

He and Melinda preceded Franz into a dining hall with three long tables stretching its length. The center table was lined with chairs, the others lined with benches. The room had a puncheon floor and at the far end was a huge fireplace with spits and floating ovens for winter use.

At least forty persons were already in the room. Women with babies sat on the benches, but most stood along the walls. In the babble of voices that greeted their entrance, he heard no English, but the word *"Schön"* was repeated several times. Surprisingly, the faces were friendly, some smiling, and a large, matronly woman stepped up and said, *"Kommen Sie, Mellie!"*

"They knows my name, Mr. Ricky."

"Yes, and they think you're pretty."

Melinda smiled, and the woman took her arm, leading her away. Big Franz touched Solomon's shoulder, pointed to a side door to the building, and motioned for the people to stand back. Solomon walked toward the door as Franz had commanded.

So, he was being conducted to his cell. He shrugged. He had bargained for this captivity. For this, he had given up his manhood, his religion, and the black girl. Now, he would embrace his prize.

Politely, Franz opened the door, and Solomon stepped into an annex built onto the refectory. Against the far wall were privy stalls, and on his right, a wash trough with cans of soap and hanging towels.

Franz had merely shown him to the men's room.

When they returned to the dining hall, Franz directed him to a seat at the center table, where others now stood behind the chairs. Franz took his place at the head of the table and stood until the matron brought Melinda to Solomon's side. Then, they all sat.

Big Franz intoned a short prayer, and when the diners all joined in the "amen," the word set off the mechanism of a giant clockwork. From the summer kitchen across the arcade, twelve women marched in, two abreast, dimpled elbows aloft bearing trays of steaming soup. Four to the right, four to the left, and four to the center table, they moved to the swing of a pendulum. With two at each end of a table, and facing each other, they advanced to the center, peeling off bowls of soup. The squad advancing from the door did an about face, and the platoon marched out.

Solomon's nose reported cabbage boiled in beef broth, and the aroma prompted him to gulp the bowl in one swallow, but he restrained the impulse and used the soup spoon.

Then came butter in huge pads dewy with moisture, freshly baked bread redolent of yeast, sliced carrots and celery, pickles and chowchow followed by roast pork, roast beef, roast leg of lamb, Wiener schnitzel, boiled tongue, liverwurst, sausages, breaded pork chops and tenderloin, boiled potatoes golden with melted butter and green-flecked with parsley, parsnips and sauerkraut, breaded fried eggplants and fried green tomatoes, string beans and peas, stewed ripe tomatoes, red cabbage boiled with sugar, peas, corn on the cob, baked yams and lima beans.

Solomon was dumbfounded by the offerings and depressed by the precision with which they were served. Every aspect of this strange community seemed directed by some invisible brain. He was in a giant beehive arranged with an orderliness as alien to the South as the language.

At the moment, the language was terse, monosyllabic: *"Brot, bitte . . . Kalbsnuss? Danke . . . Schweinefilet? Nein . . . Hachse or Schnizel? Schmorbraten! Jawohl, mein Herr."*

Closing his mind to the sound, he laid to with determination. If he were being fed as a social duty pending the arrival of the sheriff, then the lamb must fatten himself for the slaughter.

He ate until satiety slowed his pace enough for him to look around at his fellow trenchermen. Despite the gusto with which they were eating, he noticed them throwing covert glances at Melinda. She was probably the first black they had ever seen at close range and certainly the prettiest. In repose, her face possessed more animation than the German women's when they smiled. Their faces seemed molded from an excess of flesh where hers seemed carved from ebony.

One girl, near Melinda's age, approached beauty with her golden hair and blue eyes, but the older women reminded him of figures painted by Rubens, and they all looked alike.

One lad of eighteen or so, the only youth at the center table, who sat next to an empty chair to the right of Franz, could hardly keep his eyes from Melinda. He was a young Siegfried, but the glances he threw toward her were non-Teutonic; they were Italianate, Vesuvian.

"These folks don't seem like bad folks," Melinda whispered. "They seem to like us."

"They like you. And well they should. Mr. Blake will pay them money for catching you."

"How much?" She asked the question over a lifted fork.

"Two or three hundred dollars, I reckon."

"Mr. Ricky," she lowered her voice, "that pretty white boy across the table ain't thinking about money. Looks like I done cotched me a beau."

She looked at the boy and smiled. He blushed and bent his head to the plate. Solomon caught the exchange.

"What are you doing to that white boy?"

"I's just doing me a little tempting, Mr. Ricky."

He might have been offended over her boldness had he not been so concerned over his own fate. As he brooded, the clockwork women returned with huge pots of coffee and ewers of cream. Solomon watched them dazedly—he could not have looked a single Pfeffernusse in the face—but he permitted them to pour him coffee. His waitress looked in mild surprise at his plate pushed back and clucked and shook her head.

"Wir brauchen einen Dolmetscher," she said, smiling.

Solomon gave her an ambiguous nod and managed a drawn smile.

They were returning with Streuselkuchen, Schokoladen-flauf, Kasekuchen, and Apfelstrudel when he heard the clatter of hooves in the distance, growing closer. Then, Little Franz rode up to the doorway and called inside, *"Die Freundin kommt."*

Solomon had assumed that the "female friend" was Melinda, but from the hush that fell over the hall, he decided it must be the queen bee of the hive, some Brunnehilde or Lorelei.

As Little Franz rode into the compound, a buggy pulled up to the door.

Solomon rose with the others when Franz stepped out to usher a woman into the hall.

She was past sixty, gray hair drawn tightly into a bun, tall, lean, square of jaw and shoulder, and as flat-chested as a man. She waved an impatient hand to the diners, saying, *"Setzen Sie sich, bitte! Setzen!"*

They sat.

Her dress of black fustian fell below the tops of her buttoned shoes and rose to a tunic collar that covered half of her long, scrawny neck. Relieved only by a thin piping of gray around the sleeves and undecorated except for two rows of black buttons in front, the dress resembled a uniform. The resemblance was appropriate for her ramrod bearing, maintained at a slight tilt as she leaned on a walking cane.

Her face was composed but not placid. It was neither molded nor carved but etched from steel. Wellington on a hilltop at Waterloo could not have presented a more imperious figure, Solomon thought, as the young Siegfried stepped forward to take her cane and help usher her to the empty seat.

"Danke, Karl," she said as she eased herself into the seat.

A waitress offered her food, but she waved the woman away with *"Wasser, bitte."*

She turned to Big Franz with a staccato flow of German

173

which lashed the air between them and changed his smile of welcome into a shame-faced grin, which, in turn, gave way to abject embarrassment.

He lifted his hand as if to ward off her words and tried to inject an *"Aber."* Failing, he visibly wilted.

Solomon could pick random words from her flow, *"Pistolen,"* *"Kannonen,"* and *"Todt,"* that would have convinced him she was arranging his death before a firing squad had it not been for the frequent repetition of *"Dumkopf."* The crackle in her voice transcended the language, and Solomon did not need to see the cowed expression on the face of Franz to know he was getting a tongue-lashing.

Finally, a trace of smile flitted over the iron face. Her language slowed, softened, and she reached and patted his hand, saying something that brought smiles to his face and lifted the tension in the room.

"Danke, Freundin. Danke," Big Franz said.

She paused, sipped her water, and glanced at Solomon. Her eyes flicked to Melinda, registered distaste, and turned back to Solomon. Her gaze reflected neither hostility nor friendliness, only abstract intensity.

"Well, Mr. Villaricca," she said. "Better late than never."

"You speak English, ma'am?"

"Indeed. Friend Blood tells me that thee does also, and very skillfully. I am Friend Norah Gresham. I had instructed Mr. Gruber to take thee by force, if necessary, assuming that thee might be in the hands of bounty hunters. Mr. Gruber assumed that the force should be applied to thee. I was telling him what Friend Blood tells me, that thee can be a violent and dangerous man and that thee could have done him and the others harm."

"Ely must have given me a bad report, ma'am. There were three of them, and they were armed."

"A good report by Ely's lights . . . No, carrying weapons was stupid. These people are Mennonites. Their religion, as mine, forbids violence. It is stupid to invite violence with the threat of a weapon that is not loaded."

So he was not a prisoner!

Even as this intelligence was imparted to him, it yielded to self-disgust so strong he quailed before it. Solomon Villaricca had been reduced to pigeon-livered poltroonery by the mere sight of an empty rifle! Better he should lie dead at the ford than carry this disgrace to his grave.

174

She who had thrown him into an abyss of self-revulsion lifted him with her scorn.

"But as for my report, I would not give thee a passing mark for alertness. Thee habitually lie abed until six as thee were found this morning?"

· "No, ma'am. My head was in the shadow of the wag—"

"Nor did thee hear the horsemen approach. I must say, Mr. Villaricca, thee does sleep well on watch. But thy ward must have great confidence in thee, since she was also asleep.

"All men are derelict in their duties, but thee's more derelict than most. Thee ignored heaven and risked hell to sleep till noon."

Her scorn lashed him. He quailed before her as Gruber had quailed, when suddenly, her voice quivering with fear or outraged loyalty, Melinda came to his rescue. "Mr. Ricky, he good, ma'am. He protect me mighty fine. He up late learning me things."

"Hush, child. I'm speaking . . . Thee's three days late, Mr. Villaricca. What caused thy delay?"

"We had to go over the mountains at Waynesville, and we were marooned on top by a storm. Then, four miles from the Station, I was caught by sundown and had to stop for Sabbath yesterday."

"Yesterday was Friday."

"Hebrew Sabbath, ma'am."

"Ah, I see." She tapped her fingers on the table. "I must look more closely into thy odd faith . . . Mellie!"

"Yes, ma'am."

"I must tell thee, girl, thee's done more to lower the morality of East Tennessee in the last three days than all the whiskey made in these hills . . . Why's thee wearing that outlandish jewelry?"

"This is my finery, ma'am."

Melinda's hurt showed on her face, and the martinet's features softened. "Not that I approve of jewelry, mind thee, but on thee it is very becoming. Thee's a very comely girl, isn't she, Karl? *Das Mädchen ist schön, Karl. Nicht wahr?*"

"*Ja . . . Ja, gnädige Frau,*" the boy blushed as he stammered.

In a twinkling, the strange woman had crushed Melinda and raised her again.

"Mr. Villaricca, thee'll come to my house to discuss a

matter. Mr. Gruber will provide thee lodging for the night, and the girl's needs will be attended likewise."

He was dismissed. For the remainder of the meal, she was absorbed in a discussion with Franz Gruber. When, finally, she summoned him to ride with her westward, she refused his offer to take the reins. She drove, sitting rigidly erect and staring straight ahead.

She rejected conversation, answering the questions he ventured and his pleasantries with monosyllables or nods. His genuine wish to become better acquainted was defeated by her taciturnity. Her detachment was that of a general planning a battle who did not care to discuss strategy with a private.

When they came to a hand-operated ferry across the Powell, he muscled the ferry across by the cable and climbed back to the seat beside her without receiving as much as a nod of thanks.

Beyond the river, the road climbed up, then leveled off. For another two miles, they drove, his silence matching hers, until they came to cultivated fields. She said, "My farm."

At this point, he could see almost two miles ahead to a point where their road debouched onto another running generally north and south. He asked if the distant road was the Wilderness Road. She turned left into a driveway that led to an unpainted frame house before she answered "Yes."

Nearing the house, she honked the air horn, and a bearded man shambled out to await their arrival. "My son," she told him.

Her son took the reins she tossed, and Solomon jumped down to assist her, but she had edged to the ground before he could get around the buggy. As horse and buggy were led to the rear of the house, she walked to the steps with her cane and swung stiff-legged up to the porch, brushing off his offer of assistance.

She led him into a sparsely furnished and uncarpeted parlor, undecorated except for a daguerreotype of a man and woman on the mantel, and pointed him to a seat before a desk by the window. She eased herself into a chair behind the desk, which held a quill and inkwell, and took a sheet of paper from a drawer.

Her chair was higher than his to accommodate her stiff leg, and the height made him feel like a felon in the presence of a judge. His discomfiture was heightened when she dipped the quill into the inkwell and held it poised above the paper.

"This girl," she asked. "Is she a Christian?"

"Yes, ma'am."

"Mouth Christian or soul Christian?"

Solomon opened his palms outward and shrugged.

"I'm asking your opinion."

"As a Jew, I don't qualify for judging a Christian's Christianity."

"Thee talked to her of religion?"

"Yes, but rarely."

Her fluttering quill brought a Star Chamber atmosphere into an otherwise merely grim parlor and made thinking difficult. He did not care for written records, and this writing reminded him that perhaps, somewhere, a recording angel was still busy on the record of his previous night's activity.

"I don't wish to sound impertinent, ma'am, but I ask you not to enter my name in your notes. Written records can be dangerous in my business."

"I'm not entirely safe, either, and these notes concern only the girl . . . Go on. Christian, soul or mouth . . ."

"You understand, Mrs. Gresham, I didn't pry into her religious beliefs. They're her concern, not mine. Most of her religious instruction, for better or for worse, came from a white preacher entrusted with the guidance of the blacks on her owner's plantation . . ."

"This preacher. What denomination?"

"Hard-shelled Baptist."

"Wonderful! A very militant faith. Go on . . . go on."

"I felt his opinions were sophistry . . . Strike that from the record—that's an opinion of him."

"All Baptists are lackwits . . . But, go on."

Her remark seemed at odds with her previous admiration of Baptist militancy, and both seemed pointless to him. Yet, seeing he could not evade her questioning and curious about her reasons for asking them, he projected the appearance of deep thought and pontificated. "Now, is she a soul Christian or a mouth Christian, the question under discussion . . . I feel she has one of the greatest souls I've ever encountered, in any color of skin, black like hers, white like ours, or pale pink like those animated Rubens paintings over in the settlement."

Suddenly, she threw back her head and broke the precincts of silence with un-Quakerish laughter, high, whinnying, and as equine as her face. Subsiding, she dabbed tears of mirth from her eyes with a small handkerchief. "Well put, Mr. Villaricca . . . All Germans are stupid, and the Mennonites are the worst of a bad lot . . . Go on."

"I don't know whether or not her soul would meet the standards of a truly devout Christian, but I think her spiritual worth would be recognizable on the banks of the Ganges as well as the river Jordan . . ."

"Thee's being mealymouth." Her fluttering quill paused, and she looked down on him sharply. "Give me examples."

"So, I'll give you examples. She's unselfish. On the road, no matter how tired she might be, her first concern was for my welfare. She was willing to forego pork on Fridays to keep me from being dissatisfied with boiled eggs. How many darkies would make that sacrifice?

"She loves justice. In Georgia, once I smote a forward lad who threatened her defloration, and she rebuked me for my deed. He deserved better at my hands, she said, because he had worked so hard in our behalf."

"Did her behavior in this instance spring from a Christian love of justice, or," she paused and leaned forward, ". . . carnal longings? From the authority of my age and righteous concern, I ask thee, is she a fancy girl?"

Any "yes" or "no" to that one might possibly be self-damning, he decided. Friend Gresham was a Southerner, and a "yes" answer might imply that he was so lacking in manly graces that he had stooped to poontang pounding, but a "no" would be shattering in its inference that he had tried and failed.

"How should I know?" He shrugged.

"In thy opinion, is she morally loose, like all blacks?"

Her generalities cried for rebuttal, but he did not wish to become stranded in a discussion of morality when he was curious to know the reasons for her questions.

He answered bluntly. "If all blacks are loose, then she's loose because she's black. You've answered your own question."

"In thy opinion, is she more or less promiscuous than most wenches?"

Solomon succumbed to the grotesque. "Do you mean, ma'am, is she more or less promiscuous than a promiscuous

Christian girl, a promiscuous Jewish girl, or a promiscuous Chinese girl?"

Again she whinnied. "I'll declare, Mr. Villaricca, thee's a well-traveled man. Let me ask it this way. Is the girl a wanton?"

"No."

"Good! As a Jew, did thee attempt to undermine her faith in the Lord Jesus Christ?"

"No, ma'm. I encouraged it."

Surprisingly, she flashed him a look of disappointment and asked, "Why?"

"If Jesus was her shortest path to God, I felt she should take that path."

"There is only one way to God, and that is the way of Jesus. The sooner thee Hebrews admit this, the sooner will the stigma of Christ-killer be lifted from thy unfortunate tribe."

"I learned to weigh alternatives at my mother's breasts."

"There are no alternatives to Christ!"

Her thin lips clamped shut on the sentence, and he knew he was faced with fanaticism. She waited his arguments, but he sat mute while the fire of her militant righteousness died from lack of fuel.

"Thee think the girl has intelligence?"

"Yes."

"Why?"

She was not accepting general answers, only issuing general statements; but here he was on firmer ground. "She learned the first primer on reading in two weeks, and I'm not a teacher."

"Were there moral or religious instructions in the primer?"

"Moral, but no religious."

"Good!" She was writing again. "Now what did these moral preachments consist of?"

"Be kind to dumb animals. Obey your parents. Don't believe what chickens tell you because chickens are natural-born liars."

"Thee think that she's capable of further education?"

Emphatically he answered, "Yes."

She studied her notes. "Then, we have one Mellie, a slave girl of fair-to-middling morals, a good intelligence, who received watered-down religious instructions on a plantation. Apparently, thy influence has been negligible."

For a long moment, she studied the notes, tapping her fingers on the desk top. Finally, as if talking to herself, she said, "Interesting. Most interesting. She may do. Yes, she may do."

Suddenly she looked up at him, "Ah, yes, Mr. Villaricca, I have a letter for thee from Friend Blood, but first let me show thee a document that may interest thee. My son procured this from Knoxville."

From her desk, she drew a printed handbill. He took it and read.

$1000.00 REWARD

RAN AWAY FROM SUBSCRIBER LIVING NEAR CANTON, CHEROKEE CO., GEORGIA, ON 21ST OF JULY, MY NEGRO WENCH, MELLIE. SHE IS 17 YEARS OF AGE, SMALLER THAN AVERAGE, FINE-BONED. SHE HAS A STRAWBERRY ON HER LEFT FLANK AND AN EXCELLENT SET OF TEETH WHICH SHE SHOWS WHEN SHE SMILES. BLACK BUT NOT KINKY-HEADED. SHE IS BELIEVED HEADED NORTH IN THE COMPANY OF A JEW PEDLAR NAMED SOLOMON VILLARICCA DRIVING TWO-MULE CARAVAN. I WILL PAY REWARD FOR SAID NEGRESS PROVIDED SHE IS DELIVERED TO ME OR SECURED IN JAIL SO THAT I MAY GET HER.

WILLIAM BLAKE

Solomon returned the handbill, saying, "Blake must have mortgaged his farm."

"It's the largest reward I've ever seen offered for a wench," she said. "The intelligence about the strawberry mark has every young blade around Knoxville accosting wenches and hoisting skirts. 'Hunting strawberries' they call it. Was she his fancy girl?"

"I don't think so," Solomon said, "but I think his wife thought she would become so. Blake, I believe, is trying to teach his wife a lesson. Mrs. Blake is very fond of money." Briefly, he told her of his experiences with the Blakes.

"A fine woman," Friend Gresham commented. "It is unfortunate that she should be married to so weak a man."

"But he isn't a weak man," Solomon began, when Friend Gresham held up her hand for silence.

"All men are weak in the presence of temptation!" Again, her lips snapped shut with a finality that brooked no opposition. But he conceded that she had a point there.

180

"Now, the letter."

She handed him a sealed envelope addressed to S. Lomon, C/of Friend Norah Gresham, Sycamore, Tennessee. To all outward appearances, the letter had not been opened and censored. His heart rejoiced at the sight of Ely's familiar scrawl as he tore open the envelope.

Dear Sol,

I take my pen in hand to tell thee all is well with us and hoping thee's the same. Thy good wife is progressing well and mama has a touch of ague. Thy letter of the 22nd inst. received and I was happy with your choice of remedies.

Sol, I think we have been sleighted by the Popist. He came to thee a few hours before thy Sabbath and upon the eve of my busiest day. Then my Sabbath came, and I could not make inquiries until Monday. I think our friend did plan it this way.

My inquiries of Monday divulged such disturbing intelligence that I then conducted further investigations aided by members of the Society.

The gentleman in question is indeed a churchgoer. His church is in the northwest section of town and his place of business is in the southeast section. Very wisely does he keep them far apart. As thee knows, I am not well informed on such matters, but I would hazard the opinion that his place of business is the largest house of ill-fame in this sinful city. In addition to twelve fallen women from our own nation, he has a Choctaw squaw and four large, fat, and middle-aged blacks whom he keeps, in his own words, for Southern boys who are homesick for their old black mammies. Further, he has six gaming tables which are locally believed to be "on the square." My informers believe that when he plays, as he often does, there are five square tables and one with a definite bias.

In other ways, he seems to be an upright man. My friends among the constabulary tell me he has never been arrested. I know not whether this fact reflects on his good character or to the discredit of the Cincinnati police force. I have no doubt as to the purpose for which the present merchandise is consigned and no doubt as to the action we should take, particularly in view of the peculiar mortgage the Popist holds on our souls. I know thee's a man of principles, but our mercantile obligations must be subordinated. Turn the girl over to God.

Friend Gresham will assist thee. Thee'll find her an unusual Quaker and a most unusual woman. She will always let a man have the last words, as long as those words are "yes, ma'am."

Hoping to see you sooner than we both expected, I remain.

Thy obedient servant, etcetera,

Ely

"Hoping to see you sooner than we both expected." Solomon looked at the phrase and pretended to be reading as he gathered his thoughts.

So, he was to hand Melinda over to the Quakers. If this had been the old lady's wish, why had she prolonged the questioning? To soften his heart? Why had she not simply told him that she wanted the girl?

Ely's fears were groundless. Melinda had promised that she would have Kelly in the kitchen, and he believed Melinda. He also recalled the expression on Kelly's face at the mention of Melinda's name. Ely feared that Kelly would drag Melinda down, when the fact was Melinda would lift Kelly up, and Kelly's sensuality would be the means by which Melinda would effect his salvation.

So, Kelly ran a bawdy house. But Ely sold whiskey in a Quaker store. Kelly's sin was greater, but only in degree.

Ely, with typical Christian charity, was concerned over his own soul, but who was to save poor Kelly? Melinda! If Kelly's sins were of the proportion of an iceberg, they would melt before the southwind of Melinda. Kelly would marry the girl and be faithful to her. He would seek no farther.

"Seek no farther." The phrase popped into his mind and stayed there, insistently, irritatingly, as he tried to focus his mind on the problem.

Ely had made another error. He was appealing to Solomon as a godly man to ignore his commercial obligations, but Solomon had thrown away his yarmulke—and as a man of commerce, he had forestalled any deviousness on Kelly's part by the terms of his agreement. Mellie did not have to marry the man, if that was Blood's worry.

His thoughts returned to the woman across the desk. If the Christians needed a Jew to expound the doctrine of Christian charity, he could think of no better champion than himself, particularly when the weight of one thousand dollars rode on his arguments.

Solomon lifted bland eyes to the hostile eyes across from him. "Nicely written, but there are passages which might offend a Christian lady."

"No need. Friend Ely has written informing me of its contents and giving me directions. What is thy decision?"

"Should something be decided?"

"Certainly not! There should be no equivocation. Give me the girl."

"Ma'am, I was thinking of poor Kelly, alone up there in that swamp of sin with no one to save his soul from eternal damnation. That black girl could mean his salvation."

"Salvation of thy thousand dollars, more likely."

"A pittance, ma'am, a mere pittance, offered as a sop to an humble merchant who is risking life and limb."

"Mr. Villaricca, thee risks for money what we Quakers risk for love of God. If thee takes the girl to that popish whoremaster, thee'll be delivering her to slavery more vile than that from which she escaped. Thee'll deliver a soul to Satan."

He shrugged his shoulders expressively, letting compassion drop his eyebrows. "Am I a man who would deliver a girl to Satan for one thousand dollars?"

"Yes!"

His rhetorical question had been answered so unexpectedly and emphatically that it threw him off stride. Friend Gresham leaped into the breach.

"If it's soul saving thee's interested in, I'll make thee privy to my plans for the girl. The Society has a school in Michigan. I have allies at that school. The Friends will educate the girl, shape her into an instrument for bringing the lost black children to Christ. She will be my first convert to the new Society of Friends—the Quakers Militant!"

Ely should know about this woman! In the brain that burned behind those cold hard eyes, a schism was in the making. The small Quaker sect, already split into two factions by doctrinal differences, could not tolerate further splintering. Friend Norah Gresham was a keg of black powder under the Society of Friends, and the fuse was sputtering.

"Yes, I have seen the cutting edge of this Mellie. She has iron, that wench." She was breathing hard from her passion. "We'll temper her soul in our beliefs and hone her cutting edge into a hatchet of God. The wench, Mellie, is now a Gresham concern. Not for hell's dark angels, nor half the timid ones of heaven, shall I be turned from my purpose to loose her among the Ethiopes as the first Negro Quaker Militant."

The avalanche was roaring down, and Solomon decided

to get out from under, fast. He had discovered all he wished to know. "Mrs. Gresham, I can get you a very intelligent young Negro boy, more suited to the militant life, who would be ideal for your missionary work. His name's Jimmie T. He's from the same plantation. I could let you have him for less than two hundred dollars. Such a bargain you'll never see again."

He'd expected vexation from her because of his interjection of a commercial note into her heaven-slanted tirade. Instead, she softened and looked at him sadly.

"I would not give thee a half-dime," she said. "Men are too weak."

He diverted her further. Holding Blood's letter, he asked, "May I burn this at your grate?"

"There are phosphorous matches on the mantel. Thee may use one."

"Thank you, ma'am."

"I don't offer expensive matches to thee from hospitality. I want to impress on thee that we Quakers are not mercenary."

She might not be mercenary, he thought as he arose, but he was; and if she wished to deliver a sermon for the equivalent of two cents, he had listened, and he was happy to be paid.

Her matches were laid in an orderly row on the mantel beside the daguerreotype. "Is this your husband?"

"He was," she said. "He's dead."

"I'm sorry."

"Thee needn't be. He defied the will of God."

Solomon looked at the portrait with renewed interest. It had been taken not much over a year ago, since there was little change in her. Her husband had a forthright, candid appearance, marred somewhat by heavy pouches under his eyes, giving him the impression of an amiable bulldog. "He looks like a strong man," Solomon said, bending to the hearth as he lit the match.

"He was weak. Chewing tobacco killed him. I forbade him, but he would slip out to the barn and bite off a chaw. I set my son to trailing him, and whenever I found his twists, I destroyed them, but he defied me. Neither Reuben nor I could find them all. He swallowed too much juice and died of putrefaction of the liver. I told him God would strike him dead for his addiction to the sotweed, but he was weak."

Solomon, watching Ely's letter burn, lied gently. "At school, I delved for a term in pharmaceutics; tobacco juice was allowed to be a specific for liver ailments."

"What school did thee go to?"

"A Hebrew seminary," he said.

"That explains it."

He scraped the ashes into the grate with the side of his boot and walked back to his seat. "Mrs. Gresham, I don't approve of Melinda going to your missionary school. She has a spirit that could be destroyed in the strait jacket of doctrines. Her mind questions too much. You asked if I had attempted to influence her toward Judaism. On the contrary, she sort of shook my confidence in Moses."

"Did she make a Christian of thee?"

"No, but I'm thinking kindlier of Spinoza."

"I hope that's an improvement."

"Could be," Solomon said, deciding to drop levity before an audience incapable of humor.

"The girl would never submit to a rigid doctrine. It would be very hard to channel her thinking into a subsect of a subsect of a religion. As a man, I appreciate what you Quakers are doing, but I cannot approve of putting blinders on the girl."

"I did not bring thee here to seek thy approval."

"Then, why did you ask me here?"

"I wanted thy decision."

"My answer is no."

"Thee thinks, now, thy answer is no. Mr. Villaricca, I ask thee to return to the settlement. Thee'll be housed with Mr. Gruber. When thee gets there, I ask thee to pray to God and ask Him what thy decision should be and return tomorrow morning with thy consent.

"Reuben will drive thee back to the settlement." She got stiffly to her feet. "I must leave thee. Young men see visions, but we old folks must concern ourselves with constipation."

Standing, he watched her leave, swinging her stiff leg with such haste that she seemed to swagger, calling, "Reuben! Reuben!"

He went to the front porch to await Reuben. Young men see visions, she had said, yet she who hurried, stiff with age, to the privy carried with her a vision that could shatter the Society of Friends into shards.

On the ride back, Solomon was grateful for the Gresham

taciturnity which Reuben seemed to have inherited from his mother. With the gift of speech combined with a fraction of his mother's will, the man beside him might have attempted an on-the-spot conversion of the Jews, making Solomon the first Quaker Militant assigned to the Hebrews. He did not wish to become another of the Gresham concerns.

Solomon ventured no comments until after Reuben had wheeled the buggy into a U-turn before the house of Franz Gruber and sounded a ducklike quack on the air horn. Solomon, just before he dismounted, said to the man, "Sir, I appreciate your driving me here. To show my thanks, I would like to pass on an observation. I've noticed a slight puffiness beneath your eyes. I have received some schooling in the medicinal arts, and I've been told that this is a sign of a liver ailment.

"May I recommend to you sir, that before your condition advances to a serious stage, it would be advisable to cultivate the habit of chewing tobacco and swallowing a little of the juice. 'Tis a fine specific."

Reuben might or might not have heard. Big Franz emerged from around the corner of the house, pruning shears in hand, smiling and waving to the dour Quaker. Reuben tipped his hat, flummoxed the mare's behind with his reins, and drove away.

The smile on the pink face of Franz remained as he opened the gate for Solomon.

Solomon said, *"Danke, Herr Gruber."*

"Sprechen Sie Deutsche?"

"Ein wenig," Solomon admitted, *"Wo ist Mellie?"*

Franz, genuinely excited, clapped him on the back, and Solomon was suddenly enjoying the genuine, imported *gemütlichkeit.* He could afford to relax around the Germans now, for he had met the enemy. It was not Big Franz Gruber.

Frau Gruber, a pleasant little woman, came in from the kitchen to the parlor where Franz conducted Solomon, wiping her hands on her apron to greet him. She, too, was pleased that her guest could speak German, and for ten minutes, he slogged his way through the unfamiliar language, listening to their carefully spoken sentences with equal care and picking up from their context the meaning of words he could not immediately understand.

"How did you find Mrs. Gresham?" Mrs. Gruber asked.

When Solomon ventured the word *"schrecklich,"* and they both laughed, he knew he had found the right word for "terrifying."

Melinda was staying with the Meyers, he was told, because the Meyers had a daughter, Mira, of Melinda's age, who could keep the black girl company.

Frau Gruber served them tea and explained to Solomon that he would occupy the same bed as Karl, their son. When Franz excused himself to return to his pruning, she showed Solomon upstairs to his accommodations, a large room, pleasantly furnished. She invited him to lie down and rest, turning back the tufted counterpane. She understood, she told him without irony, that the men had disturbed his morning nap.

He thanked her and accepted her offer. His duel with Mrs. Gresham had tired him, and he had nothing to do before supper.

He would pray, Friend Gresham had told him, and God would point out to him the need for his acquiescence to Friend Gresham's will, but he would neither pray nor acquiesce. The sword of Solomon would oppose the hatchet of God.

Supper was not so lavish or pleasant as dinner had been. Cold cuts were served, and Melinda did not sit at the center table, which was reserved for married males. Married women sat at the table to the right and unmarried young folks at the table to the left.

Solomon spoke briefly to Melinda before supper and told her to be prepared to leave in the morning. She was disappointed because she had formed a friendship with Mira Meyers, the daughter of the house where she was staying. "I's teaching her our talk, and she's teaching me her talk. I's better at teaching than she is, but she's better at learning than I is."

After supper, he walked home with the Grubers.

Night had fallen. Around him, the hum of the voices of homegoers gave a summery contrast to the suggestion of snow from moonlight on the gravel of the roadway. From the well-lighted Meyers house across the street, someone tuned a violin. He thought of going for his own instrument and joining the group until he heard a Beethoven sonata commenced with an artistry that made him continue down

187

the boardwalk, fleeing from the competition as Marchand fled from Bach.

He sat for a while with the Grubers on their porch, listening to the music. It was a pleasant evening, with the hint of a breeze from the bottomland bringing a river smell to mingle with the aroma from the pipe Franz lighted, with the music and, between the intervals of music, the laughter of young people.

The music or the laughter brought memories to Mrs. Gruber.

"I was a young girl in Munich," she told Solomon, "before I met Franz. Ah, it was wonderful to be a young girl in Munich." She mewed the name *"München"* with love and reverence. "And in October, there was a festival in Munich. Believe me, all Munich was mad with joy and wine . . ."

Solomon strained to translate the language, and the strain on his attention, the rise and fall of her voice, the repetition of *"München,"* half-mesmerized his senses and made him peculiarly aware of the home-longing in her voice.

Finally, Franz excused himself and went into the parlor to read the Bible. She remained for a little while with Solomon, listening, before retiring, herself.

It was good to sit on the porch in the moonlight and listen to music, to feel alone and apart because he was not young anymore and had no closeness with God and no memories of Munich. He was sad in his apartness, but it was a pleasant sadness. Because he had been born with a sense of exile and because this feeling of apartness had the familiarity of an old companionship, he was less alien to this land than homesick Germans or the girl of Africa.

Only Jews and Englishmen, he mused, could ever possess or be possessed by America: the first because they had no homeland, and the second because the home they had left was far more cruel than here.

He listened until the music ended and he could hear the distant *"Auf wiedersehens"* float down the street. Then he went to bed.

Sunday breakfast was in the Gruber dining room at seven. Breakfast was buckwheat cakes piled high on a platter, with cane syrup, omelets, hot biscuits, jams and jellies, coffee with fresh cream, preserved peaches, pfannkuchen, and haferbrei. It was sunlight on the polished floor, and Maude Gruber, gayly aproned, directed teasing banter at Karl, betrothed to Mira, who was beautiful and who played the violin. Afterward, there was the clatter of dishes, a hurrying to dress, and the church bells chiming.

Franz Gruber invited Solomon to the services, but Solomon declined. He had the meeting with Mrs. Gresham, and he had to be on his way North.

Meanwhile, Karl had fetched his van.

Solomon thanked him and angled across the street to the Meyers' house to get Melinda. He arrived at the gate as the Meyers family came through the doorway—mother and father, their small son, and Mira. "Where is Mellie?" Solomon asked.

Meyers looked at him, shrugged his shoulders, and brushed past him, saying, *"Ich verstehe nicht."*

Solomon stood for a moment, perplexed, then strode forward, matching his stride with the man saying *"Wo ist das Mädchen?"*

Meyers said, *"Ich verstehe nicht."*

Solomon turned and strode back across the street. Franz and Maude were emerging onto the sidewalk when he addressed Franz in German. "Mr. Gruber, the girl is not with the Meyers. All I can get from Mr. Meyers is that he does not understand. Do you know what happened to her?"

Gruber looked at him without smiling and said, *"Je ne parle pas Français."*

The whole village was converging on the church. Solomon strode rapidly up the hill, going ahead of the others. At the church door, the minister awaited his flock. Beside him, dressed in a frock coat, stood an usher.

Solomon could see inside. The pews were backless benches, and the church was empty. He turned to the usher, asking in German, "Where is the black maiden?"

Without looking at him, the usher replied, *"Ich verstehe nicht."*

The preacher walked down to the bottom of the steps to greet the arriving congregation with silent handshakes. Solomon scanned the faces of the people as they entered. They averted their eyes or ignored his gaze. Near the end of the procession, he saw Mira Meyers and walked down to her, saying, *"Mira, Wo ist deine Freundin?"*

"Ich weiss nicht," she said, and averted her eyes, but not before he saw they were red from weeping.

In a matter of minutes, the congregation was inside. The usher asked, "Are you coming in, sir?"

"Nein, danke," Solomon said, and the usher closed the door.

Solomon stood for a moment on the steps, slapping his fist into his palm, and looking down over the deserted village. Inside, an organ wheezed the opening bars of "A Mighty Fortress is Our God," and the congregation began singing.

He walked away from the sound, down the gravel walk bordered by whitewashed stones to the street, between the precise boardwalks and the identical gingerbread houses, feeling like a fly struggling out of honey. He moved fast, remembering Mira's tear-stained face.

Mira had cried saying "good-bye" to Melinda. Since the marks of her weeping still showed, Melinda could not have been gone for long. The Germans had graveled the road all the way to the ferry, but the work road leading south was bare. If she had been taken south, wheel tracks would show on the dew-crusted dirt. If there were none, she had been taken west to Norah Gresham.

He walked rapidly toward the van when a thought made him break into a run. Melinda could have slipped away when the Quakers came for her, if she were clever enough to guess the reason for their coming; if she had escaped, she could have hidden in the secret compartment.

He opened the door, leaped inside, and flung back the lid of her chest.

It was empty, completely empty, except for two pearls which had apparently fallen from her bracelet. Her carpetbag, her book, and her Bible were gone.

Two pearls and the faint odor of verbena were all that remained of a girl who had made the van her home for nigh on a month, two pearls and the vanishing scent of verbena for a thousand dollar note that would never be collected, unless he moved fast and adroitly.

He lowered the lid of the chest, closed the van, and climbed onto the driver's seat, snaking the whip forward with an angry crack between the ears of the mules. They lunged forward.

He was angry for his loss, angry at the injustice of his

190

loss, and angry at the perpetrator of his loss. He careened past the intersection at fifteen miles an hour, seeing at a glance that the dust lay undisturbed on the road south. She had been taken to Norah Gresham. If she were not waiting there when he arrived, a Quaker Militant would know the wrath of a militant Jew.

Chapter Eight

If he was a bad Jew, he would make a worse Christian, he decided; although he had just left a church in session, he had completely forgotten it was Sunday. Rigs lined up in the frontyard of the Gresham house reminded him. The Quaker meeting was at Friend Gresham's house, and she had known this when she had made the appointment with him yesterday.

Norah Gresham would use the meeting as an excuse to stall for time.

Her trick would not work. She was relying on his religious sensibilities to keep him outside until the meeting was over, but she could not know that for him, God was as dead as Isis.

He strode down the hallway to the closed door of the parlor, swung it open, and stalked in, to find himself in the center of a group of silent worshipers. They ignored him, and he ignored them, except for a hasty glance that told him all the faces were white. His attention focused on the woman, bolt upright and silent behind the desk.

"I want to talk to you," he said.

She held up her hand for silence.

"I'm not being silenced! I want to see you, and I want to talk to you, now. We can talk here or outside, but we're going to talk. If you want to disturb your fellow mummies, we'll talk here."

She rose and went into the hallway, closing the door behind them. "Sir, thee's aware that we are praying."

"Of course. I'm familiar with your odd persuasion, and I can smell the prayers when I can't hear them. You conspired with that pig-eating herd of cattle across the river to steal my girl. I thought there was honor among thieves, but I reckon that doesn't apply to Quaker thieves. Where's my girl?"

"Thee is calling me a thief, sir?"

"A thief and a liar. You set up a meeting with me to get my decision on the girl, knowing you were going to steal the girl."

"I did not steal the girl. Thee stole her. I liberated her."

"Liberated her! To what? To wear the chains of your confounded self-righteousness? For all the filthy excuses for underhanded behavior I've ever heard, that one is buzzard's puke. You stole her, and I want her back. Where is she?"

"She's on her way . . . toward Canada," she said, "to lead a God-fearing life."

"When did she leave, and which way did she go?"

"She's long gone, and whether she's gone by way of Norfolk, Wheeling, Harpers Ferry, . . . or Wilmington does not concern thee. The girl is my concern."

"You mean you're not telling me."

"I'm not."

"Very good! There's nothing I can do to force the truth from *you*, but . . ."

"Truly," she was imploring him to believe her, "I thought thee would agree with me after prayer."

"Agree! I'll agree with you when we're both sitting on a brimstone in hell, and then I'll only agree that it's hot . . . I can't do anything to make you talk, but if you don't volunteer . . ." He put his hand on the doorknob. "I'm going back into that prayer meeting and drag that tattletale son of yours out of there and beat the information out of him. And I promise you, madam, when I get through with him, the pouches under his eyes will be bags of pemmican. Now, are you talking?"

Suddenly, she was her old imperious self again.

"I will not," she snapped.

He swung open the door and stalked into the room to stand amid the silent occupants, looking at each worshiper individually, and he found the reason for her renewed confidence. Reuben Gresham was not among those present.

He turned and walked back to the hallway. She had gone

to the front porch and was standing there, leaning on her cane, looking out into the sunlight.

He stood beside her for a moment, looking over the rigs and idly swinging his fist against his palm. Her own rig was missing.

She had added Wilmington as an afterthought, thinking to confuse him. Wilmington was east, Norfolk, Wheeling, Harpers Ferry, all were reached by going north. "Toward Canada" she had said, but not "to Canada." Being a Quaker, she could not lie, but she could confuse the truth. Reuben would head north, for they were taking Melinda to Michigan, and she would not be spirited out from the South through a seaport. Reuben would think he had more of a head start than he had, for his mother had counted on delaying Solomon for an hour, perhaps two.

He started down the steps.

"Mr. Villaricca!"

He turned and looked up at her.

"Thee has spunk. I wish we had thee on God's side."

"That wouldn't be fair to God. The two of us on God's side would bankrupt heaven."

She threw back her head in her high, whinnying laughter. Suddenly, he almost liked the woman. She lacked human compassion, she was narrow, bigoted, old, ugly, and flat-chested, but, by the devious God that she served, she was unique.

He mounted the seat of the van and headed west toward the Wilderness Road.

Reuben would probably head straight north, figuring himself far enough ahead of Solomon to have no need to waste time with diversionary tactics, and he alone knew the Underground Stations.

He should have taught Melinda to write—but what could she have written? She had no way of knowing which way they intended to take her or where.

Well, he thought, she could have left him a farewell note to remember her by, some little missive reminding him that any time you fooled around with a religious person, you got . . .

Suddenly, he clapped his forehead; who could be more stupid than Solomon Villaricca? She *had* left him a note which outlined her itinerary.

Those pearls in the bottom of the chest! One could have been an accident, and she foresaw this, leaving two. To her

194

they were priceless, and she would have overlooked them as easily as he would have overlooked two diamonds.

He pulled up at the junction of the settlement road with the Wilderness Road and climbed down from the van, searching the ground. He walked north less than ten yards along the road before he found a pearl, then five more, dropped about a yard apart, and plainly visible against the blue clay. He picked them up, dropped them into his pocket, and walked back to the mules. He turned them north on the Wilderness Road.

He looked up the long road stretching into Virginia, cutting through piney woods with the ridge line crested westward and the ground sloping to the river valley to the east. He could see for almost two miles, straight as a die, to where the diminishing streak dipped over the horizon. The Wilderness Road was aptly named. Into a wilderness of forests and mountains it led, and the wilderness had claimed Melinda. O, mistress mine, he thought, where are you roaming?

Ah, that line was the key to the forgotten stanza of *Twelfth Night* which had haunted him for days.

Leading the mules, he started walking, his legs swinging easily beneath him, his body bent forward, covering the ground in the long, loping stride that put five miles behind him each hour, from the first hour through the fourteenth, if need be. As he walked, he caterwauled to the trees:

> O, mistress mine, where are you roaming?
> Stay and hear your true love's coming,
> Who can sing both high and low.
> Trip no further, pretty sweeting,
> Journeys end in lovers meeting
> Every wise man's son doth know.

Like an old, mad, and cackling Jew, he strode northward, singing.

He found her before nightfall, four miles north of Rose Hill.

The sun was touching the mountain rim to his left when he saw the pearls, six of them, dropped a pace apart in the roadway. Next, there were three, spaced closely together, leading off the road. At the place where they had turned, a stand of chestnut had been cut and underbrush had grown up, covering a strip approximately ten yards back from the road to his right. Looking closely, he could see a narrow break in the line of trees beyond the cut-over ground, marking a wagon trail into the forest beyond—a trail he would have surely missed had it not been for the pearls.

But the pearls had told him more. Melinda and Reuben were not alone.

Mentally, he had constructed Reuben's probable method of transporting the girl, reasoning that she would be hidden under a lap robe behind the seat. This was the main road out of Virginia into eastern Kentucky and Tennessee, and Reuben would be cautious; many a Quaker had lost all possessions for helping a slave escape.

Reuben would not have told the girl of his intentions, so she had heard him talking to someone else.

Solomon led his mules through the underbrush. His quarry must have gone this way over an hour before, for he could see wheel tracks in the loam between the tufts of grass, and the bushes had sprung back up.

Once beneath the trees, the underbrush gave way, and he found himself following an old wagon trail through the forest. He went far enough into the woods to conceal the van from the road, took his spyglass, and grabbed his whip, striding along the trail at a rapid pace.

The sun was setting behind the mountains, but the light in the sky was still bright. He moved cautiously now, avoiding fallen twigs and loose stones, following the trail deeper into the forest and downward. Occasionally, he would pause, listen, and sniff the air.

He smelled the wood smoke from their camp fire well before he came upon them. Crouching low, he moved slowly, alert, tense. Before him, the trail dipped into a shallow ravine, bending left. He kept moving straight ahead, keeping the trail in view but advancing onto the promontory the trail had curved to avoid, moving out onto a rocky spine where the boles of the trees were thinned by the granite outcropping.

Crawling now, moving from bole to bole, he crept to the edge of the bluff and looked down into a clearing—a bowl-like basin margined on the far side by a brook. To the left, someone had dug into the hill for kaolin, or potter's clay. Below, about thirty yards away, was a small shack made from slab boards runing vertically on the frame of the building, probably a toolshed or bunkhouse for the abandoned mine.

Parked across the clearing, away from the shack, was

Norah Gresham's rig. In front of the shack, a fire had been built, and the evening meal was over. He could see Reuben Gresham squatted beside the brook cleaning tin dishes. Between the fire and the door of the shack, another man was hunkered down, his back to the door. There was a demijohn of whisky beside him, and he was smoking a pipe. That man was not a Quaker.

Prone, Solomon disengaged his spyglass from its case and focused it on the stranger. When the image came in focus, Solomon recognized the breed. Granted there was no art to read the mind's construction in the face, still any man could tell a pit bull from an egg-sucking hound— and the man in the glass was a pit bull.

He was lean, angular, and beardless. Jutting from his homespun shirt, his scrawny red neck was marked by a protruding Adam's apple. He was redhaired and freckle-faced with a long head and a receding chin, but the ugly face had arrogance and a cold deadliness, and there was contempt in the way he hunkered while Reuben washed the dishes.

His contempt was explained to Solomon when he reached over to lift the jug of whiskey. Lying beside the jug was a pistol belt and a holstered pistol. The redneck was neither a Quaker nor a Mennonite. He was a hired guard. Friend Gresham was no longer taking any chances with men who carried unloaded weapons.

Solomon turned the glass on the door behind the man. It was fitted with a bolt for a padlock. Though there was no padlock, the bolt was shoved home. They did not trust Melinda. She was locked in the cabin.

Behind the shack, a dense growth of alder bushes provided excellent cover. Solomon could sneak down the ravine to his right and come up from the rear. He only had to worry about the guard; Reuben was harmless.

Since he wanted Melinda awake and ready when he came, he crabbed backward, concealed himself behind a boulder, and sent their danger signal ululating down the hollow. It was one of his finest efforts—answered, almost immediately, by a whippoorwill down the ravine and another across the glade below. The answering birds pointed out the folly of a choice that had already led him to adultery. Whippoorwills sang at twilight.

He thought a moment. Then, he sent the song of the mockingbird trilling down over the glade, ending it with the warbling of the hermit thrush. Melinda could not fail to hear and recognize the signal.

He crawled back to his lookout station trying to surmise the enemy's intention.

Probably, neither one would stand guard, since they intended to sleep in front of the shack; their bedrolls were laid against its walls. A white moon hung overhead. Crawling, keeping hidden in the underbrush, it would take him less than fifteen minutes to get to the western corner of the shack. He would wait there, and when they slept, he would attack.

"Mr. Ricky, you bring my pearls?"

He skittered around to see Melinda, barefooted and hatless in her boy's clothes, squatting behind him. Her carpetbag was beside her.

"Why, child!" he blurted in happy astonishment. "How did you get here?"

"One of them old slabs was loose in the back, and I crawled out. Did you bring my pearls?"

"Most of them. Maybe all of them. But let's get out of here. If they look in and find you gone, they'll come hightailing after us."

"Not if they just looks in," she said, crawling backwards, " 'cause I stuffed that blanket full of cornshucks and put that old hat at one end and them old shoes at the other end . . . That skinny man, he mean. He told me he done shot six niggers and two white men, and he been hankering to get him a Jew."

"I'm happy to disappoint the gentleman," Solomon grinned. "Anyway, if he got me, he wouldn't be getting a very good Jew, not after you and me in the pool of Heshbon."

He had crawled forward to conceal himself from camp, and now rose and walked rapidly back up the wagon trail, Melinda trailing him. He thought she moved in panic until he heard from the gathering twilight her low and liquid giggle. "What's you now, Mr. Ricky? A nigger man?"

He chuckled.

He let her ride beside him on the driver's seat because night was coming on, it was still hot inside the van, and he was happy to see her. When they reached the road and he turned the mules to the left, Melinda looked at him worriedly and said, "Mr. Ricky, you's heading south."

"I'm backtracking," he explained. "Those men won't

198

figure I'm going south, so they'll head north. They won't even suspect until they get to Jonesville, and then they won't be certain. I'm going to drive till moonset. By morning, we should be in Kentucky."

"Won't the pattyrollers git me in Kentucky?"

"Chance we've got to take. From now on out, the Quakers will be laying for us on the road north, and there's only one road through these mountains. There are more roads through the low country, and it's a shorter way.

"Besides, we got a better chance with the bounty hunters in the lowlands. Bounty hunters want money, but the Quakers want your soul. I'll take bounty hunters any day against soul hunters.

"Anyway, I've got a plan that may make it easier for us to get through Kentucky. It's a lunatic notion and may come to naught, but I've got to do something.

"One thing I want you to remember, Melinda. The only way you'll ever get anything done in this life is to have a plan and stick to it with firm resolution."

"I'll do that, Mr. Ricky. 'Deed I will, 'cept I don't know what a firm resolution is."

"A firm resolution is something you decide to do, and do it. Back there by the pool, you made a firm resolution not to let me do it to you anymore. That's one resolution that you've got to keep. If I make a slip in Kentucky, I'll wind up on a sledgehammer, making little rocks out of big ones, and you'll end up in Georgia chopping cotton."

"I ain't going to do nothing to lose you, Mr. Ricky. I don't know what I'd do without you. You's the smartest man."

They drove in silence as the moon rose in the darkening sky. She yawned, and he said, "You're tired, child. You'd better go back in the van and get some sleep. They must have woke you up early."

"Since before light," she said. "I damned near forgot, Mr. Ricky, but I brung you a chicken leg and a biscuit."

She rummaged excitedly in her carpetbag and brought out viands wrapped in oiled paper. "Mira's ma fixed it for me," she said. "I took the skin off, 'cause I don't know if they fried it in hog grease."

He tore into the chicken voraciously, suddenly realizing that he had not eaten since early morning.

With Melinda inside the van, he felt a growing loneliness as he drove into the night. Dark and forbidding, the forest pressed in on the sandy stretch of road which stretched endlessly before him white under the moon. Above the cushioned thud of the wheels, a night wind soughed with an intermittent moaning which reminded him of the sounds of someone dying.

Weird fancies harassed him. He was driving a road without end into a night without morning; he drove the mules at a killing pace, passing the Gresham farm before eleven, the sleeping hovels of Cumberland Gap shortly after midnight. Only when he turned west toward the Gap did he get down and walk.

Walking helped relieve his sense of oppression, and the monotony of the road ended with the curving ascent. He was climbing now through the tollgate, open and unattended, and his melancholy abated when he eased over the hump into Kentucky.

On the western slope of the Cumberlands, in the last rays of a setting moon, he turned up the course of a rill that trickled across the road and followed its winding path far enough into the woods to conceal the van. He left the mules in harness as they watered themselves in the branch, fed them with nose bags, and tossed the seat cushion on the roof of the van and stretched out. He might have slept until noon had not Melinda awakened him. She popped her head up and tugged at his boots. "Breakfast ready, Mr. Ricky, and I done fed the mules."

He sat up and rubbed his eyes. From the vent forward, he smelled coffee and pancakes. The girl had not started a fire but had used the charcoal stove to lessen the danger from smoke.

He had been told that Negroes could not think and did nothing without being told. Either his informants lied, or this girl had more white blood than he suspected. She should be converted to Judaism and introduced to some nice Jewish boys.

Today, he headed northwest, figuring that he was four miles through the Gap. Ahead of him, the road went up and over a razorback ridge. At the crest, he paused and looked over the hills rolling away to the northwest, dark blue beneath the pale blue sky.

Out there lay Kentucky, the Dark and Bloody Ground that non-Christian savages had yielded to savage Christians. Out there, the country swarmed with men who would bar his way North, not only from convictions and from hope of gain but from sheer cussedness and a passion for excitement.

Ah, how easy it was to sit in an office in the North and, laying a finger on a map, say, "We'll convey the fugitive from Station X to Station Y, a mere twenty miles."

Here, where distances were measured by the slow turn of a wagon's wheel drawn by tired mules, where the heat was a blanket one plowed aside to move through, where fear made time flow like treacle, a mile was no longer a figure on a scale. One mile was a measure of pain, ten was a measure of human endurance, and twenty was a superhuman effort. He thought of the two hundred odd miles that lay ahead, and his spirit quailed.

In the manner of Gentiles, he spoke aloud and said, "To hell with them," and leaned forward to slap the rump of the mules with the reins. But the phrase was sterile, as any such phrase would be sterile, because he still would not take the Lord's name in vain.

Seeking a stronger expletive, he said, "Like sheep they'll be laid in the grave, and the righteous shall have dominion."

Somehow, that phrase seemed more satisfactory, though lately, it hardly held favorable significance for him.

So it was that he came down from the mountains carrying assorted provisions: four kegs of white lightning, one demijohn of strained honey, odds and ends of hardware, two bolts of bright red gingham, one bolt of denim, four yards of oilcloth, and one highly nubile Negress locked in his van. Locked in his head was a wild and desperate plan to escape straight through the heart of the Kentucky slave region where fugitive-slave patrols roamed day and night, where King Cotton yielded to the growing of hemp to be used in the ropes that were woven for the nooses that stretched the necks of slave stealers.

Into the town of Cumberland Ford, Kentucky, he rode on the noon of a bright August day heavily pine-scented by the heat along a road where chickens challenged his passage by moving from his path with arrogant slowness. From the shadow of a church, a sow rose with ears erect, grunting her disbelief at a human stupid enough to be abroad on so hot a day, and lay back down. He passed the graveyard and counted the headstones. Into the settlement he rode, between unpainted frame houses and log cabins with forms askew, where dogs lay and looked but would not rise and bark. On he drove, to the most impressive building in the village, a large, barnlike structure with a front porch and a false front which bore the peeling legend, "I. S. TANGLING, GENERAL STORE AND TONSORIAL PARLOR."

He pulled the mules to a halt, climbed down, and looped the reins over the hitching rack. He moved across the porch into the comparative coolness of the shaded interior, smelling the licorice odor of feed as he walked between the unattended counters. One of the rear corners had been set aside as a barber shop, and he could have found it by following the odor of bay rum, warm soap, and witch hazel.

He came at last to I. S. Tangling, the barber-merchant, in attendance upon a pimply-faced boy of fifteen who perched atop a stool, a barber's apron draped around him, its neckband stained by sweat.

Tangling turned a casual eye toward Solomon as he advanced, said, "You're next, mister," and then recognized his visitor.

He straightened up, shifted his comb and scissor to his left hand, and waddled forward. "Well, I'll be goddamned if it ain't old Solomon Villaricca. How air ye, Mr. Villaricca. Ain't seen you since two years ago last June. Thought for a minute there you were some furriner looking for a shave."

"I'm fine, Mr. Tangling. And how are you?"

Solomon advanced to take his hand with heartfelt thanks that it was not the ramp season. Tangling had an inordinate appetite for ramps, and when those delicacies were in season, the only trading done in his store was with other ramp fanciers.

"Ain't been too pert, to tell the truth. Been having a mite of trouble with my kidneys."

He stepped back, a short, chubby man, his breeches held up by a rope looped below his pendulous belly. His unbuttoned shirt revealed a navel protruding like the tip of a conch shell festooned by fallen hair. He put his hands to the back of his hips. "Right here's where it hurts. Hurts like hell. Wakes me up nights."

"Try drinking sassafras tea?"

"Drunk so goddamned much I been pissing brown."

"Maybe you're passing blood. You talk to Doc Huber about it?"

202

"Cain't. Doc's dead. Nigh onto a year ago, he went to his unjust reward."

"I'm rightly grieved to hear about that, Mr. Tangling. I counted a new gravestone as I passed the burial yard, but I didn't figure it was old Doc. Hope he died sober."

"Naw, he died drunk. Dead half a day just setting there on his front porch. Mary Ellen thought he was passed out."

"Too bad. What's Mary Ellen doing, now that her paw's gone?"

"Little midwifery. Making a few poultices. She can't set no bones 'cause she ain't stout enough. Mostly, she's taking in boarders."

"Where'd she find the boarders?"

"They opened a sawmill up the river a piece. Some of the hands boarding with her."

Solomon eased down on the waiting bench and said, "Have to go over and extend my heartfelt sympathies."

"You selling something?"

"I've got about four yards of good oilcloth. If she's opened a boardinghouse, she could use some oilcloth."

"What you want for it?"

"What'll you give me?"

"Nine cents a yard."

"That won't pay the freight on it."

Tangling's young customer turned his head and arced a shot of tobacco juice six feet through the air, landing it dead center in a spittoon set in a sand box. "Goddamn, Mr. Tangling, you gonna stand there and jaw all day?"

"Bates, this gentleman's Mr. Villaricca. He's an old friend of mine . . . Mind your goddamned manners, boy, and say 'Howdy' to Mr. Villaricca."

"Glad to meet you, Mr. Villaricca."

"Glad to meet you, Bates. I know a deputy sheriff down in Georgia I'd like to have you meet so you could teach him marksmanship."

"He's Jeff Purcell's middle boy," Tangling flicked his thumb toward the boy's back, "and he's just as foulmouthed as his paw and a bigger liar."

Nevertheless, Tangling turned and waddled back to his customer. "What's your hurry, boy? You can't do no cunt hunting on a day's hot as today."

"No, sir, but that durned loose hair's making my neck itch."

Ah, it was pleasant to be back among people—away from Germans and Quakers—where "goddamns" floated easily through the blasphemed air and tobacco juice did not invoke the wrath of God. If a woman had walked in, both the man and boy would have dropped their bravado for shyness, and their language would have become very circumspect if they spoke at all. Among themselves, their profanity was unguarded and without malice, often without any purpose except amusement, and their accents were so soft that genuine anger could only be detected by the rising pitch of the voice.

Solomon knew that an accent, a rhythm of speech, was a learned thing, a surface covering, but sometimes it seemed to him that the surface coloring went deep enough to stain the soul, and he liked the way these souls were stained.

He might have relaxed, seated and leaning against the back of the counter against which the bench was placed, had it not been for the ordeal he faced and for the merchant-barber.

Tangling was sick, far sicker than he knew, and as Solomon watched the scissors flicking deftly behind the comb-ruffled hair, noting the gentleness with which the fallen hair was brushed from the boy's neck, he felt regret and a sad finality. He knew that when he came again this way, those hands would be stilled, and Tangling's kidneys would lie beside Doc Huber's liver in the plot up the road by the church.

"Reckon if we dug old Doc up today," Tangling said, "he'd look just like he did when we laid him away. His pore old hide was pickled . . . But there was a man. Never charged a dime more than he had coming. Warn't out to grab every penny he could get. People around here loved him, drunk or sober . . . How much you figuring on asking for that oilcloth?"

"I figured on about thirteen cents a yard," Solomon said. "I'm not looking for love. I'm looking to break even."

"That's retail, Mr. Villaricca," Tangling stepped back away from the boy and turned to face him. "I buy wholesale. Now, we both know you can get it for six cents a yard in Knoxville . . ."

"Knoxville's got a railroad . . . You can get it for five cents a yard in Louisville. Louisville's got steamboats."

Again the boy spat. "Mr. Villarica, don't talk to him. I

don't want to make getting this haircut my goddamned life's work."

"Take care of Bates, Mr. Tangling, and don't put any gaps in his hair. I've got a very nice bargain for you when you're through."

Tangling returned to the boy, moving rapidly now. He swabbed the boy's neck with soap, whisked it clean with a razor, and drew off the apron with a snap and flourish.

"There you be, young'n." He reached behind him and handed the boy a mirror. "That'll be ten cents before the girls get it."

Bates carefully examined his haircut in the glass, handed it back, swung down from the stool, and gave the barber two half-dimes. "Hit'll do, Mr. Tangling," he said. "Hit ain't bad. Hit ain't no damned good, either, but hit ain't bad."

"If that gets you any extra, son, you dedicate a piece to me, you hear?"

"The fourth one'll be for you." He spread his legs, jerked his jeans upward to his crotch, and swaggered out.

"Be seeing you, Mr. Villaricca."

"Good hunting, son."

With studied nonchalance, Tangling looked at the departing boy and said, "Little bastard was telling me, afore you come, he knocked off three pieces Saddy night . . . These young'ns getting so they lie like their elders . . . How's business been with you?"

"Not good. Make a little, lose a little." Solomon shrugged. "Came over from the Holston Valley. Bunch of Gypsies been through there, selling whatever they could steal. They plucked the country so clean, I give up. Swapped more'n I sold. I figure those Gypsies owe me a mite of money."

"You'll pay hell collecting," Tangling snorted. "Them bastards off to Lexington, most likely, aiming to pick pockets at the fair."

Solomon stroked his beard with a preoccupied air. "I think I can get a little of that money back, with your help . . . How much you charge for a haircut?"

"Fifteen cents for grown men."

"How much for a shave?"

"Ten cents."

"That retail or wholesale?"

"Retail. Ain't no wholesale for services. People around here like to buy a haircut. Shows they got money."

"I'm surprised they got any left, after what the Gypsies did to the Holston Valley. Did the Gypsies cut into your trade?"

"Hell, they cut into me! Them's the fastest talking sons of bitches I've ever did see."

"They speak good English."

"Like goddamned Philadelphia lawyers . . . You know how my old lady is about God and Jesus. One of their women came to the door last Thursday, knocked as pretty as you please, and looked in when my old woman opened the door. She saw that Jesus sign hanging over the fireplace. Right away, she commenced talking about God and Jesus and how she visited the Holy Land. Before she knew it, my wife was paying her twenty-five cents for a pillow stuffed with Spanish moss from Palestine. Holy Jesus! Right today my wife won't believe me when I tell her there ain't no Spanish moss in Palestine. She won't even sit on the goddamned pillow . . . Now, what was this bargain you were talking about?"

"I'm going to give you that oilcloth, straight out, for those four pails of paint that drummer unloaded on you two years ago. I know you still got it, because I didn't see any yellow or blue cabins when I drove into town. So, I'm generous. I'll give you the oilcloth for the paint, and you throw in a shave and haircut free."

"That paint cost me twenty cents a gallon."

"That may be what it cost you, but I figure it's not paying for its shelf space. It appears to me that the campaign to beautify Cumberland Ford that that drummer got you so all-fired het up over never got off the ground. Nobody around these parts is going to use green, red, yellow, and blue paint, nobody but Gypsies, and they're gone. But I'm taking off after them to sell them that paint. You can't go after them, but you can walk across the street and sell that oilcloth at eighteen cents a yard. So, you'll be making money on the paint. I'll be getting back at the Gypsies for both of us, and for doing you that favor, I'll ask you to throw in a shave and haircut."

"Hell, I thought shaving was against your religion."

"So's lice."

"Now, Mr. Villaricca, you know if I give you a haircut and shave, you ain't just getting one haircut. I got to give you another haircut when I whack off that beard. I think you ought to pay me for one of them haircuts."

"Whacking off my beard won't take anymore skill than shearing a sheep. You can save the hair and give it to your wife and tell her this is real Spanish moss from Palestine, because I'm a Spanish Jew."

"Mr. Villaricca, you've done got yourself a trade. Step right up."

Solomon closed his eyes to the desecration as Tangling began to reap with deft and indifferent hands the harvest of his years. A full decade he had devoted to the beard. He had gone under it at the age of sixteen, and he had lived with it twice as long as he had lived with his wife, washing it, drying it, glossing it, combing it, loving it.

It was the badge of his Orthodoxy and the emblem of his faith, but it was also his trademark. Along the reaches of the Southern Appalachians and into the Piedmont, customers recognized his beard from afar. Expectations were whetted by the sight of its approach and trading instincts honed by its arrival. Fingers of babes had tugged it, young belles had thrown it sidelong glances, and mountain men had eyed it with envy. In a sense, the beard was not a part of him, he was a part of the beard. It was his character, his integrity, yes, and his beauty, that was falling to the floor.

What would Leah say? He groaned aloud.

"You sick, Mr. Villaricca?"

"A mere touch of dyspepsia, Mr. Tangling."

"I got some good five-cent lemons I'll let you have for four cents."

Even as he groaned and inwardly lamented, a question was knocking for admittance to his thoughts. Was not his beard, above all, vanity? Surely, every man walketh in a vain show; he heapeth up riches and knoweth not what manner of man shall gather them, an unworthy heir or a barber in Kentucky.

When Thou with rebukes corrects man for his iniquity, O Lord, Thou makest his beauty consume away like a moth, and all is vanity. So, if this act to which he had been forced was a rebuke from God, then this shearing, not seven years in a Tennessee jail, was his atonement for the broken Commandments.

All this has come to me, he thought, because the Lord has not forgotten me. Though I have dealt falsely with His Covenant, my heart is not turned back, neither have my steps declined from the way of the Lord.

He felt a weight gone from him and lifted his eyes to the wasp-daubed rafters, "The Lord shall redeem my soul, and He shall receive me. Selah!"

"What you blabbing about, Mr. Villaricca?"

"Just reciting an old Hebrew proverb."

"Hold it, won't you? Your jaws wagging spoils my aim."

Tangling whacked, trimmed, and shaved. Solomon, at peace, enjoyed the hot towel, the warm lather, the smooth flow of the razor over his tautened skin. He relished the tingling of bay rum and the soothing oiliness of witch hazel. When it was done, and his face was powdered and his hair combed, Tangling threw off the apron with the air of a Michelangelo unveiling the statue of David and stood back, well pleased.

"Hell fire, Sol! Under all that shrubbery, you got a phiz like Junius Brutus Booth. Goddamn, you're a young'n. I allus thought you were an old fart, like me."

Solomon looked into the mirror that Tangling held before him and saw a face he had not seen since he was sixteen. That rather receding chin he remembered had structured up and fleshed out in a clean, almost square line. He was pleased, but Tangling was excited.

"You don't look like nary a Jew I ever saw. You look like a goddamned Frenchman. Sol, this takes the cake!"

Dropping the "mister" was a breach of propriety on Tangling's part, but Solomon could understand. He had always imagined himself a mature man, but taking away the beard had taken ten years off his appearance.

There was one grave flaw in his appearance. Where the beard had been, his skin was pale.

"Well, Sol, now that we've both got a good look at you, let me take a good look at that oilcloth."

Solomon went to the van. Melinda, despite the heat, was obediently inside the chest with the lid closed. "Just a little while longer," he said, "and we'll be out of town."

He pulled out a hardware drawer in the chest across the aisle from hers and took a razor and strop. Quickly, expertly, he honed the edge of the razor, flipped it back into its handle, and dropped it into his pocket. He removed the roll of oilcloth, locked the van and went back into the store.

Tangling was perched on a stool behind the front counter, his round belly exposed, his bald head shining, the grin on his face giving him the appearance of a benign Buddha.

Tangling fingered the oilcloth and said, "It'll do. Here's the paint. 'Course, it's no good without a paintbrush. Not even Gypsies are stupid enough to buy paint without a brush. Now, I just happen to have a couple of real good, genuine China bristle brushes for twenty cents apiece."

"That wholesale to me?"

"Sho."

Casually Solomon said, "That's what I figured. But I got the brushes. Matter of fact, I need the paint to sell the brushes. I figured I'd go a little low on the brushes so I could come a little high on the paint. But since you offered them brushes to me wholesale, I got an item right here you could surely use, and I'll let you have it at cost, plus two cents. This is a razor made from genuine Toledo steel. It cost me eighty-eight cents. You can have it at ninety."

Tangling flipped open the razor and hefted.

"See," Solomon pointed out, "it's got Toledo stamped on the blade."

"Seems to me I recollect seeing a razor like this down in Lexington. Yes, I rightly recollect. It had Toledo stamped on it, and it was selling for fifty cents retail. Now, you wouldn't be trying to fool an old barber, would you, Solomon?"

" 'Course not, Mr. Tangling. The blades you saw in Lexington did have Toledo stamped on them, but they were made in Toledo, Ohio. The Ohio merchants are a smart bunch. They want you to think the steel was made in Spain, but they're just bamboozling you. This is real Toledo steel. You ever see a razor do this without being honed first?"

He took the razor and ran the blade lightly down his forearm. The fuzz, wafted off by the sharp edge, drifted lightly to the floor. "Now, that thing you shaved me with dragged like a road-grading log. You need a new razor, and that's why I'm offering this one to you wholesale."

Tangling shook his head. "I reckon those Ohio Yankees are a pretty sharp bunch. Average barber don't know Toledo, Ohio, steel from Toledo, Spain, steel. 'Course, you'd know, you being from Ohio.

"Tell you what, Sol. Seeing as how I'm a little short of cash since I sold you a dollar and a half's worth of paint for thirty cents worth of oilcloth, I'd be willing to pay you ninety cents for the razor, if you take fifty cents in cash and the other forty cents in two bundles of sassafras."

"Sassafras roots at twenty cents a bundle? Do I look like a sick man? I can get mandrake for less."

"This is real top quality sassafras."

Tangling reached under the counter and pulled out two bundles tied with string. Their sweet, sickening odor, stronger than cheap perfume, flared across the counter.

"I have no doubt about the quality," Solomon assured him, "but I don't drink sassafras."

"Niggers like it. Might be you'll run into some little nigger girl down the road who'd be powerfully obliged to you for a cup of good, hot sassafras tea, 'specially some little nigger girl with a strawberry mark on her ass."

He should have expected this. Tangling had seemed too knowing, sitting there and grinning. By now, Blake's reward posters were all over Kentucky, and Solomon was known all over Kentucky. He looked at Tangling and said, "Don't suspect that'll ever happen, Mr. Tangling, but seeing as how I'm getting it wholesale, throw it in. Here's your razor. Reckon I can cultivate a taste for sassafras tea."

Solomon drove out of Cumberland Ford with fear compounded by confusion. Tangling's trading advantage had proved Solomon correct in removing his beard, but the storekeeper had used his advantage merely to purchase a sixty-cent razor for fifty cents, throwing in five cents worth of sassafras roots as a lagniappe. He could have kept the sassafras, reported Solomon to the sheriff, and made one thousand dollars. Instead, he had taken five cents and warned Solomon.

Tangling's widow could use the half-dime to buy flowers for his grave, and welcome to it, but he would have to give up the idea of selling paint to the Gypsies. His own grave was opening. Henceforward, he would travel by night and sleep, while the girl stood watch, by day.

Come to think of it, he had swapped thirty cents worth of oilcloth for four pails of worthless paint.

His mind paused.

He would use the paint. The Gypsies were a recent memory in the neighborhood and a gaudily painted wagon might be deceptive—at least as far as Lexington, where a friend of his father lived who might help him. Parked off the road in daylight, the van would appear to belong to a wayward Gypsy and might, as such, be ignored.

He knew a field on the other side of the river where

wild onions had ruined a farmer's pasture and the clearing had been abandoned to rocks and the onions. Two miles after he forded the river, he pulled off the road and into the secluded glade, knowing he could work here in secrecy.

He was not disturbed by the prospect of losing the entire afternoon. Since the Gypsies were working the countryside, they would move much slower than his usual pace, and he wanted to stay behind them.

When he opened the door and called to Melinda, she stood blinking in the sunlight as he walked forward to unharness the mules.

"We'll spend the night here, Melinda," he said to her, and noticed the surprise on her face.

"I got shaved back in town," he said.

"I declare, Mr. Ricky, you're the prettiest man I ever did see. You makes me want to forget them firm resolutions."

"You hold onto them, girl. You're going to need them more, now, than ever . . . Now, we're going to paint this wagon from stem to stern. I'll need your help. There's a band of Gypsies hereabouts, and I want this wagon to look like a kissing cousin to a Gypsy's wagon."

Melinda, who had whitewashed a hen coop or two in her day, was enthusiastic about the task. Since it was a matter of indifference to him, he let her select the color scheme.

She gave the matter serious thought, standing with her hands on her hips and looking over the wagon from a distance, a black girl in a brown study, as he mixed turpentine into the paint. When she had made her decision, he set to work to follow it out, letting her handle the trim; although slower, she was more deft with a brush than he.

With the brilliant colors to choose from, Melinda composed the visual equivalent of a clapping juba. Red spokes radiated from the green hubs to yellow rims. Red cornerposts reached to a blue roof and framed side panels of blue around a wide center panel of yellow. Rearward, a yellow door was enhanced by a green trim, while the forward seat box of blue set off the brilliant red wagon tongue.

Work flowed smoothly through the afternoon, and when it was finished, they stood off to admire their handiwork. It was too gaudy for a Gypsy caravan and too small for a circus wagon, but the van would never be taken for that of a Hebrew merchant. Merely to look at it was to feel cheerful, and as they complimented each other, he knew why harlequins dressed as they did to lighten the burdens of kings.

For the next two days, he decided, he would risk traveling by daylight.

After supper, he detailed sewing tasks for her. With a pencil, he sketched his recollection of a Gypsy's skirt and blouse; and he added a bright red jacket for himself.

"You've got to keep inside the van. When you have to come out, I want you wearing your red skirt with a kerchief over your head and all your jewelry.

"We've got problems. You're a little bit black for a Gypsy, but I'm too white. Before my face gets brown, it's going to get burned. I can feel it itch already."

"Mr. Ricky, if you can find me a black walnut tree, I can boil some shells and make you near as black as me. Maybe we could just move in with them folks."

"They don't take to strangers," he said.

At Barbourville the next morning, he laid in a supply of provisions for the next ten days at the general store and elicited the information that the Gypsies had been through four days before, headed north. From a livery stable attendant, Solomon learned they had taken the left fork out of town, which meant they were heading for Lexington via London rather than Manchester. Solomon hightailed up the London road, striding easier with the knowledge that the storekeeper in Barbourville had failed to recognize him.

He wore a broad-brimmed felt hat he had bought to protect his face, and he knew that the hat and the beardless face had changed his appearance as completely as the paint had changed the wagon. He was no longer a plodding religious of antique mien, but a young rapscallion striding over the earth as if he owned it. He even walked differently, with his shoulders thrown back, swinging loose and free. He gloried in his rippling, tireless muscles, and for the first time in his entire career on the road, he found himself whistling as he walked.

Near the hamlet of Raccoon, he stopped at a farmhouse to trade for corn, which added to the oats and natural forage to feed the mules to Cincinnati.

While at the corn crib with the farmer, a pleasant young man, he angled for information about the Gypsies, relating imaginary complaints about "them furriners" and their shoddy merchandise. The farmer agreed with him to the extent that politeness demanded.

"Heard tell Sheriff Craig's holding one of them over in the London jail, so there must be some ruffians amongst them, but they treated Mag and me nice. One of the ladies sold Maggie some lace doilies for a dime apiece that would cost her three times that in Louisville. Come on in, Mr. Ricky, and set a spell. I'll show you them doilies."

Solomon begged off staying, but he went in to see the doilies.

If the lace were an indication of their sharp practices, then the Gypsies must be the poorest traders in the world, he thought. Four doilies, eight inches square and designed in the sol motif of *punto de Cataluna,* were bordered by margins one inch wide in *gros point de Venise,* through which were woven with delicacy and charm a strand of gold. They had been made by a Cellini of the needle.

"Ma'am," he said, "your husband said this lace would be costly in Louisville. Indeed it would, but it could not be bought in Louisville."

With a renewed sense of urgency, he bade good-bye to the farmer and his wife. Now, he had a reason to call on the Gypsies: he wanted to arrange to purchase the best lace in the country to sell at the Cincinnati Trade Fair.

To find the Gypsies was the problem. As afternoon wore on and he traveled north, no signs of old campfires warmed the spoor. Following their general direction was easy, but to find their location was another matter. They might be off the road in any hidden glade, and he would miss them.

Meanwhile, each mile was taking him deeper into the slave country. Soon, he could expect to meet fugitive-slave patrols, the dreaded "pattyrollers" of the Negroes that roamed the countryside by day and night. Any closed van would be suspect, whether driven by Solomon Villaricca or Sol Ricky. From here into Cincinnati, he would be balanced on the edge of peril, and that edge would get thinner as he neared the Ohio.

As he strode along, looking in vain for old campfire sites, fresh-rutted wagon trails leading off the main road, and the foliage of black walnut trees, his mind turned to the problem of ingratiating himself with the tribe once he had found it. Commercial reasons might afford him reason for an introduction, but they would hardly furnish basis for a friendship that would last the three days to Lexington.

He thought of the Gypsy in the London jail. Sheriff Craig, he recalled, was a gentle, dignified man of fifty whom he had met, once, when he stopped in to inquire about a farm family. Probably, the Gypsy was being held for vagrancy or creating a public disturbance, minor charges used more for harassment than punishment. Craig might release him into the custody of a dignified, soft-talking relative.

Solomon rejected the idea. Craig might recall their earlier meeting, and though he was sure he would not be recognized without his beard, it was bad policy to set a lawman wondering where he had seen a face.

Yet, if he could talk the sheriff into releasing the Gypsy into his custody, he would have a carte blanche for entry into the tribe.

It was risky, but everything was risky. If he dared and was successful, there would be far less risk as the days went by. No night patrol would disturb a Gypsy camp, and no sheriff would stop a caravan to look for fugitive slaves. Gypsies might be petty thieves and traders of low repute, but they rarely committed capital crimes; and their movement along the roads was welcomed because it meant that they were going somewhere else.

Solomon might have made London by nightfall, but he found a black walnut tree about two miles south of the town and pulled off the road to park beneath it, out of sight of the road.

Melinda had spent the day sewing. She came out of the van wearing a skirt which reached to her ankles and a red kerchief pinned over her hair. Her pearls hung in a single strand. She had sewn him a red jacket with brass buttons stitched the twin rows down the front, and she had slit his denim trousers at the bottom and sewn in a red triangle.

Before nightfall, she boiled the shells of black walnuts into a mush, which she laid over his face, neck, and back of his hands. She left the mixture on for an hour, and when she removed it, his face was very dark by the light of the lantern.

By the morning light he was swarthy, with a yellow cast to the brown. He thought he resembled a Gypsy with jaundice, and when the thought struck him, he knew what he must do. Last night he had awakened twice to the sound of horsemen on the road.

After breakfast, he sat down with Melinda and drew a map on a piece of paper, giving her instructions as he

214

drew, showing her how to reach the Underground Railroad Depot at Barbourville. "If you hear me come out of the sheriff's office shouting in Hebrew, drop through the escape hatch, crawl into the bushes, and follow the creek downstream."

Before he closed the door on her and locked it, she said, "I truly hopes it comes out all right, Mr. Ricky. I'll pray to Jesus."

"Good. I'm hoping it will, but if it doesn't, may your years be long and your children many."

He wheeled the mules and drove them down to the road, turning right toward London. A swarthy man in a red jacket with bell-bottomed trousers, a red kerchief showing beneath his broad-brimmed hat, he might or might not pass for a Rom, but he was certain he resembled no Jew or Gentile born of woman.

Half an hour later, he walked into the office of Sheriff Craig.

Sheriff Craig sat at the table reading a novel. He looked up reluctantly when Solomon entered, closing the book over his index finger to mark his place. "What may I do for you, my good man?"

His stilted, bookish tone was soothing to Solomon, who answered slowly, as if unfamiliar with the language. "I have come to inquire about a Gypsy you are holding."

"Oh, Larry. He's incarcerated."

"I would like to know what he is being held for and if his release can be arranged."

Sheriff Craig closed his eyes, rubbed them, and pinched the bridge of his nose. Solomon glanced down and read the title of his novel, *Peril on the Plains*, by Ned Buntline.

"He's being held for sheep stealing. He was charged with stealing a lamb and found guilty. His trial was held yesterday at a circuit court convened in this office. He was sentenced to ninety days or thirty dollars."

"Thirty dollars for a lamb?"

"Are you a relative?"

"Sir, I may or may not be a blood relative. I have been long away from my people, and I suffer from jaundice, but I wished to see my people again before this thing . . . worsens. I wouldn't think it of Larry to steal a lamb."

"I myself do not think the lad had any intention of stealing the lamb. He told me it had strayed, and he was bringing it back to the fold. But he pleaded neither guilty nor not guilty. He insisted that it made no difference what he pleaded, and I rather think the boy was right. Judge Smith was determined to make him an example."

"But, captain, thirty dollars for a lamb! A man could buy a flock of sheep for thirty dollars."

"Indeed, but fine was set to compensate the neighborhood for the depredations of your people. Judge Smith was prejudiced. His wife paid three dollars for a marble statue of cupid that smashed to smithereens when dropped. Tom Fields, over by Lyn Camp, paid twenty dollars for a windsucking cribber sold to him as a sound beast. That's good horse-trading in Tennessee, but we don't take kindly to it in Kentucky."

"May I speak to the boy?"

"Surely."

Craig jerked a thumb toward a door behind him and returned to the book, saying, "Go through the door, there. First cell to your left."

Sheriff Craig seemed happy to be rid of Solomon.

Solomon turned and went through the door, grateful to the graphic power of Ned Buntline.

A bushy-browed boy of seventeen, fair skinned, heavily muscled, lay on a bunk swung down from the stone wall by chains. In the corner of his cell, a guitar was propped against the wall.

"You Larry?" Solomon asked.

"Sho." The boy rolled over and sat up, looking at Solomon with pale blue eyes that were neither hostile nor friendly.

"You a Rom?"

"Sho."

"You speak Romany?"

"Sho."

"If I get you out of here, would you take me to your king, count, duke, or whatever you call him?"

"Sho."

"My name's Sol Ricky. I may or may not be your relative. That depends on you. Don't talk Romany to me around the sheriff."

"Sho."

Solomon went back into the office.

Craig was so intent on his novel that it saddened Solomon to interrupt him.

"Sheriff, I'm a poor man, a scholar of sorts, whose in-

216

come is more limited than his mortal days, and I wish to take the lad back to his people. He tells me the lamb had strayed, and he was returning it to the ewe. I believe him, as you believed him. We are both honorable men, you and I. The lad is innocent, the lamb has been returned. Under such circumstances, could you find in your heart the kindness to pardon the lad into my custody? I will give my word of honor, as a gentleman, that you will never regret the nobility and magnanimity of your deed."

Craig marked his place on the page with his finger, looked up, said "No," and returned to his reading.

Craig had presented the best argument in the world against an impassioned plea—indifference. So—thirty dollars! But thirty dollars would virtually eliminate his profits for August, already cut to a minimum by the boy's people. Rather, he should spend two dollars for a Bowie knife and cut his way to Cincinnati.

With head held high, Solomon stalked from the office.

In five minutes, he was back with a bulging poke, asking, "Will you take a five-dollar note from a Knoxville bank? The rest is hard money."

With a tired smile, Craig said, "Let me see the paper."

Solomon handed him the scrip. He examined it and said, "It'll do."

Solomon laid the remainder in coins on the desk. Craig did not count the money. He raked it into the drawer. "We are both honorable men," he said, and pulled a release form from the drawer. "What is your name, sir?"

"Sol Ricky."

"Mr. Ricky, while I make out your receipt and the release for Larry, will you take the key off the nail there and release the prisoner? Put the key back on the nail when you come out."

Solomon took the key and went back to the cell. "All right, boy, I've paid your fine. You're released into my custody. Let's go."

Larry said nothing. He grabbed his guitar and followed Solomon.

Craig had resumed reading. He said, "Thank you" as he heard the key click on the nail, finished his paragraph, and looked up as Solomon approached the desk with the boy.

He handed Solomon a receipt on which he had scrawled, "Wed., Aug. 18th, 1858. Released Larry Morgan to S.

217

Ricky, on payment of $30.00.   C. L. Craig, Sheriff, Laurel Co., London, Ky."

He arose and extended his hand to Larry. "I'll miss your guitar, son. You be good, now!"

"Sho," Larry said.

Solomon bade the sheriff "Good day," wondering if Craig had heard him, for Craig was dropping his gaze again to the book.

As he opened the door and stepped out into the sunlight with his prize, Solomon felt vaguely melancholy.

Behind him, an old, gentle, and elected sheriff who could not swagger the streets of a peaceful town where he had been known since birth walked in his imagination the streets of wilder towns, taking dead aim at desperadoes who always fell in stylized, bloodless deaths under his flaming guns.

Each man walked a dark and lonely path, Solomon thought, and each chose his own method of illumination. Solomon's candles gleamed out of a night that had settled over his people centuries ago, and a flambeau lit eighteen and a half centuries lighted the path of Norah Gresham. Craig's way was beaconed by new-lit candles bought for the half-dime from Ned Buntline.

"Over there," Solomon said to Larry Morgan.

Morgan climbed aboard the van without comment.

As he wheeled around and headed toward the road, Solomon asked the boy a direct question. "Which way?"

Larry pointed left.

In silence, they rolled out of the hamlet. In the past, Solomon's fancy had lit on London because there was a locksmith there named Barrel whose shop was next to the office of a stock dealer named Locke, and the local wags held that Locke with his stock and Barrel with his locks owned London, lock, stock, and barrel. Such tenuous strands could no longer bind his affection to a hamlet where he had paid thirty dollars for one measly lamb.

Beside him, the object of his concern sat in silence. He had not thanked Solomon for his deliverance. He had not commented on the weather or remarked on his treatment in the jail.

"You speak English?" Solomon asked.

"Sho."

"Then why don't you speak it?"

218

"I'm speaking it."

His words were a Southerner's, but the rhythm to his speech was from no section of the country that Solomon could identify, yet it seemed vaguely familiar.

"Your real name Larry Morgan?"

"Sho."

"I never heard of a Rom named Larry Morgan."

"I never heard of one named Sol Ricky."

"I'm not, but I want to join up with your tribe."

"You crazy?"

"Do I have to be?"

"Well, if you want to be, you are."

"Crazy or a Rom?"

"Both."

"Who's head man of your tribe?"

"Ramon Sanchez, my uncle."

"You know where he is?"

"No. But I can find him, I think."

He pronounced "think" as "thank," in the Southern manner, but he drew the word out as if it were split in the middle.

There was something odd about this boy, so odd that Solomon began to have misgivings. Larry Morgan was a Welsh name, and Wales was all that Solomon could see in the boy's pale skin, black hair, bushy eyebrows, and cragged jaw.

These hills were full of Welshmen. It might be that he had spent a month's income on some moonstruck boy from a backwoods cove. Even sane Welshmen were peculiar, and there was inbreeding back in the hills. It would be in keeping with that nation's character for a lunatic Welshman to convince himself that he was a Gypsy, and only a Welshman would dream up a Gypsy uncle with a Spanish name.

Spanish! That was the rhythm of the boy's speech! Solomon had heard the same lilt in the English spoken by his grandfather.

"What tribe of Roms do you belong to, Ungars?"

"Hell, no! We'uns is Catalans."

Solomon heaved a sigh of relief. Larry Morgan was a Welsh mountaineer, no doubt about that, but he was also a Spanish Gypsy. As a Spanish Jew, Solomon felt he should find some meeting ground with Ramon Sanchez.

One hour, and three and a half miles later, Solomon's relief was justified.

South of Hazel Patch, Larry Morgan pointed to a side road, an overgrown wagon trail which wound westward through the pine barrens in the direction of the Rock Castle River. Solomon followed it until it passed the chimney of a burned farm dwelling behind a cluster of oaks which had shaded the frontyard of the house.

Behind the former homesite was a spring with a brick apron, and beyond the spring was a pasture. In the pasture were the caravans of the Gypsies, lined up in two uneven rows and facing each other about twelve yards apart. Solomon counted nine vehicles, high-roofed and gaudily painted, with low turning wheels and high rear wheels. Tents had been erected behind two of the vans in the line to his left and behind three in the right lane. Farther down in the pasture, he could see the draft horses grazing on tethers.

On the avenue between the lines, the turf was trodden. Men, most of them shirtless, lounged beside wagons, and women tended cook fires. Solomon pulled up beside the first caravan on his left and parked.

Larry jumped down. "This way," he said.

Solomon walked beside the youth between the line of wagons. Some of the men looked at him, but with no more curiosity than he would have met with on a stroll down Congress Street at twilight of a summer's evening. Only one individual paid him heed, a small boy, stark naked, with a thumb in his mouth, which he removed as Solomon walked past.

"Hello, *Gajo*," the boy said.

"Hello, boy," Solomon answered.

Turning to Larry, he asked, "What does '*Gajo*' mean?"

"Gentile, I reckon."

Larry Morgan led him to the last van in the right-hand row of wagons. Before its open door, a slattern tended a pot hung on a spit over a fire. She was peeling and quartering onions to toss into the bubbling pot, seated on a three-legged stool over which her broad buttocks draped like dewlaps. She was dark-eyed and dark-skinned, and her long, oily black hair was plaited into a hawser she had hoisted over her shoulder.

"Ramon in?" Larry asked.

She threw a thumb toward the open door.

As Solomon stood back, waiting, Larry spoke into the dark interior in Spanish, turned, and walked away, leaving without a good-bye or another look toward Solomon.

Solomon stood alone by the woman, who kept flicking her dark eyes up to him as she peeled onions and wept. Solomon, looking at the doorway, saw movement inside. Slowly, pulling a suspender over his bare shoulder, a man emerged from the shadowed interior, stepped down onto a step box, and stood looking at Solomon.

"I'm Ramon Sanchez."

"I'm Sol Ricky."

Ramon Sanchez was a Spanish Gypsy. It was difficult to judge his age, because there was no gray in his hair and no lines on his face. Solomon figured he must be in his late forties solely on the basis of his air of authority. His face was thin and long, his jaw square, and his lips thin and wide. His skin was very brown with a copper tint. He had Spanish features and a Moorish complexion.

"You paid the boy out. Such a fine gentleman must be wealthy." His voice had a mendicant's whine at odds with his hauteur.

"No, I am poor and a road peddler, like yourself. I would like to drive north with you, if you are going north."

"We are going north."

"When will you go?"

Sanchez shrugged. "Does the bird know when he will fly? Tomorrow, or Friday, or Monday. But we will go."

"May I go with you?"

"Why does a *Gajo* wish to go with gypsies?"

"I am not a *Gajo*, I am a Hebrew. Your people make fine lace. I have seen it. Next year, or the year after, I may wish to buy all of your lace. I will not roam always."

"Juanita de Cordobiza, she makes the lace. She only sells to those she likes, and she is seventy years old. However, she may like you. Sometimes the old think young."

"Yehuda," the woman on the stool looked up and spoke to him in Yiddish, "you are a fine looking man. Have you a woman?"

"Yes," he answered in English, "and your stew smells good. What must I do to get a little?"

"Bet mich a bisele, bubela."

Solomon smiled. Her sentence was too charged with

221

coquetry to refer solely to the stew. He looked at Sanchez again.

"May I join you?"

"The road is free, and you are here," Sanchez said.

"I have my woman with me."

"They are good to have, if they work and don't eat too much."

"He's a candlewick saver," the woman said in Yiddish.

"My woman's black," Solomon told Sanchez.

Sanchez shrugged. "They must be some color."

He turned and went back into the van.

As Solomon walked away, the woman called after him in Yiddish, "Remember, lover, if you want a little, beg me."

"I'll remember." That much he could answer in Yiddish.

So, he thought, as he walked back to his van, I have met the king and queen. He would have to walk wide of the queen. Obviously, she was a forward wench with a roving eye, and he did not desire a knife in his back over a woman so huge and oily he would have to mount her with pitons and descend from her with rappelling ropes.

He had weighed the risks in telling Sanchez he was a Jew. The Gypsies would not have read the wanted posters because they could not read, and they would expect more from his implied promise of a trading agreement over the lace than they would expect from a Gentile. As a Jew and member of another wandering tribe, he had hoped to arouse more fellowship among the Gypsies than he could have as a Gentile, but obviously that gambit gave him no advantage.

Their word *"Gajo"* interested him. It was close enough to *"Goy"* to indicate that somewhere in the past this tribe must have had commerce with Jews.

When he reached the van, he opened the door and called, "You can come out, Melinda. We're in Gypsy town."

She came out, rubbing her eyes. She was wearing her red skirt with her scarf and her jewelry. She looked up the avenue at the wagons and the tents.

"What kind of folks is these Gypsies, Mr. Ricky?"

"I have, this moment, returned from an audience with the reigning monarch. From what I've seen of the Gypsies so far, they're stupid, mercenary, inhospitable, ungrateful, and carnal-minded. If their men act the way their women talk, you'll need a double lock on your chastity belt. Better stay close to the wagon."

She listened to his cultivated cursing with a head cocked in concentration and said, "Mr. Ricky, you know you done lost me with them words. Is they good or bad?"

"I don't know," he said, thinking there was no point in creating in her mind the apprehension in his own.

Chapter Nine

He was pounding the cooking spit into the ground for Melinda, who had gone into the nearby woods to gather twigs for the dinner fire, when the children came.

Vanguard of the horde was the naked little boy, who waddled up, followed by a girl of six, whose head was balanced by twin plaits falling below her shoulders. Both children were so dark that the whites of their eyes gleamed in their faces, and both were shyly curious.

"Hello, *Yehuda,*" the little boy said.

"Hello, boy. You his sister, little girl?"

"Yes, sir."

"What's your name, boy?"

"Pedro."

"Pedro what?"

The little boy looked at his sister, who answered for him. "His name is Pedro Sanchez, and he's three."

"What's your name?"

"Margarita Sanchez. I'm six."

"How did you know I'm a *Yehuda,* Pedro?"

"Margarita, she told me."

"How'd you know, Margarita?"

Margarita squealed with delight and shyness. "Pedro, he told me."

"Then, who told the two of you?"

Again the little girl laughed. *"Un pajarito!"*

Someone in the camp was not as unconcerned as the people he had seen. It had not taken the little boy ten minutes to waddle down the row of wagons to Solomon's van, yet in that time, a little bird had told him that Solomon was not a *Gajo* but a *Yehuda*.

He saw in the children an opportunity to breach the indifference of the adults, and he said, "You all wait here."

He climbed into his van to get a twist of licorice, and he snipped the twist into halves. Margarita said, "Thanks," and Pedro said, *"Gracias."*

They stood in silence as he finished pounding the spit, and when he turned, there were four more children, ranging from five to nine. Solomon went back into the van for more licorice, snipping the twists into thirds. He looked out and got more licorice. He emerged with a handful of sticks that did not go around. By the time he had returned with more, there were more children. When he finally completed his giving, there were sixteen children chewing on progressively shorter sticks of candy. Invariably, they had thanked him, in Spanish or in English.

Melinda returned with the firewood and he said, "Looks like we got company."

"Lordy, Mr. Ricky, where'd all them come from?"

They stood looking up at Melinda with unabashed curiosity. He said, "Children, this is Melinda. Melinda, this is Margarita Sanchez, and the little boy in the natural uniform is Pedro. Introduce yourself to the rest of them. I'll make the fire."

Melinda moved among the children, squatting to their height, saying, "And what's your name?"

Solomon went about making the fire, and when he had finished, Melinda arose from the circle of children. "Mr. Ricky, most ever' one of these children named Sanchez. Mrs. Sanchez, she must be kept right busy."

One of the little girls tugged at Melinda's skirt. "Melinda, more candy."

Melinda patted her head. "No, child. Too much'll make your belly ache."

"Are these little beggars pestering you, sir?"

A woman, almost as tall as Solomon, stood on the step box of the neighboring van. She was slender, handsome, and imperious. She wore a white blouse above a dark skirt bordered with silver brocade, and she could have been anywhere between twenty-five and thirty years of age.

"No, ma'am," he called. "I volunteered to give them all a stick of licorice."

She stepped down and swished toward them with an easy

225

grace. "Give them a penny and send them packing, else they'll pester you till the morning glories open."

"I have no pennies," Solomon said, thinking, for sixteen cents, he preferred their company.

"Scat, brats," the woman shouted.

Screeching, screaming, shouting, tumbling, the pack broke and ran down the avenue, herded by the tallest girl, who moved with the same indefinable grace as the woman who now stood and watched them, hands on hips, with a hint of a smile softening the strong lines of her face.

She turned to Solomon. "We are *Gitanos,* Spanish *Gitanos,* and the way these children beg, you would think us Ungars . . . I am Juanita Armandez. You have a beautiful van there. Such colors! It makes my earlobes dance from the music in my eyes. *Bravura!* And you are a crocus pitcher, no doubt?"

"Not quite. I'm Sol Ricky, traveling merchant, and this is Melinda."

"Ah, Melinda! Your name has the tinkle of guitars, and such a pretty girl. I shall teach you to become a witch and enchant people. Already, you cast spells. But don't let my Nicky see you. He will spit on me.

"I would ask you to have a meal with me, for it is getting on that time, but I have prepared nothing. My Nicky sleeps, and will sleep until it is time to drink again. And there will be drinking tonight, with Larry free. Of that you may be damned sure."

"I was just fixing something, ma'am," Melinda said.

"If you're alone, why don't you join us?" Solomon invited. "My woman cooks well."

"If she cooks well, she is loved well. You must stir the pot properly to have the pot stirred properly. Is he a good lover, Melinda?"

"Right nice, ma'am."

"I saw him with the children. He has the eyes of a dreamer, the nose of a nobleman, the chin of a man of action, and the shoulders of *un toro.* So, I will love your cooking."

Juanita Armandez's company proved well worth the price of the two bowls of stew that she ate. She engulfed them with words, but atop the flood came bits of flotsam that interested him.

She was intensely proud of her Spanish heritage. Spanish Gypsies, she told him, were the aristocrats of the Romany peoples; and she used the word *"Gitano"* in referring to herself but "Roms" when referring to other tribes.

Solomon looked on her pride with a double vision. His Anglo-Saxon attitudes remarked that one segment of a race should feel superior to another segment, but as a Jew, he understood. His grandparents had grieved when he had once courted an Ashkenazi girl. They had rejoiced when he had married Leah, a Sephardi whose family had been invited to Georgia by General Oglethorpe to teach the colonists industriousness and good manners—a project in which they had failed catastrophically, judging from what Solomon knew of Georgians.

Juanita was delighted that Solomon was Hebrew. She too was religious, though not many *Gitanos,* she admitted, were moved by great faith. "I have seen God with my heart," she said. "Some say, 'Prove God to me, and I will worship God.' I say to such fools that the proof of God is the facts of God. God is a tiara of dew crowning a rose. They say, 'Show me a miracle.' I say, 'Look at me, I am your miracle.' Fools! The mind that doubts God is proof of His existence."

She was a Catholic.

"Ah, they had such beautiful cathedrals in Spain. To walk into them is to feel the soul soar. God is a Gothic arch."

God she respected, but Mary she doted on.

"Poor María, the Holy Mother! Imagine what the Blessed Virgin must have gone through in her life. A virgin married! That horn of José's must have butted her from evening to dawn. Ah, she must have fought to keep her legs crossed. The temptation!"

"I hadn't thought about it that way," Solomon admitted, "but Joseph must have had a rough life himself, married to a virgin."

"Don't you worry about José," she assured him. "He got his, and plenty. But, María! And her son was a god. Now, don't you think she had her hands full? In our church, we say, 'Ave, María, full of grace, pray for us now and in the hour of our death.' That is selfish. I pray for María and the sorrow of her hours upon earth."

Melinda sat cross-legged on the ground, having yielded her stool to Juanita, and listened avidly to the torrent of words flowing from the woman who wove an eyewitness account of the coronation of Mary in heaven. To his astonishment, Solomon learned that Mary had been bodily lifted into heaven and physically crowned Queen of Angels. If Juanita could believe such dogma, then it would follow that she could truly believe in fortune-telling and palmistry; but he suspected that her religion was less a way of life than an inspiration for her fancy. So it had been with him, perhaps, until he came to a river he had not crossed.

As the stream of her language carried them along, a scrawny man, barefoot and shirtless, came out of her caravan. He walked over to the now dead fire and the group around it. "My husband, Nick. Sol. Melinda. Sit down, honey. You might wear yourself out standing up."

Solomon saw the man eyeing the stew, and he invited Nick to eat. Nick did so forthwith, as Juanita told of the love affair between Jesus and Mary Magdalene. With his wife's spoon, he ladled the stew from the pot, scraped it clean, and returned to his caravan. He had not said a word, and he had not listened. .

Solomon thought her words would never cease, when two youths and a girl, all about sixteen, came walking down the avenue, and Juanita hailed them in Spanish. They walked with the same effortless grace he had noticed in the woman, and he began to wonder if walking was a learned art in this tribe.

"Sol and Melinda, here are our lovers, Jerry and Arabella, and their boy duenna, Mike."

Mike was the runt of the litter. He was a wide grin beneath a dirty cloth cap pulled down to his eyebrows with the bill creased in the middle. Jerry, tall, slender, wide-shouldered and narrow-hipped, resembled a line drawing of a toreador. Arabella was slightly taller than Melinda, more slender, and her face had dignity and composure. Her shy smile of greeting radiated a luminosity far beyond the movement of her lips. She had a quality of loveliness which did not glitter but would never pall.

"Ain't our lovers handsome?" Juanita said. "They're jumping the broom St. Crispin's Day. I wanted St. Agnes, but it's too late for that."

Jerry looked down at Melinda with unconcealed admiration. "We're running traps. Want to come along and keep Arabella company?"

"I's so dirty the buzzards might get me, thinking I was cyarn," Melinda said. "I got to give me a washing."

"You and Mike go without me, Jerry."

Arabella was not asking, but ordering, and the two boys turned and walked on without cavil. Arabella turned to

Melinda. "I've got a swimming hole on the creek I'll show you if you'll promise not to tell."

"I won't tell nobody."

"After you wash, we can hunt mushrooms."

"All right if I go, Mr. Ricky, and take my soap?"

"Certainly, Melinda."

Solomon did not want Melinda to go, for the girl who skipped gaily into the van was his protection. Juanita would have him alone now, and that omnivorous woman might rape him. Over his mind flashed a fantastic vision of Juanita climbing aboard him, chanting psalms, and intoning Hail Marys as her liquid thighs engulfed him.

Juanita watched the two girls and said, "God is girls going swimming."

She had been facing Melinda as she talked, and now she turned to him, crossing her legs and letting him glimpse the undersides of brown thighs.

"Yes, God is everywhere, even in love-making. No, God is especially in love-making."

Her words perturbed him, now that they were alone, and her indrawn, contemplative but calculating look reinforced his perturbation, and he shifted the channel of her thoughts: "I wondered why the Romanies roamed, but if I could think my thoughts as you think yours, I too would roam forever, for then all places would be as a garden of God."

"We roam because we like to and because the road is there," she said. "God is a mountain made purple by distance . . . Ah, I admire you Jews. Three *Yehudin* died rather than forge the nails that pierced our Blessed Savior to the cross. But the fourth smithy, a *Gitano*, was frightened by the Roman swine and forged the nails. From that day, our tribe was cursed, they say, and forced to wander.

"Myself, I do not believe the tale. They do not suffer who love the punishment.

"I believe the *Gajos* have paid. They must till the fields, weave the cloth, and press the wine so we *Gitanos* may roam.

"But, ah, when the dew of the morning lies fresh on the road and the road curves toward the sunset, over the crest of a day swelling with spring, or green with summer, or golden with autumn, there is no music but the crack of a whip and the creak of a moving wheel. God is a Romany caravan rolling!"

Apparently, she had found the true name of God, for she swung into dithyrambs extolling the joys of the road, and she reminded him of birds. Bending, swaying, straightening with hauteur, pausing to pluck the right word, she was a finch, a swallow, a hummingbird poised in flight, and above all, she was a raven.

Her voice grew low-pitched as the orbit of her conversation swung again toward its central star. "Alas, good loving comes hard on the road."

She had woven a spell with her words, and her eyes seemed to speak to him above the flow of her voice. "I have waited long for you, Solomon, and there are meadows, close by, bright with summer daisies, and cool canebrakes by yonder creek. Come with me to hidden places, and I will let you feel the rhythms that buoy me as I walk. I, Juanita, the sorceress, will weave my magic spells for you alone, and not with words, not with words."

His eyes answered hers, saying: "Your plumage is black but comely, O, my raven, and you tear out my heart with your strong beak. I shall let your talons rend my thighs, but I shall sheathe my sword in your dark passion until, forspent, you flutter and fall. You have blinded my eyes with the raven-spread of your wings, and I shall come to you in the hidden places; but I warn you, after me, all others will be a shadow of your lost ecstasy, and your heart shall be branded forever with the image of a six-pointed star."

So their eyes spoke as her voice was saying, "Nick's no good lest he sleeps a lot, and he can't sleep much on the road. Strange, but a man gets sleepy after loving, and it makes a woman wake up."

His timbre quivering from the pizzicato in his groin, Solomon spoke. "Perhaps your husband is inadequate."

Suddenly, he saw the beckoning in her eyes grow stiletto-sharp and dangerous.

His voice did not falter but dropped lower, beneath the area of suggestiveness into an area of sadness. "If so, it is a burden all men must bear. For any one woman, three husbands would be inadequate." His voice rose, became professorial, as he continued, pleading for understanding for all men. "It is a physiological necessity, ma'am. The act of love takes energy from a man and gives it to a woman. So, I beg you, don't judge us too harshly. We try, but the burden is great."

He smiled his warm, endearing smile, shrugged his shoulders in a disconsolate plea for understanding for all men, and saw perplexity replace the hostility in her eyes.

"I get sleepy after I eat," she said.

"The labors of digestion," he affirmed, in his best pedagogical manner.

"Well, I got a siesta due me, so I'll haul ass. You're a good talker, Sol. 'Round here, they ain't."

"Thank you, Juanita," he said, wondering on what basis she had decided he had such talents, since his own words had been at a minimum.

He watched her walk away and turned to gather the dishes.

He had made a mistake by thinking carnal thoughts in the presence of a Gypsy who could read minds.

Would he never learn! With Phoebe Blake, he could blame soft lights and wine. With Melinda, it had been prompted by a vision of nude beauty by twilight. Here, cold sober in the blaze of noon, he had hoisted full sail to a gust of passion engendered by a flicker of a brown buttock, an avian simile, an imagined beckoning, and he had almost run aground.

When he and Melinda accompanied the Armandezes to the welcoming party for Larry Morgan on the meadow eastward of the caravans, where flambeaux had been planted and lighted in the gathering dusk, Solomon was no longer sure that his glibness had cast all suspicion from Juanita's mind. She stayed with him after Melinda had gone to find Arabella and Nick had gone to find a winebag. She acted as his hostess, but her introductions were so perfunctory that it was obvious she was shunting the people away from him. However, he insisted on talking to Juanita de Cordobiza, the lace-maker, and found to his sadness that her total production amounted to one doily a month.

Two violinists played, and he heard shouted requests for Larry to sing. Once a woman arose and did a fandango. Larry, slumped under some great sorrow, was oblivious to the requests that he sing. One of the men passed a winebag back to Solomon, who held the goatskin over his shoulder, Spanish fashion, and tongued the nozzle.

Shouts for Larry to sing were growing in number and volume, rising now to a chant of "Sing, Larry, sing." The sound was too great to be ignored.

Larry stood up, waved a languid hand at the crowd in assent, and walked to the center of a square lighted by four flambeaux. He walked slowly, his head bowed, in the manner of a man in great grief, and when he reached the center, he stood for a moment, his head still bowed.

Standing there, broad thighs spread beneath stocky

231

shoulders, his white skin gleaming in the torchlight, wearing loose ankle boots, Morgan resembled an English sailor. He strummed a chord tentatively, threw back his shoulders, and threw his face toward the stars; his eyes were closed in some secret agony of grief. The chords stood out on his neck, the cartilage of his throat was visible.

Once more, he slapped the strings and moaned to the stars, "Ohhhhh, Lord!"

Was he singing a Negro spiritual? Solomon asked himself, suddenly interested by the boy's histrionics.

Larry's fingers plucked at the strings, slowly, sorrowfully, and the music drifted into the easy, simple beat of a ballad. Then, he straightened and began to sing in a clear soprano-like alto that quavered over the heads of his listeners.

> I got put in the London jail.
> Man came long and paid my bail.
> But a good man stayed in the London jail,
> And only God can go his bail.

It was a plaintive but a lying ballad, because Larry had been the only prisoner in the London jail. Solomon felt the sorrow rising in the Gypsy hearts around him, but he could not share Larry's falsely induced compassion for a pent spirit until the last stanza.

> So, that's the story I had to tell
> Of a good Gentile in the London jail.
> No sadder fate e'er man befell
> Than Sheriff Craig's at the London jail.

Larry's grief was for his jailer.

Juanita walked back with Solomon and Melinda to the van. Nick stayed behind, "to get drunk," Juanita said with an absolute lack of wifely concern.

Solomon was more concerned. If too many of the tribe got drunk, hangovers might delay their departure in the morning.

As they walked the avenue between the caravans, the memory of Larry's voice softened the memory of Solomon's ostracism. Out of Sanchez by Morgan, out of a Spanish dancer by a Welsh bard, had come a near-angelic singer. No one had thanked him for the return of Larry Morgan, not even Larry, but he thanked himself. For thirty pieces of silver, he had lighted a dark place, and if the brutes who skulked in these wheeled caves had no gratitude toward him, his money was still well spent.

They did not move out in the morning. At nine, Arabella came for Melinda to accompany her on some secret mission, and the children came to him. Perhaps, they sought candy, but they got fairy tales and fables.

After the children left, Solomon, conceding Thursday lost, went fishing on the creek.

Inactivity bored him, but seated on the creek bank waiting for his pine-bark float to bob, he tried to accept the loss of a whole day. Regardless of whatever religion these people professed, they were Oriental contemplatives who had run out of things to contemplate.

He lost Thursday and he lost Friday. He inquired of Juanita concerning the delay, and she shrugged her shoulders. "They got a shindig Saturday night."

On Friday afternoon, he lost the children.

They had come to him for stories, and he complied, but during his narration, he noticed three of the older boys pushing a younger one forward. The youngest, about ten, edged in and waited, with suppressed excitement, as Solomon completed the tale.

"*Yehuda*," he asked, "did you have your thing cut off?"

He had been with them long enough to become inured to their frankness, and so he said, "No, only about this much."

He held up his hands about six inches apart.

"How much they leave?" one of the older boys blurted.

"About this much." Solomon held his hands eight inches apart.

He could see the boy adding the dimensions with his hands, and he looked up, saying "*Jesu Cristo!*"

Screaming in glee and astonishment, the children rose from the semicircle around him and fled, caterwauling, down the avenue, back to their old amusements. They were Orientals, every last jot and tittle of them, but they had not run out of things to contemplate.

There was another musicale in the meadow that night, but Solomon begged off from both Juanita and Melinda's invitations. At dusk, after he had washed his socks and hung them out, he lighted his candles. When Juanita came to reiterate her invitation, he declined, telling her it was his Sabbath.

He invited her to look into the van.

She looked at him. "Sol, it's so beautiful. It was made for worship. You go and worship there. Perhaps, in God's own time, you and I shall worship together, and I shall

233

provide the altar." As she spoke, she reached down, patted herself, and was gone into the darkness.

He went into the van, wrapped his shawl around him, and considered her gesture. Under the circumstances, it had not been sacrilegious or even lewd. Juanita's variety of worship was fitting and proper against the background of a spirit that pondered the sex life of Jesus. Come Saturday night, he mused, he might take her down to the canebrake and light a candle. If she liked to worship that way, he could be tolerant.

He, himself, was using candlelight to aid orderly thought.

He had been with the Gypsies since Wednesday, and they had not made a move to head northward, and they would be here, he knew, on Saturday also. Somehow, he had to communicate a sense of urgency to a people born without a sense of urgency. He had enough provisions left for only a week. To all appearances, he was marooned on this oasis; three times since their arrival he had heard patrols pass at night, but he could not stay here and starve.

His other problem was Melinda. She was at ease among the Gypsies, because many were as black as she, and was learning to tell fortunes by cards. She might be joining in rivalries within the group. Currently, she was concerned with the competition between Larry and Jerry for the hand of Arabella. Arabella was engaged to Jerry, but until the actual marriage, there was still room for competition, it seemed. Melinda, herself, had formed a dislike for Juanita, "that loud-mouth with all them big words who can't even read."

He did not want Melinda forming alliances, because allies meant enemies; already, he sensed that something had occurred. The Gypsy children's curiosity must have come from Melinda, who was propagating the same myth that Brother Smith had planted in her mind to forestall carnal relations with another "preacher."

If Juanita had questioned her alone about the prowess of her lover and Melinda had denigrated his ability, then Melinda had done the worst possible thing. Juanita would have taken Melinda's remarks as proof positive that he was the hottest Jew in Christendom.

It grew stuffy inside the van, and no thoughts came to him. He removed his shawl and sat in the doorway listening to the distant violins. The sound reminded him of his own unused violin in its rack, and he rose and took it down. By

234

playing himself, he might let his mind lie fallow, and some plan to speed his departure might come to him.

He started with a few of the Gypsy melodies he recalled from the musicale of Wednesday night. Since the sadness was there, he exploited it with an orchestration borrowed from *Eli, Eli,* using measures to follow the notes of the ancient chant. Improvising, he got a rather sad little Gypsy melody which spiraled up and down.

When he had finished, he took the instrument down and cradled it in his arms, marveling at the tone it had produced.

Suddenly, the darkness around him shook with the sound of applause, and he looked up at a semicircle of listeners before him in the starlight. Out of the darkness, Ramon stepped, saying, "*Yehuda,* your playing drew us from the flambeaux. You must join us with your playing, for to-morrow night Arabella dances."

"I'd be right glad to, Ramon."

He turned and was gone, and with him went the tribe. Only Melinda remained, and she said, "I stood back there with them *Gitanos,* and your playing made me right proud of us *Yehuden.*"

"Thank you, Melinda."

He went to sleep that night with the hope that his decision to play the violin had been inspired by God.

Nearing midafternoon Saturday, he had completed a new violin composition and was preparing to leave for the cane-brakes to rehearse it, when Mike came by and told him that Ramon would like to see him.

Ramon had never impressed Solomon with his imperial grandeur, but he was deferred to by the tribe, and Solomon felt that the summons was an honor, although Ramon prob-ably wished only to discuss the program for the evening.

Solomon's supposition was borne out by the presence of another musician, Tomás, a withered, scrawny little man, advanced in years, who squatted with Ramon by the door of the van. A few feet from them, the Romany with the oversized rump on the undersized stool sat as she always sat, tending the pot.

Ramon greeted him without rising. "So, you have come. Sit, *Yehuda.* Tomás, here, admires your music very much. Tomás is old and wise and he knows the violin but not much English. If you wish to speak to him, I will inter-pret. He thinks you are an artist."

"Tell him that I think he, too, is an artist, and my hope is that someday I may play as well as he."

235

Ramon looked over at the old man and said to him in Spanish, "He compliments you like a Spaniard. Shall I talk to him in the Spanish manner and tell him what he wants to hear, or shall I talk like an American and tell him the truth?"

"Tell me the truth," Solomon said to Ramon in Spanish.

Tomás spread his toothless mouth and cackled. Ramon, nonplussed by his exposure, grinned also.

Speaking in English, Ramon said, "*Yehuda,* I want my people to be happy, and they are not happy. Tomás here is the father of Juanita. Nick paid him two hundred dollars for the hand of Juanita, but Juanita is not happy with Nick. This makes Tomás unhappy. But he is old and poor.

"If you will give Tomás two hundred dollars to repay Nick, Nick will be happy. He can buy much wine. Tomás will be happy because Juanita will be rid of Nick. Juanita will be happy because she can divorce Nick and marry you."

Solomon, hunkering before the two men, listened attentively. So, Juanita *had* been guarding him—she had staked him out as her private claim.

"If Juanita marries you, she will be happy. You are not happy with the black, but you will be very happy with Juanita. She would put her soul into loving you. As every *Gitano* knows, Juanita has a very big soul. With her soul in her love-making, *Yehuda,* she would be a volcano."

"So am I, *Yehuda,*" said the wife of Ramon Sanchez in Yiddish.

"Silence, woman!" Ramon barked at her.

"But I don't have two hundred dollars," Solomon told Ramon.

"For me, twenty dinars, and we throw in the wagon," said the Yiddish-speaking Greek chorus.

Ramon had turned to interpret Solomon's answer to Tomás.

"Be gone," Solomon managed to say in Yiddish. "I cannot parley in three languages."

"I go," she said, throwing back her greasy hair and laughing, "and I will wait for you in the canebrake."

She arose and waddled away in the direction of the creek.

Ramon looked at Solomon with admiration. "You have great force with women."

Solomon shrugged and smiled sadly. "The children believe I have my member severed. Perhaps the women have heard and pity me."

"The children also say your stub is worth two men. . . Perhaps the women have heard that, also."

Solomon, on his haunches, considered the situation. From politeness, he could not turn down Ramon's offer flatly, because the father of Juanita sat across from him. Besides, he did not wish to offend Juanita.

"Juanita says you have a great soul," Ramon said, "and Juanita should know. She understands souls."

"Juanita is very attractive," Solomon said, "but I don't have two hundred dollars." These men were serious, and if he played the game correctly, he might turn their offer to his advantage. He took a bargaining stance. "Besides, my *calla Yehudni* is worth much."

"We know. She would fetch a good price from the *Gajos*."

Ramon's remark was not a threat, Solomon figured, but a door left ajar for further bargaining.

With the ease of long practice, he feigned interest as he pleaded poverty. "I would like Juanita, but I cannot afford her. I am a poor man, a peddler."

"We know that, and we, too, are poor. So, we have decided to help you buy her. Mike would like your woman, but Mike is but a boy. His parents are poor. He cannot pay you over one hundred dollars."

"The girl, Melinda, is worth much more."

"Ah, yes. She is worth much more, and we are poor."

As two powerful forces of weakness confronted each other, Solomon thought: He had heard tales of Gypsy traders and their persuasive powers, and the mask of compassion and understanding on the face of Sanchez was the mask of an expert. To persuade Solomon Villaricca to give up a two-thousand-dollar girl plus an extra one hundred dollars for a woman he did not want would take the talents of the greatest woman trader in history. Solomon was interested in selling techniques, and he was eager to see how Sanchez went about the task. Besides, he thought he could glimpse in this situation a chance to speed up the movement to Lexington.

"The black is worth thirty times one hundred dollars," he said flatly.

"But only to the *Gajos* and as a slave. No wife is worth that. There are bulls that cost more than Juanita, but only cattle breeders buy them."

"I take your point as well made," Solomon said, "but

237

how do you put a price of two hundred dollars on Juanita and only one hundred dollars on my black?"

"Juanita is twice as big and twice as strong."

"So, we are back to the bulls. Are we buying and selling women by the pound?"

"Your point touches my heart," Ramon said, and his face reflected great sadness—greater sadness, Solomon was sure, than any he had ever genuinely felt in his life. "We cannot sell by weight that which cannot be weighed."

Ramon paused and looked into the distance. A philosopher's glaze coated his eyes. Inwardly, Solomon alerted, sensing that the pitchman's talent was being focused.

"What is a woman?" The Gypsy's question was rhetorical. "A woman, *Yehuda*, is what we make of her. We pour into a woman our own soul's richness, our own imagination, our love, our trust, our fidelity. But for most of us, the crock has cracks.

"In the beginning, it is always a trifle that ensnares us, a manner of tossing her head, perhaps, a sudden sadness that clouds her laughter. We are charmed, and from such strands, we weave our tapestry of dreams. Often, the tapestry is far more beautiful in our minds than the fabric will let it be. But we are not blinded forever. We take her, and we learn to know her as she is—lazy, shrewish, ill-tempered —and the tapestry unravels. So, we know we have been slighted, but we are our own tricksters.

"Not so Juanita. She was richly woven from the beginning. In four days of dukkering at the *Gajo's* fair, she will have your hundred back with interest."

"I don't take a woman's money as my own," said Solomon.

"But with Juanita, it is not the money. It is the soul. You are a gentleman, *Yehuda*, with a finespun soul. Your soul's richness will harrow hers, and your two souls will grow together, become as one."

"My soul's my own," said Solomon.

"Yes, but you are a musician. You cannot play the grand notes upon one violin. Juanita will be your orchestra."

"I'm a solo player," said Solomon.

"Let me tell you, *Yehuda*, Juanita has been touched by God. He who loves and is loved by Juanita is doubly blessed, here and in eternity." Ramon leaned forward, his eyes burning with intensity. "Where will you stand on Judgment Day, *Yehuda*? On the right hand of God or the left hand of God? Don't tell me. I know. You are a man among men, and your soul is stained.

"But on the day you stand before God, Juanita will whisper the words of your salvation in His ear . . . Juanita can fix the Judge!"

He had met the world's greatest salesman, Solomon decided. For one black girl and a hundred dollars, he got a free ticket to heaven—the greatest bargain ever offered a man. Unfortunately, he was going to Cincinnati.

"A saint interests me," Solomon admitted, "but still, I do not have one hundred dollars. However, I have a friend in Lexington, a general of militia and a powerful man in politics, who might lend me the one hundred dollars, if we can get to Lexington quickly."

"We will go to Lexington soon."

"There is something else," Solomon said. "I would not think of selling Melinda for one hundred dollars, and I would never offer merely two hundred for such a woman as Juanita. I am offering five thousand and one hundred dollars for Juanita."

Sanchez smiled and spoke to Tomás in Spanish. He turned back to Solomon. "The black is very pretty, and Mike could learn to love her very much. So, we will offer five thousand for the black."

"I shall tell the *calla Yehudni*, and she'll be pleased."

"I shall tell Juanita, and she'll be pleased . . . But we must see that each shall not tell the other."

"Then, I suggest," Solomon said, rising to go, "that someone shoot the little bird that flies over this camp."

"The bird shall be shot," Ramon promised gravely. For a moment, he looked regal.

Solomon returned to the van and went into the woods to practice his composition, on a direct line away from the canebrake.

His mind focused on his composition as the afternoon wore on toward twilight, and suppertime, and Saturday night in a Gypsy camp.

The flambeaux cast their shadows almost to the end of the avenue, and Solomon, striding beside the free-swinging Juanita and the easy-slogging Nick, felt life grow as taut within him as the strings of the violin he carried. There were no clouds and no moon, and the stars were bright, and he was acutely aware of the grace of the woman beside him.

"Look at the stars," he said. "They are candles lighted on God's altar."

"You talk well, Sol," she said, and her voice when she spoke was soft and gentle. He had never considered the word "altar" a suggestive word, but Juanita had turned his world upside down.

As they neared the gathering place, he could hear the voice of Larry Morgan soaring above the sorrows of his guitar.

> The head must bow and the back will have to bend,
> Wherever the darky may go;
> A few more days, and the trouble all will end
> In the land where the sugarcanes grow.

Solomon found Melinda seated cross-legged on the grass with Arabella and Jerry in the semicircle formed by the audience upwind from the torches.

"What ails you, Melinda? You look peaked."

"Larry, he been singing some right sad songs, but don't you pay me no mind, Mr. Ricky. I'm enjoying my cry."

Solomon patted Melinda's head and walked over to the camp stools reserved for players where Arabella's father and Tomás sat. They greeted him in English and Spanish and motioned him to a seat beside Tomás. Tomás spoke to him in Spanish, "We'll let Larry set the tempo with the guitar, and we'll come in with the violins after Arabella comes on stage."

Larry got up from the center of the flambeaux, where he had been sitting as he played the preliminary songs, and brought his stool with him. Jerry and Arabella arose and went into the darkness, moving in different directions. Melinda, dry-eyed, got up and came over to sit on the ground beside Solomon.

Solomon adjusted his screws as Tomás explained, "Larry will pace the dancers. When we come in, we'll follow his tempo."

They were done, all instruments were tuned, and the hum of conversation around them had drifted into silence.

Larry was long adjusting his shoulder strap, and Solomon realized his activity was nothing more than stage business. Larry was letting the tension grow in the audience.

Suddenly, loudly, he strummed the guitar.

Solomon almost jumped at the sound.

It was followed by silence.

Beyond the torchlight, the darkness seemed to wait.

Again the guitar, louder, more insistent, and the silence.

Louder, longer, more urgently, the guitar pleaded to the darkness and the silence. Some magic in the music had turned the darkness into a live thing, and it was the darkness that answered, coyly, with the lone click of a castanet.

Now the guitar was happy. It sprang to life at the sound, joyous, whirling, rhapsodic, wheedling the castanets out of the darkness, luring them, begging them into the circle of light.

The castanets answered, flirtatiously, seeming to say, "Beg a little harder. Cry for me, then I'll come."

The guitar cried its loneliness, its sadness, its despair, and the castanets answered with a shy longing that sent the guitar into a frenzy of pleading. Here, in this darkness, the castanets spoke with a feminine sibilance and yielding which matched the masculine impetuosity of the guitar.

Now the castanets were merging with the rhythm of the guitar, speaking of an end to loneliness, and Arabella flowed out of the darkness, swirling to the click of the castanets. The guitar was mad with joy.

Guitar, castanets, and the dancer were one, and the thud of her bare feet on the turf flowed into a perfectly cadenced pattern of sound, and the swirling, lithe, and sinuous figure of the girl was a blur of grace and harmony.

Silence.

Sounds and motions stopped with such split-second simultaneity that it was as if both had crashed into a wall of silent immobility. The girl stood, her spine arched backwards, her eyes on the stars, one arm curved above her head, one curved below her hips and behind her. From the silence and frozen motion, her castanets clicked twice. From the darkness came two answering clicks. Her castanets chattered and stopped. The hidden castanets answered.

Jerry leaped into the circle of torchlight, and male and female began a slow, circling, stately movement clockwise, back to back, and the castanets were talking in the tender language of lovers.

When the guitar whirled into life, the dancers responded, Arabella swirling with abandoned grace around the stately Jerry, and when he warmed to her coquetry, she became prim and coy. Basically, his movements were a foil for hers, accenting her grace and her suppleness by his decorousness. Now the violins joined the guitar, and the dancers flowed with a more liquid rhythm.

Solomon, knowing the tempo, joined in, and the violins

and guitar were simple background orchestrations for the castanets, their assonance not music but an agency for transmuting and transmitting the movements of the dance into enlarged and enriched currents of sensuality that the music, alone, did not contain and that the lissome, swaying, and untouching bodies could never have expressed. The alchemy of the castanets changed motion to emotion, and the very air around him seemed charged with the voluptuosity of the dance.

He felt himself confronting a vast tidal wave, crest curling above him, bending toward him, breaking.

It stopped; there was silence without motion.

Out of the darkness came one spontaneous *"Olé!"* and the dance and the music were done.

Solomon turned and reached behind him for the violin case, laid the instrument inside, and snapped the latches shut. He had been here before, he thought, on the banks of the Little Tennessee when Melinda had sung in the twilight. Each time this happened, he emerged from the experience with his angle of vision slightly altered, his viewpoint broadened.

More to the moment was Larry Morgan, Welshman cum Gypsy, the changeling. There had been a talented male dancer in the torchlight, a girl whose gifts approached artistry, and three violinists in the wings. But there had been only one artist whose genius was woven through the entire texture of the night—the boy with the Spanish guitar.

Walking back to the van, Melinda said, "Mr. Ricky, that Larry Morgan, he sure does make that guitar talk."

"He does more than that, Melinda. He gives it a soul."

"Arabella's learning me to dance, and Larry plays. When he plays, my feet can't help but do things."

"How long has he been playing for you?"

"Off and on, two or three days."

"You learning well?"

"Yes, sir. Larry, he say I's a better dancer than Arabella, but he don't want me telling Arabella."

"Why not?"

"She's spiteful."

"Who told you that?"

"Larry, he told me."

They fell silent, but Solomon was worried by a vague unease.

He had not known that Melinda was learning the fandango, which was no particular cause for concern, but the

242

criticism of Arabella by Larry might imply that Melinda was being manipulated into the current of tribal rivalries.

Larry was capable of acting from long-range motives. His mind had dimensions and could work from hidden purposes to create schisms and weld alliances.

Genius was supposed to carry with it its own sense of responsibility, but in the psyche of the Gypsy, no such sense existed.

It was his mood, Solomon decided, compounded of the night and the music and the torchlight casting shadows on dark faces, which had led to this sense of impending evil. His dark thoughts came from the guilt he felt from his enjoyment of a pagan festival, a most un-Jewish delight.

Obviously, the little bird had winged straight to Juanita with his offer of five thousand one hundred dollars for her hand in marriage, for she had become demure, and ladylike, and somewhat awed. He rather preferred the old hellraiser, but when she invited him over Sunday afternoon to enjoy a spot of wine with her and her present spouse, he accepted with formality.

As the wine loosened the tongue of Juanita, Solomon steered her into a discussion of Larry Morgan, initially complimenting the boy on his beautiful voice, musical ability, and stagecraft. Once the subject was introduced, Juanita attacked it with her old volubility. Larry's father, a Welshman who had floated downriver from the hill country, had joined them shortly after the tribe arrived in Louisiana from Spain. He had fallen so deeply in love with Larry's mother that he had forsaken his own people.

"Poor Andy. Being a *Gajo*, he wanted to boss his wife, but his wife wished to boss him. They were not happy. Then, his wife's sister's man ran away, and Lucia wished to come and live with them. Andy thought this would be good. They would fight each other, and he could rest, for he was tired.

"Ah, Lucia, María's sister, doted on Andy. He was a big man. His skin was like milk. His hair and eyes were blue. Then María grew jealous. She wanted her share of Andy.

"For a little while, he was happy. He had two wives working for him. True, he now had two bosses, but he no longer cared. They brought in much money. Much whiskey. If he was with Lucia, then he had to be with María. That María is a pig! When her turn came, she would grunt and squeal, and Lucia would have to go again.

"Poor Andy! He got thinner and thinner. He got weaker

and weaker. He coughed a lot. He no longer mounted them. They mounted him. That boy was always flat on his back. Is that not true, Nick?"

"*Si*, Juanita."

"Soon, he would not even open his eyes. He knew who was on him by the feel. I will say this for the boy, he did not mix them up. It was always 'Thank you, María,' or 'Thank you, Lucia.' He kept to the *Gajo* ways.

"One day, when they both grew tired and he did not open his eyes, they brought Juanita de Cordobiza, she who makes the lace—she was old, even then—and put Juanita on top of him. When he had had his pleasure, he said, without opening his eyes, 'Thank you, Juanita.'

"This made María and Lucia very angry. They wanted to beat Juanita because she had lain with their husband, but she was too old. They wanted to beat Andy because he had been unfaithful, but he was too weak. But the color came back to his cheeks, and he grew much better. So, they brought Juanita in, often, and he had three women.

"He died, but I will say this for the man, he never disappointed any of them. Is that not true, Nick?"

"*Si*," Nick said. "He was the only dead man I ever saw with a hard. In his coffin, he was a skeleton big with child."

"He died beautifully," Solomon said.

So, he socialized until the wine was gone and Nick departed without ceremony to take a nap. When Juanita left to go into the bushes, Solomon ambled back to his caravan, drowsy from the drinking.

He lay in the shade of his van and dozed until late afternoon, until awakened by the sound of footsteps. He sat up and somewhat to his surprise found that Larry was his visitor.

"Howdy, boy."

"Howdy, Mr. Ricky. I heared you playing t'other night, and you did right well. Mind playing that tune tonight you were sawing on yestiddy evening?"

"Happy to, boy."

"Melinda's dancing tonight. I reckoned ya'll might he'p us celebrate our Sunday."

"You think Melinda can dance good enough to entertain the people?"

"She can, sir. She sho'ly can."

He turned and was gone.

Larry announced him that night, and Solomon played

his composition. Politely, his audience clapped for an encore, and for no reason known to himself, he fiddled "Oh, Susanna." He was surprised when they sang the tune. Their spontaneity prompted the "Blue-Tailed Fly," and he bowed out with the group in a happy mood.

As he seated himself with the other musicians, he thought, in a happy frame of mind, they would be more tolerant of Melinda's efforts when she danced.

Tomás said to him, "No violins tonight. Only the guitar."

Larry used no dramatic devices to bring Melinda on. He sat in the center of the flambeaux with his guitar, and he asked Melinda out of the crowd. There was no prelude, no tension in the crowd, just the girl Melinda standing in the center of the light, with Larry seated beside her. She wore her Gypsy skirt and the low-cut blouse he had once been chary about. She wore a coin anklet lent by Arabella, and she had no castanets.

She stood there, nervous and frightened, glancing down at Larry with an imploring look. For the first time, Solomon saw Larry smile. His smile had a debonair quality, as if it were saying to her, "To hell with them, girl!"

He slapped his thigh with his open palm and began to strum the guitar, slowly, easily, quietly. Almost reluctantly, as if she moved in mud, her feet padded the ground. Larry watched her face as he gradually stepped up the rhythm, gauging her emotions, allowing her time to overcome her stage fright and to lose herself in the dance.

He must have seen her relax; he increased the tempo, and she glided into a slow, shuffling form of flamenco buck-and-wing, arms loosening, moving with an easier rhythm and freer motion. Morgan was a puppet master, controlling the girl by guitar strings. Solomon relaxed slightly, and though she had little of Arabella's grace, she had more natural rhythm.

Suddenly, she raised her hands upward in a quick but graceful movement and clapped twice, arching her head and shoulders back in a manner that distorted the haughty arch of the fandango. The staccato sound cracked over the heads of the onlookers, and they leaned forward. Her shuffling movement became more sinuous, abandoned, as Larry stepped up the tempo.

Now the guitar was strumming a steady, incessant beat augmented by the thudding of her feet, as her hands glided up the length of her body, slapping her thighs, strumming against the taut muscles of her stomach, caressing the rise of her breasts, and leaping upward as she flung her head back and her pelvis forward at the two-clap of her hands.

Olés rang from the crowd.

Four times she moved thus, her hands flowing downward, slapping, to rise again to the explosive two-clap. The repitition was hypnotic, the strumming of her hands, the sudden pause, and the clap-clap. On the fifth movement, she clapped thrice, and the guitar swung into a faster tempo.

She was moving into a strange fandango with a juba pat, Africa's answer to Spain; it was not dancing—it was sorcery.

Into a glade in Kentucky, dark, dissolute, and long-dead gods were being summoned. Her hands pounding against the taut muscles of the stomach were tom-toms throbbing through the jungles of the Congo, calling for Kuwa, for Tara, for Cagn, calling to Mumbo Jumbo.

She rippled now in undulations as her legs spread to bring her closer to earth, her hands crossing and uncrossing to beat a tattoo on her knees and against her thighs. Closer she came, arching her body backwards, opening her body to the fecund earth. Her hands lifted to the darkness as her torso lowered, came almost parallel to the ground, and the incredible shimmying continued. With the folds of her arms and the rippling of her body, she caressed the night, which had become a living thing, and though she clapped no longer, Solomon could hear, or thought he heard, beneath the strumming of the guitar the clicking of dry bones on dry bones, the witch doctor's rattle.

It was lewd, bestial, and beautiful.

"La Zarabanda!" Old Tomás whispered beside him.

She held her hands upward in supplication, and slowly, she began to rise, as if lifted by invisible hands; and when she stood, spread-eagled upright and quivering, the music stopped to freeze her in the classic pose of the fandango, but the dry bones rustle of the voodoo charm continued, out of the night and the darkness.

Suddenly, and with intense relief, he pinpointed the sound. Melinda was making it with her teeth.

When the music resumed, it was at a slower tempo, and she moved with the languid grace of satiety back into the conventional movements of the fandango. Solomon, watching, felt alienated from her. This girl was not his student. She was not the girl he had seen naked in the twilight and had taken. He had never known this woman.

The music ended, and Melinda returned to the body, bowing shyly in the slow bend of a curtsy, leaning forward until her hair fell below her extended knee, her palms spread outward. The dance was over.

Instead of applause, there was a concerted rush forward to grab the girl. Solomon, fearing they meant her harm, leaped to his feet, but they were lifting her to their shoulders, passing her from hand to hand above the crowd, as the night rang with *olés*.

They passed her to him, and he took her on his shoulder as he tucked the violin under his arm. She was leaning down and asking, "Did I do all right, Mr. Ricky?" even as they patted her and complimented her in English.

"You hear their answer," he shouted to her above the din as he moved easily through the gradually dispersing crowd.

He carried her all the way to the van on his shoulder, and when they stood alone, he asked, "Where'd you learn that dance, Melinda?"

"I don't know, sir. Some I learned from Arabella, some from Larry, and some I just made up. It was like I was remembering something."

"What else have they been teaching you, other than to snare rabbits and tell fortunes?"

"Lordy, I don't know, Mr. Ricky. I'm dukkering real good, and I reckon I learned their dancing."

"I reckon you did," he said, lounging on the chest as she went to the drawer for her playing cards.

"They been teaching me a little of their jibe too. *'Sar shan'* means 'hello.'"

"That's more than I know," he said, thinking he had been remiss. Involved in his efforts to get the tribe moving, he had left her to her own devices. He had tolerated her fortune-telling in the hope that cards would make her more familiar with numbers, but that could be an error. One of his aims as a teacher had been to rid her of superstition.

"You don't really believe in those cards, do you?"

"I looks at it this way, Mr. Ricky, if I believe and they's right, then I'm right. If I believe and they's wrong, then it don't make no difference, 'cause they's wrong."

"Do you still believe in ha'nts?"

"Not in the daytime. When I's by myself, at night, it don't hurt none to believe just a little bit."

"You're afraid of witches, aren't you?"

"Yes, sir. I sure is."

"All right. If you can tell fortunes by cards, that would be divination, foretelling the future. If you can practice divination, then that is witchcraft. Do you want to be a witch?"

She thought for a moment, apparently trying to follow his logic. "Would I get to ride a broom?"

"Yes."

"I'd like to ride an old broom. I'd hop on that broom and fly over the trees, all the way to Cincinnati. None of them pattyrollers gonna catch me, no sir." Her eyes glowed with the fancy that had struck her. "Yes, sir. I'd surely like to be a witch."

Logic had only an incidental place in her thinking. She was mostly imagination, dark or bright, and with a half-tinge of remorse, he regretted trying to disenchant her. He said, "Well, since you're committed to a life of witchcraft, I might as well join in the fun. Tell my fortune, Melinda. I've got a dime here, and I'll cross your palm with silver. That's the tradition, I hear."

Genuine fear flashed in her eyes. "I don't want to tell your fortune, Mr. Ricky."

"Why not?"

" 'Cause it might be bad."

"Are you scared for me, Melinda?"

" 'Course I is, you's all I got."

"You got the Gypsies."

"I don't want them Gypsies."

"I thought you were doing right well with them."

"That boy, Jerry, he scares me. He looks like he wants to eat me."

"He likes you, Melinda, and little Mike's offered me five thousand dollars to let you be his wife."

"That boy ain't got a pot. But I don't mind little Mike. He's nice. Larry's smart. But that Jerry, he ask me why the wagon don't shake nights."

Solomon was suddenly alert. "What did you tell him?"

"I told him you took it slow and easy."

"Now, you wouldn't have just let drop a little remark that I had my thing cut off?"

She giggled. "That's what I told Arabella when she asked me why the wagon didn't shake. Them people must stay up all night waiting for our wagon to shake."

Solomon laughed. "You made me the five-day wonder of the whole tribe with that little remark."

"Mr. Ricky, I been thinking. Maybe, 'fore we go to sleep tonight, we maybe can jump up and down a little bit, after

248

we blow out the light. Then, they won't think you is no good."

"Right sure it's me you're worried about?"

"Maybe," she said. "But it's me Jerry's after, and he's done plaited his troth with Arabella."

"Plighted his troth . . . Don't worry about what the Gypsies think, Melinda. You going to tell my fortune?"

"I better not."

He rolled over to a sitting position. "Honey, I've got to get this superstition out of your mind. If those cards tell us anything bad, then we'll know what to be ready for. We'll be prepared, and that'll be good for us. If they tell us good, it'll make you happier, and it won't make me lower my guard, because I don't believe them, good or bad."

He moved over beside her and sat down. "Deal me a hand."

"You deals them," she said. "I don't. And you shuffles them."

She handed him the cards, and he riffled them together. He tapped them into an even pack and set them on the chest top.

"Keep shuffling," she said.

He resumed a slow shuffle, and she leaned forward, studying his face and his eyes.

"Stop."

He quit shuffling and tapped the cards into a neat pile. Still looking into his eyes, she reached over and drew the top card.

"Now, you keep shuffling."

He resumed the shuffle, but Melinda refused to turn the card over. She looked down at the card and continued to look as he slowly shuffled.

"Turn it over," he said. "It's not going to change spots."

" 'Course, one card don't mean nothing," she assured herself, and flipped it over.

It was the king of diamonds.

She almost leaped from her seat in excitement, clapping her hands with joy.

"That's you, Mr. Ricky. That's you. Just yesterday, I was talking to little Mike, and I told him if there was any card in the deck that was you, it was the king of diamonds. That means nothing's gonna stand 'fore you. Least not for long it ain't. That means you gonna get us to Cincinnati sure as hell."

"One card don't mean nothing," he reminded her.

"I'd rather have that rabbit foot with me than against me."

She drew now, with more confidence, a ten of spades she laid to the left of the king and a four of spades she laid to the right. She studied the cards with a dubious expression on her face and said, "They say you been sick, but you gonna get well. I don't remember nothing like that."

Suddenly he was interested. To Melinda, sickness was an ailment of the body, but there was a sickness of the soul.

Suddenly her face brightened. "That four telling me you been real worried, but don't you worry none. That little old four of spades says we gonna get to Cincinnati."

Suddenly, he liked the feel of that rabbit's foot in his pocket.

"Now, we gets to the future."

She was optimistic, selecting three cards which she placed above and to the right of the king's trio, three to the upper left, three to the lower left, and three to the lower right, working counterclockwise. She flipped the cards as she picked them, and did so with the crisp movement of a skilled card player.

She made no comment and revealed no emotion until she flicked over the final card, a nine of spades, which she laid in the lower right-hand corner. Her hand paused slightly as she placed it, and anxiety flickered in her eyes.

He watched her as she assumed an air of solemnity and deep concentration. She resembled a little girl playing at cards, a continent and eons removed from the sorceress whose dance had woven a voodoo spell over the camp less than an hour ago.

"Now," she said, "looks like you got a woman waiting for you in Cincinnati, and you gonna make a lot of money. Or maybe you gonna lose a lot of money. Them cards say you got a dark lady in your life . . . Your wife dark?"

"Her hair is."

"Now, that jack there's a girl, 'cause it faces a seven of hearts. Them cards say you got woman trouble coming." She looked at him disapprovingly. "Mr. Ricky, you fooling around with some woman up North?"

"Of course not. I'm faithful to my wife."

" 'Cept that once. Now don't you go stepping out on your wife with nobody else."

"Just tell my fortune, Melinda, and forgo the advice."

"Yes, sir. Now, down here," she pointed to the lower left

trio of cards, "they's two men fighting over you, and that ace of spades means it's a powerful fight, . . ."

Her remarks about the women were hogwash, but the two fighting men could well be Kelly and Blood.

". . . a fight between an old man and a young man. That young man. Looks like he's redheaded."

His nerve ends tingled at her remark. Kelly was red-haired, and he had not told her of the conflict between the two men.

"What about that nine of spades?" His question was sharp and abrupt. "Is that the card of death?"

"There ain't no death card," she said with forced casualness, "leastways, not for Gypsies. 'Course, I don't like all them spades. Too many spades mean trials and tribulations."

"We're not making this trip for our health. We've got to expect trials and tribulations."

Her face suddenly brightened from its troubled perplexity. "Ain't no nine of spades gonna stand up to no king of diamonds. That king knock that nine of spades on he's ass. Why, Mr. Ricky, that king of diamonds . . ."

Arching out of the darkness in a leap that brought him three feet inside the van to land in a semicrouch on the balls of his bare feet, Jerry Romano stood in the lantern light, shirtless, the lantern playing on his sinewy muscles and glinting against the knife in his hand. His eyes were flaring with strange lights, and he was licking his lips. "I'm cracking your woman, *Yehuda*. Get out or get your guts slit."

Calmly, Solomon asked, "You know what you're doing, boy?"

"You goddamned right I do. *Vamos!*"

Solomon rose, slowly, turning, and the boy leaped on the opposite chest, saying, "Crawl along the chest. Stay out of the aisle."

Solomon crawled the length of the chest, eased off the end, hearing Melinda say, "Why, Jerry, honey, Mr. Ricky won't fret none if you wants a little jelly roll. You just lay down that old knife and come over here."

She giggled, low, thrilling, inviting. "Let the old man watch from outside, honey, 'cause he can't do nothing but watch, nohow. You just come right here, baby."

Still moving slowly, sickened as much by the purr in the voice of the girl as by the madness of the boy, he stepped down into darkness, hearing her caress the lad with words.

"I been hankering for that thing of yours ever since I first seed you. You just drop your pants and come to your little old bird's nest. I ain't had no real loving since I left Georgia."

Well, Solomon thought, he had scored a victory of sorts. At least she had said "loving."

"Hey, old man," she called derisively, "want to see how it's done? Maybe you can learn something."

He looked in and saw that she had scooted the edge of the cabinet, saw the boy lower his trousers, his buttocks lost in shadow but the knife still glinting in his hand. He saw Melinda's legs lift and open in brazen invitation as the boy moved forward, his breathing audible outside the van. Then, he saw the boy flying backward, his trousers at half-mast, and tumble and fall on his back as she kicked his shoulders.

"Watch the knife," she screamed, and continued to scream, meaninglessly, as her kick had propelled the boy's head through the door of the van and Solomon had swung his fist viciously against the exposed chin.

He grabbed the head and jerked with such force that Jerry's heels cleared the floor of the van in a straight line, and there was a sickening thud as the unconscious body hit the ground. He raised his boot to smash it into the face.

He halted, not because of the advancing lanterns bobbing through the darkness but because of the knowledge, certain and sure, that the skull he crushed under his boot heel would be the wrong skull. The boy who should die for this deed was Larry Morgan.

Chapter Ten

When the lanterns reached him, the evidence was spread before the gathering crowd—the unconscious boy, the knife lying beside the outflung hand, the girl moaning hysterically in the van. Solomon kicked the knife away from the hand as Jerry's mother ran through the crowd and knelt beside the boy, repeating *"Devla! Devla!"*

As Jerry stirred, the encircling Gypsies stepped back for Ramon, who walked up to Solomon and asked, in Spanish, "Was he trying to rape the girl?"

"Si," Solomon answered.

"And he drew the knife on you?"

"Si."

Ramon turned to one of the men and said, "Go get a rope and truss him up. Tie him to the oak tree by the spring. There'll be a *kris* at eight in the morning. You can all go home now. It's over."

"He didn't hurt the girl," Solomon said. "He only frightened her."

"The girl does not matter," Ramon said. "He drew a knife on one who is not a *Gitano*."

Whimpering and still murmuring "God! God!," Jerry's mother rose and walked into the night.

Solomon stood and watched as the man returned with the rope and tied the boy, who was moaning and conscious now. They bound his hands behind him, and they bound his feet, and then, they secured the bindings together so that his legs and arms were doubled behind him.

Observing the device, Solomon ventured anew to gain

253

some consideration for the boy. "Ramon, he did not hurt me. Why bind him so?"

Ramon turned to him, speaking with impatience and sincerity. "No, he did not hurt you, *Yehuda,* but he hurt us. We live on the edge of oblivion, and we must walk carefully. If he had cut you, the *Gajos* would have been down on us like wolves. We have our laws, *Yehuda,* and they must be obeyed . . . Take him!"

Two men lifted Jerry and carried him into the darkness, led by Ramon carrying a lantern. Solomon stood alone in the lantern light falling from the open door of the van and listened to the sobbing of the frightened girl.

He climbed back into the van. She was lying on her stomach, her face cradled in her arms, sobbing convulsively. He sat down on the edge of the chest beside her and placed a hand on her shoulders, patting her slowly, abstractedly.

He, too, was shaken, but not by the violence. It had happened so quickly and was over so quickly that the entire episode was dwindling in his memory with the speed of an express train.

The aspect of the episode that left him dazed had been the behavior of Melinda. She had not swooned, and she had interposed her own body between him and the knife. Melinda, of no name, had acted in a tradition of bravery that would have done honor to a European queen.

Her sobbing was slowing now, and he asked, "Why did you risk getting slashed with that knife?"

"He was mean mad, Mr. Ricky. I was scared he was going to cut your guts out with that knife. I kept thinking 'bout that nine of spades."

"You could have been killed, girl."

"Don't make no difference 'bout me. I's just a nigger. You's a fine gentleman, and you helps colored folks."

O Lord, he thought, have You touched this woman?

She had not even acted from personal motives. She had offered up her life for an abstract good—her estimate of his value to her people—yet knowing him a mercenary hired to carry her to freedom.

Mimicking her dialect, he slapped her idly across the neck with the back of his hand. "If you ever think of yourself as a 'wuthless nigger' again, I'm going to whup hell out of you."

Lethargically he arose, thinking, in her dark shell burned a spirit whose worth was beyond his power to measure.

He took the candlestick from its compartment and the candles from their drawer. He raised the globe of the lantern and lighted a candle, placing the candlestick on the forward cabinet. He lighted each candle in turn and inserted them in the candlestick. This girl whom he had badgered, cozened, inspired, berated, and tutored might well be what the Catholics called a saint. It might be that through her he had walked and talked with God.

He turned back and sat down beside her.

"Melinda, your Jesus spoke in parables, a little story with more than one meaning. They may not be factual stories, but they're always true stories. I want to tell you such a parable.

"When I was a young man, I was standing on the corner of Front Street and Butler, in Cincinnati. I had just gotten off the packet from Pittsburgh, and I didn't know my directions too well. But an address had been given to me, and I inquired of a constable.

"As I remember, he told me to go north on Butler to High Street and cross the canal to Ellen.

"Following the constable's directions, I found the house, a shabby little frame building painted a dingy white with green shutters. A few pickets were missing from the fence, I remember, and a few shingles had been blown from the roof. I walked up to the door of that mean little house on that shabby street and knocked.

"God answered the door."

She lay silent for a moment, and then she asked, "What'd He look like?"

"She was black," Solomon said.

Melinda giggled.

She had missed the point of his story, but he was happy that she laughed.

"Say, Melinda, you remember that sad little song you sang on the banks of the Little Tennessee back in North Carolina?"

"Yes, sir. That was sure a sad song."

"I remembered that second stanza when I went looking for you along the Wilderness Road. Listen."

Seated beside her, he sang both measures to "O, Mistress Mine, Where Are You Roaming?"

"That's real pretty, Mr. Ricky. You sing right well."

She lifted her eyes to the candles. "You gonna thank God?"

"In a manner of speaking," he said.

255

He went to the door and stood for a moment looking out at the stars above the serriform skyline of trees. The night was clear and cloudless, and the stars seemed remote and cold and as indifferent as God. Looking at them, he felt the continuity of generations, for these same stars had guided the legions of Caesar and had shone with equal brightness on the camps of the Assyrians and the camps of the Jews. Tonight, they would not quiver in their courses for all that he might do, and Leah, his beloved, would sleep beneath them undisturbed.

He pulled the door toward him, hooking it slightly ajar, and deliberately and completely he disrobed, feeling free and unashamed in his actions. There was no longer need for furtiveness. He knew what he had to do, and he would do it without fear of remorse. Standing above her, he said, "Turn over, Melinda."

With a slight sigh that told him she had been watching, she turned on her back. Her head remained pillowed on her arms, and her eyes were closed, not from modesty or shame, he sensed, but to draw a curtain on the night's violence.

As gently as a surgeon unfrocking a patient for an operation, he reached down and lifted her skirt, moving it upward over her thighs as she arched her body for its passage. She held her hands up as he cleared her head, and he folded the garment neatly and laid it on the cabinet across the aisle. He turned back to her. Her hands were again clasped behind her head and her eyes closed. When he touched her, there was a sharp intake of breath, and the tempo of her breathing increased. His long fingers fluted gently over her, caressing, manipulating, and convulsively, she reached down and took him in her hand.

There was no urgency in his actions. He felt natural and free and innocent, until she said, with almost a plea, "I's ready, I's truly ready."

He stretched out beside her, cradling her in his arms and kissing her neck. She cringed and giggled her low, liquid giggle, saying, "I knows you're a Yankee now."

In the traffic between them, no more articulate words were said, and none were needed. Whereas in their first encounter he had ridden a whirlwind, he felt, now, as a swimmer gliding without effort and without haste down a wide, warm, and dark river, moving slower as his passion mounted to prolong his sensations. After her initial and lonely flurry wherein she felt like a covey of quail released beneath him, she grew remarkably compliant, and he learned what Ramon had meant when he spoke of the love that drew on the resources of the soul. In learning, he was, unbeknownst, adding to the lore of the Gypsies; for this night would be long remembered throughout the tribe as The Night the Wagon Shook.

Solomon awakened shortly after dawn and lay on the pallet listening to a mockingbird rage at the sun. He smelled the dew-heavied odor of wood smoke and buckwheat batter from Melinda's breakfast fire, and he tried to sort from his memory the sensations of the night before, the music, the dancing, the fighting, and the carnal jousting. After a Gentile's weekend, it was pleasant to lie on a pallet with the cool humidity cloaking him in a weightless mantle that trapped the perfume of Melinda.

"Mr. Ricky, breakfast about done."

There was his ten-minute warning.

He stretched and rose.

In every man, there was a Melinda to be succumbed to or to be exorcised. He would succumb now, but he would be freed of her charms once the free-flowing Ohio was crossed.

After his toilet, he returned to watch her weave the magic of her deftness over the fire.

"Want me to fry you a little ham this morning, Mr. Ricky? Ham goes good with sorghum."

"No, thanks, Melinda."

"Reckon I ain't much good at converting."

"Brother Smith's methods don't work on me."

He sat down at the table, and she placed the platter before him. "They's holding court this morning over Jerry. Juanita yelled over to tell me I ought to come and bring my man. Why she call you 'my man'?"

"A little bird's been talking to her."

"Reckon I ought to dress up to go to court, Mr. Ricky?"

"Wouldn't be a bad idea. Shows respect."

She sat in silence for a moment, watching him eat.

"You kissed me last night, Mr. Ricky."

"Think I'd forgotten?"

"How you like them hot cakes?"

"Delicious, as always. Aren't you eating?"

"Don't reckon I's hungry."

"Hungry or not, eat something."

"I'll just have a sip of coffee."

"Why aren't you hungry?"

"Can't say."

"You know, but you can't say?"

"Mr. Ricky, I don't wants to sound disrespectful, but you's the prettiest man I ever did see."

"Then why're you fixing to tune up. You should be happy."

"I loves you, sir."

" 'I love you.' Not, 'I loves you.' Quit adding an s on your verbs. Why do you do that?"

" 'Cause that's the way I talks."

"Quit talking like that."

"I love you, Mr. Ricky."

"Now, that's better . . . It's fitting and proper that you should love your fellowman."

"Last night, you were telling me you loved me by the way you did it. You won't doing that to no man."

"I don't deny what I told you last night. But you're spoke for, so forget it."

"I ain't never going to forget it, Mr. Ricky, 'cause you meant it. I knows what I know."

"I didn't say I didn't mean it."

"Is Mr. Kelly nice as you?"

"Now, just how would I know that?"

"He's a Yankee, too."

"He's a different kind of Yankee. I've compounded an error. I'm a Hebrew Yankee."

"You don't talk like no Yankee. Your voice sounds soft, like Larry and me, and Miss Phoebe, and Massa Blake."

"I spend most of my time in the South."

"Why for you don't want me to talk like I talks?"

"I don't argue with your accent. You do all right, one word at the time. When you start stringing them together, that's when you play havoc with the language."

"What's 'play havoc'?"

"Make a mess out of."

"You sure done played havoc with them buckwheat cakes. Want some more?"

"No, thank you. I've had a sufficiency."

"Couldn't I fix you just one little bitty piece of ham?"

"Melinda, why do you keep on me to eat pork?"

" 'Cause I wants you to come to Jesus."

Out of the bright morning and the singing birds, the light talk of love and lighter talk of grammar, a deep sadness had come. With surprise and dismay, he saw the tears forming in her eyes, and he reached across the table to take the hand she was clenching and unclenching.

"Child, do you take your religion that seriously?"

"It ain't that, sir. I just don't want to go to heaven if you ain't there. I so does want to see you when I's an angel and we's both white."

"Melinda," his voice rang, "fry me a slice of that damned ham!"

For once, her movements were not graceful. She bolted from her camp chair, overturning it in her haste, and leaped to the oilcloth where the ham was laid. Feverishly, she sliced it, slapped it into the pan, and in a trice, her tender pink passport to the Christian heaven was lying on his plate.

In ecstasy, she watched him eat. He, feigning gusto after six buckwheat cakes, pronounced the ham succulent, tasty, and without a doubt the best ham he had ever eaten in his life. Finishing it, he slid back his plate.

"All right, Jezebel Jones, now, when we meet in heaven, I'll be pleased to greet you, and if these people don't move pretty quick, that may be sooner than you think."

She went inside to dress up. Over coffee, he wondered if after Kelly, after the tides of male passion had rolled over her, she would remember him and this summer's idyll. She might remember, for she was in the springtime of life, and the remembered roses of spring were always brighter. She might forget his name—did not, in fact, know it—but she would remember him, and in the pantheon of her sex heroes, he would be enshrined somewhere close to Brother Smith.

Court was a cleared area before the caravan of Ramon where a table with four empty chairs had been set. A whitewashed semicircle before the table defined the limits for spectators, and for once, Mrs. Sanchez did not tend the pot.

Bright red, green, or blue kerchiefs draped the necks of men wearing yellow, red, and purple shirts. He had assumed the trial would be an occasion for gravity, but from the colors around him, he concluded that a Gypsy court was a carnival.

Around him, the Gypsies were talking amiably, complimenting Melinda on her dance of the night before and complimenting Solomon for owning such a *Yehudni*, either avoiding the topic of the crime in their conversation or forgetting it. Precisely at eight, Ramon stepped from the door of his caravan, and the crowd grew silent.

He wore a red bandana tied around hs head beneath his hat, a red scarf around his neck, a silk shirt of lemon yellow, a belt studded with silver, and shoes. Casually, relaxed, he walked over and sat at the table.

Accustomed to the black-robed judges of Anglo-Saxon courts, Solomon breathed easier for Jerry when he saw the colorful dress and marked the informal manner with which Ramon took his seat. Black was the color of death, and any prisoner who looked up to a judge on an American bench looked up to doom. A prisoner looking down on this pied magistrate could reasonably expect little more than a friendly reprimand.

Ramon was joined by three others: Pedro Sanchez, the father of Arabella; old Tomás; and a lanky, pale-skinned gypsy whom Solomon remembered only as Juan. The council of the tribe of Sanchez was in session.

After the others were seated, Ramon made an announcement in the Romany language. Shortly thereafter, Jerry, flanked by two men, was ushered into the semicircular clearing before the bench. He walked with an easy erectness, but anxiety showed in his eyes.

Jerry faced Ramon and nodded several times in assent, apparently, to questions asked. The Rom jib was a language, incomprehensible to Solomon.

Ramon dropped his questioning of Jerry and turned to a discussion with the council.

For a while, the members were voluble, waving their hands, interrupting each other, and sometimes appealing to Ramon for assistance. Gradually, the conversation tapered off, and Ramon rapped on the table with his knuckles to get attention.

He turned to Jerry, talking easily and, judging from his expression, paternally to the boy. Once he smiled, but there was little affability in the smile.

He paused, and his face assumed a solemn expression. Jerry perceptibly straightened to attention as he spoke.

Jerry shrugged his shoulders, muttered an answer, and slumped.

He turned and walked away, took a deep breath, and straightened. The men who had escorted him into the trial area again stepped up beside him. As the crowd moved away, Solomon turned and walked over to Juanita, asking, "What happened?"

"Ramon was very kind. He gave Jerry his choice between leaving the tribe and taking a good whipping. Jerry will be whipped."

Solomon, relieved, asked, "Who'll give him the whipping? His mother?"

"Oh, no," Juanita laughed. "His mother was not offended. You were offended, but you cannot whip the boy because you are not a *Gitano*. So, the family of Arabella was next offended, because Jerry is betrothed to Arabella. Now, Pedro Sanchez cannot whip the boy, because he is of the council. Then it must be either Pedro's Romany or Arabella. That will be decided by the family of Pedro."

"When will the sentence be carried out?"

"Right now. It would be cruel to keep the boy waiting."

They did not keep the boy waiting.

They led him to the oak tree beside the spring where he had been tied for the night and where the mockingbird apparently nested, for it had gone berserk, caroling with frenzy from the highest bough of the oak.

Jerry took off his shirt and extended his hands. They took the rope still lying under the tree and tied his hands. They hoisted him by his bound wrists from a limb until only the balls of his feet touched the ground. Solomon saw his back muscles ripple under the weight of his body on his taut arms.

"Who will wield the whip?" Ramon asked Pedro.

"Arabella," replied Pedro.

With the thin, delicate girl wielding the lash, Solomon felt that her lover's punishment would be mild.

"What they gonna do, Mr. Ricky?" Melinda asked.

"I'm afraid Jerry's in for a flogging."

"Mr. Ricky, I done seen a flogging. I got to watch this one?"

"It might be bad manners not to. Anyway, I suspect it's only a ritual whipping. Arabella's going to use the whip."

"Mr. Ricky, I see that girl pick an acorn off a high limb with that whip. I sure wouldn't want no whipping from her."

There was no expression on Jerry's face when his executioner was named and none on the face of the onlookers, who were forming into two lines about ten yards apart with the polite attentiveness of cricket watchers on an English lawn. Only Arabella evinced an emotion as she stepped forward to take the whip which had been brought to Ramon. Her face was set in anger.

She walked forward and accepted the lash, fourfolded, looked over at the almost-suspended body of the boy, and walked away to stand, hands on hips, to gauge the distance of her target. She took the whip and flipped it backward, uncoiling its length. Even in her small hand the lash was ugly and seemed lethal.

It was a Spanish *querta* with its short stock and braided thongs tapering to a point, and it was the bullwhip of a Georgia or Carolina cracker in its length. But it was too big and too heavy for so frail a girl. The size of the instrument would be a brake on her anger, for its weight would wear down her energy.

She arched back slightly, throwing her whip hand behind her and her free hand forward to balance her torso, and brought the whip forward with the easy, overhand motion of an expert fisherman casting a fly. The whip snaked off the ground, looped through the air, and swished down the aisle of onlookers. Whipping past her head, the tip of the whip was barely above her head, forming a narrow-troughed, elongated U down which the tip uncoiled, on a straight line, with a speed which seemed incredibly out of proportion to the effort behind it. When the braided tip thudded against his flesh, Jerry's body shook from the impact. As the lash coiled back, Solomon saw a lurid, inch-long welt growing below the lad's right shoulder.

Jerry made no sound when the whip struck.

Arabella stepped back slightly to adjust her aim, and again the whip snaked off the ground to swish through the air, but now the swish ended in a sharp crack. From the sound, Solomon thought she had missed, but as the whip flowed back in its easy arc, he saw a thin trickle of blood swelling from a spot adjacent to the welt, and he knew he was wrong.

She had found the range with the second stroke, and the whip no longer touched the ground. She moved into an effortless rhythm. Her shoulders swayed backward, pivoting easily on her hips, and then forward. Her legs spread apart, her back to Solomon, there was hardly movement beneath her pelvis except for the tensing and relaxing of her buttocks, the coiling and uncoiling of the muscles of her lower legs. Framed in a panel that excluded her victim, she would have been grace and swaying rhythm, but above the body bending forward and arching back, liquid in its ebb and flow, Arabella's face was frozen into a mask of hatred and scorn. With each forward bend of her body, a new globule of blood sprang up on the back of the boy.

Jerry Romano was not being flogged, he was being flayed by a fury-driven machine of torture.

Blood flowed in the crevice down the small of his back. Dammed by the cord that held his tousers in place, the flow spread to stain the edge of his trousers, the stain growing. Bit by bit, with professional detachment, Arabella was tearing his skin to ribbons, moving slowly across and down.

Eastward, the sun had risen high enough to find holes through the leaves of the tree, and the light dappled the blood on Jerry's torso with leaf patterns. The mocking-bird, silenced by the initial sound of the lash, had grown accustomed to the steady, demonic swish and crack and had resumed singing. Muted sunlight and birdsong touched the scene with tranquility.

Solomon did not know whether the soaking of the blood or the cutting of the lash loosened the rope Jerry used as a belt, but the trousers slipped and fell to encircle his ankles. Bare, white, and unbloodied, his buttocks gleamed in the tree-splattered light.

The sight of unmarred flesh stirred Arabella to greater fury, and she stepped forward, sweeping the whip with a sidearm motion. The lash swished forward, curled around his hip, and slashed downward toward the hidden groin.

He moaned, and the sound was his undoing.

As the lash raked backwards from his body, his pinioned ankles combined with the blood-slick turf to loosen the grip of his feet. His body swung to the pull of the back-drawn whip, swinging as easily as a vane in a breeze, to expose his side, his forehip, and finally his pubes. As the whip stroked steadily against that too-delicate flesh, his moans rose to a high, keening whimper of animal agony.

He was exposed to the eyes of the crowd and the tip of the merciless whip, and there was no doubt, now, as to the target of Arabella.

She stepped back, resuming the overhand motion that forewarned Solomon of the deadly crack. Frozen a split second by horror at her intention, he lunged forward and lunged too late. The whip struck.

Jerry screamed with a sound that died too quickly.

Before Solomon reached her, Arabella pivoted in a half circle, facing in his direction, bending at the knees, her skirts flaring as she dipped in a travesty of a curtsy from which she did not arise.

She sank to the ground, arms spreading apart and palms upward, her skirt flaring around her like the opening petals of a rose, her head dropping forward. The sun cleared a gap in the leaves, and the rays caught her fallen form in a spotlight, illuminating her shoulders and the top of her hair, extending down into her drooping blouse to reveal the nipples of her breasts, circled with sparse hairs and swollen in tumescence. Her shoulders heaved and subsided in exhaustion, and standing above her, he could hear the sough-sough of her breathing.

She might have been a ballet dancer taking her bow had it not been for the bullwhip, which dropped from her hand and snaked away coiling and sinuous to the feet of the bleeding boy who dangled from the tree limb, spinning slowly above a pool of blood.

Solomon kicked the handle of the whip away from the girl and looked over the line of stolid faces across from him. He saw Larry Morgan, mouth gaping, lips wet, eyes glazed, and turned and walked over to him, saying to him in a voice hoarse with anger, "You're the son of a bitch who should have been tied to that tree."

Morgan turned and walked away.

Solomon walked back to Melinda, who stood with bemused horror to watch the Gypsies lower Jerry to the ground.

"We'll take our chances with the Gentiles," he said, "because I'm not staying with these brutes any longer."

"Yes, sir," she said, but she did not move. She was watching the litter-bearers move forward, carrying a tarp supported by sapling poles, where two men waited with the limp body swung between them.

He took her arm and steered her away from the scene, back toward the encampment and the van. They walked over a carpet of clover still scented by the morning's dew and heavy with the hum of bees.

"That Arabella, she's mean," Melinda said. "She sure played havoc on Jerry's back."

His anger subsiding, he fumbled at an attempt to ameliorate her horror. "I don't think she was mean, Melinda. I think it was sort of a ritual flogging that got a little out of hand . . . She let her enthusiasm kind of carry her away."

"I don't know some of them words," Melinda said dubiously, "but if they means she ain't mean, I sure as

264

hell don't know what you mean. She popped his peter, Mr. Ricky. She didn't have no call to do that."

His rhetoric had been no better than his rationale. He tried again.

"I meant," he said, "that even though Arabella was mad at Jerry, she wasn't mad at him because he had done her wrong, not entirely. She was working out something deep inside her. He'd not only wronged her. He'd wronged her people, his people. She was punishing him for that, too."

"What's that?"

"I don't know," he said, "but the whipping was something Jerry needed. Something he wanted."

He was attempting to explain the inexplicable, he thought. Jerry had been tried for violating a taboo, the violation of which had imperiled the safety of the group, but connotations of tribal betrayal in his act had turned Arabella from an executioner into a torturer.

For no crime at all, but for the mere intention to commit a crime, an untutored boy had faced torture rather than expulsion from his tribe. Solomon Villaricca could not plead the innocence of ignorance.

He had also betrayed his tribe. Twice, he had broken the law against adultery. He had forgotten Sabbath, borne false witness, lied, stolen, dishonored his parents, practiced covetousness, contemplated murder, denied his God, and he had made a mockery of the dietary laws of his people.

Solomon Villaricca should have been tied to that tree. Leah should have wielded that whip, and the Congregation of the Temple of Judea should have watched in silent approval.

"Hear me, O God, for my sins are many."

"You talking to yourself again, Mr. Ricky?"

"I was talking to the Lord, honey, in Hebrew."

"You talk English, Mr. Ricky. Jesus don't understand them foreign tongues."

He could not desert Israel. Great were the Greeks with their logic and mighty the Romans with their laws, but the Children of Israel had led humanity out of paganism. Only his people, among all the barbarians, had held to the image of one God, and that God universal, and that God just. Yet, he had thrown away his yarmulke, while a boy had faced death for the integrity of a tribe which held not a single claim on human history.

His course before him was plain. He must turn again to face Israel and lay the ghosts of this sinful August before the free-flowing Ohio was crossed.

He put an avuncular arm around the tiny black girl.

"Child," he said, "we'll be facing the patrols from now on out, and my love for you must be as a brother to his sister. Do you understand?"

"You swearing off again, Mr. Ricky?"

Half lifting his face to the heavens, his voice rolled with awesome solemnity as he answered, "Yes, I have sworn."

"Oh, shit!" Melinda said.

He filled the water cask and pried up the cooking spit as Melinda stowed the gear and went about mopping the van. He left her stowing the gear and walked moodily back to the pasture for the mules.

He had come to the shank of August, wasted six days and provisions for six days, thrown away thirty dollars, and still had to face the fugitive-slave patrols alone.

Slowly, reluctantly, he returned with the mules and harnessed them to the wagon.

For a while, they sat in the cool interior of the fresh-mopped van as he drilled Melinda in the place-names of the towns through which they would pass. He drew a map and explained to her the routes she must take from various points along the way in the event that he was apprehended and she escaped.

He gave her the name and address of a Quaker family in Covington, knowing that if she reached Covington, alone, the collection of his fee from Kelly would have long since become academic. Then, he broke the bad news to her, telling her she must stay in the chest, day and night. "There'll be pattyrollers everywhere, all the time, so it must be done."

"Don't you fret none, Mr. Ricky. I'll do right well."

"Very well, Melinda. In you go. Remember, if I'm stopped, wait for nightfall to attempt your escape. Follow the North Star."

She took her primer and her slate into the chest with her, maintaining that there would be light enough through the airholes for her to practice reading and writing her name.

"You decided on your name yet?" he asked.

" 'Bout to, Mr. Ricky. 'Bout to."

"If I'm not stopped before nightfall, I'll see you 'round

about Walnut Valley. If not, may your years be long and your children many."

"If I has a lot of children, I's going to name my first boy after you. I's going to call him Big Peter."

Her giggle was cut off by the thud of the closing lid.

He paused for a moment before he climbed upon the seat, wondering if he should walk over and bid Juanita and Nick farewell. He shrugged his shoulders, stepped up, and grabbed the reins. He had wasted enough time already with these brutes.

He wheeled the mules in a short turning circle, casting a farewell glance down the avenue of caravans. Lined up in the bright morning sun, they were gaily colored and embellished with wood carving. To the eyes of a casual artist, the scene might have been charming, but connotations warped his vision. Yet, gazing down the vista, he felt a sadness for the disparity between reality and appearance . . . Then, it struck him that there was something wrong with the scene, something missing!

No gypsies lounged in front of the wagons, and the tents were gone from behind them.

He reined the mules up and sat for a moment, watching.

Far down the avenue, beyond the encampment, he could see men moving in the pasture. Even as he watched, he saw a distant figure emerge, leading a horse, then another, moving purposefully, moving toward the caravans.

The camp was moving out.

He tapped three loud and solid strokes on the side of the van, leaped down, and went back, unlocking the door.

"Put your scarf on, girl, and come on out! We're riding to Lexington in style."

In a matter of minutes, they were flowing past him in a river of color, and the teams were led by grinning Roms who waved to him as they passed. In the cool, clean air, Melinda sat beside him on the seat as they watched the caravan go by, the gay caravan, the grand caravan, the glorious caravan, rolling, and rolling north.

Solomon rolled with them.

Into the long afternoon, the caravan snaked over the hills, looped around them, dipped into valleys, passed farmhouses where frightened dogs cowered under porches, passed slave gangs toiling in fields of tobacco or hemp. Moving north with the unhurried haste of an army confident of its might, *vardos* rolling with an easy jounce and sway, the caravan rumbled on into twilight and dusk. When

267

only a flicker remained to the day, it pulled into an abandoned field and parked.

Because of the ease and joy of his walk without fear into the Bluegrass Region, Solomon's antipathy toward the Gypsies was blunted from acute to abstract, but he did not mingle with them around the campfires, and Melinda held herself aloof. However, Juanita, the irrepressible, paid a visit and brought the latest gossip, which cheered Solomon

Arabella, who had walked all day with the wagon of Larry, was tending the wounds of Jerry with poultices. Jerry would live, Juanita said. "You can't kill a Gypsy."

Arabella had wept when she entered the van of the boy and had kissed his wounds.

"I hope she covered them all," Solomon said. "The boy'll be scarred for life, fore and aft."

"She will only love him better for his scars," Juanita said, "because a boy cannot become a man until he is scarred. And the last one, the one that made him scream, that one will give her greater pleasure for the rest of her life."

That night, Solomon lay across the aisle from Melinda with the door and window open to the night breezes. The caravan lay near the road, and before he slept, he heard a squad of horsemen go clattering by. Later, he was lulled to sleep by the faraway baying of running hounds.

On Tuesday, they rolled through the villages that bore the place-names Melinda had learned in desperation and in haste. From the seat of the van, she was able to watch the passing of Walnut Valley, Kingston, Rogers, and Richmond. At nightfall, they camped north of Richmond.

He who set a killing pace for himself was amazed at the speed with which the Gypsies moved. With no forays into the countryside, no long delays for meals at noon, they drove from dawn to dusk to reach predetermined campsites. At their current rate, they should reach Lexington by noon tomorrow. He would then be within two days striking distance of Cincinnati, plenty of time to be home with Leah for the Sabbath with an extra thousand dollars in his pocket.

They moved out shortly after sunrise on Wednesday, with Solomon's van midway in the procession. He had discovered that there was no particular order in the positioning of the *vardos* other than the fact that Ramon's van always was in the lead.

He was third from the lead wagon when the caravan passed through Walnut Hill. Beyond Walnut Hill, a side road branched off for Nicholas Village. Standing at the road junction was a sorrel. Astride it sat a huge man. Behind him, another man of lesser size sat aboard a smaller roan. The man in front raised his hand to halt the wagon of Ramon.

When he held his hand aloft, Solomon, at a distance of forty yards, could see the tin star glinting on his shirt. Solomon turned and waved Melinda into the van and walked forward as Ramon halted the train behind him with an upraised hand.

Solomon kept in the background, well behind Ramon and Pedro, but close enough to hear what was said. He was confiident that his red shirt and bandana would disguise him, but if the sheriff was looking for him, the loyalty of the Gypsies would be very dubious. No doubt, they would inform on him unless they still held a lingering hope that he'd be worth one hundred dollars and the girl in Lexington.

Suddenly, he felt calm. Ramon was no fool. If he told the sheriff that Solomon and Melinda were with them, then he could be fined a thousand dollars for harboring a fugitive slave. Ramon would keep quiet unless he trusted the sheriff implicitly, and Gypsies did not trust *Gajos* implicitly.

The sheriff said, "Hello, Ramon."

"Hello there, cap'n. Good to see you again. How's things in Lexington?"

"Fair to middling," the sheriff answered. "How're things with the clan?"

"Fine, cap'n. Just fine. Y'all getting ready for a good fair in Lexington?"

"Yeah, Ramon, we'ns are, starting right now."

King Ramon, Solomon noted, who had acted with such imperiousness in arresting the boy and having him whipped, was whining in an accent that mirrored the sheriff's own, bowing, scraping, and "captaining" the sheriff at every opportunity.

"Y'all know fair opens tomorrow?"

"Yes, sir, cap'n. We'uns thought we'd come over and treat you to some dancing and do a little horse-trading, if the cap'n don't mind."

"The cap'n minds, boy. I ain't here as official greeter. I'm here as official stopper. You'uns ain't going to no god-damned fair, leastways not in Lexington, you ain't."

"Why cap'n, I'm surprised to hear you say that, nice as you've been to us."

"I reckoned you might be, but maybe you ain't."

"Cap'n, if it's fees or a little assessment . . . Well, cap'n, you know we's poor folk. We could scrape up maybe forty dollars for you and your boys."

"I ain't taking no goddamned bribe this year, Ramon. I let you in last year for twenty dollars, and you stole my old lady's purse. I don't mind you being a goddamned swindling horse trader, a lying fortune-teller, or a dirty sneak thief, but one thing I cain't abide's an ungrateful son of a bitch."

"Why, cap'n, you know we're honest. Anytime anything gets stole around the fair, ever'body's blaming us. That forty dollars is for you with another forty for your boys. You know we're fair and square, cap'n."

"Well, there's two sides to every story, Ramon. Lots of folks in Lexington come to the conclusion that you'ns is liars, pickpockets, and thieves. I try to be fair-minded, Ramon. I know some people think you're honest and maybe a little put on, but people who think that is mostly Gypsies. I hold with the aforementioned majority opinion.

"Now you take your passel of mongrels and haul ass down that road to Jessamine County."

"Why, cap'n, we'll surely do that."

"I'm glad you're reasonable, Ramon. So I'll be reasonable with you. I'm giving you fair warning. I don't want nary a goddamned Gypsy at the Lexington Fair this week. If'n one of your boys gets lost and happens to stray into town, accidentally or on purpose, I'm sending him back to you in a goddamned box."

"Thank you, cap'n. We'uns'll mosey on down the road."

Ramon, without remarks, walked back to his van and led his horse forward, taking the road to the left, southwest toward Nicholas Village.

Southwestward, the pace of the caravan was much slower. Near midday, well over the line into Jessamine County, they stopped a few yards south of the junction of the side road with the road from Nicholas Village into Lexington.

Solomon, in a mood that had frozen his mind, stopped with them, while Melinda boiled him eggs. He parked away from the group and sat under a tree, not wondering any

270

longer what his next move would be but simply gathering a minimum of mental force to assault the problem. Now, whatever he did, he would have to wait for nightfall, but he was not going south.

Melinda brought him his eggs already peeled and a piece of hotcake. As he sat absently munching his meal, Mike walked up, the grin for once gone from his small face, and said, "*Yehuda,* Ramon is holding council, and he would like for you to come."

Solomon laid the remainder of his food on the plate and got up to go with the boy.

Solomon found the council hunkered in the grass before the caravan of Ramon. He nodded to the four men and squatted beside them.

"*Yehuda,*" Ramon said, "usually our council talk is in Romany, but out of respect for you, we will speak in Spanish so you and Tomás will understand."

"*Gracias, señor,*" Solomon said.

"We have decided to go south, but we know you cannot go south with the Negro. She would be taken from you, and you would be taken by the *Gajos.* We do not wish to see this happen, for you are a great violinist. If you are taken by the *Gajos,* your hands will be useless for the gentle touch on the violin.

"We know, too, from the way your wagon shook that you would not be content among us, even with the soul of Juanita, and Juanita feels that her fire could not match your fire.

"We have heard from the children that there is paint in the side boxes of your van. We have a plan, *Yehuda.* Among us, there is a man who is very good at drawing letters. Is that not so, Tomás?"

"*Si,* Ramon."

"You cannot go into Lexington as a Gypsy, but you can go into Lexington as a *Gajo.* If you will permit the man to use a little of your paint, he will transform your van, and it will not be as a Gypsy's van."

So soft and compassionate was the voice of Ramon that Solomon came almost to tears. "Of course, you can use the paint, Ramon, but it will not help. I am sought by the *Gajos.*"

"So, we felt . . ." Suddenly, he turned and yelled at Mike, "It is good."

As Mike turned and hurried away, he looked again to

271

Solomon. "In this country, there are many traveling medicine shows. We can letter a sign on the side of your van, and the people will think that you are a seller of liniments and ointments."

His quietly spoken words electrified Solomon. The scheme was so simple and so apt that he was amazed that he had not thought of it himself.

"True, Ramon, very true. In town, there was a man who said I resembled a Frenchman. Could your artist letter for me, on the sides of the van, some such wording as 'Monsieur Hugo's Therapeutic . . .'"

"No, no!" Old Tomás interjected. "Therapeutic would not do . . . Elixir of Life . . . No, it should be Elixir of Youth . . . That would be the word. Then, old men like me would think you bring lead for their pencils."

"But the old men would stop him on the road," Pedro Sanchez protested. "He does not want to sell the elixir."

"Why not?" The man called Juan spoke up. "If he can skin the *Gajos,* let him. We have those small bottles I used in Nashville. We can fill them with good wine. The old men would not know, and after they drank, they would not care. You have the port, Ramon."

"But that is expensive port."

"So?"

Around him, Romany voices babbled with excitement as they suggested and contradicted methods and measures, hammering out a plan not only for him to escape the country but to exact a toll from it as he ran.

"I do not like 'Hugo,'" Old Tomás told him. "It is the name of a calf or a dog. And 'monsieur' I do not like as much as I would like 'doctor.'"

"What about Doctor Maurice Ravenal?" Solomon suggested.

"I do not like Maurice," Ramon objected. "Solomon is a good name among the *Gajos,* and you would not fail to answer. Maurice you might forget."

"Then, let's make it 'Doctor Solomon Ravenal, sole purveyor of the world famous Ravenal's Rejuvenating Elixir of Youth.'"

"Keep it short, *Yehuda,* for our artist must work fast. And you must spell it out for him."

"Let us adjourn to the van of the *Yehuda,*" Ramon said.

Paced by the excited Solomon, the council of elders strode briskly to the van, where Melinda was cleaning dishes from the midday meal. Already, the artist was there, looking over the side panel. Solomon brought out the paint buckets and went into the van for Melinda's slate.

Seated cross-legged on the camp chair, Solomon lettered:

DOCTOR RAVENAL
SOLE PURVEYOR
RAVENAL'S FAMOUS ELIXIR OF YOUTH

"It will be a very simple matter, Ramon," the artist said, looking at the slate. "I do not need to change the color of the panel, which is beautiful. I will letter in bright blue over the yellow on both sides."

"How long will it take?" Ramon asked.

"About an hour."

"Hurry, for we too must be departing. Now, *Yehuda*, let us go and toast your departure with the elixir of youth. But, first, you must change your clothes. One so dressed cannot be a man of medicine."

Solomon ducked inside and changed swiftly. When he emerged, wearing a boiled shirt, four-in-hand, gray suit, and broad-brimmed hat, Ramon beamed.

"You are the picture of a French doctor, *Yehuda*. Come, let us drink a toast of farewell, and when the *calla Yehudni* is finished, let her come to my *vardo*, also, for the people will want to tell you both good-bye. You are a great violinist, *Yehuda*, but Melinda is a great dancer, as the scars on Jerry's back will long stay."

After Ramon's woman filled the dozen half-pint bottles from the flagon in Ramon's van, there was enough left for each man to have a cup of the very excellent port.

When the toasting was finished and Melinda came, the council adjourned and went outside. Now the tribe was gathering from the scattered vans, flowing up to the invisible line that drew a half-circle around the door of their leader's van.

Ramon stood in the doorway and anounced to the crowd, "Come, give your farewells to the *Yehuda* and the *Yehudni*. They are leaving us for the frozen wastes of the North."

The Gypsies came forward to shake his hand, the women to hug Melinda; and many women wept. Melinda's eyes misted politely in return.

No Gypsy male adult was content with a mere "Godspeed." They took his hand and clasped his shoulder, Spanish style, as he responded automatically, and they vied with each other in their farewell addresses.

"*Yehuda,* your soul has lighted our souls with the fire from your violin. May the memory of our fire warm your journey into the North."

There was a religious note. "I embrace you, *Yehuda,* and bid you farewell in the name of the Father, the Son, the Holy Ghost, Moses, Abraham, Isaac."

For some, Solomon said, "Thank you." To others, "*Shalom.*"

He had not been aware that such sentiments existed in the hearts of these people. Some of the older people went through the line twice. Arabella was there, begging Melinda's forgiveness for the behavior of Jerry; she presented Melinda with a polished coin anklet.

Only Jerry and Larry were absent.

After almost an hour of handshaking, Solomon was glad that even two were missing, and when the artist came down to bid farewell, Solomon felt a surge of relief.

"Now," Ramon said, "let us see what our artist has wrought. You, Juan, may bring the magic tonic."

The artist had wrought well. Using only a slate for a guide, he had done a superb job of lettering.

Solomon unlocked the van and put the wicker basket filled with bottles inside. He permitted Melinda to ride beside him until they had cleared the area, driving between the lines of waving and weeping Gypsies, doffing his hat as he made his royal exit. Once on the roadway and around the bend from the Gypsies, he put Melinda inside and went to the head of the mules, slogging with the easy stride of the Gypsies.

It had been a wonderful experience, and he would always remember the tribe of Sanchez as he had seen it last, waving to him in their varicolored dress, and he would hold to that image as the truth.

In this final act of generosity and graciousness, the spirit of God had shown. Solomon had erred in judging them by their crudities. God was expressed in them through their dancing and their music, and these attributes carried them as close to heaven as any of earth's peoples.

God was a Gypsy's violin.

Moreover, he had learned from them.

Call it craftiness, call it guile, or call it original thinking, the simple idea of transforming his van into a medicine show had been a stroke of genius. It had taught him the value of a fresh approach to a problem, had lifted him from despair, and had inspired a plan of his own: As a traveling medicine show, he would go to Lexington and take the steam train into Covington.

It was not yet three o'clock. He had plenty of time to get to town, have supper, take a bath, and get a shave and haircut before arranging for the transportation for himself and the van on the night train.

Shortly past four, he topped a rise and looked northward to the spires of the churches of Lexington.

The road from Nicholas Village was not a main-traveled road. Seeing no other travelers in sight, he stopped the mules and went back into the van, lifting the lid of the chest to tell Melinda, "We're coming into Lexington now. You might as well try to get some sleep, but if you feel yourself riding in a boxcar, don't be upset. God willing, I'll waken you tomorrow, in Cincinnati."

"Yes, sir," she said drowsily.

He unlocked his money cabinet; he'd need at least seven dollars to get him to Cincinnati, calculating the fare for himself, rental on the boxcar, his meals, and the ferry fare across the river. He'd spare himself the cost of the girl's breakfast by driving straight to the tavern. With the girl hidden inside, he could collect his money from Kelly before he pulled the prize out of the box.

He opened the cabinet and looked inside to the money box bolted to the floor; there was no money box bolted to the floor because there was no floor.

Someone, it must have been Larry, had bored a hole in the bottom of the wagon large enough to get the blade of a hacksaw through and had sawn out the square of planking to which the box had been bolted.

Every dime he had, eight hundred and thirty of them, was on its way to Danville, Knoxville, Nashville, Memphis, or Natchez.

Now he understood the prolonged good-byes, the old ladies who had come twice through the line to wish him Godspeed. Now he understood the ceremonial drinking and the concern for the hands of the beautiful violinist.

So, he could report the theft to the sheriff in Lexington, tell him the details of the theft, and spend seven years having his beautiful hands calloused beyond redemption.

He locked the van carefully and walked forward to the

front of his mules, clucking them forward toward the city beckoning in the sunlight, but the city that beckoned in the sunlight was no longer a pleasant way station on an overnight jaunt to Cincinnati. He could not buy a corn fritter for his caved-in stomach, much less a ticket to Covington.

Suddenly, he remembered—he was not alone in Lexington.

Cassius Marcellus Clay was here.

Chapter Eleven

Through the southwestern approaches to Lexington, Solomon led his mules down lanes bordered with white board fences, past green pastures framed in white fences, and white frame houses set in green groves. Around him, the simplicity of green and white, ordered woodlands, and geometric meadows gave the landscape of rolling hills a Doric restraint that enlarged the magnificence of the grazing horses. To a casual visitor, the serenity and classicism of the scene might have denoted peacefulness and a high order of civilization, but Solomon had been here before.

It was hot and getting hotter as he trudged into the residential streets of town, where shade trees grew in single file and the frame houses yielded to structures of brick and stone.

He had never cared for Lexington. Here, slaves were kicked by poor whites, who were cuffed, in turn, by tradesmen, some wealthy in hemp, tobacco, and horse-trading, who suffered the arrogance of the landed gentry toward any man in trade. In Solomon's opinion, the top bracket of the social order in Lexington, from the point of view of training, breeding, and even intelligence, was occupied by horses.

He would not have voiced his opinion. Whatever sentiment that Lexingtonians might lack, it was not a tender ardor for violence. The high sheriff and chief bribe collector had not boasted when he promised to send any interloping Gypsy back in a box. As the sheriff's words had expressed the will of Lexington, the six-shooter hanging from his belt expressed the town's spirit. To Solomon's expert knowledge, Fayette County was the only county in four states that supplied its constabulary with such modern armament, and the sheriff of Lexington needed it.

He turned right at the railway station and headed toward the Clay house.

Passing in the shadow of the courthouse, he raised his eyes to the statue of blind justice above the building's portal.

For the slavocracy, the symbol of justice should have been a mole. In its blind burrowings below the sunlight, the mole sometimes uprooted noxious weeds by accident. So, in his maltreatment of the Gypsies, the sheriff had been administering justice unconsciously, though with too much lenity. He should have shot them all.

For a moment, Solomon's mind was buoyed by the image of the tribe of Sanchez laid out in pine boxes painted a Lexington white.

Perhaps on the scales of God, justice was balanced in the South by weights invisible to mortal eyes. It was conceivable that an apparent injustice might administer justice. The Gypsies' theft of his money, grievous though it was to him, would have been considered justice by Bill Blake. There were subtle forces at work in this region—certainly, no one deserved Southern sheriffs more richly than Southerners.

He reproached himself for doing his Southern brethren an injustice. The same breed that produced a sheriff of Ellijay or of Lexington also produced a Burl Gaines and a Cassius Marcellus Clay.

He thought of Cash Clay, his father's friend.

Clay was a typical Kentuckian—he resembled no one. A younger cousin of the Great Pacificator, Henry Clay, he had freed a quarter million dollars' worth of slave property and hired most of them back at wages to prove that slavery was an economic evil. He had failed to prove his point because he had almost gone broke, not necessarily because of his ideas, but because of the impetuous generosity of his spirit and because he had become a newspaper publisher.

He might have made money with the newspaper by exercising some discretion in his editorial policy, but at a time when antislavery agitators were being mobbed in Boston, he had started an emancipationist newspaper in the slave region. Even so, he had one talent which had insured his success in the field where staying alive, not making a profit, was the only true gauge of success. Clay was an artist with a Bowie knife.

Clay had been a house guest at the home of Aaron Villaricca, Solomon's father, when Solomon was a boy. Solomon's father had, at that time, been engaged in assisting Clay to sell the printing presses of the emancipationist paper which had been shipped to Cincinnati by the citizens of Lexington while Clay lay abed with fever. Solomon remembered well his visitor, at whose feet he had set to be regaled by tales of the Mexican War, of *caballeros* and *señoritas*.

Clay might not remember Solomon, but Clay would surely remember his father, Aaron Villaricca.

He parked in front of Clay's house, a sprawling, one-story stone structure set well back on a shaded lawn. Gray with age and choked with ivy, the building resembled a cottage constructed by a castle builder.

Solomon's knock was answered by a colored man, slow with age and dignity, whose homespun frock coat challenged the heat. "I seek an audience with Mr. Clay."

"Yes, suh. Who I say's calling?"

"Mr. Ravenal of Louisiana—a distant cousin of Mr. Clay's wife."

"Won't you step in, sir, out of the heat?"

Solomon walked into an octagonal-shaped reception hall as the old man went over to a door Solomon assumed to be the door to the study and rapped twice before entering. He closed the door firmly behind him.

From his position, Solomon could see through a large, open doorway opposite the study into a parlor where a woman sat at a tambour desk, her back to Solomon, bent over a letter she was writing. No doubt, it was Mrs. Clay. At the distance, she could not have heard him announce himself as her relative; yet, she might come at Clay's summons, and there would be stuttering embarrassment as Solomon was unveiled as a fraud.

"What may I do for you, sir?" The question was coldly formal, and it came from the entrance to the hallway behind him.

Solomon wheeled, and Cash Clay stood behind him, feet spread in a fighter's stance, body bending slightly forward, his arms aligned tensely behind his torso. He wore a magnificent black beard that might have aroused nostalgia in

Solomon had not his emotions shriveled from the hostility in Clay's eyes.

"May I speak to you, sir, on a matter of urgent concern—to me?" Solomon's gentle voice turned Clay's hostility into vexation.

"In there," he said, pointing to the study.

Uneasily, Solomon entered a book-lined library. A littered desk was next to a window, and another door, ajar, led into a dining room. Through that door the Negro had vanished, and through it Clay had gone to the hallway to stalk his visitor from the rear.

Very gently, he turned to face Clay, still on guard in the doorway, and said, "Forgive my intrusion and my deception, Mr. Clay, but I am not Solomon Ravenal but Solomon Villaricca, son of Aaron Villaricca."

Only then did Clay smile, in relief as well as in greeting, and stepped forward to shake hands. "Why, Sol! I declare, you've grown. How old are you now, boy?"

"Twenty-six, sir."

"You've made quite a name for yourself in twenty-six years. I've been reading about you, Sol. Might say you're famous in these parts. But why did you deceive me? You're no criminal to me, although others might disagree. Where did you get the alias—Ravenal?"

"It's the name on my van, sir. I had to gain an entree. When I saw your wife in the parlor, I feared she might come and uncover my fraud."

"You made a mistake, all right," Clay grinned. "My relations with my in-laws are a little strained at the moment. However, the lady in the parlor is a house guest, Mrs. Pamela Foreman, previously known as Pam Sherwood, here to sing a few patriotic airs at the opening of the fair."

Solomon stood silenced by the flow of information. He knew from gossip that Mrs. Clay periodically left the household in protest against the fiscal, philosophical, and political attitudes of her husband, and he had not expected to find Pam Sherwood in Lexington, singing a "few patriotic airs." He had heard her sing in Cincinnati. Her specialty was British public house ballads in their pristine prurience.

"Sir," he finally said, "are you willing to help a runaway slave girl?"

"Well, that depends," Clay said, "on which way she's running."

"She's running in the right direction, and I got her outside in my van."

"Then, we should get her out of the heat. Let's go to the van, and I'll direct you to the alley. Her quarters are prepared and waiting, in the stable."

Clay stepped back and motioned for Solomon to lead the way, saying, "I'd write her a manumission certificate, but I've already written four hundred, and my father left me only one hundred slaves. Besides, there's that strawberry mark."

"You've read Blake's handbill?"

"Your nemesis is a genius."

Together, they walked out into the blazing sunlight, and Solomon sketched his adventures and explained his financial position after the theft of his money. Clay listened with sympathy, which became guarded as Solomon touched onto his financial condition.

"Fifteen dollars is all you'd need," Clay said, "and I can understand why you can't write home. Under usual circumstances, I could advance you the money. At the moment, one dollar would embarrass me, and five would bankrupt me, at least until I sell some of my horses at the fair. Turn right at the elm tree."

Solomon, geeing the mules, felt a ground swell of compassion under the ocean of his misery. He had heard that Clay was financially embarrassed, but obviously "embarrassed" was a Texas euphemism.

"However, I still have credit in Lexington, somewhere . . . perhaps." Clay knitted his brows, trying to think of an untouched source.

"Mr. Clay, I'm not without resources," Solomon interjected. "Before they stole my money, the Gypsies gave me a dozen bottles of best quality port wine to equip me as a cheap-jack selling a medicinal tonic, and I have four kegs of whiskey and two demijohns of strained honey."

"Turn in there," Clay pointed as they rolled down the alley. "The Gypsies must not be entirely without honor. They did a professional job on the van. They gave you a surefire idea for making money. They donated the inventory to start the campaign.

"The Ladies Temperance Union of the Campbellite League shoved through an ordinance banning the sale of whiskey on the fairgrounds. Your wine's no good, too obvious a fraud. If you mix a little honey with whiskey, sir, that's good for the ague and therefore a medicinal alcohol. If you were not above becoming a cheap-jack, I might persuade the chairman of the fair committee to rent you a stall for your van and defer payment till later."

"Mr. Clay, it would surprise you what I would do to get out of Kentucky in one piece."

"Then, I've conferred with the chairman of the fair committee. You've been advanced credit on the stall rental."

"You're the chairman?"

"Indeed, sir. Pull to the far end of the stables and drive the mules all the way forward . . . I propose that you charge twenty-five cents a bottle for the tonic."

"At such a price, sir, I'd be charging forty dollars a keg."

"Not at all, sir. You'll be adding two gallons of honey to the batch. It's your skill in blending that the public is buying."

"I have some excellent sassafras. A touch of sassafras in the concoction would add a medicinal flavor."

"Indeed, sir! Your talent for blending is so remarkable, perhaps you should charge thirty cents."

"But, I'll need bottles. I'll empty the ones they gave me . . . May I present you with a house gift of excellent port?"

"Indeed, you may."

"If this plan works," Solomon said, "twenty percent goes to the house."

"A magnanimous offer accepted with magnanimity. Now, bring forth the prize girl."

Solomon went to the rear and opened the door, calling for Melinda to come out. He saw her pop out of the box and walk forward, mopping her brow. "Mr. Ricky, I damned near stifled to death."

She had not seen Clay behind the opened door, and he said, "Mind your language, Melinda. I have a gentleman with me, Mr. Clay of Kentucky."

She came out dressed in full Gypsy regalia, with her pearls and coin necklace draped around her neck. " 'Scuse me, Mr. Clay, sir. I didn't know we had company."

"We're the company, Melinda. Mr. Clay has kindly consented to take us in. The Gypsies sawed through the floor of the wagon and took my money box. We're on poor relief."

"So, you're Georgia's prize darky. Welcome to Lexington, girl."

"Thank you, sir." Melinda seemed suddenly shy, perhaps

overly demure, in the presence of the handsome Clay, and alarm bells rang in Solomon's mind.

"I thought them old Gypsies was carrying on something awful 'bout us leaving, Mr. Ricky."

"Girl," Clay interjected, "will you henceforth refer to your guardian as Mr. Ravenal. Can you say 'Mr. Ravenal'?"

"Yes, sir," she said.

"Then say it, girl."

"Mr. Ravenal."

'Now, girl, you're from Baton Rouge, Louisiana. Can you say 'Baton Rouge, Louisiana'?"

"Baton Rouge, Louisiana."

"Good, an intelligent girl, Sol, and well-mannered, though a little given to profanity. You'll sleep here, girl."

He shoved open a door which led into an annex to the stables. Melinda went inside, and Solomon followed at the nod of Clay, entering a small room with a small, high rear window, a sand floor, a bunk without bedding, a table and two chairs, and a wash stand in the corner beneath the window with a pitcher and washbasin. There was a small wood stove with the remnant of a woodpile from winter in a box beside it. A stovepipe snaked through a hole in the rear wall.

"Have you more modest clothes than those, Melinda?"

"Yes, sir. In the van, I got my bag."

"Get into them, then, girl. The pump's outside the door. Draw yourself a basin of water and wash up. I'll take you in to meet Reba. You can help her around the kitchen."

As Melinda went about her tasks, Solomon and Clay sat at the table and discussed procedure.

It was a unilateral discussion. In short, emphatic sentences, Clay laid down his dicta with the forcefulness of a general, which he was, and the forcibleness of a lawyer, which he was.

Melinda's clothing and jewelry would remain in the van. So, also, would Solomon's, except for those items he needed immediately. Melinda would dress plainly and refrain from idle conversation with the other servants. She would prepare the special dishes Solomon required for the observance of dietary laws of his nation whenever the household fare conflicted with such laws, and she would explain her actions on the grounds that Solomon was a French Huguenot—Melinda pronounced "Huguenot" successfully when she came in to get the water pitcher—Clay's servants would not know a Huguenot from a hawkshaw, anymore than did their master. Melinda must stay on the property at all times. Sheriff Whitcomb could not and would not come onto Clay's property without a search warrant. He would have to have evidence that a fugitive was on the premises. No one among the servants would volunteer such information, but inadvertencies must be guarded against.

To guard against inadvertencies, Clay insisted that Melinda not use the name "Mellie" or "Melinda" while staying with Clay. Modestly dressed, Melinda entered with her filled water pitcher, and Clay asked, "Girl, how would you like to have an alias?"

"Just fine, sir. I always wanted one of them things."

"She means she's been trying to think of a name for herself ever since we left Carolina. You named yourself, yet, Melinda?"

"Arabella, she wanted me to name myself 'Arabella,' but she already had that name."

"Well, what about Arabella for a little while?"

"That'd be right fine, Mr. . . . Ravenal."

"Arabella it shall be," Clay said. "When you get through washing up, I'll show you to Reba, and, Monsieur Ravenal, I'll introduce you to Mrs. Foreman. If the storm passes swiftly, I trust I'll be permitted to introduce you to my wife before the fair is over."

Solomon, carrying his hamper of wine bottles and a ditty bag, was escorted with Melinda to the kitchen, where he was introduced to Reba and George. From the kitchen, Clay led him down the hall to his bedchamber. As Solomon washed, shaved, and changed to fresh linen, Clay explained the presence in his home of Mrs. Pamela Foreman, formerly known to the entertainment world as Pam Sherwood.

She was returning to the boards after an unsuccessful marriage with a planter on the Georgia Sea Islands. The marriage had taken place at the height of her career, which she had launched in the music halls of London and which had carried her to this side of the Atlantic.

Three weeks of close association with the South's peculiar institution had turned her against slavery, and the boredom of plantation life had reinforced her aversion. She had left Mr. Foreman but had retained his name in an attempt to reach higher levels of musical expression than those she had found as Pam Sherwood.

Presently, she was occupied in correspondence with various persons in an attempt to revive interest in the new Pam Sherwood.

"She has quoted the glowing reviews she received from the Lexington paper at the opening of the fair. She is not being dishonest. The reviews shall be published as written, for I wrote the reviews."

It was good, Solomon thought, as he dried his face in a fluffy towel, to have friends in influential places.

"Now, to the parlor, Monsieur Ravenal, to meet this beautiful and tragic woman. Don't forget your Creole airs."

So it was that Solomon was ushered into the parlor to await the arrival of Mrs. Foreman, at present retired to her chambers but in the process of being summoned by Bob.

Clay used the interval to get a map of the fairground from his study.

The fairground was a cobblestoned quadrangle enclosed by a high board fence in front of the grandstand of the racing oval. On the north side were exhibition stalls for horses and domestic animals which were stabled beneath the grandstand. East and west sides were taken over by exhibits and the "shows." The entrance gate was on the south side facing but almost a hundred yards back from the Paris pike, and it was taken over by a reviewing stand erected for the opening ceremonials.

Solomon, analyzing the fair's layout, felt that the horse stalls would produce the greatest collection of potential tipplers. He favored an area close to the stalls.

"True," Clay said, "but when a horse-trader's looking at a horse, he's a dedicated teetotaler. Now, here's the admission gate. People coming in will tend to go to their right as they enter, making the traffic counterclockwise around the yard . . ."

Bob entered bearing a decanter of the Gypsies' port and three glasses. "Mrs. Foreman sends her compliments, sir, and says to tell you she'll be with you directly."

Solomon's thinking was interrupted by the appearance of the wine, and he said, "Let me taste that . . ."

"I had the same thought," Clay said, and hastily poured a bit into a glass. "You taste it, Sol. I'm no connoisseur."

Solomon took a sip and was gratified to nose the bouquet and taste the genuine body of port. "It's the true Hippocrene."

Cash handed the glass to Bob to replace with a fresh one

and turned to Solomon. "Now, back to the fairground . . .

"Foot traffic should be counterclockwise. Over here," he pointed, "you'll get the swains while their pockets are still jingling, and what could impress a young lady more than a twenty-five cent purchase made in an offhand manner?"

They discussed the pros and cons of available locations: If too close to a shooting gallery, noise would interfere with Solomon's spiel; too close to the hog exhibit would be noisome.

Then, they considered the possibility of a hasty exit. Since an entrance fee was charged, the gates would be guarded.

Clay solved this problem with his knowledge of the terrain.

Concessionaires' stables were west of the grounds. With a stall against the western fence, a barrier eight feet high, Solomon could leap to the top of his van and vault over the fence in event of a disturbance that might bring the law. Thus, his mules would be only a few yards away.

He chose the western fence, sacrificing the swains for the stables.

"Sol, I've got an idea! This will bring you customers no matter where you're located and will weed out all but the sporting gentry . . ."

Suddenly, he laid aside the pencil with which he had been marking the paper and stood erect, "Our lady comes."

Solomon turned to face the doorway as Mrs. Pamela Foreman entered the room.

She filled the parlor with her presence, advancing with a prim grace as if to restrain the animalism beneath the bones and stays of her garments. She moved forward with a sidewise motion, her dignity confining to a sway a movement that was kissing cousin to a flounce.

Her green eyes were cool and reserved. Chestnut hair brushed back to a cluster of curls gave her a Grecian profile. She acknowledged Clay's introduction in an English accent spoken with the low, mannered voice that marked her a lady of breeding despite her public profession. British regality merged with Greek classicism in her face and manner, but beneath her head and slender neck, her body, tightly corseted and pneumatic-breasted, surely must have been harvested during a vintage year in the Soho public houses.

As Solomon exchanged pleasantries, he spaced his remarks lest he infringe on her conversation and be rebuked with a sudden, "Silence, royalty speaking!" Recent victim, himself, of skirmishes between head and body, he forced his gaze to focus on her eyes to avoid the swellings that peeked above a neckline which would have been modestly high in a lesser woman.

As they lamented the weather in the language of decorum, he felt a sudden nostalgia for areas of communication beyond language. With this morality, he thought, a man might defy mortality in the dalliance of self-complete moments, might discover the metaphysical by probing the physical.

As he dabbed his brow in the languid manner of the French, his mind grappled with concepts it could not define, but there was one fact, hard, cold, crystalline, that denied all cavil: Whoever Mr. Foreman had been, he was the most unfeeling oaf in Christendom to let this one get away.

"We do hope you'll stay long enough to hear us sing," she said, "though, I daresay, we're a bit rusty after being ever so long away."

Relishing the sweet modesty of her imperial "we," Solomon assured her, "Ma'am, if you sing with half the grace your person commands, wild horses couldn't drag me away from your recital."

"You are *très gallant, monsieur.*"

Her cool green eyes sparkled with royal pleasure, but Clay cut the budding lines of communication.

"Mrs. Foreman, Mr. Ravenal and I are plotting to enrich the larder. We do not wish to detain you further, ma'am, from your studies. With your permission, we'll excuse ourselves and withdraw."

"For such a noble cause, you're surely excused."

Once in the study, Clay explained his abruptness. "The thought struck me, Sol, that the lady was baiting you. I feared you might get carried away, sir, with your disguise, and try to talk to her in French. She would have trapped you, for she speaks the language like a Joan of Arc. You're a third generation Creole, if she should ask, who can't speak a word of French."

"Do you doubt the lady?"

"I doubt them all, God bless them. She's with us on the slavery matter, but her involvement is a matter of the heart, and I never trust the heart in a showdown with the purse. Your girl in the kitchen could earn Mrs. Foreman ten times what we're paying her, and our lady is a woman. The hand that rocks the cradle grabs the purse.

"Now, as to our venture . . . Be seated, sir, and hear me out."

Clay was walking back and forth, not looking at Solomon, declaiming in a low-pitched, rolling voice. "True, a quarter-dollar is more than many of the fair visitors make in a day. For that reason, we're eliminating the worthy working-man, the housewife, the industrious yeoman."

He turned, looked directly at Solomon, and lowered his voice further to emphasize his remarks.

"So, for those who buy, no hardship will be worked and our consciences shall be clean."

He resumed the leonine stride, hands folded behind his back, head bent, pacing back and forth. "Now, bear me out, for this is an abstruse point . . . Vouchsafing to man a passing interest in the arts, sciences, and politics, two concerns hold his interest from birth to death—bowel movements and erections."

Clay wheeled and held up his hand for silence and to warn Solomon to think upon this profundity.

"Mark my words, Sol, if they have faith in your tonic, it will work. For twenty-five cents, they will have faith.

"Tell them it is the best constitutional ever devised by man, tell them loudly, tell them long, and tell them often. And then," Clay lowered his voice, "you slyly insinuate that the elixir is an aphrodisiac as well as a purgative. Do you know what an aphrodisiac is, sir, or are you too young?"

"I can gather from your context, Mr. Clay."

"Good. Now, drink, as the Bard says, provokes desire and takes away the performance, but you are making no claims for the performance. So, you will bring the old sports back, possibly to buy a spare bottle for their wives.

"The young sports in the audience will be eager to prescribe a bottle of the tonic for the girls they are courting.

"Some gentry will recognize the tonic at the outset, but that happy band will be back with deliberate haste to purchase from the only van dispensing spirits on the fairground.

"The timid, bucolic swains will be emboldened by the tonic. Romance will bloom for him in the desert of his shyness. Perhaps, for him, Ravenal's Elixir of Youth may well be a lifetime boon.

"So, for a mere quarter-dollar, all this, plus a gratifying trip to the outhouse."

"Mr. Clay, how can I work all this into a lecture with ladies present?"

"Ah, sir, you have asked the question which was the genesis of my stroke of genius. There'll be no ladies present.

"Tomorrow, I'll go early to Ed Beauchamps, the printer. Since I'm already indebted to the gentleman, he will not risk jeopardizing future payments to deny me this credit. With the bottle labels, I'll have him print handbills which can be posted on the fairground and elsewhere. Those handbills will advertise a free lecture by Doctor Solomon Ravenal, appending your degrees, for male adults only. Sol, no red-blooded American male old enough to read could resist the salaciousness implied by such an invitation . . ."

All the vast sweep of a general officer's mind had been brought to bear on the acquisition of fifteen dollars, and Solomon was amazed at his friend's fertility of invention. Clay was a true general, albeit without an army, and his unbroken flow of suggestions were impelled by an enthusiasm that swept Solomon along with him despite Solomon's rock ballast of reservations.

"Now, in reference to your lecture; keep them smiling, not laughing. You're not a clown. You hold degrees from Oxford, from Heidelberg, but not from Harvard or Yale. There might be some listener present who knows someone who is related to someone who went to Harvard or Yale."

In the end, before adjuring Solomon to retire to his chamber and concentrate, concentrate, concentrate on writing the lecture, Clay persuaded Solomon that he would need one hundred labels for one hundred bottles, basing his estimate on the probable attendance at the fair.

Solomon, now captivated by the sweep of Clay's imagination, buttressed as it was by facts, figures, and projections, agreed to the huge amount. Yet, one hundred bottles represented twenty-five dollars, or five dollars a day for the five days of the fair. Clay figured ten of the twenty-five dollars would go as expenses, leaving the original fifteen Solomon had set out to earn.

Solomon did not need fifteen dollars to get to Cincinnati. Clay had estimated Solomon's expenses on the Clay standard, Solomon traveled on the Villaricca standard.

Solomon went to his room, laid out the handbill and label, and wrote and revised his lecture until the dinner bell sounded.

During the dinner, at which Clay ate one-third of the omelet Melinda had prepared for her Huguenot master, Solomon was preoccupied even in the presence of the incomparable Mrs. Foreman. Afterward, over coffee in the parlor, Solomon listened to social gossip with half an ear, until the lady retired.

Clay was so impressed by Solomon's literary effort that he offered his own manuscript, a treatise on the art of fighting with a Bowie knife, for Solomon's criticism. Such sentences as "Your opponent will find it disconcerting if you give the blade a sharp twist after inserting it beneath his rib cage," so awed Solomon that he could not parse them.

After the goodnights, Solomon lay spread-eagled on his bed, his mind warming to the glow of the afternoon's events which had interposed between him and the sickening loss of his money.

He was still penniless in Lexington. All that had been solved was the immediate problem of provisions and shelter for him, Melinda, and his mules. He was still destitute, still one hundred savage miles from home, but hope had trounced despair, and he thanked Jehovah for Cassius Marcellus Clay.

Then, Solomon's dybbuk gazed through the window and asked if it were really true that hope had conquered despair, or had truth been hornswoggled by a false dream?

Clay's enthusiasm had been an anodyne against reality, but, tomorrow, reality must be faced. Solomon was not a crocus pitcher. He had never handled a large audience, and a quarter was a horrible price for four cents' worth of mountain dew. To mark valuable merchandise up fifty or one hundred percent was honest trade, but to square the price of worthless merchandise was fraud.

It was easy for General Clay to sit inside his study and plan a campaign, but Private Villaricca would be on the field of battle, tomorrow. Private Villaricca could not carry his general's enthusiasm into the conflict when the bayonets clashed and the fighting began. It would be the blood of Private Villaricca flowing over the cobblestones.

He stirred restlessly.

He was no longer an infant, and he had whimpered his last whimper. Tomorrow he would go forth as Elijah went forth, or as David, and though he might be beaten, he would not be conquered.

Past midnight, he exhorted himself to the pitch of battle, but resolution wavered in his mind as fitfully as the curtains bellying in and out by his open window. When finally he found peace, it was not in the example of the heroes of

Israel but from the image of himself as Hector, foredoomed but unconquerable, walking alone beyond the portals of Troy to give battle to Achilles.

It was a stirring image to go to sleep by, but many-fingered dawn pried open the lids of the same old Solomon Villaricca, who lay in a sweat on his mattress, depleted, inadequate, and frightened. The same resources of the harassed, anxious, and self-doubting Jew forced him to his feet, rising with all the *élan* of a veteran soldier who had never won a battle.

"*Ave* and *vale*, Hector," he said aloud, wondering if the recumbent Trojan understood Latin.

Shaving soothed him. There was a therapy in cutting edges.

Washed, dressed, shaved, powdered, he entered the breakfast room at the sound of the triangle, feeling slightly less incapable than he had felt upon awakening. Clay charged in with the same enthusiasm he had taken to bed, and Pamela in the morning was more radiant than Pamela in the evening. She wore a blouse with a laced bodice, above which her superfluity of flesh heaved and shimmered beneath the folds of a peignoir-type waistcoat.

As Clay outlined the schedule and informed Mrs. Foreman of their plans, some of Solomon's depression left him. After breakfast, when Melinda brought his dark suit cleaned and pressed to the bedroom, he began to feel the self-assurance of formality.

The fair opened at two, preceded by a parade escort of the guests of honor, which included Clay and Mrs. Foreman. Solomon had to get to the fairground before one o'clock to set up his lectern, which George was constructing, even now, in the backyard.

Clay was to see to the printing of the labels and handbills and to arrange for additional half-pint bottles for the elixir. Solomon was to mix his batch and bottle it in the bottles, which would be hauled from the the distillery by George's boy, Willie, in his two-goat goat cart.

While Reba boiled a very strong concoction of sassafras tea, Solomon set up his laboratory adjacent to the woodshed, using cups for measuring vials and gallon buckets for beakers. When the tea was ready, the entire household, with the exception of the absent Clay and Willie, gathered to watch the shirt-sleeved alchemist perform.

Solomon mixed four formulae in cups, using his nose to

evaluate the formulae, and asked the congregation to vote on each batch. Mrs. Foreman tested first, alternating a sip from each cup, followed by Bob, Reba, George, and Melinda. They voted by secret ballot, and all five voted for the cup which Solomon's nose had rejected because of the emphatic odor of alcohol.

A few drops of vanilla extract from the kitchen further reduced the odor, and the addition of a food dye added an exotic red color to the beverage. Solomon poured the first half-pint to present to George for excellence in carpentry.

Then Willie came rattling into the yard with the additional bottles. Solomon mixed while the women poured with cider funnels. Within half an hour, he had fifty dollars' worth of merchandise poured and stoppered, awaiting the labels. By eleven, the printer galloped in with the labels and handbills in his saddlebags. When the crew ceased for lunch, the medicine show of Doctor Ravenal was ready for the road.

After dinner, Clay prevailed on Solomon to wear a tall silk hat from his collection. "I'm not sure that doctors wear these, but I'm confident that the well-dressed doctor should."

Clay also pressed onto Solomon a large and impressive book to be placed on his lectern for effect. He assigned George to drive Solomon to the fairground and set up the lecture platform.

On the twenty-minute ride through the residential streets to the outskirts of town, Solomon, dressed in his freshly-pressed suit, gleaming boots, and high hat, felt every inch the gentleman and doctor as he rode beside the rigid and frock-coated George, who handled the reins.

When they arrived at the gates, the ticket taker looked over the permit Clay had written, directed him to the assigned area, stepped back, and saluted. Gravely, decorously, Solomon Ravenal, Doctor of Comparative Physiognomy, College of Medical Science, New Iberia, Louisiana, *et al.*, tipped his hat in answer and told his boy to drive on.

Solomon directed George to the space reserved for him across the cobblestoned quadrangle. It was plainly numbered in whitewashed lettering against the fence. George maneuvered the van within two feet of the fence, putting the top of the boards within easy vaulting distance from the top of the van. As his assistant went about setting up his platform, Solomon unhitched the mules and led them back

292

through the gate and to the stables, putting them in stalls as close to the fairground as possible.

George's work had proceeded apace during Solomon's absence. He had set up the platform extending from the back door of the van and running parallel with the van almost half its length. From two upright posts at each end of the platform, he had strung a tarpaulin tacked to the van's roof to give Solomon a sunshade. As Solomon walked up, he was stringing red, white, and blue bunting along the edge of the platform to hide the unsightly underpinnings. Solomon brought out the lectern with the impressive tome and pinned his notes to the center spread.

When George had finished, Solomon complimented him and promised him the proceeds from the first bottle sold. The rostrum was fully as impressive, on a smaller scale, as the bunting-draped speakers' platform built beside the front entrance.

Solomon set George to nailing up handbills announcing his lecture on bare spots on the fence, and taking a sheaf of the notices in his hand, he set out to survey the area.

Across the quadrangle was a pyramidal tent with broad red and white stripes that narrowed as they neared the apex to end in a blue circle below the center pole. Its entrance was shaded by a tasseled marquee above a carpet. On the left of the marquee was a platform for the barker, and on the right was a ticket booth. Below the ticket window was a sign: "The Great Mustafina—See her death-defying cobra dance with live king copras. Admission, 10¢."

Inserted in a slot above the ticket window was a notice which read, "First performance, 3 P.M."

Two areas north of Solomon on the west side of the fence was another show tent, less imposing than the pleasure-dome across the quad but flashing a gaudier sign.

See the Original
UNCLE TOM'S CABIN
Presented for the first time south
of the Mason-Dixon Line.
LEARN THE SHOCKING TRUTH ABOUT
LITTLE EVA
Presented by the Roanoke Puppeteers
Six Performances Daily
Four—Count Them—Four
Minstrel Banjos
Admission 10¢

Meandering among the early arrivals, he caught the odor of whiskey several times. At first, he was disturbed, but logic restored his equanimity. Some were bound to bring bottles into the grounds, but they were the heavy drinkers, and soon, they would be in short supply. These premature imbibers would be his best customers.

He wandered near the speaker's stand and looked through the gate down the long approach road from the Paris pike. Casually, his gaze swept the parking meadow to the right of the road, and he saw that a wide plank supported by two barrels had been set up under a jerry-rigged tarpaulin. Behind the makeshift bar, a huge man wearing a leather apron was hoisting a barrel onto a block.

Blatantly, not fifty yards from the entrance to the fair, a blind tiger was opening.

Not only was the eyesore a flagrant insult to the ladies of the Campbellite League, it was an injustice perpetrated on a legitimate merchant inside the grounds who had paid good money, or used good credit, to purvey medicinal tonic.

He had one advantage. The proprietor of the blind tiger could not solicit business inside the compound.

Forthwith, he moved among the crowd near the speakers' platform, passing out handbills, introducing himself where convenient, extending private invitations to his lecture to the more prosperous and intelligent-seeming gentry. So impressive his manner and so cordial his handshake that thrice he was invited to take a swig from private bottles, but inwardly his spirit drooped. Ravenal's Elixir must now stand or fall as an aphrodisiac and constitutional; he had no corner on the whiskey market.

His soliciting was stopped by the roll of drums and the whirl of fifes.

An usher shouted, "Stand back of the line!"

Around him, word was carried through the crowd. "Back of the line, folks! Stand back of the line! Make way for the Lexington Rifles!"

Through the wide gates, he could see the vanguard of the Lexington Rifles swinging along the Paris pike with its ragtag escort of pickaninnies and arabs, banners flying, bayonets gleaming, long rifles slanting in precise rows. As he shuffled backward from the press of the crowd, he heard the company commander's "Col-yum . . . LEFT!" and saw the color guard swing on the pivot with the precision of a hinged door, the band behind, to move straight toward the spectators, who were drawing back to clear the passageway.

Company A of the 1st Battalion of the Lexington Rifles, Kentucky State Militia, swung crisply left and marched toward the fairground with a rapid swinging stride, each lad over six feet tall, each dressed in gray buckskin with fringed sleeves, coonskin hats, and moccasin boots. Cadenced footsteps were falling to the beat of "Yankee Doodle," and the rifles, at "shoulder arms," were as steady and as evenly spaced as pickets on a fence.

The tall man in the plug hat moving back in the crowd responded in emotions though not in the same manner as the excited, tumbling pickaninnies and white ragamuffins, doffing the hat and placing it over his breast as Old Glory neared.

Banners and drums gave new dimensions to his thoughts, and though he knew that those advancing bayonets guarded much that was bad, they guarded much more that was good. Although he was an Ohio Hebrew and these lads were Christian sons of Kentucky, all divergencies became compatible under the flag that waved above them. He had no other countrymen than these boys, and nowhere, not in Spain, not in Babylon, not in Judah, could the sound of drums so hallow for him the soil he walked on.

They were swinging into the quadrangle, the thud-thud of their measured footfalls as clear to his ears as the now subdued tattoo of the drums, with their striding captain bellowing, "Companeeeee," and the lieutenants echoing "Platooooon"—"Halt!"

"Leeeeeft . . . FACE!"

"Order . . . ARMS!"

With a thud and a snap, the rifle butts hit the ground.

"Paaaraaade . . . REST!"

One hundred twenty-eight feet moved left, and one hundred twenty-eight rifles jutted forward in a single motion.

Through the gate rolled four barouches, escorted fore and aft by mounted officers of the Lexington Rifles. Four black coachmen, dressed almost the same as Solomon, assisted by four black footmen, handled the carriages with self-conscious rigidity and pride. In the first carriage, the mayor and his wife faced another dignitary and his wife. In the second carriage, bedecked in black, rode Sheriff Whitcomb beside his wife, a matronly little woman whose unofficious bearing had once cost her a purse, and they

295

faced aft to the leonine face of Cassius Clay and the regal beauty of Mrs. Pamela Foreman. Following came the dignitaries of the Fair Committee.

Slowly, the coaches passed before the troops.

"Company!"

"Platoon!"

"Attench . . . HUT!"

"Preeeeesent . . . ARMS!"

The coaches rolled to a halt before the speakers' platform. Footmen leaped to the ground to open the carriage doors, and the mounted officers alit and walked back to assist the ladies. As the dignitaries mounted the steps, the drums rolled a slow tattoo. There were cheers and good-natured jeers for the mayor, unalloyed jeers for the sheriff, a mixture of both for Clay, but Pamela Foreman got three cheers and a tiger.

Solomon pushed his way toward the black barouche with the black horses occupied by Clay and Mrs. Foreman. He doffed his hat to the lady, who espied him in the crowd and blew a kiss in his direction. Even as he thrilled to the intimacy of her recognition, his eyes, dropping to view her trim ankles as she exited, spotted two sets of leg shackles bolted to the floor of the vehicle.

Sheriff Whitcomb's official carriage doubled in black as a paddy wagon.

For him, Solomon thought, there was never a meadow of daisies without its sprig of nightshade.

"At ease!"

Clay rose and announced the mayor, who spent fifteen minutes introducing the gentleman from his carriage, who, it developed, was the district's representative in Frankfort. For twenty minutes, that gentleman regaled the crowd with a word picture of the future of the Bluegrass Region, and the crowd grew restive. Someone yelled, "Knife him, Cash!"

Finally, it was announced that Mrs. Foreman would sing "The Star Spangled Banner." The major ordered the captain, who ordered a lieutenant, who ordered the bandmaster to strike up the band. Mrs. Foreman rose.

Her voice was a husky contralto which could not reach the upper levels of her song, but no one objected, since her swelling chest was an adequate compensation for the inadequate vocal range. However, her rendition of "My Old Kentucky Home" was superb. Her voice fitted the range of the song, and its huskiness enhanced the song's sadness with an impact no soprano could have achieved. She brought tears to the eyes of the Kentuckians and caused a slight mist in the eyes of the visiting Ohioan.

She was cheered as she was led down the steps to the waiting barouche by Clay, and the soldiers snapped to attention to honor her.

The soldiers were faced about, and with a "hip-hup" and a roll of drums marched back to the armory.

The Fayette County Fair was opened.

Dr. Ravenal commenced.

"Right this way, folks," he chanted to the dispersing crowd in a loud singsong, "to Doctor Ravenal's edifying and amazing lecture on the comparative anatomy of male and female and the ailments attendant on the aging process, a lecture given in secret to five of the crowned heads of Europe and never before delivered from a public rostrum. Gentlemen only, please. Step this way, folks. Learn the real reason for our president's nickname, Old Buck. Yes, I have been a visitor to the White House, albeit after dark and by the rear entrance."

He mounted the rostrum, moving with slow dignity but continuing the patter as he walked. At least a dozen listeners had followed him, and more were congealing around the original core.

Speaking in the manner of a man accustomed to the attention of his audience, he introduced himself. "Gentlemen, I am the world famous Doctor Ravenal, late of Heidelberg, Sorbonne, Oxford, and the University of Madrid. I've got more degrees than a Fahrenheit thermometer, in addition to the Order of the Garter bestowed upon me by Queen Victoria. Unfortunately, I lost the trinket."

Feigning confusion, he looked around him, continued talking, and plucked a bottle of the elixir off the stand.

"Gentlemen, I do not hold with the authorities that this tonic which bears my name is the greatest scientifico-medical discovery of modern times. If I were a cheap-jack practicing quackery, I might agree that this powerful and potent beverage is the greatest medicinal tonic of all times, but I will not lie to you in German, French, or English, although I've been known to tell a few whoppers in Spanish.

"In addition to the rejuvenating qualities of this potent tonic, it is a cure for ague, chilblains, nervous disorders, pains of gout, liver, lights, intestinal obstructions, and all diseases of the skin. It has been known to cure smallpox, but for that, I make no claims, since I am a responsible Doctor from Heidelberg, etcetera, etcetera, and do not engage in quackery. However, I withhold my full approval of the tonic, gentlemen, for Ravenal's Elixir does not cure leprosy. No, gentlemen, Ravenal's Elixir of Youth cannot cure leprosy.

"Now, gentlemen, I have excluded the ladies from this audience, for I must make a confession. I take credit for augmenting the formula and making it known to the western world, but this secret was stolen by a Gypsy girl who fell madly in love with me and fled from her tribe, bringing me a phial of this undiluted essence of eroticism as her dowery.

"Gentlemen, I pause a moment for tears . . ." He did not pause but merely wiped his eyes. "To the memory of the beauty of the dear departed who died of a surfeit of love. Look upon this scarlet potion, gentlemen!" He cuddled the bottle in his arm, looking down with deep admiration, love, and regret.

"For this, my beauteous Romano expired in these arms upon our wedding night, for I had taken an overdose. Yes, this is it, gentlemen, the one, the only, the original Gypsy love potion fortified by the distilled essence of the comfrey plant to render it the true, the universal constitutional."

More spectators had been drawn by his flight into drama, and he could feel, with his salesman's instinct, the crowd swinging toward him.

"Ravenal's Elixir is dangerous, gentlemen, if used indiscriminately, and as a Doctor of Heidelberg, etcetera, etcetera, I must warn you. I have been licensed by the Medical Society of North Adams, New Hampshire, as the sole dispenser of this elixir on a professional and confidential basis to all save bridegrooms, nubile maidens, lads from twelve to fourteen, and unmarried females under sixty. It is not recommended for married gentlemen over eighty, unless wed to younger wives."

"Hey, doc, is that stuff surefire on dead-sure virgins?"

His questioner was a blond young man wearing pimples and a red waistcoat.

"How old are you, my good man?"

"Seventeen, sir."

"Sir, the physiological emoluments of Ravenal's Elixir are independent of age, innocence, or prior condition of chastity."

"What's it worth?"

"Its worth is priceless, but its price is low. Because of rare ingredients imported from the mysterious and exotic Orient, price has been set by the committee in North Adams at fifty cents [Groans], but as an introductory offer, I was prevailed upon by the governor of Kentucky to cut the price in half, or two bottles for fifty cents, four for a dollar."

"Four bottles!"

"Pass back four bottles, gentlemen, to the handsome gent, from who knows where, with the red waistcoat and the golden hair."

"Give me two bottles . . ."A wizened little man bent over a walking stick edged forward.

"Your age, sir?"

"Seventy."

"Mighty young-looking for your age, sir . . . Two bottles, please, for the youngster with the swagger stick."

Hands were being raised now, holding up one, two, or three fingers. As Solomon passed back the bottles and collected the coins, he continued, nonchalantly, with his patter.

"Last week, on the occasion of a lecture before a medical group in Nashville, I dropped in to visit an old gentleman of my acquaintance who complained of rheumatic pains. Having, by chance, a bottle of Ravenal's Elixer of Youth upon my person, I poured him a couple of swigs and went on to give my lecture. Returning by his domicile, I stopped in to inquire of the old gentleman's health and found his wife packing for her departure, swearing she would divorce her husband on the grounds of lechery. 'Thrice he has assaulted me,' quoth she, 'and even now he has treed the maid in her upstairs bedroom and is baying at the door.'

"I proceeded upstairs to chastize the old gentleman . . . your change, sir . . . but after observing the distraught state of his mistress, I poured her the remainder of the elixir . . . one bottle for the gent with the bifurcated beard . . . and proceeded posthaste to the upper floor, where I found the old gentleman pounding at the maid's door. Even as I watched, the door crashed in, but, alas, the maid had flown, climbing from her window to slide down the woodshed roof, her treasure still intact, though perhaps pierced by splinters.

"Turning to the old gentleman, I commenced to upbraid him, but he looked at me in such a manner that I was forced to retreat backward. As I reached the first flight of stairs, I heard the clatter of advancing footsteps. Casting a hasty glance behind me, I saw his wife advancing on my rear. Trapped, as it were, between Scylla and Charybdis, I made a hasty leap over the rail and fled the house.

"Pausing at the door, I looked up to see such billing and cooing going on on the stairway that I knew that domestic tranquillity would reign forever in that household."

He was succeeding. The crowd was with him, laughing at his oldest jokes and most artless puns. He knew how an actor must feel when a play flows so easily and loosely that even missed cues bring sympathetic applause and the admiration emanating from beyond the footlights is liquid, ambient, and sustaining.

But his feeling was not entirely placental. Here was a dynamism and an interaction that required an effort to keep it flowing, to keep the quarters coming and the bottles going, yet the effort was as pleasantly given as yachtsman's hand to a tiller when the wind's astern, the sails filled, and the sea runs with the craft.

Suddenly, the fetus was ripped from the womb, and a crosschop capsized the boat.

Three hands were waving at once when the minstrel band in the area down the fence shot a salvo of banjo plunks into the crowd. Four, count them, four banjos began strumming as one, and his audience fled en masse. Only the halt and the lame heard his final joke, and they heard it departing.

He brought out his camp chair and sat beside the lectern mopping his brow. Twenty-three bottles gone, sales enough to pay the day's expenses, give George a quarter and fifteen cents to the Clay exchequer. His net of sixty cents was not exceptional, but his gross of five dollars and seventy-five cents was a fair week's work on the road. On his next sortie, during the musicians' break, his gross would be his net.

He never made the next sortie.

From across the quadrangle, keening above the charivari of the banjos, came the notes of a flute.

The sound drew his attention to the platform before the pleasure-dome. A fakir sat before a wicker basket, his boney legs crossed, a diaper around his loins, and a turban around his head. As he fluted, the lid of the wicker basket opened, and the head of a cobra appeared, swaying to the music.

As the snake reared upward, its hood spread, the crowd drifted toward the site, slowly, drawn by ancestral dread and fascination.

From the shooting gallery, the firing ceased, and the banjos dwindled into silence.

"Oohs" and "ahs" rose from the gathering crowd as a second cobra lifted its head beside the first, rising higher and falling behind the first snake, overreaching it. The two snakes undulated to the rhythm of the flute. As the tempo of the music stepped up, the cobras lunged and recoiled in a motion so rapid they seemed to be pecking. Then, the flutist slowed, and the snakes began to sway in a reptilian travesty of a waltz, slower and slower, until the waltz became macabre.

Spontaneously, the crowd applauded, and the snakes bowed, turned to face each other, and kissed.

Before the crowd could yell "fake," the cobras' hoods broke into five segments, became gloved fingers, and a raven-haired woman, her face veiled, lifted her black-gloved arms and slithered upward from the false bottom of the basket, keeping to the rhythm of the flute and seeming to climb the air with her undulations.

The Great Mustafina, exponent of the cobra dance, uncoiled from the basket with a flash of thighs through her beaded skirt, revealing her trickery to the crowd and making them applaud.

Her blouse of blue silk covered her breasts and arms down to the gloves. Her face was hidden by her veil. Her skirt of beadstrings reached to her ankles and was draped low over her hips. Between the bodice and the skirt was a bare midriff accented by a navel blackened with lamp-black.

With the snakes gone and the woman revealed, the minstrel band renewed its harassment, but the lone flute continued to dominate the banjos. The flute had something besides the snakes to augment its sound—it had the belly button of the Great Mustafina.

Her hands moved to the rhythm of the flute, her legs coiled and uncoiled, her shoulders swayed and her thighs shimmied, but the navel remained motionless.

More compelling than imagined cobras, that unblinking eye around which her body contorted stared at the crowd, mesmerized it, and lured it inside to watch the death-defying dance performed with live cobras.

Solomon had seen a professional's exhibition of the carnival pitchman's art. He was appreciative, but he was not awed. Aesculapius had yielded to Apollo, and Apollo had succumbed to Terpsichore, but on the morrow, Aesculapius would return, supported by Apollo and Terpsichore. Tomorrow, the god of healing would command the field.

When the crowd emerged from the tent, the banjos summoned them to the puppet show, which lasted long enough for the cobras again to work their magic.

Casually, Solomon went behind his van and loosened two boards on the fence to permit them to swing outward unobtrusively when pressed. They were the boards closest to the escape hatch of the van.

He sold two more bottles before he left the grounds early, both to the young man in the red waistcoat who confided, "Doc, if I warn't an old elixir drinker, I'd swar this was whiskey."

At supper in the Clay house, Solomon voiced melancholy over the turn the day had taken after its bright beginning. Mrs. Foreman, who was staying over for the military ball at the armory on Saturday night and who still glowed over the compliment Solomon had polished for her on his drive home, essayed optimism. It was the first day of the fair, she pointed out, and the backcountry folks would be arriving soon. He could count on larger crowds Friday and Saturday. Although the fair was closed Sunday, on the following Monday and Tuesday, everyone would have seen all the variations on the puppet show and snake dance and would be ready for the deeper joys of his edifying lectures.

Clay's remark was closer to Solomon's thinking. "What you need is a larger minstrel band and two Persian dancers."

After supper, Solomon arranged a conference with Clay in Melinda's quarters in the girl's presence.

Solomon opened the meeting with a polite falsehood.

"Your remark, sir, at supper set me thinking. I don't

think it's a matter of overpowering my competition with sound alone. One flute was worth four banjos, because it attracted attention to the lady's bare skin. Thereafter, her belly button bore the burden."

Clay, remarking on Solomon's alliteration, accused him of being impressed in the pitchman's mold.

Solomon laid his plan on the table. Putting absolute trust in the gullibility of crowds, he proposed to introduce Melinda, alias Arabella, as a Nubian princess and let her perform her dance, to the music of his violin, as an educational demonstration of Nubian fertility rites.

His plan was received with enthusiasm by Melinda, but Clay expressed reservations.

"Sol, you'd be exposing to public view a girl with a price on her head. If you're caught, you won't be cited for violating a city ordinance, you'll go to prison, and the girl will be sent South. For both your sakes, I can't approve."

Clay, the lawyer, was mulling over the problem. Solomon enlisted the aid of Clay, the soldier.

"Mr. Clay, this is a war I'm fighting, against the blind tiger outside and the competition inside. No battle is fought without risks. There's lots of money out there, and we all need funds.

"Sir, I'm the field commander, and it's my duty to estimate the tactical situation. I know I can sell to those people if I can get their attention. I know they'll believe anything that I tell them, and they'll believe Arabella is a Nubian princess. I know her dancing will attract an audience.

"General, the issue is in doubt on the field of battle. I am hard-pressed by the enemy. Sir, with your approval, I request permission to bring up the artillery!"

"By God, man, spoken like a true Anglo-Saxon!"

Solomon relaxed as he saw the joy of combat rising in Clay's eyes. He smiled. "Sir, after that remark, I don't know whether to thank you or challenge you to a duel."

Clay rose to pace the room, saying, "Now, hear me. We'll clear the debt to the printer but save the bottle money to pay the sign painter. We print new handbills, something about exotic dancers of the Nile . . . the only Nubian princess in captivity . . . No, that word is too suggestive. She's a free and noble princess of the Nubian line. Princess what? Arabella, of course. The name means 'little Arab,' and if memory does not fail, the Nubians had an influx of Arab blood.

"Now, I observed at noonday you had a tarpaulin unfurled as a sunshade. How long's that tarp? . . . Eight by four, good! Our sign painter can label it, 'Commencing immediately, Princess Arabella of Nubia with her dance of the Nile.' Concentrate, sir. The appropriate lettering will come.

"George can nail stanchions to the side of the van, four feet above the roof level, and you can hoist the sign at the beginning of each performance. Attract attention!

"The girl must wear shoes. The noise on the boards will attract, and the shoes will dispel any hint of the Gypsy in the girl's costume. We must stir no memory in the mind of the sheriff . . ."

Clay's magnificent mind was harvesting the grand designs. Solomon gave thanks for the military analogy that had set Clay aflame.

After writing and revising, Solomon lay down and slept soundly on the eve of a venture far more desperate than that which had kept him sleepless the night before. He arose to frantic after-breakfast activity, George pounding, the sign painter lettering, the printer printing, and rehearsals on the sandy floor of Melinda's room.

Clay was so enamored of the military metaphor that he bade Solomon good-bye with the words, "Captain, your general will be waiting at field headquarters, tonight, for first reports from the field."

"Aye, aye, sir," Solomon saluted, mixing the metaphor.

General Clay did not have to wait until nightfall for the report from his field commander. First reports dribbled in from Willie, who had visited the fair in his goat cart, where he was given free admission as Clay's boy. He spoke of his adventures to his mother. Reba told Bob, and Bob told Clay, "Marse Clay, something's going on over at the fairground. Willie says Arabella's done caused a commotion."

"Send the boy to me, Bob."

Willie came into Clay's presence wide-eyed with excitement. "Mister Clay, they was whooping and yelling something fierce ever' time Bella danced."

"Sheriff didn't get anybody, did he, Willie?"

"No, sir. They's happy crazy!"

Clay did not know whether the boy meant the crowd was drunk or simply applauding Melinda with whoops and hollers, but he suspected he was hearing a good report.

His suspicions were verified in the late afternoon, when Solomon thundered into the backyard and brought the careening van to a halt, leaping from the driver's seat with Melinda's valise in his hand. As Melinda dashed for the privy, Solomon rushed in to meet Clay coming down the hall.

"Sir, I asked for the artillery, but you sent me a whole new division. Princess Arabella was sweeping the enemy from the field when I ran out of ammunition."

"Ah, a breakdown in logistics," Clay commented, as Solomon steered him into Solomon's bedroom, opening the valise to spread coins and script on the counterpane.

"Mr. Clay, they were throwing the money onto the platform, and I was tossing the bottles back. The puppeteers and the Persian dancer begged for a truce. We've split each hour into twenty-minute segments, one for each show."

Standing back, he scratched his head. "Seems I've won somewhere in the exchange. Here's ninety dollars for eighty-seven-fifty's worth of merchandise . . . Sir, it's a gold mine. You found it, and you deserve the royalties. Henceforth, the house gets a full twenty-five percent cut on the gross."

"You've got your fifteen dollars, Sol. Are you leaving Lexington?"

"Sir, I've found means of recouping my entire loss and augmenting the treasury of the house. If you're willing to risk my presence, I'm willing to risk the stay."

Clay said brusquely, "Put ten more dollars on the bed, and I'll close the blind tiger."

"Thank you, sir."

"To the distillery," Clay said. "My buggy is hitched and waiting. I have a fast horse."

Solomon counted out ten dollars and laid it on the table beside the twenty-two and a half dollars he had already placed there.

They bought two barrels of aged bourbon and two bottles of grenadine syrup which would substitute for honey while holding the ruby glow of the elixir. They cleared the distillery of its supply of half-pint bottles, six hundred odd.

Clay enlisted all hands to assist in bottling a new batch, but despite their haste, Solomon wheeled into the quadrangle with only half an hour remaining before the booths closed. He backed the van into position alongside the platform, leaving the mules hitched as he hoisted his tarp and lighted the torches at the corners of the platform.

Spectators surged as he stood forth to invite the audience to a ceremonial swig before the fertility rites of ancient Nubia commenced, and the clamor came for bottles. His was the last twenty minutes of the hour, so he prolonged his spiel in order to sell the entire batch, but the crowd grew restive.

"Get on with the show," someone called from the gathering shadows.

"You got all our boodle, Doc," another yelled. "Bring on the burrhead."

For the few bottles still unsold, he could not risk a riot. He reached for his violin, and he played the brief, introductory notes, hearing the door of the van open behind him. Melinda's shoes began to thud to the music.

In the flare of the torches, he saw the eyes and the half-opened mouths below him. He felt the crowd lean forward as Melinda bent backward in the beginning movements of her symbolic orgasm. These men were ominously silent. Heretofore, her horizontal shimmying had brought cheers and cries for more, but now the watchers seemed more intense and far more attentive.

Although his music did not falter, Solomon felt a growing alienation from the crowd. All day, he had been a puppet master, and they had been his puppets; but he was no longer their master, and they were no longer puppets. Darkness and the flickering torchlight was working against him. They would need a diverting finale, and quickly.

He drew from the instrument the notes of the finale, knowing she was bowing to the crowd and that her bow was the crisis.

Quickly, he stopped, raised his hands, and shouted to them. "Gentlemen, the princess has learned a few words of our language, and she wishes to honor you with a familiar song."

He bowed to her, lifted his bow, and began to soothe them with the familiar strains of "My Old Kentucky Home."

Looking toward Melinda, he prayed she would remember the opening lines of the song.

Hesitantly, she stepped forward, but she sang:

> The sun shines bright in the old Kentucky home,
> 'Tis summer, the darkies are gay.

As her tremolo, poignant, appealing, startling, quavered over the crowd, a few drunken voices responded automatically.

> The corn-top's ripe and the meadow's in the bloom,
> While the birds make music all the day.

Others joined in to drown the music from the violin.

Solomon laid the instrument on the table beside his unsold bottles of elixir and walked to the edge of the platform to lead the chorus. All were singing now, their voices growing in volume. Still pacing the tempo with his hands, Solomon walked back to the table, dropped his hands, lifted the table, and carried it into the van. Inside, he grabbed his tin cup from the peg and emerged, waving his hands aloft in time to the singing.

He stood beside Melinda and through unmoving lips said to her, "When they get to 'Weep no more,' start backing toward the door of the van. When they sing 'good night,' bow, step inside, and lock the door behind you."

He turned back to conduct the chorus. Still conducting, he walked over and stood beside the remaining torch.

Melinda timed her exit perfectly and naturally. Before the echoes died from the final "good night" of the last stanza, he cupped the remaining torch and called out, as he swung aboard the wagon, "Good night, gentlemen, we'll see you, tomorrow."

He drove off at a princely trot, leaving the stupefied chorus to face an empty platform in the darkness.

As he rolled through the lighted gate, he removed his hat to wipe the perspiration from his forehead. He remembered the climb up the Great Smokies when the witches laughed, and he wondered if the thing he had sensed tonight in the mob had been real or his imagination. If it were real, he hoped the girl had not sensed it. Tomorrow would be a long day, since the fair opened at nine in the

307

morning on Saturday, and if she became terrified, her worth to him would be ended. Unrestrained abandon was the basis of her art.

With a feeling approaching dread, he heard her fumble at the latch, unhook the windows, and push it open.

"Mr. Ricky?"

"Yes."

"What you mean when you say 'etcetera, etcetera'?"

He grinned in relief and answered with the spontaneity of a born crocus pitcher. "Way I use it, girl, it means I'm well qualified as a pecker raiser."

"That you are, Mr. Ricky. That you sure are."

Chapter Twelve

If circumcision dulled the pangs of lust for Jews, as Maimonides averred, then heaven help Gentiles, Solomon thought as Mrs. Foreman turned toward him in the candlelight with admiration in her eyes. Clay had completed a toast to Solomon with an invitation to tomorrow night's dance at the armory.

"I beseech you to come, Mr. Ravenal. I do adore military balls, and if you're not there to dance a set with me, I'll just die."

"I shake a mean leg at the bayou shindigs, but I may be a little shy at town dances."

"Don't let his modesty confuse you, Mrs. Foreman," Clay said. "As one whose line goes farther back than the Bonapartes, he has the grace of breeding that will make him the natural leader of the cotillion."

"Modesty in a Southerner is refreshing."

"In me, ma'am, I expect it's timidity."

"Not so," Clay protested. "Sol's father was an expert duelist, given his choice of weapons, whose reputation ranged as far north as Cincinnati."

And as far south as Covington, Solomon thought, as long as the choice of weapons was words.

Solomon bent to the roast lamb Clay had ordered, with the claret and candles, to celebrate his success. Clay, as a gentleman, would not lie, but he presented facts in such a manner that a Hebrew peddler fleeing Georgia emerged as an epic hero of the Louisiana aristocracy.

"I think it wonderful, Mr. Ravenal, when a gentleman can engage successfully in trade."

"A sordid business, ma'am, but justice of a sort. I am righting a theft with humbug and fakery."

"Never fret, sir. The public loves to be deceived."

Over coffee, Solomon outlined his evening to Clay, whose servants he had retained to complete the bottling left unfinished from the afternoon. Night work was necessary because the fair started early on Saturday because of an afternoon recess for horse racing. Clay voiced confidence in Solomon's ability to handle the crew, alone, and excused himself to work in his study. Mrs. Foreman graciously volunteered her services as a taster, which Solomon accepted with alacrity.

Solomon gathered his labor force in the backyard, and by lantern light, the work went smoothly apace. Bob gathered the filled bottles and wheelbarrowed them to the van, where Willie stowed them in the wall rack George had built during the afternoon.

Solomon mixed in a wooden bucket and adjusted the ingredients according to Mrs. Foreman, who tasted each batch with a ladle. She insisted that Solomon approve her final decision with a sip himself.

From the beginning, he found her taste infallible. By the end of three hundred bottles, which required samplings from eight batches, he was finding her taste exquisite and telling her so.

At the three hundredth bottle, Solomon called a recess, and the crew was so complimentary of the quality of the elixir in the two bottles Solomon donated that he added two more in appreciation of their appreciation. Work commenced on the final two hundred bottles in a spirit of camaraderie which combined the loftier sentiments of a revival meeting and an all-day-singing-and-eating-on-the-ground.

By the eleventh batch, Mrs. Foreman's British reserve had yielded to the spirit of the occasion. She did a graceful little schottische to the music of her own singing, bowed, and presented the ladle to Solomon with an impromptu ditty.

> Take a little sip,
> Take a little sip,
> Take a little sip,
> Right now!

Her vivacity so charmed him that he drank and swung her into a few graceful whirls with an answering ditty.

> It is very good,
> It is very good,
> It is very good,
> I trow.

The crew clapped.

Mrs. Foreman pronounced his final batch his masterpiece.

"I declare, Solly, I've never tasted such ambrosia. Really, I cawn't express my admiration for your genius. You are the most handsome, witty, and skillful elixir mixer I ever did see."

She had the most delightful accent he had ever heard, a combination of British precision and Southern languor which reminded him *exactly* of a box hedge blooming with magnolia blossoms.

"The inspiration of your proximity and the exquisite sensibility of your taste buds is solely responsible for the success of this delightful, desire-provoking, and potent potion, ma'am."

"Desire-provoking and potent, quoth he. 'Tis a combination devoutly to be wished."

"May I offer you the last two bottles of Ravenal's Elixir of Youth to fortify you against chilblains, ague, colic, nervousness, and the slings and arrows of outrageous fortune?"

"They've been spoke for, Solly. You promised them to our hardworking darkies."

"Indeed, Pam, ma'am, but there's a bucket left from the batch. Crew, a bucket in the bulk repay you for the loss of two half-pints, bottled?"

"Yes, sir," came the chorus.

"Fetch us cups, Reba, We'll gather around the wassail bowl."

As Reba rushed to fetch the cups, Solomon paid the crew and took inventory. He had a full barrel of whiskey in the van plus an eighth remaining from the barrel he had mixed. "Would you tap this partial barrel, sometime ere morn, George, and, Willie, if you'll patrol the fairground tomorrow, I'll pay you a penny for each five empty bottles returned."

He poured the remaining grenadine and sassafras into the barrel. "I'll hold this in reserve to be served from the spigot. If we sell out our bottled stock, Arabella can fill Willie's empties between dances."

"Speaking of dancing, sir," Mrs. Foreman said, "I cannot wait till tomorrow night. I challenge you to an immediate waltz."

"We'll have a drink to that, from my private stock . . . A toast, children, to Mrs. Foreman, Britannia's gem from over the ocean."

He ladled from the barrel, and the cups were filled.

They toasted her, then him, then they toasted each other, and Solomon asked, "Does anybody here play anything?"

"I fiddle, sir," Bob said, "and George plays a harp."

"Y'all know, 'Down in the Valley'?"

"Yes, sir."

"That ought to do for a waltz."

Bob filled his cup and went to get his fiddle. George filled his cup, pulled his harmonica from his pocket, and flipped it against his thigh. George filled his cup and gathered the lanterns, and Reba and Melinda made for the porch swing, giggling in their cups. Willie tailed along with half a cup.

Solomon ran the impromptu band through a few bars, keeping the music low in order not to disturb the master of the house or the neighbors, and found they played with passing skill.

He swung his lady into the waltz.

Waltzing with Pamela Foreman was a surge, eddy, and ebb. An inexpert dancer might have clung to her waist and been swept into the flow of the music, and Solomon was not inexpert. He moved into the music with her, feeling as Oberon might have felt waltzing with Titania on a moonbeam.

"You dance divinely, sir," she said.

"And you, ma'am, are as light on your feet as a leaping fawn. I concede you the victory, but beg your leave to fight a little longer."

"Granted, sir. What a lovely waltz they're playing!"

"An old song, ma'am, well-known hereabouts," he said in a tutorial manner to a wide-eyed attentive student. "It has words, ma'am."

Suddenly, he was singing, low, and for her alone, and a

312

pleasant tremor came into his voice when he reached the stanza:

> Roses love sunshine,
> Violets love dew,
> Angels in heaven
> Know I love you.

Impishly, his erstwhile student answered:

> If you don't love me,
> Love whom you please.
> Put your arms round me,
> Give my heart ease.

Her quaint deception charmed him. He was speaking to her now, in the impersonal intimacy of a love ballad, singing *con amore fervente:*

> Build me a castle
> Forty feet high,
> So I can see her
> As she rides by.
>
> As she rides by, love,
> As she rides by.
> So I can see her
> As she rides by.

She squeezed him, warmly, in a gesture that told him she understood, and Solomon glided now to the rhythm as lightly as a fallen leaf whirling on the surface of a stream. From the night, the music, the lanterns, and the waltz, the lady of fire and ice had woven a charm around him that split for a moment the veils of reality to let him glimpse the cloud-capped towers of Prospero. If he had been Faust, he would have said to this moment, "Stay." But he knew that it would not stay, and he did not want it to pass without some monument; and so he said to the weaver of dreams, "You are as beautiful as a cloudscape which the sun tints with dawn. You're more glittering than the night stars when the moon's hid away."

She was gazing up at him as he spoke, and a sadness and softness veiled her eyes. Too overcome by his compliment to speak, she nestled her head on his shoulder and squeezed him gently. In silence and in tenderness they ended the waltz.

313

She turned away from him, after the bow and curtsy, and said to Bob, "Can you play 'Good Night, Ladies'?"

He could, and standing beside him, she sang to the group. They thanked her and departed to their quarters.

She took her bottles from the banister and his arm, and he led her into the house. Passing the kitchen, he said to her, "You must have been the belle of the Sea Island balls."

As he spoke, he remembered that she had never mentioned to him a word about her life on the Georgia plantation, but she failed to notice his intrusion on her privacy.

"Oh, I was happy, Solly, deliriously happy, for three weeks. I shall always love Fair Oaks, and I shall remember the life there as a happy, happy life. I have hidden the scars. You can see no scars on me, can you, Solly?"

"None at all, Pam."

"You're a gentleman, and I'll trust you into my chamber. Come, let me show you my scars."

"I'd be right proud to see them, ma'am."

She ushered him into her unlighted bedroom and said, "The light is over there, but first, yield to a whim. Hold me close and kiss me in the darkness."

Strangely, he was not flabbergasted by her request. It seemed a natural development from the evening, the dancing, and the dreams.

He did not bend to her shyly, but with ardor, cupping her regal head in his long, artistic fingers and bending, *con fervente,* to the white column of a neck arching upward out of the darkness, the soft lips, the faint perfume of grenadine. He felt her pneumatic breast heave in a prolonged sigh and felt all the sweet machinery of love expanding, the hissing, the sighing, the drive rods moving, the rails shining before them, and the lights flicking green. But there was a flaw attendant on the beginning locomotion. Somewhere, a valve developed a leak, and as his arms twined around her, as one hand sought and found the hard, smooth, upward rising of buttocks tensed on toe tips, he felt an insensate urge to relieve his bladder.

It was a weird juxtaposition of desires. Bending over a warmly ardent and adoring woman on tiptoe for a longed-for kiss, how did one, as one enwrapped her thighs and thrilled to the heavings of her truly mammoth mammae, stoop to her and whisper, "Madam, unclutch me, for I must hie myself to the privy?"

314

At long last, she disengaged herself and said, "You may light the lamps, Solly."

"Madam, tonight you've lit such a lamp as all Lexington won't put out, but excuse me . . . My matches are in my coat, and my coat is in my room."

As rapidly as possible, he returned and lighted the lamp.

She was seated near the head of the bed, her bottle uncorked. "Bring us glasses from the washstand, Solly. I took a nip from the bottle while you were gone in a most unladylike manner. I don't dare bark my shins looking for glasses in the dark."

"A sensible precaution, ma'am."

He brought the glasses and divided the scant remainder left in the bottle after her nip.

He was amazed at her capacity, not so much as to where she put it but as to where she kept it. She had not excused herself all evening, and she had consumed, to his knowledge, two glasses of claret, two cups of coffee, a glass of water, and an approximate quart of the elixir. He had drunk less of the bourbon than she, and he was far over his quota.

She rummaged in the drawer of her night table and tossed a daguerreotype on the bed beside her. "Fair Oaks!"

He sat beside her and picked up the photograph. It was a picture of her and a man, taken at a distance, standing on the top steps of a veranda. The columns lining the porch were Mobile, Alabama-sized columns, bigger around than a hogshead.

"Henry," she barked, and tossed him the picture of a long-faced man, light-haired and light-eyed, with the far-focused gaze of the dreamer.

"Thelma!"

An old Negro woman.

"Marse Henry and his blushing bride."

Over the fourth daguerreotype he spoke. "Then, as now, you were beautiful, and he's almost handsome."

"Aye, he was a bloody toff, all right! Without his drawl, he might have passed for his lordship, minus the royal pox, ill-met in Soho."

She was burning with rage, and she was not acting.

He stacked the photographs and handed them back to her. She fanned them out in her hand in the manner of a card player. "Carte de vista from hell!"

Suddenly, her voice went soft and her eyes grew dream-lost. "Ah, but it was a lovely, lovely spot. Nothing can ever change that . . .

"After our strange honeymoon, after we were joined in love and in beauty, Henry used to take me sailing along the inner channel. At night, when the moon was full and the water so still you could hear the splash of fish, the live oaks dripped with Spanish moss above the sea marshes —silver on silver in the moonlight. I do wish one could pluck segments from their memory, tear them from their anguish, and preserve them in some amber apart . . . Do you like me, Solly?"

Intent on her narrative, his curiosity aroused by her words, "strange honeymoon," he blurted, "Indeed, ma'am, very much."

"Why, Solly?"

On guard, he answered, "Because you say such things as 'preserve them in amber apart.' "

"You're the sweetest thing, and ever so understanding."

She bent a gaze on him that would have melted him had he been less intent on her curious honeymoon.

"Do you know, Solly, that women in public life are often lonely. Rarely do eligible men come near. Ah, there are always men, managers, sycophants, commission men, who come to us for private gain or public notice.

"At that time, I was only twenty, but the toast of two continents, as the papers said. Gentlemen would take me out to dinner, behave most circumspectly, take me straight home, and then the bastards would go bragging how they took my virtue.

"At the time I met Henry, quite by accident I had a frightful reputation, but Henry did not travel in circles where a lady's reputation was discussed. When I met Henry, he didn't know Pamela Sherwood from Good King James.

"I'm supposed to be beautiful, you know, but my parts don't quite match. I have an English head on an Italian body, and my nose is a bit too long, don't you think?"

"No, ma'am, Pam. Your nose is pree-cisely the right length."

"Thank you, kind sir . . . Henry took me to dinner three times before he even ventured to hold my hand. It was not until our second date that he even mentioned that he owned a 3,356-acre rice plantation in Georgia with two hundred thirty-seven slaves.

"He was so modest and ever so understanding. Oh, he was weak, Solly, but I didn't care.

"Did you ever notice, Solly, that the men women really fall in love with are weak. Oh, they can admire and even learn to love a strong man, but nothing stirs their emotions so deeply as a frightened little boy who comes to have his bruises kissed.

"I could have been his companion, his lover . . . Why do you like me, Solly? Tell me true."

"Your cultivated mind, ma'am. You're the only member of the fair sex I've ever met who can quote Shakespeare."

"Pshaw! Any aspiring actress can quote the Bard. I just love William."

"So, but how many are on a first name basis with him?"

"Could you love me, Solly?"

"You're a very beautiful woman with your classic face, and your eyes have a shade of green . . ."

"And you, sirah, have melting brown eyes, a clean-cut jaw, a thin, patrician nose above wide, sensual lips, and I thrill to your lustrous and curly black hair. But I ask you a question."

"You wouldn't want my love, Pam. Its currency is debased. For you, I have a coin of brighter mintage."

"Prithee, a pretty phrase, 'My currency is debased.' By such a measure, my own love is worthless . . . Dead soldier?"

"Kill it."

She finished the first bottle by squeezing its contents and topped the glass with the fresh bottle.

"Those three weeks at Fair Oaks were my Golden Age . . . It's not debasing love to give it, but it's degrading to have that love spurned for an evil passion.

"I said Henry was weak, but in ways he was strong. He ran his plantation without a whip, and he used his own slaves as overseers.

"When we arrived at Fair Oaks on that bright morning, the field hands gathered before the house, the men coming forward to shake his hand, as if they were white, and the women hugged and some even kissed him. They were weeping with joy.

"I was overwhelmed by their greeting. It seemed to me that they worshiped him, and I suppose, in a measure, they did. But there was more to their greeting than unalloyed love. It took me three weeks to find the reason for

317

this . . . this greeting they gave him. The horror of it! The horror of it!"

She was recoiling from some abyss in her memory, and he asked gently, "What was the reason for it?"

"Thelma," she tossed back a daguerreotype. "That black bitch! I should have skewered her on a silver spike, but I was pigeon-livered and lacked gall to make oppression bitter."

He looked again at a face which, except for the eyes, he had seen a thousand times in the South. The proud defiance in the Negro woman's eyes was that of a captured general overwhelmed by an inferior foe.

"When Henry was born, his mother, a wispy, frail old lady whom I hardly met during my stay, lacked something in her milk. Thelma, being then with child, was brought out of the fields as a wet nurse. She was kept in the house with a white baby at one breast and a pickaninny at the other. After the babies were weaned, she never left the big house.

"But I was not resented there. No, they doted on me. I didn't lift a finger except for my own pleasure. I had nothing to do but ride, hunt, go boating and fishing. I set out my own lobster traps. Have you ever fished for lobster, Solomon?"

Fearing a dissertation on lobster fishing, he lied. "Yes, yes, but please go on . . . You mentioned, Pam, that your honeymoon was strange."

"Strange, yes, but most interesting.

"We boarded ship at New York and sailed to Savannah, in adjoining staterooms. It was Henry's wish that our marriage be consummated in the master bedroom at Fair Oaks, where his father and grandfather had taken their brides.

"It was refreshing to find someone with such a delicate regard for tradition. I was weary of gluttons. If he wanted me at a ceremonial banquet, I felt pleased and honored. Tenderness, Solly, means much to a woman . . . What's this about a new coin you wish to give me?"

"Later, Pam. It's too intimate for now."

"Too intimate! I adore intimacies. Tell me, in all intimacy, why, truly, do you like me?"

Laughter in her eyes triggered a spontaneous sincerity in him, and he answered. "All attractions bow before your magnificent breasts. Ma'am, your bosoms overwhelm me."

She had asked for the truth, and with a scholar's integrity

318

he answered, expecting to be reproached for his brazen words; but Pamela Foreman lay back on her elbows, threw her head to the ceiling, and rippled silvery laughter. Wiping her eyes, she sat up, smiling. "Solomon, one thing I never expected to hear was truth from the tongue of a Frenchman. Sir, we'll spread no more horse manure about Shakespeare and souls . . ."

"Please, Pam. The honeymoon."

"So it was that we came to Fair Oaks. On our wedding night, he came to me with reverence and tenderness, and I responded with awe and modest delight. Henry never once suspected that I lost my maidenhead at fourteen to a goat from the city who hid his horns under a bowler hat and broke my hymen with his furled umbrella.

"I loved his shyness and his reverence. His tenderness was rapture. I responded until I slept from a surfeit of love.

"In the morning, there was only snuggling and cuddling, for we were both spent, and we rose to romp like children over the acres. The darkies beamed at the happiness of Marse Henry, and Miss Pamela was their goddess. We galloped the oak-shaded lanes on blooded steeds. We picnicked by the ocean on the wide sand beach. That was the twelfth day of September, 1854."

There was such depth to her poignancy that her voice broke when she named the day, and Solomon feared she might lose her self-control; but she continued in a prosaic tone, as if relating a tale that happened in another country, to another person.

"He never made excessive demands on me, but when I felt the need for him, he would sense my need and come.

"After the first night, we kept separate bedrooms because he suffered nightsweats and bad dreams and did not wish to discomfit me. He always let me know, by the way he patted my hand or the way he stroked my hair, that he understood when I wanted him and that he would come to me.

"On such a night, he always took a stroll around the grounds. He had something of a poet's nature, he said, and by taking these walks alone, he could prepare himself to approach my couch with the reverence due my worth. Ah, he was a skillful dissembler, he was. Truly, I was in love . . . Have you ever been in love, Solly?"

"I've been through there," he said, hiding his impatience, "but I was on a train going to another town."

"One night, he had given me the signal, when a rain-squall blew up, suddenly, as they do in Georgia.

"He was a man of strange fears. He killed a man once in a duel, though I didn't learn it from him, but he was afraid to get up on the left side of his bed in the morning, and he cowered before electrical storms. That night, even I was alarmed by the lightning which came in such constant flashes that the night was almost turned to day.

"Yet, I heard him leave the room as the appointed hour neared and quietly close the door behind him to go for his walk. My bed lamp was not lighted out of deference to his modesty, and I arose to see where he was going.

"I'm a trusting soul, Solly, but I'm also an inquisitive woman. It seemed more than strange that he should be walking on such a night, and I could hear the floor creak from his footsteps as he passed my bedroom going down the darkened corridor.

"I followed him at a distance and lost the sound in the crash of thunder which was shaking the house. When I reached the end of the corridor, I found the exit bolted from the inside.

"He had not left the corridor.

"Very quietly, I walked back up the hall, and very slowly.

"Then I heard what seemed, at first, to be moaning sounds between the rolls of thunder, sounds so low I could have never heard them had not my ears been straining for a sound.

"I paused a moment outside a door. At first, I thought perhaps he had gone alone to an empty room to pray or to weep in fear, and then I realized that I was standing outside the door to Thelma's room.

"I could hear my husband making the moaning sounds, and then I heard the voice of Thelma saying, 'Now, don't you fret none, sugar. You gonna be all right. There's nothing to worry about, baby, purely nothing to worry about.'

"Up to that point, I thought he had fled to his old mammy in terror, but then she said, 'Miss Pam's a nice lady. You told me yo'self she 'preciates my baby. Ain't nothing to be afraid of, sugar.'

"I cracked the door and looked in. There was no light in the room, and there was no need with the lightning flashes.

"There on that bed my husband lay, stark naked, and that old beldame had his head cuddled on her lap, one scrawny arm holding his head up, the strap of her night-gown lowered, and one of her leathery breasts was out. He was sucking her breast and mewling like a child.

"That filthy old crone kept crooning to him, 'Now, honey, it's soon be ready for Miss Pam. Now, don't you let this old lightnin' scare you none. I done put a conjure on this lightnin', and it ain't gonna hurt my baby.'

"I don't know how long I stood there, listening. The old woman's crooning was strangely detached, yet it was warm and loving.

"At one point, she was almost giving him a report. I remember she said, 'Sugar, don't you worry about old Ralph. You just tell him, come morning, he ain't gonna get over he sick till he quits soldiering. If I conjure that lazy old nigger, I sho can conjure a little old lightnin'.'

"He was gurgling now, happy and contented. And she was exhorting him, 'You's almost there, sugar. It's a-comin' up. Now, I's gonna sprinkle a little hoodoo powder on it, and you is gonna go in there and give Miss Pam the best she ever got. You just believe that, sugar, 'cause yo' old mammy ain't never gonna lie to her baby.'

"Solly, I could stand no more. I turned and fled down the hall. When he came to me, I told him I was frightened by the storm, and he withdrew.

"The next morning, I got old Ralph to drive me down to Darien, and I caught the stage for Savannah. Henry knew then that I knew, and he didn't offer to kiss me good-bye to save me the embarrassment of refusing him. He just stood on the veranda and watched me go, the saddest, loneliest man in the world.

"That was the third day of October."

He saw she was bordering on hysteria, and to calm her, he said, matter-of-factly, "You must understand him. Your husband was just a late-weaned child, ma'am."

"But, Sol, her paps were old and withered. Yet my husband, my beloved, was tugging at that old black dug and gurgling with delight."

Even at this distance in time, her eyes held a look of dazed disbelief as she said softly, almost to herself, "He had to use those old black titties to get a prickstand, when he had this!"

With a sudden, convulsive movement, she reached down

into her blouse and lifted. Into the lamplight, into the full view of his astonished eyes, plopped one of her magnificent breasts. She was not wearing a corset.

"And this!"

Like two full moons on the horizon, they gleamed in the lamplight.

"Her witchcraft ran that plantation, and her black dugs had given him the prickstand he brought to our marriage chamber."

"Pam, he was not turning away from those delectable orbs. It was not lack of love of you or lack of appreciation for those wonderful mounds. On the contrary, he was a sculptor who had fears that his dull tool might chip inaccurately. So, he turned to his old black mammy, and she honed the tool from which he hewed his monument of affection for you."

"Are you making excuses for that depraved son of a bitch?"

"No, ma'am! What he did was inexcusable, but it did not spring from a lack of love for you. Believe me, it would have been impossible to spurn these."

To underline his sincerity, he reached over and stroked her breasts, letting his fingers come down and focus on the point, fluting his fingertips around her nipples, and he saw them growing erect.

Her voice was softer, calmer when she spoke. "They got you ready the minute I put them against you. Why wouldn't they work on Henry?"

"The poor lad was called upon to play a violin sonata on an unstrung instrument. Remember, dear Pam, I play the violin."

"Solly, boy, what was that new-minted coin?" His therapeutic kneading had worked. Her hysteria had vanished.

"A quality of desire, ma'am. I know that in your regality and beauty, you can pick and choose among gallants, but of all the men in the world, there is not one who burns with as pure flame of desire for you and for these as I do now."

"Oh, Soollly," she sighed to the deft kneading as he rolled the nipples in his fingers, "I bet you tell that to all the girls."

"How could I, dearest? There has never been a woman born with such a bosom, and these words will never be summoned again to eulogize such beauty."

322

"I'll declare, Sol, are you just going to sit there and squeeze me out of shape. Here, unbutton my bodice."

She whirled with a graceful motion, spinning the delightful orbs from his grasp, and twisted to turn the immaculate arch of her back to him.

He fumbled at the tightly-buttoned bodice, asking hoarsely, "Who buttoned these buttons for you?"

Her laughter tinkled at the suspicion in his voice, "Reba, you silly boy. Who did you think? Willie?"

Her left hand reached behind her and patted his knee, her fingers fluttered along the inside of his leg, caressingly, when a loud and imperious knock sounded on the door.

"God damn," she whispered. "Mr. Clay!"

Solomon's tumescence plopped like a soap bubble.

Clay's attitude toward the fair sex was typical of the South and precisely the reverse of the attitude that the South had taught Solomon: Clay believed every woman was a lady until she proved differently. He could see the Lion of Lexington outside the door, Bowie knife unsheathed, waiting in his fighter's stance to avenge the honor of his house guest.

"Let me handle this," Solomon whispered to a lady who was stuffing her breasts back into her dress with unladylike haste.

He went to the door, glanced back to see that the lady was now modestly sheathed, and opened it.

"Melinda! What in heaven's name are you doing here?"

"Mr. Ravenal, somebody's done tapped the full barrel."

Solomon clapped his hand to his forehead in anguish and in self-exasperation. He had intended to lock the van, but his intentions had been diverted by the waltz.

He turned a stricken face to Pamela. "Excuse me, ma'am, but somebody's tapped the main barrel."

He exited and closed the door, loping behind the scooting Melinda past the kitchen, into the yard, and sprinted for the stable and the van.

She was right. The full barrel had been tapped, and also the partial barrel. George had outdone himself, doing too much too early.

He cast a quick glance toward the bottles on the wall rack George had installed, and the solid rows of filled bottles indicated no pilfering.

The whole interior was plainly visible in the light of his seven-pronged candlestick, which flickered above the end

323

cabinet. His tallis was folded on the chest beside it, and atop the tallis, supported by paper wadding, gleamed the black dome of a yarmulke.

"How much straight whiskey did George pilfer?"

"I give him just a little bitty bit, 'bout half a cup."

"Who lit the candles?"

"I did, sir."

"Where'd you get the yarmulke?"

"I made it."

"Why?"

"I reckoned you'd want it, sir, seeing as how it's Friday and you been busy."

"Who gave you the prerogative to act as my conscience?"

"I don't know them Hebrew words, sir, but I just knowed you'd want to get in there and say a little prayer, 'cause you told me, once, you didn't never want to forget another Sabbath."

He looked down at her.

This was trickery, vulgarity, unmitigated insolence and gall on the part of the presumptuous little wench. To contain his rage, he focused his attention on the candles.

The golden light, twice beautiful from his double vision, ameliorated his fury. It was, indeed, a beautiful scene, made more dazzling by the reflections from the bottles of grenadined bourbon which glowed a deep purple in the candlelight.

"I should flail hell out of your black ass for this! You know what I'm going to do?"

"No, sir!" She looked up at him, tiny and sullen, her arms folded across her chest, her head tilted back, frightened but defiant.

"I'm going to crawl in there and say a little prayer."

He crawled. It was safer than attempting to step into the van.

Mrs. Foreman would have to wait a little longer while he spent a few minutes with the Lord. About time he was giving thanks for some of the blessings this day had brought, for it was written—something about an ungrateful son. Perhaps, it might be wise to ask God, in His wisdom, to grant him an added measure of tenderness to take to his tryst with the lady, who did so appreciate a bit of tenderness.

With his shawl around him, his yarmulke cocked at a rakish angle atop his head, Solomon rose to his knees before the altar and assumed a Christian attitude of prayer, albeit supported by one arm in the manner of a slouching anthropoid. He attempted an invocation in Hebrew, but the warmth of the confined quarters and the fumes from his own breath heightened the impact of the alcohol, and for him, Hebrew became temporarily a dead language.

Hebrew was a presumptuous language for a third-generation American, and a Sephard at that. It was as bad as Latin in the pope's church. Next thing he knew, the pusselgutted rabbis would have him counting beads. When a man talked to God, he shouldn't have to strain for a word. God understood English. With all that profanity pouring up from Georgia, He would have to learn English to keep track of the blasphemy.

What did the rabbis know about God, anyway? Had they ever looked down a Dutchman's rifle barrel? Sweated in a Georgia jail? Kicked a cracker in the nuts? Coldcocked a Gypsy? No!

No? They had known the ghettos of the Pale, Cossacks' sabers, Turks' knouts, and Spanish fires. They knew something, those rabbis. For one thing, they approached God with respect and didn't pray while falling-down drunk.

Tears of remorse started forming in his eyes, when he remembered that he had promised himself never to whimper.

Stand up, take it on the chin like a man. After all, he was one of God's children. When a son came home drunk, what did papa do? Gave him a good talking to, that's what papa did. Well, he'd just sit here and talk to Papa, pass it off like nothing had happened. He'd have a good Man-to-man talk with God. Nothing serious. Just light conversation.

He rocked back and sat on his buttocks, tipping his yarmulke forward, and wrapped his arms around his knees.

He began his new-style prayer, feeling the warm compatibility of God flowing from the candle flames.

"Now, God, I got a little problem . . . You think you got problems, Villaricca? You should see the problems! . . . Well, this isn't much of a problem. It won't take You away from Your stars. I'd just like to get Your thinking on a little matter.

"As it is written, the love of money is the root of all evil . . . Lord, God, do I know THAT one. I took advanced studies in it from the Gentiles. Now, I want to give some of my expert knowledge back.

"God, I got this little potation I'm selling for twenty-five cents a bottle. I could sell it for a dime and make a good profit. Now, Lord, I know it's unethical to sell the stuff for a quarter, but if I'm going to be unethical for a quarter, I might as well be unethical for fifty cents. You can't get more unethical than unethical. What I mean, Lord, is that there are no degrees. Either you're unethical or you're not. I am.

"Well, that's ethics, but there's something beyond that. It is written that faith moves mountains, and, Lord, those people have faith in Ravenal's rejuvenating juice of joy. Lord, it works!

"God, a couple of swigs of this stuff, and you just naturally forget all your aches and pains. This evening, an old fellow came hobbling up on a cane and bought a bottle. Next time my girl danced, he came back without his cane. 'Lost it som'rs,' he said, 'and didn't need it, nohow.' Third time he came back, he was jumping up and down and yelling to Mellie, 'Throw it my way, Princess.'

"My thought was this: If those people have faith at twenty-five cents a bottle, wouldn't they have twice as much faith at fifty cents a bottle?

"Ravenal's Elixir of Youth would be worth it, every thin dime of it. It woud cure chilblains, ague, croup, colic, the gout, the nervous debilitations and infirmities of old age. O Lord, it's worth it! What You say to going fifty cents, Lord, one half of a dollar?"

"Mr. Ricky, I brung you some coffee."

"Girl, don't you know better than interrupt a man at his prayers?"

"You ain't praying, Mr. Ricky. You trying to sell God some of that hooch."

He whiffed the aroma of coffee and clambered upon the chest where she had set the coffee cup and saucer and was pouring for him. Gratefully, he lifted the cup as she sat beside him holding the pot.

"One thing you'll never learn, Melinda, is the subleties of theology. From now on, I'm praying in my language, straight from the shoulder. None of your hosannas, hallelujahs, amens, and selahs. You ever hear of Martin Luther?"

"I knows a Luther Jones."

"He won't do. Martin Luther was a great man, a Catholic priest, and he figured the Church was getting too far away from God with its icons and liturgies and masses, and he said to his fellow priests, 'To hell with you, boys, I'm going to play this tune my way. I'm talking direct to the Old Man.' And he did.

"Girl, you're looking at a Hebrew Martin Luther. From now on, I'm going it alone."

"Amen, Brother Ben."

"Go get yourself a cup. You know I don't like to drink alone."

"Give me your saucer. It ain't stopping your slopping, nohow."

He sat beside her, sipping, the hot brew slowly bringing his thoughts and vision back into focus.

But for the help of Melinda, he would have forgotten another Sabbath. He was grateful to her. Obviously, she had been suspicious of his activities in the lady's boudoir, else she would not have gone to such extreme lengths to extricate him. It was necessary to keep her goodwill, lest her resentments mar her dancing. He decided to placate her.

Smiling, he turned to the girl. "You know, you broke up a most delightful talk I was having with the lady. We were discussing books. A cultivated man enjoys a lady who can carry on an intelligent conversation about books. I want you to remember this, so you'll keep up your reading after you're married. Books are never-failing friends, Melinda."

"You'd better call me Arabella, Mr. Ricky, so's you won't slip up. You done called me Melinda in front of that Gentile funky-butt."

"Watch your tongue, girl! How dare you refer to the white lady in such a manner? Are you out of your head?"

"No, sir. But you damned near was out of yours. Them was mighty big and mighty funny looking books y'all was talking about."

"Were you spying on me through the window?"

"No, sir. I just went out for a walk in the garden."

"Walking in the garden at eleven o'clock on a cloudy night, with no moon yet. And what did you expect to see in the garden in the pitch dark?"

"I was smelling."

He shook his head in disgust. "You're all alike—black, white, Gentile, or Jew. Why do you have to act like you owned me?"

"Mr. Ricky, you got a nice Jewish lady waiting for you at your house. You start fooling around with that Gentile funky-butt, and that nine of spades going to get you yet.

Them cards had a dark woman in them who's going to cause you trouble."

"I've got a dark woman who's causing me a lot of trouble."

"I can't cause no trouble, leastways not with your wife. But that Gentile, she sure can, and she will. She's after your money and some of that etcetera etcetera of yours. I got that nine of spades past Jerry, but I can't get it past her, if you don't help."

"Listen, Melinda, she's a gracious lady. I told you once that some women could make money by singing. Mrs. Foreman does just that."

"I 'spect that ain't the only way she makes money."

"You're being insolent, girl. No more of these snide remarks about the lady, you hear? Now, blow out the candles and get to bed."

Huffily, he scrambled from the van and walked across the yard to his quarters, feeling himself far more in possession of his faculties on his way in than he had been on his way out.

Let a woman get the slightest claim on a man, and she would take full possession. Thereafter, any other woman who might be kindly disposed toward him became a designing strumpet, and any relationship with her was given a sordid interpretation by the claim-holding female's low, vulgar, and, likely as not, accurate estimate of the situation.

Disgustedly, he strode down the hallway and turned the knob of his door, but he did not enter. The rotundity of the knob aroused recollections that opened sea-cocks of desire. He walked down the corridor to her room and rapped lightly on the closed door. As he waited, he was suddenly struck by the stupidity of his behavior.

No woman would rise at midnight to give an official greeting to her illicit lover. Boldness was expected, boldness and gentleness, the masculine virtues. He turned the knob and pushed.

The door did not budge.

An inadvertency, nothing more. From force of habit, she had locked her chamber door, forgetting, for the moment, that he would return. He rapped again, louder, and waited.

Silence.

He stood there, toying with the idea of kicking the door down, but the thought of Cassius Clay stayed him. Any man, awakening to hear a lady's door kicked in at midnight, might assume that the intruder's intentions were something other than social. Clay might arise and extend to the lady the protection of the house. In short, Clay might degut him.

Solomon reconsidered.

In the forty-five minutes of his absence, the point of the lady's eagerness had dulled, and she had yielded to the euphoria of alcohol. Pamela had passed out.

Here he stood, his spear atilt for the jousts of love, loins quivering for the sweet encounter, while his love lay sleeping. This night would not deny him flesh, must not, could not.

He turned and slithered down the passageway, moving with fluid urgency, heedless of the sleeping house, out into the voluptuous darkness where clouds hung from the lowering sky like udders. He oozed into the dark slit between the van and the stable wall, into Melinda's room, where her white slip was visible through the gloom.

"Melinda?"

"Yes, sir."

"Get your drawers off, girl. I'm back."

"What you come back for?"

Her voice was sullen, hostile.

He sat on the bunk beside her, sliding his hand under her petticoat, up her tense, unyielding body, until he found her breast and cupped it.

"Why'd I come back? Well, I went in to go to bed, and I figured I'd been ungrateful. I wanted to come back and thank you for saving me from that Gentile funky-butt. She's got teats like a heifer, and I'm hankering for the melons of Melinda. Besides, honey, you know good and well that you're the only girl I do it to on Sabbath."

"Now you talk sense, Mr. Ricky," she said, sliding her petticoat up to her neckline. "Leastways, you ain't catching no clap from me, less'n you give it to me, last time."

"No," he agreed, "not from my little old black mammy."

He grinned at his own riposte as he dropped his trousers, not removing them or his boots. "This one's got to be quick, mammy. You got a hard day coming up tomorrow, and you'll need your sleep. Besides, I got to keep you a little hungry, because you shimmy better when you're wanting it."

"You hush up, honey. You been a bad boy tonight, but your old mammy's been keeping it warm and juicy for her baby."

She giggled her low, liquid giggle, but there had been a motherly tone to her voice that was strangely comforting. For a moment, some objective area of his mind detached itself from his body's urgency, and he understood the dark compulsions of Henry Foreman. In those brief seconds of detachment, before the frenzy of Melinda claimed him, he also felt a pang of sympathy for those magnificent breasts, alone and untended in the big house, which seemed destined to lose, forever, to the withered paps and unripened pomegranates of little old black mammies.

Chapter Thirteen

Saturday brought clouds scudding from the southwest, bellying low over the Bluegrass Region, and the day was dark and ominous. At the fairground, the reds, greens, yellows, blues, and whites of the exhibits struggled upward against the gloom like organic things. Many of the faces that passed glanced upward to the clouds, and to Solomon, it seemed that the umbrellas blossomed in relief when, nearing eleven, a flurry of drops hissed over the cobblestones of the quadrangle. But the shower ceased as quickly as it had begun, and uncertainty returned.

Solomon, huddled in his camp chair on the platform, felt as gray and as futile as the clouds. Clay's ten dollars had closed the blind tiger, and even though the early morning crowds were made up mostly of solid burghers, exhibit-owners, and track attendants, he had averaged a take of almost ten dollars a performance. But enervation and nausea from his night's drinking and the memory of his sacrilege, lechery, and adultery made him listless and remorseful.

"So," he thought, "and what's new in Kiev?"

He had considered Phoebe Blake's antidote for the morning after, but with a wagonload of bourbon behind him, he could not risk a cure more catastrophic than his sickness. Once he had toyed with the idea of going into the van to seek solace in the Bible, but he had rejected the impulse. Reading the Bible to help allay a hangover while surrounded by bottles of whiskey to be sold on his Sabbath under a false label in the presence of his concubine struck him as futile.

He should worry about last night. They were all drunk. Mrs. Foreman had been too indisposed to attend breakfast, and Reba had left the preparation of breakfast to Melinda. Melinda would have been ill, herself, had she not spent the evening in the rose garden.

Solomon's spirits got a boost from a spurt of business that occurred just before the races commenced. Several customers stopped by to buy bottles of elixir without the stimulus of Melinda's dance. One brazenly ordered, "Two bottles of panther piss."

Perhaps as a sop to her conscience after failing to meet the roll call at breakfast, Reba sent over two hampers of food via goat cart, one of roasted chicken and one of pork chops with turnip greens, baked sweet potatoes, butter beans, plus a crock of buttermilk with biscuits and jelly.

Solomon and Melinda ate inside the van as Willie went around the fairground salvaging empty bottles. The mildly acid taste of buttermilk soothed Solomon's stomach, and he commented on Reba's selection of food.

"She knows you Hebrewnots don't eat pork," Melinda said.

Solomon alerted.

"Reba didn't help you sew my skullcap, did she?"

"No, sir. I didn't want to make out like you was a Jew-Hebrewnot."

Solomon chewed on a chicken leg and thought of Alexander Pope.

Clay's choice of Huguenots had been a clever choice for anyone with a slight knowledge of Frenchmen who wished to name an esoteric sect to confuse others with even less knowledge, but Solomon himself should have foreseen that Melinda might confuse "Hugue" with "Hebrew."

If Reba had set her mind to the problem, she might have figured out that Solomon was a Jew and spread the word to her family. It would follow, then, that Willie would have spread the word through the neighborhood. Any white in the surrounding area with a grudge against Clay would possess information that Solomon and Melinda were his house guests. For a thousand dollars, the neighbor would not need much of a grudge.

Guardedly, he said, "I reckon, with all the trouble I put

332

George and Reba to, they must call me that old Hebrewnot to my back."

"No, sir," she assured him. "They calls you that Hebrewnot gentleman."

"Actually, Melinda, the word's 'Huguenot.' Not 'Hebrewnot.' "

"Them big words mix me up."

"Anyway, I'm right glad they like me. George and Reba are nice, and Willie's a smart little pickaninny."

"That Willie, he's a sight. He's just like Jimmie T."

"I notice he's always hanging around you. He ever try to help you with the cooking, or sewing, or sweeping out?"

She picked up the bone to gnaw. "He didn't see me sewing no skullcap."

Suddenly remembering, Solomon asked, "Speaking of the skullcap, was it in your room this morning?"

"No, sir. You had it cocked over your ear when you left the altar last night."

"Wasn't I wearing it when I came back to your room?"

"I couldn't see nothing in the dark, Mr. Ricky. You was etcetering me so good I didn't have no time to do any looking, anyhow."

"But it wasn't on your floor or on your bunk this morning?"

"No, sir. I made my bed up real careful."

"It was probably on my pillow this morning when Reba made my bed."

"Reba ain't made no bed, I bet."

Solomon cautioned himself against panic.

He was setting up in his mind an elaborate set of hypotheses leading to his unveiling as Villaricca, the Jew, and anyone of his ideas could be wrong. Granted, he had been remiss in covering his trail, he could not lose his head and flee with an entire vanload of bottled goods to be sold, plus an untapped barrel of bourbon.

His train of fears was interrupted by the clatter of Willie returning with a cargo of empties.

Exercising calmness, Solomon said, "Excuse me, Melinda, while I settle accounts with my supplier."

"Maybe he'd take the baskets back, Mr. Ravenal."

Solomon stepped outside, carrying the hampers, where Willie waited before the platform with a full load of empties.

"Looks like I got damned near a thousand, Mr. Ravelin!"

"Looks like it, boy."

Willie had one hundred eighty bottles.

Solomon counted out thirty-seven cents, all in coppers. "Lots of money there, Willie."

"Most I ever seen."

"Your ma's going to take most of these. How'd you like to make a silver dime, worth ten of these, and a lot easier to hide?"

"I sho would like that."

"Good. Now, when you take these hampers back to your mama, you slip down the hall to my room. I left my black cap in my bedroom. It's a small cap, about so big, and it doesn't have a bill.

"If you find that cap and bring it back here to me as fast as you can, you'll have yourself a dime. But I want you to keep this a secret, because that's my conjure cap. If you tell anybody you found it, I'll tell your mama you got an extra dime."

"Yes, sir!"

Solomon carried the bottles inside the van as Willie wheeled the goat cart around and rattled over the quadrangle, and said casually, "After the races, the fast crowd will be here to spend their winnings.

"Some of the people are going to get drunk, and they might get a little ornery. If that happens, you slip out the hole, crawl through the fence, and head for the stables, taking your carpetbag with you. I'll cache the money in your bag. You hide in the stables, under the straw where the mules are, and you wait until I come and get you. When I tell you to scoot, you scoot, and take the bag with you."

"Want me to take your bag, too, Mr. Ricky?"

"They won't be after me."

"You think they going to get mean?"

"They could . . . At least, we've got a plan if they do. Maybe we'll never have to use it, but if we do, it's there."

He knew from the night before that a riot was a grave danger, but the word "Hebrewnot" and the missing yarmulke was giving him more concern. He feared the yarmulke as the seal of doom until the irrepressible Willie, face aglow, came clattering back to exchange the skullcap for a dime.

"You didn't tell anybody?"

"No, sir."

"Was my bed made up?"

"No, sir."

"Where'd you find it? On the floor?"

"No, sir. It was folded over your doorknob."

"Outside or inside?"

"Outside, Mr. Ravelin."

"Well, thank you, boy."

"Yes, sir."

Willie wheeled and was gone.

He had been in no condition to do any folding last night.

He walked over and sat down in his camp chair. If Clay had found the yarmulke, he would have hidden it and chastized Solomon for carelessness. Any of the servants would have taken it inside and laid it on his night table. Only Pamela Foreman would have folded it and refrained from entering his room. No doubt it had fallen from his head as he stood outside her door, and she had discovered it when she awakened.

She knew what it was. She knew to whom it belonged, and he had called Melinda by name in her presence.

Without the shadow of doubt, Mrs. Foreman knew who he was, she knew Melinda was with him, and she needed money.

Clay had not trusted her because her feelings against slavery were emotional and not from intellectual conviction. Mrs. Foreman despised slavery because it had taken her husband, had lured him from her with a peculiar love more powerful than her charms, and last night he, her would-be lover, had left her at the precise moment she had offered those charms to him, and he had left her at the summons of a Negro girl.

She was a woman scorned, and it was written that hell had no fury like a woman scorned. For a woman of her infinite capacity, no hangover could have kept her from the breakfast board. Shame and the shattered pride of a woman who had twice lost lovers to blacks accounted for her absence.

He got up and went into the van.

"Listen, Melinda. Take my bag, too, if you have to run. Also, when you get to the stables, wait for me for half an hour. If I'm not there in half an hour, you leave my bag in the stable, and you go back down the road to that railroad track and turn right.

"Don't go back to Mr. Clay's house. You go north on that track. Travel at night and follow the North Star. When you hear a train coming, get off the track.

"You ought to get to Covington in three or four days. If you can't get some roustabout to smuggle you over the river on the ferry, then go to that Quaker family I told you about. Let them get you across.

"But don't stay with the Quakers. And don't go to Kelly. I want you to go to a colored man's house. His name is Tom Braden, and he runs a rooming house at 510 Pierson Street. Repeat after me, 'Tom Braden, 510 Pierson Street.' "

"Tom Braden, 510 Pierson Street."

"I'm going to write him a note and pin twenty dollars in the note and put it in your bag. You give Tom that note, but don't let him or anybody else know how much money you got."

He took a pencil and paper from the cabinet drawer and wrote, "Tom, get this girl to Amherstburg, right away!" He signed it, "S.V."

He took two ten dollar scrip notes on a Cincinnati bank, folded them in the note, and pinned the note inside her bag.

He turned to her. "Now, who're you going to see, and what's his address."

"Tom Braden, 510 Pierson Street, and I ain't telling nobody how much money I got . . . Mr. Ricky, you expecting trouble?"

"Not expecting it. Just preparing for it. You've got to have a plan, Melinda, if you're going to succeed in this world."

"Yes, sir. I knows that."

"Yeah, I know you know it," he said, remembering the candles.

He put his own valise inside the secret chest beside hers, opened the exit hatch, and walked back out to the camp chair.

He could be completely wrong about Mrs. Foreman, and he would not flee again from empty rifles like that gutless Jew in Tennessee. He had lost his last imaginary battle.

So it was that he braced himself for the onslaught of a difficult evening, and his evening began with ease. There was time for three performances after the races ended, and the first performance was marked by an air of friendly cooperation and conviviality. Most of the persons gathered even squatted to sip their way into a frame of mind compatible with the spirit of the Nubian fertility rites. Although the group was smaller than the crowds of yesterday, it consumed one hundred forty bottles of elixir in the twenty minutes allotted to his show, and it tossed five dollars on the stage to show its appreciation of Melinda. By the end of the show, the spirit of the crowd was boisterous but not rowdy.

Suddenly, the obvious reason dawned on him. He was playing only to the winners at the day's races. The losers had gone home.

Then, another thought struck him. He had doubted Pamela Foreman's loyalty. By now, she was probably taking her bath preparatory for the night's dance at the armory. It was approaching twilight. If she had intended to betray him, she would have betrayed him already.

Truly, it was the eye of childhood that feared the painted devil.

While *Uncle Tom's Cabin* played to a hissing, jeering, and cheering audience inside the minstrels' tent, the Great Mustafina paid Solomon a visit.

Close up, wearing a dingy robe over her costume, the houri who wriggled from the basket so enticingly was a haggard, sad-faced woman in her early forties who spoke in a gravelly monotone with such a bare minimum of lip movement that Solomon assumed she had either been a ventriloquist or was afraid to crack her greasepaint.

"I've got an ailment, Doc, and I need some medicine."

"Certainly, ma'am. It's a great specific, good for anything that ails you, truly the closest thing to a universal panacea ever devised by . . ."

"Cut out the bullshit, Doc. I'm family."

"Precisely, ma'am, and I was just on the verge of telling you, as one performer to another, that too big a dose might upset your equilibrium."

"Hell, that ain't my ailment," the Great Mustafina said, pulling the cork with her teeth. "I just can't abide the smell of whiskey on a man's breath less'n I've had a few swigs myself. That goddamned reek near bowls me over when they come barreling into my tent, yelling at me to take it off."

She took a robust draught, almost half the bottle, and smacked her lips.

Down the line, Uncle Tom was getting whipped, and the crowd was cheering Simon Legree with vehemence, yelling, "More whip!"

The Great Mustafina listened and said to him in her laconic drawl, "We'uns oughta give you a medal. Your elixir has stepped up business something powerful. Ten minutes from now, they'll haul ass into my tent, crying their poor hearts out over poor Eva. Damned glad I don't come on after your show. My ass would get chewed worse than Eliza's."

She spoke in the accents of the South, though not with the restraint of a Southern lady, and an easy professionalism to her profanity encouraged him to enter areas of conversation he otherwise would have avoided.

"Do you have trouble with the carnal impulses of your audience, ma'am?"

"Reckon that depends on what you mean by trouble, Janie's trouble is Joanie's joy. Hell, I'm selling carnal impulses.

"Long about sundown, I start having to fight them off. Lamplight seems to set them on. 'Course, I got a man-ape to help me, but, trouble is, they's gorillas in the audience. You play 'em, though. Go easy when they get hard, and go hot when they get soft."

She took another swig and stared toward the lowering west with her tired, unshockable eyes and delivered herself of a life-learned observation. "Fightin' and fuckin's all they think about. Hell, I should care less. They pay their money, and they take their choice."

She cocked an ear toward the sounds from the show tent. "Well, they's cheering Eliza now, or maybe the hounds. I'd better haul ass. Gimme another bottle, Doc. It's gonna be rough out tonight."

In a surge of camaraderie, Solomon handed her the bottle and said, "This one's on the house."

She smiled, and her waxen features glowed with astonishing warmth. The voice that came from her animated lips was warm and throbbing. "Why, sir, this is most kind of you, and I surely appreciate your generosity."

God had turned on the footlights, and with a slight straightening of her spine, a changed angle to the droop of her shoulders, a backward toss of her raven hair, and an upward tilt of her chin, the vulgar jade was suddenly a lady of compelling beauty. She turned from him with her bottle, arched her head back toward him, winked, and strode across the quadrangle, lithe, animalistic, and lovely.

"People love to be deceived," Pamela Foreman had said, and Solomon, remembering her remark, remembered the cool distances of her green eyes which matched the flat opacity of the Great Mustafina's. Pamela's uninhibited swear words were cast from the same mold as Mustafina's, and their facile expressions were generated by the same magneto.

Pamela Foreman and the Great Mustafina were sisters in the sad sorority of illusion-makers who had few illusions themselves.

He arose and went into the van to talk with his own femme fatale, who accomplished with youthful enthusiasm what the older women practiced with ancient skills.

"Melinda, I just had a talk with the snake dancer across the way. She set me thinking."

"She can't dance! Take away her belly button, and what she got?"

"She got skill!" He mimicked her for emphasis. "Once she had beauty and youth, enthusiasm and energy, talent and intelligence. All but her talent and brains gave out, and when her ass gave out, she had brains enough to shift her talent to her navel.

"You've got skill, backed by youth and energy. You've made me more money in two days than I could make for myself in two months on the road, because you've got my brains directing your skill.

"If you keep up your education, you can make all this money for yourself, dancing and singing.

"But she told me something. They get rambunctious once the torches are lit. When they start yelling to you to throw it to them, you just start throwing harder. Now you've got to quit that. You've got to help me keep this crowd in hand. When they start getting too loud, you ease up on your shimmy. If they quiet down, then you speed it up. You follow me?"

"I's way ahead, Mr. Ricky."

"You help me keep this crowd in hand tonight, and come Monday, we'll finish off that last barrel and drive out of Lexington in style . . . What you tuning up for, girl?"

"I don't wants to . . ." She put her head into her hands and began to sob.

Solomon sat down beside her and put his arm around her.

"I just have to have me a good cry, now and then."

"Well, quit it. You're messing up your face."

He went back to the platform and stood by the halyard, prepared to hoist the announcement as soon as the exodus began from the pleasure-dome. A few nonpaying hanger-ons had already gathered at the platform, and a few who had seen all the variations on the other shows and were saving their money for old reliable dream potion.

He thought of Pamela Foreman.

Tonight, he would tell her of the Great Mustafina and her mesmerizing navel and suggest that she augment the beauty of her voice with an artful display of her charms. It could be done with ladylike discretion, he might suggest, to prevent her from inferring that he was suggesting that she should return to the old Pam Sherwood. He would develop the theme with such fervor and sincerity that she would stand convinced that his adoration of her lobes was second to none and that before their radiance all the dark charms of the Africa maidens vanished as the shadows beneath the chariot of Bucephalus. Then let the uniformed dandies at the ball chaffer for her amorous wares; he was seeing the lady home.

Sustained as a Cortez by his vision of new hemispheres to be explored, he embarked on his spiel with gusto, and the audience responded with rowdiness. Near the end of her dance, as Melinda bent backward in her shimmying invocations to the gods, her pelvis slung forward, someone threw a bottle. Solomon alertly dropped his bow and caught the missile before it struck the girl, and when the music stopped, Melinda straightened, bowed, and skittered into the van with her exit trot.

Far from being contrite, the assailant yelled up at Solomon, "If you hadn't blocked my shot, I'd hit the goddamned hole."

"Gentlemen," Solomon shouted above the laughter, "may I invite your attention to a new showing of *Uncle Tom's Habit* by the minstrel puppeteers? They've given a new and stirring twist to the drama. Eliza will be fleeing from Ohio to Kentucky's fair shore to support the aging darky's addiction to that potent potion sold only in Lexington during the current week, Ravenal's Elixir of Youth."

He was saved by his fraternity. The ministrels, in attendance and drinking heavily, strummed their banjos and, like four Pied Pipers of Hamelin Town, the four pie-eyed plunkers of the Lexington Fair led the crowd away.

It was second nature for these rubes to throw things at performers, usually rotten eggs, rotten tomatoes, and cabbage heads. This crowd was drunk and drinking from bottles. Melinda's next performance would be the final performance of the fair, and there would be no remaining attraction to lure the men away. They would create their own attraction, unless he created it for them. He would hold his last ten bottles to toss to the crowd after the dance. If they were catching, they would not be interested in pitching.

He explained his scheme to Melinda during the recess and told her, "As soon as you've made your exit, lock the door behind you, slip through the hole, crawl through the fence, and head for the stables with the money and our bags. There could be trouble, even after I've tossed the hooch. If there is, I intend to save my own ass and worry about the van later."

At the final performance, the crowd that drifted into the light of the torches aggregated about forty men, the heavy winners of the sporting crowd augmented by horse traders and booth-owners dropping by for a sip of merriment before the closing of the fair until Monday.

He strode forward on the platform and spoke to the gathering crowd in the nearest thing to a stentorian voice he could summon.

"I'm asking you, as Kentucky gentlemen, to refrain from lewd, loud, and suggestive remarks in the presence of Her Highness. In the first place, your remarks are useless, since she does not understand our tongue. If you must curse in her presence, gentlemen, please do so in low and well-modulated voices, and I will translate your remarks as praises.

"Secondly, the tribal rites of Nubian virgins are sacrosanct and should be treated with reverence. They are presented solely for your edification on the subject of esoteric rites in other lands and to demonstrate the potency of the secret distillates in the elixir on the regenerative machinery of the human anatomy. Note, gentlemen, that I say human anatomy. No sex specified.

"Take a bottle home to the lady of the house, gentlemen, and bank the cooking fires in preparation for a very late supper . . . Two bottles for the leonine gentleman with the illuminating nose . . . I said the lady of the house, sir, not ladies."

"Say, Doc, I gave a bottle to my girl, and she got half tight."

"If a half-pint makes her half tight, sir, perhaps a whole pint will make her hole tight."

"My girl needs a barrel."

341

"Then use your head, sir, and wriggle your ears."

He weighed the crowd as he talked. He wanted to ease off on the low remarks, but he had to hold their interest, and seemingly, they enjoyed low humor.

Then, by the merest of accidents, he struck another métier.

One gentleman, waving a dollar, ordered four bottles, and Solomon passed the bottles forward, saying, "Four bottles for the gentleman with a nose for horses' noses . . . My compliments, sir. Skilled betting bespeaks a gentleman of judgment. Is the four-bottle gent, the best judge of horse-flesh, or is there a six-bottle better in the crowd? Do I hear a higher bid?"

"I'll take two dollars' worth!"

"Ah, an eight-bottle man. Sir, if any one of your eight bottles fail, and you'll bring me a signed certificate so stating from the local madam, come back tomorrow for your refund, same time, same place."

"Two dollars, two bits . . ."

The element of bidding infected the crowd. Vulgarity was forgotten, and he, too, was infected by the enthusiasm. His last bid was for ten bottles. He could only meet the bid halfway by using his last bottle, and he awarded that gentleman the championship despite the lack of supplies. He had sold his last bottle of elixir, and there was nothing left to throw to them.

He grabbed the violin and began to play, hearing the patter of Melinda's feet behind him and feeling fear swell inside him like an obscene fungus. Since the heavy buyers were passing around their bottles as gifts, he figured every man jack of them must have at least a pint and a missile, and most were drunk to begin with.

As he played, empty bottles went sailing through the gathering darkness to explode and tinkle on the cobblestones, but, so far, none were directed toward him or the girl. Out there in the darkness, a beast was snarling in its chains, and the chains were breaking.

Yet, he was strangely alert as he played, analyzing above his growing alarm the possibility that he might wear down their energies by prolonging the dance. He repeated the middle bars of the Gypsy tune to give him time to think and delay Melinda's grand finale. Above all, he feared the results on the crowd of her projecting pelvis and the target it offered.

Then he saw, clearly and plainly in the gaslights flanking the entrance to the fair, a long black barouche drawn by a team of black horses pull up to the edge of the quadrangle.

He would have known the vehicle from a mile away, and he knew the tall figure that stepped down from the driver's seat. Sheriff Whitcomb had come to the fairground at closing time, driving the paddy wagon with the ankle shackles.

Solomon did not falter in his playing as he watched the sheriff pause briefly in the lamplight, hitch up the gunbelt beneath his frock coat, and start walking across the quadrangle with the deliberate, measured tread that bespoke official duty. He was walking in a straight line toward the van.

Pamela Foreman was an informer.

He backed toward the dancing girl, still playing, and said to her, "Hit the hole, right now! Scoot!"

With an artist's sense of unity, he finished the tune with a flourish as he heard her skittering footsteps behind him, heard the door of the van close and the latch drop in place.

He raised his hand above the surprised, silent, and disgruntled crowd, welcoming now the hostility he felt.

"I promised you alleged Kentucky gentlemen a surprise after this dance, and now I'm giving it to you.

"Inside, the princess is disrobing. She's wanting it pretty bad . . . She was nursed on elixir. She's spreading her royal crotch for the first man to get through that door.

"I'm a Heidelbergian, Oxonian, Sorbonneian, etcetera, but I'm also a bayou tiger, half horse and half alligator, and tonight's my night to howl. I can whip any six men from the Bluegrass Barrens, and I'm hankering for Kentucky wildcat. Come and get her, boys. It's first come, first served, to any lily-livered varmint that can get by me."

Sheriff Whitcomb was twenty yards away.

At first, his audience was taken aback, but as the terms of his proposal sunk into whiskey-fogged brains, they responded. As a man, the front rank charged, clambering onto the platform from all angles. Torches were toppled. The stanchions broke, and the platform tilted under the crush as the second rank grabbed the first rank and heaved it back into the third rank. In the preliminary struggle for position, one giant clambered up the tilting boards and was reaching for Solomon when he was tackled by a wiry lad whose size belied his strength, but the two had cleared an approach on

343

Solomon's port quarter, where an agile behemoth came bounding through, his fist drawn back. Solomon made a flying exit. Protecting his violin with this body, he dove toward the southeast over the heads and flailing fists of the mob to land eight feet from the platform.

He landed on his feet, crouching low, violin and bow in his left hand, protecting his ear with his right, and tried to worm outward through the swirling mob. Around him, the night was alive with groans and grunts, the thuds of flailing fists and boots. His course was southeast, but it veered when a lunging body fell against his thigh and a knee against the side of his head swung him about, back toward the platform, and a boot propelled him four feet northwest.

The scene was lighted by the glow from the burning bunting which was igniting the pine boards of the platform. Through the reek of sweat and whisky, he could smell the oily odor of burning pitch, and above the yells, curses, and thuds, he heard the sheriff bellow, "Stop, in the name of the law. Stop, in . . . Oh, you son of a bitch!"

Somebody had slugged the sheriff.

Solomon made toward the spot where he had last heard the sheriff, bouncing from one flailing body to another, protecting his groin now with his free hand. He was almost to the edge of the perimeter, when a vicious kick in the thigh propelled him back toward the center, but he heard the sheriff yell again. "Cut it out, I'm your sher . . ."

Again Sheriff Whitcomb was silent, and Solomon, undeterred by bruises and trailing his violin, worked his way toward the sheriff, moving now in the rising glow from the burning platform. Off to his right, he heard a battler screech in panic, "Let me at it! That pussy's going to fry afore I git it!"

He knew, then, the van had caught.

He was working against time. He had to get to the sheriff before the fire got to the barrel of whiskey. Once the barrel was touched off, the crowd was going to disperse in a hurry, and he needed the cover of the crowd.

Risking a broken neck, he stood upright and spotted the tall form of the sheriff locked in the arms of a giant who was being pummeled in the ribs by the lawman, who was yelling, "Let go of me, you son of a bitch, I'm your sheriff."

Bodies were falling now and not rising. New ones were coming in from the outer perimeter or being thrown in. Crouching low, Solomon circled, coming up on the sheriff's blind side. He stepped on and over a fallen body and inched closer.

He saw Sheriff Whitcomb break his opponent's grasp and shove the man backward at the precise moment that an elfin little drunk, either seeking refuge or from hostility, leaped on the back of the sheriff.

In a sequence of split seconds, Solomon acted. There was an open space in front of the sheriff that the big man had cleared when he fell backward. Whitcomb's head was turned to throw off the leech on his back when Solomon stepped in, moving with the precision of a ballet dancer, and violated his standing instructions to students by leading with his right.

His entire body was behind the blow, uncoiled with the coordination of a coldly sober and trained boxer. His fist, whistling upward, connected flush on the point of the sheriff's chin as it came down. He felt the head kick back, heard the crack of breaking bones, and he knew the sheriff would be out for a long, long time, maybe forever if the bone had been his neck.

Whitcomb's knees buckled. Gently, he bore the dwarf on his back downward, to deposit him on the ground as the barrel in the van went with a swoosh that illuminated the scene as vividly but longer lasting than a lightning flash.

His van was gone, but Solomon had no time to lament his loss. The crowd stampeded outward, sensing that tragedy might end the harmless Kentucky lark, but they stampeded still fighting. On the outer edge of the perimeter, his mission completed and safety almost within his grasp, the battered Solomon found himself no longer in a quiet area, but the spirit of the mob had possessed him.

Still clinging to his violin as a symbol of lost sensitivities, he laid about him with his free fist, thrilling to the crunch of flesh and choosing his targets at random. Fighting freely, fighting happily, he smote many Gentiles before a whistling boot found his crotch and a malletlike fist came out of the darkness to administer the *coup de grâce*.

Melinda in the stable had problems. He'd told her to wait half an hour, but she had no clock. She couldn't tell time by the sun at night.

He wanted her to walk to Cincinnati, least a hundred miles. Hell, it would take three weeks to walk a hundred miles. She'd starve to death. She was hungry already.

She could get lost. He'd showed her how to find the

North Star, all right, but how could she find it when it was cloudy and setting-in to rain.

Rain was beginning to patter on the roof now, softly, like it was going to rain for a long spell. Maybe that Ohio would be out of its banks.

She got into her woolen dress and threw his shawl over her head.

He ought to be here. She had all of his money, and she sure didn't want to carry all that money away. It was heavy.

He ought to be coming in, about now, if he just got into a little old fight. A man couldn't fight all night. Either he won or lost. Maybe he was beat up, back there, and bleeding to death.

Then a new thought struck her. Maybe he'd won, and he was going back to the house to get that big-titted Gentile and take her to that dance they'd all been talking about. He ought to be ashamed, rubbing bellies with that Gentile when he had a nice Jew lady.

That man, he gave her more trouble.

He wouldn't mind if she went back and took a little peek through the fence. If he was still fighting, she'd come back and wait another hour.

She covered their bags with hay and crept out of the stable, moving cautiously toward the fence. Rain was coming down in a fine mist.

Across the distance, she could see the glow from the fire. Maybe he was staying to put out the fire.

If there was a fire, nobody would pay her any mind. It must be a big fire because it was burning in the rain.

With renewed concern, she trudged toward the fairground, soon seeing she would not have to lift any planks to peek through the fence. There wasn't any fence. A whole stretch was burned down, and that big fire in the middle must be the van.

She ran. If he was in the van, she wanted to get there and pull him out.

She stepped over the charred and hissing embers of what had once been the fence and walked into an arena lit by the flames from the van.

Lordy, what a mess! The van was gone, nothing left but a pile of burning lumber. That pretty van.

All around her, bodies were sprawled. Some of the men were sitting up, moaning, and one was drunkenly trying to tug a friend away from the fire, but he was making little progress because he was pulling from a sitting position. Melinda went over and grabbed the man's legs and pulled them away from the fire. His friend, eyeing her drunkenly, said, "Thank you, Your Highness."

"You welcome, sir."

She went about her task, walking among the fallen like a dark angel of mercy, shaking her head in sympathy at the overly-bloodied.

One man sat with his wrists draped over his knees, a bottle in each hand, looking into the fire. He looked up and waved a bottle toward her in an invitation to drink.

"No thank you, sir," Melinda said.

Lordy, Mr. Ricky must have fought hard to knock out all these folks. Some of them were beat up bad. 'Course, lot of them were just drunk and sleeping it off.

She worked outward from the van, and finally, on the outer perimeter of the circle, at the point where he had almost fought his way to safety, leaving the littered bodies behind, she found the fallen hero.

He lay with a cheek cushioned on an outstretched arm, a dark bruise on the side of his face, a thin trickle of blood coagulated from a torn ear. His shirt was in tatters, and his body was curled around the neck and twisted strings of his violin, which he held in his left hand. His keen, aristocratic nose nestled among the cobblestones.

He looked so peaceful, like a little boy asleep, his face so pale and handsome in the light from the guttering fire that she almost wept. He was too young and pretty to go to sleep forever.

She took his handkerchief from his picket and mopped the blood from the side of his face. Bending, she turned his body over to let the rain wash his face. Gently, she took the remnant of his violin from his hand and folded his hands across his chest. Then she sat, cradled his head on her lap, and started to comb his hair. Lord, he was the prettiest man!

Melinda lifted her eyes to heaven and prayed.

"Jesus, honey, I ain't never asked nothing, but I'm sure asking now. Let Mr. Ricky live, 'cause he ain't half bad. He's a white man, Jesus, but you knows he's got a black heart.

"Take me, Jesus, baby, if you wants me, but, Lordy, let this poor man live. He ain't never hurt nobody, 'cept that

347

Georgia boy and a little tap for Jerry. These gentlemen around here, Lord, jumped on him because he was just trying to protect my honor."

She liked her last phrase.

"Yes, sir, Lord, this man just protecting my honor. I tempted them men, Jesus. You take me, and let Mr. Ricky go. Give him a long life, Jesus, honey, and let his children be many.

"I know he's a Jew, Jesus, but you won't mind. He's your kinfolk, Jesus."

"Where am I?" Solomon asked.

"Honey, don't you know where you is? You is at the fairground. Lord, be praised. Thank you, Jesus."

"Where's the light coming from?"

"Your wagon caught fire, sir. It burned up a little bit."

He turned his head toward the fire. "Three hundred dollars," he said, "gone to hell."

"You going to be all right now, Mr. Ricky, 'cause you's worried about money."

"My candlestick! Where's my candlestick?"

"Gone to hell, too."

"Well," he said, struggling to a sitting position, "I can salvage the silver. Where's my violin?"

"Right in front of you, Mr. Ricky."

Solomon looked over to where she pointed, and new anguish clouded his eyes. "Well," he said, "that ought to make Beethoven happy."

"I don't know her."

"She's a friend of Martin Luther."

"I heard about him . . . Mr. Ricky, you done whipped about forty or thirty men. You sure some fighter."

"Only about eight of them are mine," he disclaimed, "not including the sheriff. The sheriff's mine . . . He came out here to arrest us."

He tried to struggle to his feet, and she put a restraining hand on his shoulder. "You ain't fit to walk, Mr. Ricky."

"But the sheriff, Melinda. We've got to get out of here, right now. When he comes to, our goose is cooked."

"Don't worry none about that sheriff, Mr. Ricky. That sheriff, he dead."

"Are you sure?"

"Yes, sir. I know they's dead when they's dead. They eyes stay open, like my mammy's was when she died. I put pennies on that sheriff's eyes to hold he eyelids down."

"Oh," he groaned, "for this night's work, I've earned the gibbet. Help me up, child. That sheriff has deputies, and they're probably over at Clay's house waiting for us to get there."

"How they find out about us?"

"Mrs. Foreman told them."

"How you know?"

"I guessed it. I guessed it from the very first."

"Oh, no, sir. Reba say that white lady just despised slavery. She's for colored people."

"She's against slavery, all right, but she hates black mammys. She thinks black mammys are the ruination of the South."

"But why she tell on us?"

"She needed money."

"Hell, Mr. Ricky, everybody need money now, 'cause you got it all—over there in the barn."

"Help me up, girl."

"Where you going?"

"Help me, for Christ's sake, and shut up! We're going to Cincinnati, after I fish my candlestick out of the ashes."

"At night, Mr. Ricky?"

"At night!"

"In the rain, Mr. Ricky?"

"In the rain!"

"You done gone crazy, Mr. Ricky?"

"I'm not crazy, I'm scared."

"You scared, Mr. Ricky?"

"Of course. That sheriff."

"He can't bother us. He dead."

"I'm not worried about him. I'm worried about my neck when they find him . . . Look around here. See if you can find an umbrella. There were plenty of them in that crowd. And go fish my candlestick out of those coals."

Through a tunnel of churning night, he booted the jack out of Lexington toward Paris down a pike so dark that the girl on the jenny tied behind his mules was lost in blackness. Providentially, the rain had ceased after softening the earth for the hooves of their beasts, thus muting the sound of their passing, but the clouds which blotted all light threatened a deluge. The clouds were allies, for no casual wayfarer would be abroad tonight, and no posse could find them.

349

He did not run the mules but walked them, holding a pace that wolfed the miles, and when the jack flagged, its rider booted its ribs. His mules seemed to sense the urgency of their master and seldom slackened. When his own energy swung low and weariness threatened, he focused his mind on a vision of a man turning slowly at the end of a rope, the head distorted by a broken neck, its sightless eyes staring at the sun.

Centerville was passed before ten. By midnight, they slogged through Paris, turning due north for Cynthiana. Cynthiana was behind them before dawn. When gray light seeped through the clouded east strongly enough for him to distinguish Melinda, he turned off the road and beat his way up a narrow glen, seeking a place to hide.

They bedded down in a blackberry patch, well away from where he tied the mules, bending the vines into an arbor above them. With their bags as pillows, they stretched out, facing each other to increase their area of hearing.

In bright sunlight, they would have been shaded. Under the lowering clouds, they lay in filtered gloom. It was a nest for hiding hares, and by now, the hounds were baying.

At least two men had seen him strike the blow that killed the sheriff, the small man riding the sheriff's shoulders and the large man the sheriff had pushed backward. They had seen him by the flare of the blazing whiskey barrel, and they had surely recognized him. He had been the famous Doctor Ravenal, late of Heidelberg, etcetera, and he had carried his violin in his hand. At the inquest, this morning, the two would name him to spare themselves further involvement.

Any fool could piece together what had happened after Pamela Foreman's story became known. Whitcomb knew he had gone to the fairground to arrest Solomon Villaricca, the slave thief, and the girl he had stolen. They would understand the meaning of Solomon's challenge to his audience, and they would know that he had intended to use the resulting riot as a cover to do away with the sheriff.

At this moment, the telegraphs were clicking out a description of Solomon Villaricca, wanted for murder. Melinda was no longer the star of their duet, she was merely an added inducement for his capture, a tag line further describing the chief actor. The little disagreement between him and the Federal Government over the Fugitive Slave

Law had led to a duel to death between the People of the State of Kentucky versus Solomon Villaricca.

A wise felon would ditch the girl where she lay and hightail it out of the state, but there were other considerations. He might have abandoned her two hundred miles farther South, but his overnight leap of fifty miles added an element of geography to the humanitarian and economic arguments for staying with her. She was a little girl who would be lost and alone in the world without him. More important, she was worth one thousand dollars to him in Cincinnati, only sixty miles away.

If the weather continued as it was, at tomorrow's dawn he would be ten miles from home, if he could hold the pace. With an extra thousand added to the two hundred and twenty dollars he carried, he could put a lot of distance between him and Lexington, say the distance to Halifax, Nova Scotia. Then, a coded letter to Ely Blood, and Leah would join him en route to Argentina.

His fate was balanced on the knife edge of the weather. If the rains came, he would be marooned. If the skies cleared, the patrols would be out in force. Meanwhile, he would lie here and try to sleep through his hunger pangs and wait the transit of the sun.

"Mr. Ricky, I's hungry."

"A rest will do your stomach good. Saints have fasted forty days, deliberately, to get a glimpse of God."

"I'll be talking to Jesus in two more days."

He dozed and awakened throughout the day, but always, the friendly pall was above him, and the rain did not come.

Night came slowly, staining the dark day like bluing seeping through dirty water, and when only a tinge of gray remained of the day, he roused Melinda.

"Mr. Ricky, we going to run all night with nothing to eat?"

"Certainly."

"That sheriff can't catch us. He dead."

"What do you think I'm running for?"

"I thought you wanted to get me to Mr. Kelly 'cause we's burned out of elixir."

"Quit thinking."

He hoisted her onto the jenny and swung aboard the jack, irritated at his own irritation. She had not seen him swing the blow that had killed the sheriff, and she had a right to

351

complain. By now, she was probably the only person in Kentucky who did not know that he had murdered Sheriff Whitcomb.

When they broke from the underbrush onto the road and turned right, he kicked the ribs of the jack, and it ambled forward. He kicked again and the jack continued to amble. His third kick convinced him that the mules were setting the pace. They would not pass through Falmouth by midnight; they would be lucky to get there by two in the morning, and they would still be forty miles from Covington.

His one-day jaunt to Covington would take two days.

Through the long Sunday evening they jogged, moving slower than he would have normally walked, but now he could not walk. His hunger pangs had long since ceased, but thirty-six hours without food had deprived him of energy, and he knew his lassitude was dangerous. If apprehended, he would have to fight, and that fight would be to his death if he did not conserve what little energy he had.

It was past one o'clock, and they were still south of Falmouth when the rain struck.

He could hear it coming in the darkness, rustling through the forest southwest of the road with a sibilance more sinister than lightning or thunder. Inwardly, he braced himself as the sound grew to a rustle and the rustle rose to a murmur. There were a few preliminary drops around them, and then a sheet of almost solid water rolled over them.

Two days and nights of frustration were vented by the clouds in the first few minutes of the downpour. One moment, the mules were plodding along on a fairly dry road. Moments later, they were splashing fetlock deep in water falling faster than it could drain from the road.

Solomon leaned forward to protect his carpetbag with his body, feeling the palpable weight of the water on his back and freshets flowing down his neck. One minute after the cloudburst began, his clothes were sopping wet, down to his drawers, and seconds later his drawers went. Water squished inside his boots.

Over the twin visions of death by rope and death by hunger, a third image was impinged, death by lung congestion. The rain was very cold.

Last April, he had passed this way, and he knew of a church with white gateposts by the roadway opening onto a parking area.

The church was a quarter mile south of Falmouth and

would be on his right. Solomon dismounted. His mule was slipping now on the treacherous footing, and he had to get closer to the right side of the road to enable him to see the gateposts through the darkness and rain. He knew where the church stood in relation to Falmouth, but he was not sure where Falmouth was.

He knew he had crossed the bridge over the south fork of the Licking River, but that was ten minutes before the rain hit, and he did not know in the darkness how far he had come. Slipping and sliding beside the mule, he could not even estimate his present rate of progress.

Forty yards or a hundred and forty yards farther down the road, he found the gateposts and led the mules between them to the rear of the building. He hoped for a projecting eave behind the church to give his beasts some protection from the rain and to conceal them from wayfarers on the road if he and Melinda were forced to remain in the church on the morrow. He knew their tracks would be washed away by the pelting rain in a matter of seconds.

He was fortunate. There was an empty woodshed built onto the rear of the church big enough to shelter all but the hindquarters of the mules.

He tied the animals and grabbed Melinda's bag, leading her into the church through the back door. In the pitch-black interior, he stood for a moment, relishing the sound of rain on the roof before he felt his way forward toward dimly espied pews.

"I've got matches in my bag," he said, "if they'll strike. There should be candles under the altar."

"I can't see no altar."

"Feel your way down the platform. It should be near the center, wherever that is."

As he unstrapped his bag, she called, "I found it. They ain't no candle, but they's a lamp here. It's got oil."

"Count to ten," he said.

He groped through the darkness toward the sound of her voice and found her on the count of six. The match struck, and in the glow of the lamp, they moved back down to the pews, shielding the lamp's glow from the front window by the back of the pews.

They stripped, rubbed themselves dry with towels, and changed into dry clothes. In ten minutes, the lamp was out, and they lay on the pews, listening to the drumming on the roof.

They had found shelter for the night, but if tomorrow broke bright and fair, it would still be a day before the roads would be passable, and he had no assurance of a fair tomorrow. He had only the assurance of a hungry tonight.

"Mr. Ricky, I been thinking . . . You know, back there at the fair?"

"Yes."

"Most ever' one of them men lying around there was dead, dead drunk."

"May their hangovers last till Wednesday . . . Go to sleep."

"I can't go to sleep. I keep thinking about watermelons."

"I been thinking along those lines, myself, for the past few hours."

"Mr. Ricky, this place reminds me of Brother Smith."

"You keep thinking about watermelons. I'm tired."

"Remember that dinner I fixed for you and Brother Smith . . . I thought you was the prettiest man I ever saw. Remember your beard? Mr. Blake, he told me not to put no lard in that cornbread, so I used butter. I didn't know how in the hell that cornbread was going to come out."

"Ah, come on. You fixed that meal for Brother Smith."

"Well, yes, sir. He too. He sure like to eat. He eat like a hog."

He remembered the meal. Somehow, it satisfied him to think about it. He could remember the taste of the cornbread melting in the soup, the honey oozing from the candied yams.

With his eyes closed, he could recreate the entire scene: Phoebe Blake with her then gracious charm; Bill Blake arguing against Harriet Beecher Stowe; Brother Smith, with his turned-around collar and beads of sweat sticking out on his forehead, gulping his soup. Good thing he didn't wear a tie with that collar. The tie would have been in the soup.

"Mr. Ricky, you ever tell a lie?"

"I sold about three hundred dollars worth of lies at the Lexington Fair."

"It a sin to tell a lie, if a lie's a good lie?"

"Really, child, I don't know. You can lie without opening your mouth, or you could tell the truth and be lying. Sometimes, lies are mighty handy little things to have around.

"You go to sleep now. Tomorrow, I'm going to buy you a whopping breakfast in the Falmouth Tavern, and you're going to eat in the dining room with white folks."

354

"That ain't no nice lie, Mr. Ricky."

"That's no lie at all. In the morning, you'll breakfast at the Falmouth Tavern. Before eleven o'clock, you'll be in Covington. You'll have dinner in Cincinnati, and you'll sup in Kelly's tavern."

"Now I know you's lying, Mr. Ricky."

"Melinda, I swear on the bosom of Abraham these things shall come to pass. Now, sleep."

Chapter Fourteen

Melinda tensed when the whistle blew and the engine, three cars ahead, spurted steam from its pistons. When the train lurched forward, her gloved hand tightened on the windowsill. Behind her veil, he saw her eyes widen as the click of the wheels over the rail joints increased in tempo and kept increasing. The car began to jounce and sway, and the landscape immediately outside the window blurred with speed, thirty, thirty-five, forty miles an hour.

"This damn thing ever going to slow down, Mr. Rickey?"

"The engineer'll top her off, by and by. Right now, we're going faster in an hour than we make in a day with the mules."

She relaxed slightly when the clickety-click of the wheels over rail joints leveled off. Then a bird flying past the window parallel to the train caught her eye. "Looky, Mr. Rickey. That bird flying backward!"

On this stretch of line, the Central Kentucky Railroad followed the Lick Valley, downgrade most of the way with a solid ballast to the track, and the engineer was running ten minutes late. Quite a change, Solomon thought, from the Marietta and North Georgia, where ten minutes late was an hour ahead of schedule.

"Look out the window ahead, and you can see the engine," he told her as he felt the train slowing for a curve.

Adapted now to the feeling of motion, she put her cheek to the pane and stared ahead. They both saw the locomotive on the bend, sparks flying from the smokestack, drivers

356

invisible from the speed of the wheels—a behemoth of iron charging down the valley.

"God damn," she breathed in awe, "look at that son of a bitch go!"

"Watch your language, girl."

"Yes, sir, preacher. 'Scuse me, sir."

"Slump down and dab your eyes. Here comes the conductor."

By the time the conductor reached them and tipped his hat, she was sobbing genuine tears. The conductor took their tickets, looked down on her in a kindly manner, and asked, "Your nigger, parson?"

"No. She belonged to one of my flock, dear soul, who passed away last Saturday. Left the girl to her sister, near Covington. The girl's nigh broken up over the death of her mistress."

"Pretty little thing," the conductor commented. "Sometimes they act like people."

He punched Solomon's round-trip ticket. "Coming back on the night train, parson?"

"No. I think I'll lay over for a day or two. My team's in a Falmouth stable. The rain caught me."

"Seems to be clearing. Well, hope to see you on the return trip, parson. Enjoy your visit."

"Thank you, sir. And if you have a newsbutch, I would like a paper."

"Send him right up, parson."

He entered the vestibule for the car behind, and Melinda said, "That turned-round collar gets you nothing but 'howdy dos.' You ought to thank God for God, Mr. Ricky."

Solomon bought the *Kentucky Gazette* and a *Cincinnati Commercial* from the newsbutcher. For Melinda, he bought a peach in a paper cup, which she thought too pretty to eat.

Solomon was surprised to find the front page of the Lexington detailed events of the military ball without mentioning the death of the sheriff. Skimming through the paper, he found no hint of a riot at the fairground.

Amazed, he turned back and read the feature story with more avidity than he had ever felt for a narrative detailing a social event. Mr. and Mrs. Cassius Clay were present—apparently the general had sold his horses for a good price. Mrs. Pamela Foreman, radiant in a gown direct from Paris which was described in fulsome manner by the reporter, was escorted to the ball by Colonel Pickering of the Lexington Rifles.

His mind paused so long over a vision of lost loveliness that he almost failed to notice in the last paragraph, which was a routine listing of dignitaries present, that the sheriff and his lady were named as being present.

He did not believe the report.

Probably, a proofreader had not checked his facts, or perhaps the paragraph had been a preset potboiler thrown in to meet the deadline.

Carefully, he rechecked the back pages. Tucked away on the third page, he noticed a story he had overlooked because of the heading: "Science Set Back in Lexington."

He dropped his eyes and read the story.

Our local paragon of law, the high sheriff, is on record as opposing vulcanized caoutchouc for upper dentures. The sheriff, proud possessor of the first set of the above mentioned item in Lexington, is now returning to his metallic plates for greater durability. His new dentures were wrecked beyond recovery early Saturday night whilst he was engaged in quelling a free-for-all on the fairground whither he had gone to investigate reports that spirits were being sold illegally. His old metallic plates, he opined, would have survived the stress of official duty with ease, whereas the new-fangled contraption failed miserably.

So, the crack had been his dentures exploding and not the vertebrae in his neck. Sheriff Whitcomb was alive, hale, and hearty, sans only his vulcanized rubber dentures. Solomon almost giggled in relief. Sheriff Whitcomb had known what Solomon was peddling. That stride of his had been official, all right. He was coming to collect a little pin money for the evening's festivities. Sheriff Whitcomb was having a mite of trouble collecting bribes from the Lexington Fair —must be the Gypsy curse.

"Melinda, are you right sure that sheriff was dead when you laid those pennies on his eyes?"

"Naw," she confessed. "Didn't see no sheriff. I just wanted to make you feel good."

Without comment, he turned to the *Commercial*. So, in the imaginary battle, he had fled the field, but his flight had almost won the war.

He still had the Ohio to cross, but he was bouyed now by confidence. It was an hour before Covington, and he had no plan to get them north of the river, but necessity was the mother of invention, and he was an inventive man with a great need.

A brush fire had threatened the observatory on Mount Adams. Harrison Turnpike was being macadamized west of Mill Creek. Surprisingly, the *Commercial* seemed to favor Lincoln over the incumbent Judge Douglas in the Illinois Senate race.

It was good to be back in the stream of history, back where things were happening, after weeks of boredom interspersed with moments of terror in the South.

One item which drew his scrutiny was the story of a runaway, Willie, a small Negro discovered in a large coffin artfully equipped with food, water, and built-in sanitary facilities. The coffin had been consigned to Akron, Ohio, and Willie had been apprehended at the Walnut Street landing when a cargo officer unloading a steamboat had heard snores coming from the coffin.

Obviously, Solomon was not the only clever fugitive smuggler in the business. Too bad the trick had been discovered. He himself could have used it. What would be more natural than a minister of the Gospel assisting a bereaved family by delivering the last remains of the dear departed in person? Now, and for the next three months, there would not be a coffin crossing the river that wouldn't be opened.

Yes, he thought, a lot of coffins would be opened, many under protest . . .

His rig was fourth in line when the ferry gates opened, with two buggies and a haywagon ahead of him. He clucked his rented team of mules forward, taking the left lane around the boiler room. The dividing flow of traffic put him second behind the haywagon and ahead of a primly erect old lady in a buggy. He noticed her age with satisfaction. She was old enough to get crochety and protest any delay. He would be blocking her and at least six other vehicles if he were delayed untimely.

Rolling forward on the wagon deck, he relished the odor of river water, the fruity smell of wet pilings, and the metallic clang of hot iron against his nostrils from the engine room. Of all the river smells he cherished this odor most because it was the odor of the Ohio River.

"Mr. Ricky, I's scared."

359

He turned to Melinda, perched atop the coffin behind, and said, "You just play dumb and sniffle now and then. Leave the rest up to me."

"I ain't scared of getting caught. I's scared of meeting Mr. Kelly. 'Spose he don't love me no more?"

"He will, honey, five minutes after he sees you."

"I needs to get cleaned up."

"I'm taking you to Tom Braden's rooming house and getting you a room. While I'm gone to get Kelly, you can take a long bath with sweet-smelling bath salts and get real prettied up before your fiancé arrives."

"You ain't taking me straight to Mr. Kelly?"

"Not when every Quaker in Cincinnati knows you're headed there."

There was a prolonged blast from the ferry whistle, and the boat began to tremble with vibrations from the engine room. Sidewheels churned. Pilings of the landing slid aft, and the boat headed away from the shore, swinging upstream toward the Butler Street Landing.

Relaxed now, Melinda said, "Maybe after I's married, you and your wife can come calling."

"So you and she can compare notes about me over tea?"

She giggled, but there was a plea in her voice when she said, "Maybe you can come by yourself."

"That's a definite possibility . . . Look out there to the left. That's Cincinnati."

"Lordy, Mr. Ricky, what's holding them damned buildings up?"

Solomon would have known he was in the North when he saw the deputy sheriff coming down the ladder from the passenger deck. The deputy leaned over and looked and saw the coffin with the mourning girl atop it and came down, slowly, almost reluctantly, moving along the ramp beside the haywagon back to Solomon. He was a small man, apologetic of manner, who could have been a bookkeeper as well as a sheriff, and he tipped his hat when he reached Solomon.

"Parson, you ain't got no runaway niggers in that coffin, have you?"

"No, sheriff. I'm taking this casket to gather the earthly remains of this girl's mistress, who passed to her reward while visiting in your city. She was one of my congregation, and a saintlier soul never lived than Mrs. Henry Ashburn, late of Falmouth, Kentucky."

"It's empty, then?"

"Indeed, sir."

"Then, you wouldn't mind if I took a little peek inside?"

"Sir, I have gone to some trouble to lash it securely to the dray. I tell you it's empty. Don't you accept the word of a man of God in Cincinnati?"

"Yes, sir. I do. But I got orders to check on all coffins, full or empty, that's coming into town from across the river. It ain't me, parson. It's my orders."

"Sir, you may take your orders back to the man who issued them and tell him I refuse to desecrate the last resting place of Mrs. Henry Ashburn because of his whims."

"Preacher, I just want to look. I ain't aiming to desecrate."

"Sheriff, I understand no desecration's intended, but I don't relish the implication that I am a liar."

"I'm not calling you a liar, sir. You say the box is empty, and I believe you, but maybe a nigger slipped in while you warn't looking."

"Sir, the box is lashed down. The girl's been sitting on it. How could a nigger get in?"

The deputy raised himself to his full height. "Parson, in the name of the law, I'm asking you . . ."

"In the name of what law?" Solomon's voice rose in anger.

"By authority of the sheriff of Cincinnati."

"May I call your attention to the fact, sir, that we are not in Cincinnati. We are upon a free-flowing, navigable stream. We are, in effect, upon the high seas. Is your authority vested through letters of marque? Not only are you calling me a liar, you are proposing piracy! I swear by the sacred remains of Mrs. Henry Ashburn that her last resting place shall not be desecrated by nigger-hunting buccaneers!"

"Looky, parson, I'm just a deputy sheriff. I don't know nothing about the high seas, but these is U.S. waters. There's a man on board who speaks for the whole country."

"Wrong again, sir. If he supports these practices, he does not speak for me."

"Nor me, neither, preacher," the beldame to the rear screeched. "Stand up for your rights. Hallelujah, and three cheers for the free states."

Sadly the sheriff turned, walked back to the ladder and climbed wearily to the passenger deck. Draymen and deckhands began to edge along the ramp to get a better view of the proceedings.

The United States marshal who returned with the sheriff moved with a more imposing tread than his predecessor. His movements were brisk, assured, and officious. Since he wore no badge, he produced the warrant from his pocket which had commissioned him a marshal.

Solomon read the extended papers carefully and handed them back. "As a representative of the Federal Government, I salute you, sir. Do you have a search warrant?"

"Of course not. I wish to search nothing. I want to look into an empty coffin."

"Then, as an officer of the United States, you are no doubt conversant with the Constitution of the United States. Are you aware of its provisions against unlawful search and seizure?"

"Sir, I'm not here to get a Supreme Court decision on an empty box. There'll be no search and no seizure unless you've got a nigger hid in that coffin. If there is, then you're violating the law of the land, and you'll be a felon, liable to treatment as such. Now, order that girl off the coffin, or I'll throw her off."

"I'll so order her. Girl, get off the coffin."

Solomon stood up and pointed to the driver's seat for Melinda to take her position there. As she stepped around to the seat, he stepped over and sat down on the coffin.

The marshal shook his head in disgust.

"Preacher, I hate to use force on a man of the cloth, but if you don't come down off that coffin, I'm going to remove you."

"Sir, I have vowed on the spirit of Mrs. Henry Ashburn that her resting place shall not be defiled!"

Staring straight ahead, Solomon continued to sit.

The marshal took off his coat and laid it over the rail of the wagon. Beneath his coat, he wore a pistol belt with a pistol and holster, which he also removed and draped over the side panel. When the marshal had finished his preliminaries, Solomon got an unwanted and unexpected ally in the drayman who had moved down from the haywagon. He stepped politely between the marshal and his weapon and tapped the marshal on the shoulder as the official prepared to step up onto the wagon bed.

"Marshal," the teamster asked, "do you see that section of the railing over there just in front of the paddle wheel?"

The marshal turned at the gentle voice and said with vexation, "Of course, I see it. Do you think I'm blind?"

"I'm right glad you ain't, because if you lay ary a hand on that preacher, you're going over the rail at that spot. When that paddle wheel gets through with you, you'll be either beat to death or drowned, or both."

The teamster was considerably larger than the marshal. His face was the battered face of a plug-ugly, and his arms were roughly one-third the diameter of the mainmast of the Royal Oak. The marshal's complexion went a shade whiter, but he retained his official composure.

"Are you interfering with an officer of the United States in pursuit of his official duty?"

"That what you are? I say you're a flunky for the goddamned slaveowners. You ain't got but one witness, that pip-squeak of a deputy. He won't be no good, because he's going to accidently fall over that rail right behind you."

It was Solomon's turn to know fear. He spoke, and the only note in his voice was one of gentle concern. "Gentlemen, I'm a man of peace. I don't wish to cause trouble to appointed officers of the law, and I surely don't want to involve my friends in some impetuous act."

Behind him, the banshee wailed. "Stand your ground, preacher. Three cheers for the free states."

"I wish to effect a compromise. Although I've taken an oath that the coffin shall not be opened, I appeal to your sense of justice and your sense of touch. Sheriff, if you and the marshal wish, you may lift the coffin. Its weight will convince you there's no fugitive inside, and if you shake it, he will rattle. Such a compromise will permit me to retain my honor and convince you that the box is empty. Gentlemen, I appeal to you to accept this decision and avoid violence or bloodshed."

"That suits me, marshal," the deputy said gratefully, "if it suits you."

"Get off the box," the marshal said.

Solomon got off the box.

The ferryboat was swinging toward Butler Street, blasting a signal to the ramp tender, as the marshal and the sheriff clambered onto the wagon and untied the coffin. With muscles tensed for the strain, they hoisted the casket, freely and easily.

"It's empty," the marshal said.

As amused teamsters clapped and hooted and the

female called for cheers for the free states, the marshal and the deputy lashed the coffin down again. They departed with far less authoritativeness than that with which they had come.

Solomon drove up the ramp onto Butler Street and trotted the team toward High Street, waving to the drayman as he passed.

"I declare, Mr. Ricky, you is the smartest man. How you think of that?"

"I read a story once about a man who hid a letter by laying it in plain sight. Then, I read in the paper that coffins were suspicious items in Cincinnati. So, I furnished the law with a little diversion. They were looking for the runaway in the coffin when the runaway was in plain sight.

"You can learn a lot from reading, Melinda."

His lecture was lost on a girl whose interest had become focused on the buildings and traffic as they rolled onto Third Street.

Sentimentality was the albatross around the neck of the Jew, he thought, as the razor cut its swathe through the soap. He should be more concerned over the disappointment his beardlessness would cause Leah than worried about how to tell the black girl upstairs good-bye. To a Bill Blake, there would have been no problem, for Blake would have felt no impulse to go upstairs—but maybe Bill Blake would not have had the courage or endurance to bring the girl here in the first place.

He was through apologizing to himself for his sensibilities, he thought, as he spread the cleft of his chin to the blade. He owed it to the girl to explain her rights to her, and if she got sentimental, he could always leave.

Fluffing the drying towel over his face, he felt another problem might be brown eyes. His could never attain the piercing indifference of blue eyes, and her brown eyes could melt.

Well, he could look at her teats.

Splashing bay rum over his face, he decided to explain cheerfully to her that if she wished, she could cancel the engagement and make her way north through a land whose language she could barely read. He would keep her happy. Regale her with the possibility that she might end up as a whore instead of a bride. Laughingly, he would delight her with an alternative: Instead of Kelly, she might accept the Quaker school and spend ten hours a day learning to become a hatchet of God in the Gresham manner.

Yes, happiness would be his theme, he decided, as he briskly mounted the stairway to her room. He would fill her chockablock with wedding plans, focusing on details of dress, and he would leave her quivering with anticipation to meet her lover on this beautiful September afternoon.

He knocked and entered at her low bidding.

Freshly bathed and in a white slip, she sat before the dressing table brushing her hair. Looking into the mirror, she said, "Why, Mr. Ricky, honey, you don't need no knock."

"Custom of the country. You 'bout ready for that great jubilee?"

"I been thinking what to put on."

Her clothes, freshly ironed by Braden's woman, were spread on a cedar chest.

He walked over and picked up the white dress with ruffled sleeves that Mr. Gaines had given her. "White, by all means. White is the color that virgins wear."

"I was kind of hoping I wouldn't have to put that on for a little while."

"Should I go to my wife after five and a half months from home with a satisfied smirk, smelling of French bath salts? Into that dress, girl."

She shimmied more than was necessary as she slithered the dress over her head and down, but it *was* a close fit. It made her seem more full-breasted, and she arched her back to enhance the effect as she posed before the mirror.

"Think I's tempting, Mr. Ricky?"

"If I planned to be gone more than three hours, I wouldn't leave you here with Tom Braden, despite his wife."

She hardly heard him, so engrossed she was in preening herself, wrapping the pearls around her neck, twice, three times. She was going for four when he interrupted her.

"Put the pearls down, Melinda! You can dress when I'm gone."

She laid the pearls on the dresser and turned to him.

"You coming back, ain't you?"

"Yes, but I'll be with Kelly. Once you've seen him, you won't want to talk to me anymore."

"I done seen Mr. Kelly. I likes talking with you."

"Talk won't buy you bacon . . . Now, listen.

"Before I went to get you, I told Kelly you didn't have to marry him if you didn't want to. He's Catholic, and he'll have to publish bans and arrange for you to take instruction in his church. Meanwhile, if you don't want to marry him, hide some money I'm going to give you and go to Mr. Ely Blood's store. I'll pin his address to the money. You won't have to explain anything to Mr. Blood. Just get to him.

"Now, if Kelly tries to do it to you before you're married, don't let him. No matter how bad you want to, don't let him do it. He might think you're so good he'll want to share you with his friends, and you'll be giving it to twenty or thirty men a day for about two dollars apiece. But you'd see precious little of the money."

"How much is thirty times two, Mr. Ricky?"

"Sixty dollars, but you're . . ."

"Lordy, sir! That's much as we made selling elixir."

"If they paid that to see you dance, Melinda, you can see what they'd pay to . . ."

"God damn! Mr. Ricky, I's setting on a gold mine!"

"I fear our friend Kelly might have that thought."

"Mr. Ricky," she looked at him with dubious amazement. "You say I make money singing and dancing. Now you say I make money letting them do it to me. I's going to like it up North."

"But if you sell it, you'll be a whore and not a lady. That's bad, and if you think Mr. Kelly would approve of you doing that, you go right over to Mr. Blood. He'll send you to a school where they'll teach you how to act like a white lady and how to get to Jesus. You'd like that, wouldn't you?"

"I sho would, sir."

"I'm giving you your choices. You can marry Kelly or go to school. You take a beauty nap while I go get Kelly, and think over what I've told you. I'll be back around five. You don't have to decide anything, right now, but think about what I've told you. Make your plans, Melinda. You can never succeed in this world without a plan."

"Mr. Ricky, I done been thinking. If Mr. Kelly spurns me, why don't me and you go sell elixir at them fairs?"

"I intend to set up a store in Cincinnati."

She weighed the problem. "Maybe you could use a cook. I's a good cook."

366

"You're the best, and I'll miss your cooking the rest of my life, but I can't afford a cook."

"Hell, Mr. Ricky. I'd work for nothing till you gets rich. I'd keep your house clean and etcetera etcetera." An impish grin leaped to her face, and he laughed.

"Girl, you just got hired, and you just got fired . . . Mr. Kelly loves you very much. If I took you away from him, he'd have the police come and send you South or steal you and sell you South. He wouldn't take to me getting his girl."

"Yes, sir. I likes him, much as I remembers, but I never met nobody I likes like I likes you. When you come in, I's going to tempt hell out of you, but I can't do no tempting when I's feeling sad and lonesome . . ."

"Now, Melinda! Don't start tuning up!"

"I's trying not to, Mr. Ricky. But I been thinking. If I die before you do, I's going to hang around them pearly gates and wait for you so's you won't feel sad and lonesome when you gets there. I's going to come out and meet you and take you by the hand and lead you straight up to the throne of Jesus.

"I's going to walk right up to Jesus, and I's going to say, 'He's here, honey. Mr. Ricky's here. Don't you scorn him 'cause he's a Jew. He's your kinfolk, Lord, and he's the kindest man what ever lived.'

"By God, Mr. Ricky, if Jesus don't put no crown on your head, I'm going to walk right out of there, over to the Jew place, and I'm going to say to your woman: 'There ain't no giving or taking in heaven, so you'll just excuse me, ma'am, while I set here and listen to your man talk.'

"Bless your heart, honey, when you gets to your dying day, don't you get scared, 'cause you going to have a friend waiting for you. I ain't going to let you get lonesome . . . Mr. Ricky, what you tuning up for? You know I cry when you cry."

She was trying to convey to him a truth out of her own anguish, telling him that if human love existed beyond the grave, her tiny ghost would be waiting to lead him through the dark lands of death up to the throne of God. Her compassion for him opened the weirs of his compassion. A flood of *Weltschmertz* tore him from the grip of the Clays and Blakes of the world to submerge him, and he drowned.

He moved beside her on the bench and placed his head on her shoulder so she could not see him weep. As he wept, his aloof and analytical other self sat in judgment, but the judgment was kind.

He did not weep because he was maudlin. He wept from relief that an effort was over and sorrow that the effort was done. He wept for Melinda's loneliness and his own aloneness and for all good friends who must part.

He wept for the journey each must take, weeping more for the girl than for himself, and not weeping solely for either. He wept for all travelers into dreams and night, brides in fresh veils and soldiers with banners, Don Quixote on the roads of Spain, and Childe Harold coming alone to the dark tower.

Caught in a rising abstraction of grief, he wept for their two peoples, one scorned and enslaved, the other doomed to an unending exodus toward an ever-receding Promised Land.

He wept for forests he had never known by mountains and rivers he would never see, weeping no longer for this place and time but for his fathers in an older captivity by the waters of another Babylon.

Finally, he wept for God.

He directed Braden's man to let him off at Horn and Front streets when the boy turned for the ferry with his rented rig and walked the few blocks to Kelly's tavern, a rambling two-story structure with a porch running the length of its front.

He walked into the lobby and asked for Kelly. The clerk pointed toward the bar.

The barroom stretched the length of two boxcars and was twice as wide as a boxcar's width. On his left, the bar with its brass rail and spittoons gleaming stretched to a distant bandstand beneath a huge wall painting illuminated by hanging lamps. Tables on his right, covered with green-checkered oil cloths, were lighted by wall lamps.

He caught the mixed smells of sawdust, tobacco juice, cheap perfume, and the skunky odor of beer. He pinned down the source of the perfume when a twitter arose on his right. In a darkened corner, a covey of whores fluttered around a table.

Solomon approached the bartender. "Mr. Kelly in?"

"Ain't seen him."

"Know where he is?"

"Can't say."

It occurred to Solomon that the bartender might consider him a member of the force or perhaps the kingpin of a rival gang of knuckle-dusters. "My name's Villaricca. Kelly's expecting me."

The bartender leaned over the bar and yelled down to a man swabbing the dance floor. "Hey, Bennie. Run over to Shanihan's and tell Kelly Villaricca's here."

Solomon turned and walked down the bar, passing four solitary drinkers strung at wide intervals along its length.

He was drawn to the painting by the boldness of its colors and its use of a religious theme in a barroom—it depicted Christian maidens being fed to lions before a Coliseum crowd.

As he neared the painting, he could tell at a glance that the artist had been an American taught in Europe. Flesh tones and torsos of the women were done in the manner of Rubens, whereas the background of Roman spectators was done in the literal-idyllic manner of the Hudson River School. The dominant dramatic element was a female in the foreground, her body arched backwards over the forepaws of a lion. Her upper dress had been torn away, and the lion was beginning his meal on a delicacy which reminded Solomon of Mrs. Foreman. As a critic, Solomon adjudged the expression on the face of the lion's meal as an aesthetic flaw: No woman in such peril would evince coyness.

A closer inspection of the background details showed Solomon he had erred as a critic. He had misjudged the artist's intent.

Details were handled with the exuberance of a Brueghel woven into the nightmarish patterns of Hieronymus Bosch. Like figures in a dream, distant maidens fled pursuing beasts. Some had been caught.

From the emperor's box in the distance, the courtiers were not turning thumbs down; they were pointing index fingers up. One maiden, on hands and knees in supplication before Nero, was being humped by a lion. Elsewhere in the painting, lions were feasting on human flesh but not with their teeth. Solomon noticed with approval that the artist had integrity as well as talent, for no hint of Lesbos marred the pure bestiality of the scene. All the lions had manes.

Solomon turned away feeling ennobled, as he always felt in the presence of art. Through a savage August, he had come to this depraved September with growing concern over his moral dissolution, but as long as an artist could paint such a canvas, a patron buy it, and the public view it, there was hope for the soul of Solomon Villaricca.

He strode past the bar, emptied now of all save one patron, and sat down in the lobby. For half an hour, he fidgeted before Kelly arrived in swaggering haste, dressed conservatively in a suit of Kelly green. He advanced smiling, and Solomon matched his crushing grip with a crushing grip.

"Sorry to keep you waiting, Mr. Villaricca."

"No trouble. I was in admiring your painting. Is that a Jack the Artist original?"

"It's raw," Kelly grinned, "but the trade likes it."

"Helps business for the girls, too, I imagine."

"That's the main idea," Kelly admitted. "You bring Mellie?"

"I brought her. You got the money?"

"I don't carry a thousand dollars in me pocket. I got it in the office there. Where's the girl?"

"In a rooming house on the west side waiting for you and me."

"Not questioning your judgment, Mr. Villaricca, but wouldn't it been easier to bring her here?"

"Some people who knew I was bringing her here are mighty opposed. They figured you might be setting the girl up as a whore. After seeing those ladies in the barroom, I think maybe they're right."

Indignation and compassion in the Irishman's voice surprised Solomon.

"Mr. Villaricca, them poor things in yonder have to make a living. It's pretty easy for a wealthy merchant like you or some biddy up on Orchard Hill to look down on them poor girls, but suppose you were a poor female and not very bright—you'd sell ass or starve!

"Our Blessed Savior wouldn't give them the back of His gentle hand, so no hard-knuckled Mick like me's going to cuff them, either.

"If I'm man enough to help them wayward lambs, them nontalking, nondrinking, nonfucking Quakers ought to keep their snouts out of my business. Them pious bastards been sticking to me like flies. But Blood sent one over Saturday who won't come back; I converted the bastard. I got the son of a bitch drunk and got him bred.

"Far as Mellie's concerned, she won't be allowed in the saloon."

Solomon sensed a hidden worth in this Irishman, but harshness had brought forth his apologia, so Solomon continued harshly, "You keeping her in the back with the other black mammies?"

"No, sir. Them blacks would turn her in quicker than a cat can lick its ass. Me wife ain't associating with no whores and no niggers."

"Mr. Kelly, I told you last spring I would not bring you the girl for purposes of fornication. If you don't marry her, I'm coming back after her."

"On the grave of me dear mother, I swear I intend to marry the girl."

"I'll have to take your word, but on the record your word's not worth much. You said you offered two thousand for the girl. Blake told me it was three."

"Them Southerners brag."

"One more thing: I've been fighting to keep men out of that girl's drawers since before I left Georgia because you wanted a virgin. My caravan, worth three hundred dollars, was wrecked and burned by a mob trying to get to her, and I think that's a loss you ought to reimburse me for."

"If it's my bartender who's letting a fight break out, I'm not about to dock him for my losses. I pays my tab without whimpering.

"But out of the generosity of me heart, for I know it's been a hard and weary journey for you, and grateful I am for the lass, I'm willing to throw in an extra hundred."

"At these prices, Mr. Kelly, believe me, you are getting a bargain. The girl is a great cook, and she's very apt."

"That I know, Mr. Villaricca. May the Lord strike me if I ain't about to be hiring her a tutor."

Of all felicitous remarks Kelly had made, for Solomon the last was the happiest of all. His voice softened. "Mr. Kelly, I would like an invitation to your wedding sent to me in care of Blood's store."

"Gladly, but don't bring that pious bastard with you!"

"Very well, Mr. Kelly. Now, I'll take you to the girl."

"Then I'll get the money."

As Kelly disappeared into his office, Solomon sat and reevaluated the Irishman. He had broken his own rules by permitting Blood's opinion of Kelly to shape his estimate of the man. Always, Solomon had maintained that human worth was independent of wealth or social standing, and Kelly demonstrated, as Melinda had done, the proof of his belief.

Kelly emerged holding a tin box and grinning, "There's loads of money here, Mr. Villaricca, but they're the happiest dimes I ever spent."

On the veranda, they paused to let their eyes adjust to sunlight, and as they started down the steps, Kelly said, "Mr. Villaricca, you'd better take the box. I may need me fists."

Solomon followed Kelly's gaze and saw Blood approaching in his buggy at a trot. "I think he wants to talk to me. I gave my name to the bartender and an unfriendly Friend must have heard. He's a Quaker. You need fear no violence from him."

"Hell, I ain't afraid of violence. I likes to hit them and feel them crunch . . . You don't have to talk to him."

"He's my friend . . . or was."

"Then talk, but don't keep Mellie waiting. The poor lass is alone in the city."

Solomon waited as Kelly put the money box behind the seat and climbed into his buggy. He watched as Ely brought his buggy to a halt behind Kelly's, preparing an attitude for whatever face Blood presented. He could be truculent if need be, for he owed the Quaker nothing except two extra weeks of sweat, hot and cold, the theft by the Gypsies and a lost caravan.

Nevertheless, he felt absurdly happy when the Quaker smiled and extended his hand. "Welcome home, Solomon."

"Thank you, Ely."

"Thee's been inside, I hear. Think it a fitting home for the black?"

"Better than the one she left."

"Think she'll like it?"

"She adapts well."

"I tried to stop thee and failed. Moses must have more weight than Jesus between the Cumberland Gap and Covington."

"Both are conspicuously absent."

"Solomon, I know thee has an obligation to this man, and I think thee's taking him to the girl. Friend Gresham writes that the girl's Godliness is sound and that she yet may be saved. May I go with thee and talk to her in the presence of this man with thy permission?"

Kelly spoke over Ely's head to Solomon. "I ain't got no objections, whatsoever, to Mellie talking to Protestants . . . Let's go, Mr. Villaricca, the lass is waiting."

"She's at Tom Braden's rooming house, Ely."

In the religious wars of the Christians, Solomon was glad to be neutral, and he climbed aboard Kelly's buggy with relief. Personally, he cared little who won the argument. Ely was a man of principles, but Kelly had said nothing that Solomon did not agree with wholeheartedly.

There were depths to this innkeeper not dreamt of in Ely's philosophy.

Though his horse was fresh, Kelly did not press the pace. Instead, he looked behind at times to see if Blood was keeping up. He drove in silence, except for a single remark at the outset of the journey. "That Quaker stuff's no religion for a nigger. Niggers like to shout and sing."

Solomon enjoyed the silence. His ordeal was ending, the last physical barrier overcome with a ferry ticket, the Quaker opposition melted, and his friendship with Ely had apparently survived. Now, they trotted down the streets of home without a constable in sight.

Truly, it was the eye of childhood that feared the nine of spades!

Soon, he would pay his last tribute to Larry Morgan by staging an entrance for Melinda. Tom Braden would summon her to the dining room of the boarding house, and he would whisper to Tom to tell her to walk like Juanita. Consummate actress that she was, Melinda would float down the stairs in her white dress; and, in her own pungent phrase, the waiting litigants would "do it in their drawers."

Melinda could judge their arguments. He trusted her instincts more than either of these men's reason.

They entered the house together, where Kelly was immediately diverted by Braden's dining room, the tables with their checkered tablecloths and wrought iron candleholders, the serving window cut through the wall to the kitchen. "Be Jesus," he said, speaking only to Solomon, "I could cut such a window between me bar and dining room."

Braden's wife was in the kitchen, and Solomon stepped to the window. "Ruth, Tom around?"

"Why, yes, sir. I'll fetch him."

In an attempt to thaw the silence, Solomon stepped back and said, "She'll come down those stairs, wearing a dress appropriate for the occasion, and you'll discover, Ely, why she threw a halter over Kelly. She's got everything but a light complexion. Her grace beguiles without need of wiles. Easy to please and pleasing, she's kind, clever, and congenial. In short, she's a gollywhopper."

His sally was so unsuccessful it embarrassed him, and he welcomed the entrance of Tom Braden.

"Why howdy do, Mr. Villaricca," the Negro said in mock surprise. "Howdy, Mr. Blood. What can I do for you gentlemen?"

"Mr. Kelly's with us, Tom. He's all right," Solomon said.

"I declare, sir. I mistook you for the police."

"I been mistook some in my day," Kelly laughed, "but that takes the cake. Go get the girl, boy! Tell her Kelly's come."

Braden looked at Solomon and said, "Would these genlemen mind, sir, if I spoke to you alone for a minute?"

"Certainly not, Tom . . . One moment, gentlemen."

They went down the hall to Braden's office and closed the door. Solomon saw Melinda's ring on the desk, weighting two sheets of foolscap.

Braden turned to him in confusion. "Mr. Villaricca, Mellie's done gone to Canada."

"In the name of heaven, how?"

"I sent her."

He reached into his pocket and pulled out a crumpled sheet of paper which he handed to Solomon, "You wrote this, didn't you, sir?"

Solomon glanced down and read, "Tom, get this girl to Amherstberg, right away! S.V.

"Yes," Solomon was equally confused. "But this was for an emergency which never came about."

"Right after you left, sir, she come down, all packed and ready to go. She give it to me with twenty dollars pinned to it, so I knowed it was from you.

"I took her over to the depot and give the conductor ten dollars to put her in the baggage car on the Toledo train. I give her the other ten, and she asked me to write you a letter for her, that one there." Tom pointed to the foolscap.

Solomon looked over at the top sheet, saw squiggly lines running in all directions, and asked, "Didn't you suspect anything?"

"No, sir. Leastways, I didn't till I wrote the letter, then

I just couldn't try to stop her, Mr. Villaricca. She knowed them gentlemen was coming, 'cept she didn't know Mr. Blood's name.

"I had to help her with some of the words, but I wrote mostly just like she told me. I hope you can read my script, sir. Most people can't."

Already Solomon was aware that he stood firmly with the majority, and he groaned, "Tom, I got some tall explaining to do. Kelly's waiting out there to marry the girl."

"I knows that, sir. It's in her letter . . . Mr. Villaricca, that's a nice letter. It's wrote to you, but it's wrote to them, too. It ain't nothing personal. She left that ring to Mr. Kelly. That letter will explain things, maybe. If I was you, I'd let them read it."

"I'll give Kelly his ring," Solomon said, "but you'd better read the letter to all of us."

They returned to the dining room where Solomon said simply, "Melinda's gone. She dictated a letter to Tom which I hope explains things better than I can. She gave you this ring, Mr. Kelly, and Tom will read the letter, since I failed to bring my reading glasses."

Without looking at it, Kelly took the ring and threw it aside. His face was set and hard.

Tom Braden read easily from his own handwriting.

Dear Mr. Villaricca,

I been thinking, which aint easy when I aint got you to help me. I reckon I is going up north where my people is free.

I appreciate Mr. Kelly sending for me. He's a nice man but I can't rightly keep his ring. He ought to give it to some nice white woman and get married up right so's he can have children to take care of him in his old age.

Tell Mr. Kelly I'd truly enjoy all them nice men doing it to me, but I wouldn't charge them nothing. I is a giving person and I aint got much to give nobody. What I got worth giving I wants to keep to give to people I wants to give something special to.

Tell them nice Quaker folks that I respects them wanting to educate me like a white lady and lead me to Jesus but I don't want to be no white lady. I got just enough white in them pearls you give me and I reckon I can get to Jesus just as quick black.

I is going to get me some learning so's I can sing and dance by myself. I is taking my belongings and the money. I knows you can get more money. You is the smartest man I ever did see. You do damn near anything you sets your mind to.

May your years be long and your children many, and I thanks you, I truly thanks you, for showing me the North Star.

Your obedient servant, etcetera,
Melinda Blake Ricky

"That's all she had me write," Tom said, "but she signed it herself."

He took the letter, looking down at her Spencerian script. So, she had honored her hero, tutor, and hired benefactor by naming herself with his imagined name. He held in his hand a signature which had now cost him $1,320.00. For that money, he could buy Shakespeare's.

Behold the nine of spades! The dark lady had struck!

"What the hell you crying about, Villaricca?" Kelly asked.

"Should a pincushion laugh? I lose my wagon, my fee, and money out of my pocket. Should I be laughing?"

"Jesus Christ! You should worry. I'm out a piece of ass worth ten thousand a year for ten years."

"So, you did not intend to marry the girl?"

"Sure, and married to the wench I wouldn't be giving her a cut."

Solomon turned and issued a formal statement: "Mr. Kelly, in my considered judgment, you are a Goddamned son of a bitch."

"Mr. Villaricca, I'll be letting no Hebe insult me mother!"

His left hand grabbed Solomon's collar as the mallet on his right piston cocked and slammed forward. Before Solomon broke the Commandment, Blood had reached for a candleholder, and now he was swinging it high. Solomon caught Kelly's fist with an upward flick of his palm and swung his right fist into the Irishman's unguarded rib cage. His fist connected with the easy spontaneity of exploding joy.

A rib cracked with the sound of a breaking broomstick and Kelly staggered back, bending to clutch his rib cage as Solomon swung again. For the second time within forty-eight hours, Solomon's fist, coming up, connected with a chin coming down, but Kelly was a lighter man than Whitcomb, and he was not ballasted by someone riding his shoulders. His body seemed to rise and sail through the air to land on a table top which shattered in an explosion of legs.

376

Supine on his oval bier and shrouded in checkered cloth, the unconscious Kelly looked beatific.

Solomon straightened from his half-crouch and turned to the Quaker. "Ely, why did you pick up that candle-holder?"

Blood looked down at the object. "I hope I did it to keep him from injuring his spine when he landed on the table."

Solomon turned to Braden. "Tom, how much I owe you for the table?"

"That table's on the house, Mr. Villaricca."

"I thank you, Tom. I truly thank you . . . Would you be so kind as to bring my bag and candlestick? Ely, would you bring Mr. Kelly's money box?"

Solomon bent and hoisted Kelly to his shoulder. He carried the Irishman out of the house, down the walk, and dumped him into the buggy seat. He turned and took the metal box from Ely and put it in a corner of the buggy box, folding a lap robe over it. He tied the reins to the whip post and slapped Kelly's horse on the rump. Obediently, the horse moved away, beginning its trek homeward. To a casual or an interested eye, Kelly was another drunk being drawn homeward by his faithful dobbin, a not uncommon sight on the streets of Cincinnati.

"Thee should have thrown him in Tom's trash bin."

"I always treat my customers with courtesy."

"May I drive thee home, Solomon?"

"Indeed, Ely."

It was pleasant to sit behind the swaying rump of Ely's horse on the last mile home. Ely kept silent for the first part of the journey, but finally, he asked, "I suppose thee'll be needing money, now, to open the Trade Fair."

"About what I lost today."

"Well, thee's wiser for this day."

"For thirteen hundred and twenty dollars, I should be so smart."

"How was the South?"

"It almost converted me."

"Thee's welcome to our church."

"I'm only a Christian in the South. Down there, my *landsman* deserves more than He's getting."

"Were they warlike in their feelings toward the North?"

"Toward the North and toward the next county."

"But I do think God's on our side."

377

"God's a loaded cannon," Solomon said, remembering Juanita. "He fires in any direction."

"Has thee kept His other Commandments?"

"I haven't worshipped any graven images."

Ely lapsed again into silence. They had crossed the creek and were nearing Horn Street before Ely spoke again.

"Thee's troubled, Solomon. Thee should be happy. Thee's home."

Solomon stroked his chin. "I fear the wrath of Leah. Ely, how do you break the news gently that you have shaved?"

"Tell her thee had lice."

"I used that tale in Cumberland Falls."

"Stay Christian. Tell her it's no concern of hers. If she berates thee, cuff her. Make a Christian of her, and thee both can join the Society."

"I cannot desert Israel, for I was born afraid of women."

They turned north on Horn Street and east again on Kemble. In the slanting light of late afternoon, the white house with the green trim was visible two blocks away. Ely lashed the mare into a trot and the whirr of the buggy tires was a song for Solomon.

Leah's old maids were blooming in the front yard, which meant the roses were gone. The box hedges by the front porch needed trimming, and a picket was missing from the fence.

Leah was in the kitchen, he could tell from the smoke rising from the stovepipe. He would be home in time for supper and to feed the mare.

It was all familiar and commonplace and beautiful.

Ely swung the buggy to the north side of the street and parked in front of the house. Solomon took his bag, shook hands with Ely, and stood by the gate to wave him farewell. He opened the gate and walked up the walkway.

He wanted to run in two directions, away from the house and toward it. Facing Leah without his beard was harder than facing the mob in Lexington.

He would play the serpent and be the trembling flower above it. He was done with humility, Maimon notwithstanding, and his stride grew bolder. Audubon and Maimon and Shakespeare had gone south with him, he thought, but only Shakespeare survived the journey.

He set his bag down and rapped with authority on the door.

He could hear Leah's footsteps approaching with definite, decisive sounds. Melinda bounced and Phoebe swayed, Juanita glided and Pamela swung, but Leah Villaricca walked to get from one spot to another—her footfalls had character.

He heard her fumbling at the door. When she opened it and peered out, the sunlight fell on her eyes, and she blinked from momentary blindness.

"Ma'am, does Solomon Villaricca live here?"

"Solomon!"

She was through the door, and he lifted her, smelling the lilac scent of her hair made poignant now by the memory of his farewell on a road in Tennessee, loving the legality and propriety and decency of her arms around his neck, feeling the ample pressure of her breasts—the too ample pressure!

Even as he muscled her out to look, she was saying, "Be careful, Solomon."

"When did this happen?"

"A month before you left, but I didn't know it. I wrote you."

"I didn't pick up my mail in Wheeling. I fell behind schedule and came back through Lexington . . . You'll be light in December. I've only four months to prepare!"

"Now, don't be worried, Sol. You'll be all right. Where are the mules?"

"I was caught by a rainstorm and left them in Falmouth and took the train home. Here, let me get you inside. The evening dew might be harmful . . . I wrecked my van in Lexington, and it caught fire. A total loss. I salvaged my clothes and my candlestick. Are you having a boy or a girl?"

"One or the other, or maybe both . . . You won't be needing the van anymore . . . Shall I heat your bath water?"

"I'll do that. No more heavy work for you."

"You look tired, Sol. I'll declare, you're handsome without that beard."

"Why won't I need the van?"

"When I found out, I went down and checked our bank account. Did you know we only needed a thousand dollars to open the store? I didn't want you going south,

379

not with the baby coming. So, I wrote to Papa. He's going to sell his shop and lend us the money we need to open. I know you didn't want anybody else in the store . . ."

"You're right, I didn't."

"Papa and Mama are getting old. They want to come live with us, anyway, and I'll need Mama to help with the house and tend the baby when I'm at the store . . . We've got more room here than we need. Now, that room you use to saw away on the violin . . . The violin's burned, isn't it?"

He laughed at her hopeful expression. "Smashed to smithereens, honey. My musical career is ended."

"Then you won't be needing the room, and we can make it into another bedroom . . . Oh, my supper! . . . You look tired, Sol. Why don't you stretch out on the settee?"

"Have you fed the mare?"

"Half an hour ago."

She answered him departing for the kitchen, and he turned into the bedroom, putting his bag in the closet and his candlestick on the mantle. He returned to the parlor and sat, removing his boots slowly and luxuriantly.

He was happy though somewhat chagrined by her reaction to his missing beard, and he was disappointed about Papa horning in on the Trade Fair. Papa would want a part of the business. Papa was a good cobbler, and he knew shoes, but what did Papa know about general merchandise? Papa would get the shoe department at the Trade Fair, and that's all Papa would get.

He fluffed the pillows and stretched out.

Papa would get the shoe department, and Solomon would get a lot of free advice from here to eternity. But it was his own fault. If he had been just a shade luckier, or a little more honest, he would not have been done in by a darky.

All credit to Melinda, if he had told her that he was getting another thousand dollars from Kelly, she would have let him collect the money, gone home with Kelly, and out the back door to Canada.

The trouble with Melinda was that she took everything he told her to heart. She made a plan and she stuck to it.

Leah came back from the kitchen, saying, "Sol, I forgot to tell you. Goldie's been talking to Rabbi Wise. There's talk about a reformed synagogue. So many Sephardim are drifting away. You won't need a beard. I'd get to sit in the

same section with you. I'd have to, you're so handsome . . .
Here, put your head on my lap. Poor Solomon, you look so
tired."

"Not much sleep last night. Slept on a church pew."

"We've got to decide on a name for the baby. If it's
a boy, I can't decide on Aaron or Isaac."

"Why either? Why not Hector?"

"Hector's for bulls or dogs. Hector, oh heck!"

It was good to lie and listen to a woman's voice give
a breathless grace to trivia, to lie stretched out, unashamed
and unafraid, with no thoughts of pattyrollers, sheriffs, or
husbands.

He let her voice flow around him, over him, submerge
him, as she chatted on, self-absorbed. "If it's a girl, I want
to name her Beth. I loved your mother's name. I loved
Grandmother Gratz, but her name was Sarah Rebeccah,
and I can't abide Sarah. Rebeccah's nice . . ."

By now, Melinda would be approaching Toledo.

He hoped the lake crossing would not be choppy. If
she ate pork chops, she could get seasick below decks. Below
decks! She'd probably be up in the captain's cabin, telling
him what a nice man he was.

"What do you want to name her?"

He detected the question from the changed tempo of
her voice and, half asleep, answered, "Name her Melinda
Blake Villaricca."

"A Gentile name for a Jewish girl? I should say not!
I think it should be either Beth Rebeccah or Rebeccah Beth."

It didn't matter—Melinda needed no memorial.

But he would miss going south. With Leah's parents up
from Chattanooga, he'd have no call ever to cross the
Ohio.

"Let's call her Beth Rebeccah," he said.

He would never come again to Carthage. He might
bemoan her dear-remembered rocks, but he would not
weep, as Ajax wept, for his lost country. The land he
knew and loved would change, its hills erode, its young and
violent people grow old and die, but his loss would be
repaid in a coin that would not tarnish.

In his memory, the South would stand inviolate. Red
roads of an eternal Georgia would loop hills forever green,
and along those roads, a tall, unaging Jew would follow a
girl whose beauty could not fade toward the unchanging
Blue Ridge Mountains of his mind. And if Hector, cum

Aeneas, cum Ajax, ever dared forget that land and the girl it had given birth, there would always be Papa around the store to remind Solomon Villaricca of seventy dollars swindled in Ellijay, thirty lost in London, eighty-three stolen in Nicholasville, two hundred burned in Lexington, and 1,220 fled from Cincinnati.

"Beth Rebeccah sounds like a synagogue," Leah said. "We'll call her Rebeccah Beth."

"All right, Leah, we'll compromise," he said, drifting into sleep, "and call her Rebeccah Beth."

Solomon Villaricca was home.

Other Good Reads in SIGNET

☐ **ROMANCE by Joseph Conrad and Ford Madox Ford.** Two of the great masters of English literature tell the story of a daredevil outcast determined to win back his fortune and honor, and to capture the hand of a fiery Spanish beauty he cannot forget. Afterword by Arthur Mizener. (#Q3685—95¢)

☐ **THE CHARGE OF THE LIGHT BRIGADE by Cecil Wood-ham-Smith.** The bold story of the Crimean battle immortalized by Tennyson, in which 600 men galloped down a Turkish-held pass and into one of the most appalling slaughters in history. A United Artists movie release. "A masterpiece of creative history. . . ." —Saturday Review (#T3618—75¢)

☐ **THE PRESIDENT'S LADY by Irving Stone.** The tumultuous love story of Rachel and Andrew Jackson by the bestselling author of **The Agony and The Ecstasy.** (#Q3373—95¢)

☐ **THOSE WHO LOVE by Irving Stone.** The bestselling love story of Abigail and John Adams—two people whose devotion to each other was equalled only by their patriotic passion for freedom. By the author of **The Agony and The Ecstasy.** (#W3080—$1.50)

☐ **THE GREAT MUTINY by James Dugan.** A vivid re-creation of the most dramatic mutiny in history, when 50,000 British seamen refused to weigh anchor, leaving England defenseless against an invasion force from France in 1797. (#Q3082—95¢)

☐ **ISLANDIA by Austin Tappan Wright.** A young American goes to live in a 20th century Utopian society where the people are technologically primitive, but highly sophisticated in their understanding of life's meaning. "One of the most remarkable examples of ingenuity in the history of literary invention."—Clifton Fadiman. (#Y2870—$1.25)

THE NEW AMERICAN LIBRARY, INC., P.O. Box 2310, Grand Central Station, New York,, New York 10017

Please send me the SIGNET BOOKS I have checked above. I am enclosing $————————(check or money order—no currency or C.O.D.'s). Please include the list price plus 10¢ a copy to cover mailing costs. (New York City residents add 5% Sales Tax. Other New York State residents add 2% plus any local sales or use taxes.)

Name————————————————————————

Address—————————————————————————

City————————————State————Zip Code————

Allow at least 3 weeks for delivery

Outstanding SIGNET Classics

☐ **WAR AND PEACE by Leo Tolstoy, translated by Ann Dunnigan, edited and with an Introduction by J. O. Bayley.** A distinguished new translation of one of the towering novels of all time, with an informative introduction by a Fellow of New College, Oxford.
(#CJ404—$1.95)

☐ **ANNA KARENINA by Leo Tolstoy.** This classic love story also contains the nucleus of Tolstoy's philosophy. Newly translated and with an Introduction by David Magarshack. (#CQ34—95¢)

☐ **A TALE OF TWO CITIES by Charles Dickens, Afterword by Edgar Johnson.** Rich characterizations drawn against the dramatic backdrop of the French Revolution's bloody strife by England's popular 19th century author.
(#CP416—60¢)

☐ **CRIME AND PUNISHMENT (Complete and Unabridged) by Fyodor Dostoyevsky, translated with an Afterword by Sidney Monas.** A brilliant new translation of the classic story of a murder and its consequences, a profound study of pride and rebellion, guilt and redemption.
(#CT362—75¢)

☐ **DON QUIXOTE (abridged) by Miguel de Cervantes.** The picaresque adventures of Don Quixote and his long-suffering squire, Sancho Panza, in a brilliant translation with Foreword by Walter Starkie. (#CY273—$1.25)

☐ **FAR FROM THE MADDING CROWD by Thomas Hardy.** The classic story of a beautiful young woman whose shortsighted marriage choice leads to tragedy. An MGM motion picture starring Julie Christie, Terrence Stamp, Peter Finch, and Alan Bates. (#P3273—60¢)

☐ **THE HOUSE OF THE SEVEN GABLES by Nathaniel Hawthorne.** A tale of sinister hereditary influences within an old New England family, by America's first great novelist. Afterword by Edward C. Sampson. (#CD58—50¢)

THE NEW AMERICAN LIBRARY, INC., P.O. Box 2310, Grand Central Station, New York,, New York 10017

Please send me the SIGNET CLASSICS I have checked above. I am enclosing $_____(check or money order—no currency or C.O.D.'s). Please include the list price plus 10¢ a copy to cover mailing costs. (New York City residents add 5% Sales Tax. Other New York State residents add 2% plus any local sales or use taxes.)

Name_____

Address_____

City_____State_____Zip Code_____

Allow at least 3 weeks for delivery